# Othermoon

# Othermoon

## NINA BERRY

KENSINGTON PUBLISHING CORP.

www.kensingtonbooks.com

KTEEN BOOKS are published by

Kensington Publishing Corp.
119 West 40th Street
New York, NY 10018

All Kensington titles, imprints, and distributed lines are available at special quantity discounts for bulk purchases for sales promotions, premiums, fund-raising, educational, or institutional use.

Special book excerpts or customized printings can also be created to fit specific needs. For details, write or phone the office of the Kensington special sales manager: Kensington Publishing Corp., 119 West 40th Street, New York, NY 10018, attn: Special Sales Department; phone 1-800-221-2647.

KENSINGTON and the KTeen logo are Reg. U.S. Pat. & TM Off.

ISBN-13: 978-0-7582-7693-3
ISBN-10: 0-7582-7693-1

First Trade Paperback Printing: February 2013

10  9  8  7  6  5  4  3

Printed in the United States of America

*For John Mark Godocik*

# ACKNOWLEDGMENTS

Thanks to Elisa Nader for her invaluable help during all stages of this book, from brainstorming to fine-tuning. Much gratitude also goes to Jen Klein for her insightful thoughts on the first draft.

Fellow writers like Brigid Kemmerer, Jennifer Estep, and Marni Bates have been great support, as have my fellow Apocalypsies, particularly the fabulous Los Angeles contingent.

Particular thanks to my agent Tamar Rydzinski and my editor Alicia Condon, both women of discerning intelligence and constant kindness.

Then there is the army of people who, every day, provide support that I couldn't do without. Jackie Berry and Paul "Doc" Berry, Mom and Dad, are first and foremost, constant in their love. But my friends are family too: John Mark Godocik, Brian Pope, Michael Musa, Shelley Zimmerman, Wendy Viellenave, Diane Stengle, Jennifer Frankl, and Katherine Munchmeyer. Thanks also to my inspirational and encouraging gaming group: Scott and Pam Paterra, Maritza Suarez, Frank Woodward, David Haynes, Jim Myers, and Meriam Harvey.

*I have seen the movement of the sinews of the sky,*
*And the blood coursing in the veins of the moon.*

—MUHAMMAD IQBAL, 1920

# CHAPTER 1

The night before we moved away, I couldn't sleep. Not bothering to turn on the light, I sat up in bed at three a.m. and put my earbuds in to blast the audiobook for *The Tempest*. Rain beat down on the jacaranda tree in our front yard. I resolutely gazed out at it to avoid seeing the walls of my room, which had been stripped of all my posters and photos, leaving nothing but uneven holes and sticky tape residue.

The man reading Shakespeare's play had a crisp English accent, but his voice didn't have the depth of Caleb's. No one's did. No one human, anyway.

*Caleb*. Thinking his name sent a stab of longing up from my heart to tighten my throat. We'd talked till midnight, but I hadn't laid eyes on him in weeks.

> *"Our revels now are ended. These our actors,*
> *As I foretold you, were all spirits, and*
> *Are melted into air, into thin air . . ."*

Something glinted in the corner of my eye. I caught sight of a gray van slipping into the rain-soaked fog down the street.

We'd stolen a van like that, a white one, from the Tribunal, my otherkin friends and I, after we burned their compound to the ground. But the Tribunal had other sites, other acolytes.

*Crreeeeeee . . .*

I tapped the headphones. Electronics and metal gadgets tended to break down around me. That last noise was more like a creaky floorboard in a horror movie or the rusty door to my medicine cabinet than Shakespeare. The iPod snapped on again.

> *"We are such stuff*
> *As dreams are made on . . ."*

A shape glided through the downpour outside. The gray van was back, but now the headlights were off. The downy hairs on the back of my neck stood up as it came to a stop across the street.

*Creeeee . . .*

*That didn't come from the headphones.* I popped them out of my ears and rolled silently to my feet, senses alert with fear. For a moment the only illumination came from my iPod, the only sound the interrupted lines of Shakespeare coming faintly from the headphones.

Then, down the hall, light as a feather falling on grass, came a footstep. And another.

Someone had been in my bathroom at three a.m., opening and closing my medicine cabinet, and was now heading toward the living room.

It couldn't be my mother or Richard. I knew every variation of their footsteps, and neither one had any reason to search my nearly empty medicine cabinet.

I used all my training to move quietly to my bedroom door and turned the knob. I didn't want to wake my parents. Perhaps there was an innocent reason for the sounds. If not, I could deal with the Tribunal. And if I couldn't, better it be me that was taken or killed.

The hallway was dark and empty. I stilled and heard the footfalls again in the living room, moving faster now. Half-running down the hall, I kept my body out of sight as I peered around the doorframe.

To my night-sensitive eyes, the living room lay before me as clear as day, unfamiliar territory now that packing boxes and bubble-wrapped furniture dominated. The front door creaked open, and a hooded figure was silhouetted for a moment against the dim greenish streetlight before it stepped outside. Gray hood, gray camouflage, the slender waist and broad shoulders of a man. But why would he leave without trying to kidnap or kill . . . ?

"Desdemona?" Mom's sleepy voice came first, then the creak of her bedroom door opening. She had always had a motherly sense for when I was restless at night.

That was all it took. The gray figure took off, slamming the door shut behind him.

"Stay here, Mom!" I shouted, and ran. In a heartbeat, I had the door open and leaped down the front steps, blinking against the rain. The hard, heavy drops were icy cold and drenched me instantly.

The figure sprinted straight for the van, rounding the jacaranda tree. I was fast, inhumanly fast in short spurts, but he had too big a head start. Then his foot bumped hard against one of the tree's roots, and he sprawled facedown onto the grass.

"Thanks, tree," I said, lunging for him.

He rolled out of reach, brown eyes behind his muddied ski mask very wide, and scrambled to his feet. I knew those eyes. The sound of his breath coming hard and fast brought back a memory of a tall blond boy, his arm broken, his once angelic face sneering to hide just how lost he was. It was Caleb's half-brother.

"Lazar," I said.

He pulled off the soggy ski mask as I moved between him and the van. Beneath it his wavy blond hair was already dark with rain, curling against his forehead. Droplets raced down his temples and aquiline nose, collecting on his lips as they tightened in a familiar way. The gray trousers clung to his lean hips and thighs, and the wet gray shirt outlined the taut definition in his shoulders and chest. His breath misted briefly in the rain as it came fast and even. A muscle in his jaw clenched as he stared at me, and for a moment he looked so much like Caleb that my heart skipped a beat.

Then he spoke, and his voice, harsher, more guarded than Caleb's, broke the spell. "Desdemona. Let me go." It was a warning, not a plea.

I glanced over my shoulder. Behind me, steam rose from the van's exhaust pipe, but no one emerged. Maybe they hadn't seen us in the darkness and the deluge. But that didn't explain why Lazar hadn't summoned them on the communicator every member of the Tribunal wore on every mission.

His slightly tip-tilted eyes, with their thick, rain-spiked lashes, were the same size and shape as Caleb's, but with rich brown irises rather than black. His gaze flicked up and down my body.

Water ran down my face, plastering my T-shirt to my skin, and I realized I was only wearing that and my underwear, my usual bedtime apparel. My cheeks grew so hot under his stare that I was suddenly grateful for the icy rain. A month ago that would've been enough to send me running for safety. Now I ignored the blush and stood my ground. *Who cares? Let him look. And if I have to shift, it means fewer clothes to shred.*

"What were you doing in my house?" I demanded.

He lifted his eyes to my face, a tiny smile playing around his mouth. I realized I'd never seen him genuinely amused before. It lit up his dark eyes and carved dimples into his cheeks, highlighting his high cheekbones and strong chin. "I'd love to stand here all night discussing my activities with a beautiful half-naked girl," he said. "But I don't think my father would approve."

His tone made me want to smack that look off his pretty, pretty face. *Focus, Dez.* Lazar was an objurer, which meant that his voice, like Caleb's, was a powerful instrument, able to persuade, anger, or paralyze in just a few words. Objurers were specially trained by the Tribunal to manipulate the minds and bodies of shifters like me. Every word he spoke was a potential threat.

"Still Daddy's little boy," I said, and was glad to see his smirk drop away. "It doesn't look like you took anything, but maybe you planted something. Is there a bomb in my house, Lazar?"

He considered me, eyes narrowing. Then, almost imperceptibly, he shook his head.

I frowned. The gesture seemed oddly sincere. But it couldn't be. Was he trying to throw me off, delay me?

"If we wanted you dead," he said, "you would be."

"Your father tried a couple of times and failed," I said. "How is Ximon, Lazar? Does he beat you now that your sister isn't available?"

"Amaris." His voice softened when he said his sister's name. Something in his face changed.

A weird stab of pity hit my gut. Lazar's estrangement from his sister had been sudden and violent. Amaris had chosen to come with us, her supposed enemies, rather than live under her father's thumb and marry a man she hated. Lazar had wavered for a heartbeat, but ultimately he'd chosen to leave her with us and escape with Ximon. When I imagined how it felt to be raised by such a monster, all I could feel was sympathy.

"She's doing well," I said, even as I wondered whether reassuring him was a good idea. "She says she misses you. Though I can't imagine why."

His face hardened. "Let me go. Don't make me call the others."

"Go ahead." I bared my teeth, fingers curling like claws. "Call them, and I'll kill you all."

"Desdemona?" My mother stood on the porch, arms crossed to keep her robe closed. "Are you okay?

I startled, turning my head toward her. Lazar seized the moment and ran down the middle of Kenneth Avenue, away from me, leaving the Tribunal's van behind.

"I'm fine, Mom!" I shouted. "Get Richard out of the house!"

The van's tires made wet sucking noises as they began to roll, following Lazar. So they weren't here to hurt Mom and Richard, which meant I could tear after Lazar. I bolted down the sidewalk, outpacing the skidding van, and kept my ears peeled to make sure it didn't head back toward my parents.

Ahead of me, Lazar raced flat out, cutting left into the park. Behind me, the van was gaining. No time to waste. I'd never shifted while running full speed before. But I needed to find out what Lazar had been up to in my bathroom, and I'd never catch him this way.

I kept sprinting as I sent my mind down into the darkness that always roiled at my core, blacker than a night sky without stars.

I asked. A blazing answer of power poured forth, shooting up my spine, along every limb. Then my feet were feet no longer, but great striped paws. My clothes ripped and fell away as I gathered my back legs to leap forward thirty feet per stride. It felt so good to stretch and run. The rain bounced off my coat, no longer a nuisance. Darkness was my time to hunt, and every sound, every scent, every current of air bent to my will.

I laid my tufted ears back, shook my whiskers, and roared.

At the sound, Lazar pelted across the grass even faster. But my great galloping bounds ate up the ground between us. He ran past my favorite tree, the lightning tree, and I heard another engine rev. My ears flicked forward. The gray van was still behind us, keeping to the road, but ahead, alongside the park, another van waited, engines on, but headlights off.

*Damn it.* The Tribunal was thorough.

Just three more leaps, and I'd have Lazar between my paws once more. The side door of the van up ahead slid open. A figure in gray aimed a rifle at me and fired.

I zigged left, putting the lightning tree between me and the gun. Something thunked into the trunk, and I smelled the silver-laced tranquilizer the Tribunal used on shifters. So they weren't trying to kill me. Yet.

No time to wonder why. Lazar was steps from the van. I gathered all the power in my back legs and jumped.

Lazar ducked into the van as I left the ground, while the man with the rifle followed my arc with his gun and pulled the trigger. But I was going faster, farther than he reckoned, and the dart zoomed harmlessly beneath me.

I went farther than even I had wanted. I'd asked my body for all it had without thinking enough about accuracy, and instead of launching myself into the van, I arced completely over it to land on the other side. In my astonishment, I stumbled slightly as I hit pavement, then rolled, coming to my feet.

I looked up to see Lazar staring at me through the rain-smeared window of the van, eyes wide in amazement. Then the tires spun hard, and the vehicle took off. I lashed my tail and sent them off with a roar that made the raindrops fly.

The van vanished into the mist. Still energized with anger, I turned and ran at the lightning tree, jumping onto its rough, familiar trunk, digging in my claws to climb higher. The tree was closely linked to Othersphere, vibrating with shadow, and it drew me like the scent of blood. Better the neighbors saw a naked girl than a tiger in the treetops. But I didn't want to shift back to my human form just yet.

Being a tiger felt so right, so perfect, especially near the lightning tree. A current of power seemed to flow from deep within it up through my paws. I was atop the world now, invincible, at one with all, yet more myself than ever.

As I watched Lazar's van screech toward the freeway, I felt as if I could leap onto it even now and tear its roof off with one swipe.

"Desdemona!" I turned to see our sedan headed toward me, Richard at the wheel, my mom in the passenger seat, her head out the window, yelling.

*So much for Tiger Queen rules the world.* I climbed down and then dropped to the ground as Mom got out of the car, clutching a thick terry-cloth robe, and ran on her tiptoes across the squelchy grass to me.

"Are you all right?" She patted my neck as I butted my head into her waist, automatically marking her as mine. "What the hell were they doing? Richard couldn't find anything different about the house. They didn't take anything we could see, and left nothing behind."

She draped the robe over my long back. It was drenched already, as was she, but when I shifted back to my human form, at least I had something to cover me up.

"It was Lazar," I said, pushing long damp strands of hair from my face.

"Caleb's brother?" She blinked back water drops, one hand massaging her stomach, looking faintly sick.

I nodded. "I have no idea why he was here. And he seemed kind of . . . I don't know. Different."

Mom's eyelids fluttered more rapidly. She looked pale, even considering the greenish light of the street lamp. "Are you okay?" I asked.

"I . . . something's wrong," she managed to say, staggering a few steps to lean against the lightning tree. Then she clutched her stomach with both hands and doubled over.

"Mom? Did they do something to you? Richard!" I screamed at the car.

Mom gasped. "I feel this way in dreams, sometimes. . . ." Then, as if the texture would sustain her, she ran her hands up the bumpy bark of the tree, tilting her head back to stare up into its branches, her eyes glassy.

Then she curled her fingers into the tree, and I saw long, shiny claws cut into the wood. Thunder boomed deafeningly as lightning flared just a few feet away, knocking me flat on my back. A smell of ozone cut the air.

But my mother still stood by the tree, looking somehow taller than usual. Her hair, which should have been brown and limp with rain, looked long and red. Another bolt of lightning shot up between her feet, illuminating yellow-green eyes that were usually hazel.

"Mom?" I said, suddenly not sure who stood before me.

"The storm." It came out of her like a growl. Her voice, normally sweet and slightly high-pitched, now sounded like she'd spent her life drinking whiskey and smoking cigarettes. She swiveled her head to me with an odd, unnatural suddenness, like a marionette. "I came in the midst of the eternal storm that I might speak to you, my daughter."

"Who . . . ?" I started to say. Richard was getting out of the car. He'd be here any second. "What's going on?"

"I can only speak to you briefly here and now." Lightning stabbed up at the sky all around her, raising the hairs on my arms, and haloing her head like a crown. Thunder shook the ground.

Richard came to a pounding halt beside me, one arm up to shield his eyes from the terrible brightness. "My God, my God, Caroline!"

"Even I, who rule here, may not long endure this tempest," she said, in that dusky voice that cut through the crackling and rumbling. "But you must learn who you are."

My mouth went dry. "Who are you?" It came out as a whisper, a gasp.

A bolt of lightning bigger than the tree itself thrust up from the ground where she stood. The deafening boom knocked Richard to his knees.

Mom screamed in agony, draining every ounce of blood

from my heart. Then she cried out something as more light-ning danced around her, but I couldn't hear through the ex-plosions. I caught just a word here or there, like the voice on my malfunctioning iPod. "Never . . . belong . . . Amba!"

Then the lightning was gone, and the thunder and the claws, leaving nothing but my tiny, wet mother leaning against an old oak tree in her bathrobe. She crumpled into the mud and lay still.

# CHAPTER 2

According to the doctor in the ER, Mom's tests showed that she'd had a seizure but would suffer no long-term effects. Her MRI showed activity in what he called "some unusual areas" of her brain. We took her home later in the morning armed with pointless anti-seizure meds and a mandate to keep her hydrated.

Richard and I didn't say much to each other as we made her comfortable in bed, but we both knew this wasn't a case of dehydration or a sudden onset of epilepsy.

It was all my fault. I'd brought her to the lightning tree. Somehow her proximity to it or to me had triggered something from Othersphere. Something that called me "my daughter" and used the word "Amba." Both my teacher Morfael and my enemy Ximon had used that word when referring to me.

I didn't allow myself to think too much just yet about who or what had been speaking through Mom. She had adopted me when I was nearly two years old from a Russian orphanage. No one knew who my biological parents were, and no tiger-shifters had been heard from in over twenty years. The remaining otherkin whispered that they'd all been wiped out by the Tribunal, that I was the last of my kind.

I'd always hoped that wasn't true, that one day I'd meet more people like me. Now I didn't know what to think. Why couldn't my biological parents have been teenagers who forgot the condom or folks with too many mouths to feed? People like that wouldn't pose a danger to Mom.

Not for the first time, I wished Morfael had a mobile phone. Not only did the mysterious head of our school look like a ghostly apparition, he behaved like one too. Like Caleb, he was a caller of shadow, with the power to conjure objects from shadow and force shifters to take their animal form. But Morfael had other, unexplained abilities, and a long history of watching over me without ever quite telling me why. He was my best chance to find out what was going on with Mom. Not that he'd necessarily tell me, even if I could reach him.

I texted Caleb briefly, then put the phone down. Keeping it near my body might kill it before I could get an answer. When it chimed mid-morning, my heart leaped, till I saw it was from Siku, not Caleb.

*"Trib visit last night, no casualties,"* his text read. *"You?"*

And right after that, one from November: *"Some bastard sneaking around here last night. Nothing's missing. Weird."*

I seized the phone, fear pulsing with my heartbeat, and typed back. *"Same. No idea why. What about L and A?"*

Even as I sent that, another text came in, this time from London. *"Obj snuck into house last night. Mom killed him but others got away. You ok?"*

An objurer from the Tribunal in London's house in Idaho too! I copied them all on the next text, and included Arnaldo and Caleb. *"I'm ok. Coordinated home invasions on me, N, L, and S. A, please respond. Need to know why."*

I got up from where I'd been sitting next to Mom's bed to pace. More texts came in from Siku, November, and London. All three invading objurers had rummaged around our bathrooms, but they'd left nothing behind and had appeared to take nothing. No one's aspirin or water appeared to have been spiked, no traps laid, no cameras planted.

Caleb finally texted back that they'd seen no Tribunal activity in or around Morfael's new school. So for now that appeared to be safe. He sent me a personal text, *"Making sure—you okay?"*

I texted back:*"Ok, but not great. Will call soon."* No way I could tell him about Lazar or Mom via text. We'd have to talk on the landline later. Strange events were piling up too fast.

An hour went by. Mom woke up, asked for water, and didn't remember anything after seeing me shift back to human last night. Richard had postponed the move till tomorrow to give her a little more time to recover. But he didn't want to wait longer than that. The sooner we were off the Tribunal's radar, the better.

And Arnaldo never responded. His family lived in a very remote part of Arizona, so his cell reception might be bad. Also, his father hated everyone who wasn't a bird-shifter, so he might've taken Arnaldo's phone away at the first text, or forbidden Arnaldo to respond.

Or Arnaldo and his whole family could be dead or kidnapped.

That was something else I couldn't think about right now. Events were rolling along quickly, and I wanted, *needed,* to make a plan. The Tribunal was up to something awful, no doubt. If we were quick and smart, we could get ahead of them. For too long the otherkin had allowed their enemies to take the initiative.

Then London texted in all caps: *"JUST FIGURED OUT— THEY TOOK MY HAIRBRUSH! WTF??"*

I stood there for a moment, not quite believing it, but knowing, somehow, exactly what it meant. Then I pelted into my bathroom and slid open the side drawer where I kept a comb and a hairbrush.

The comb lay there. The hairbrush was gone. The drawer was otherwise empty. Everything was packed up for the move. But under the comb I spotted something white. I opened the drawer farther and pulled out a small, folded piece of paper. Goosebumps pricked on my skin as I slowly unfolded it.

The handwriting was so like Caleb's it took my breath for a moment. But the lines were slanted the opposite way, to the left, and the pressure was darker, as if he'd pressed the pen very hard into the paper. It said only, "I'm sorry. Maybe someday you can forgive me. For everything."

The last two words were crammed into the corner, as if they'd been added later. No signature. But I knew who had left it. An uneasy mixture of anger and pity flooded through me. Lazar had taken my hairbrush and DNA on orders from the Tribunal.

Then he had apologized.

Grabbing my phone, I blasted a text to everyone except Arnaldo, in case his father had taken his phone: "*My brush gone too. They want our DNA. Can everyone meet in Las Vegas tomorrow? First we get Arnaldo, then we get answers.*"

A flurry of responses pinged in. Siku and November's toothbrushes were gone, sealing my conviction that the Tribunal had been after things that held our DNA. No way to know why yet, but Ximon's old compound had held a laboratory, and files filled with scientific jargon. We'd burned them all, but there were other compounds, other labs, other experiments.

If the objurers had succeeded in taking something from Arnaldo's home too, that would mean they had DNA from all five tribes of otherkin, and from each shifter member of the group that had raided Ximon's compound. Caleb had been there too, but the Tribunal held a special hatred for shifters. Callers like Caleb were essentially identical to the Tribunal's objurers, and thus not considered demonic, only misguided. And Caleb was Ximon's son. That was half his DNA right there.

I was planning to drive to Vegas the next day with Mom and Richard. I didn't know exactly where Morfael's new school was yet, but it was close enough for Caleb to meet us there. My friends all agreed to convene at the entrance of the Luxor Hotel. Caleb said the crowds would be useful if we needed to lose anyone who might be following. And we couldn't meet at the apartment Mom and Richard had taken. The fewer people who knew where that was, the better. So the Luxor it was. From there we could head to Arnaldo's, a few hours south.

By nightfall, Mom felt well enough to get up and share Thai takeout. I told them I needed to meet my friends and go to Arizona, and they didn't like that at all. I tried explaining how Arnaldo might be in danger from the Tribunal, but that only made things worse.

"You want to walk into a trap and probably get killed?" Mom said. Anger made her cheeks flush. She looked healthier than she had all day. "I won't allow it."

"Arnaldo's like family to me," I said. "All my friends from Morfael's school are. You know that. I told you how Ximon, Lazar, and their Tribunal troops attacked us at the school and kidnapped Siku."

"You all risked your lives to save him," she said. "I know, honey. I know how much you love them."

"Then you've got to see why—"

"Your mother just got out of the hospital," Richard said. "She needs you."

"That's the thing," I said, my voice dropping low. "I think Mom might be safer not just away from the lightning tree, but away from . . . me."

That drained all of the color from Mom's face, and then I

really did feel guilty. She sat down heavily. "None of this is your fault, Desdemona," she said.

"We don't know what happened to you, Mom," I said. "Until we do, maybe we should keep you away from anything or anyone connected to Othersphere. Including me."

Mom opened her mouth to protest, but Richard put his hand on her shoulder and said, "She could be right, Caroline."

Mom looked back and forth between my face and Richard's, then dropped her head and sighed. "I still don't think it's you. But okay. You just have to promise me you'll look carefully for any signs of a trap."

"I promise," I said.

After that, we ate, sitting on boxes, not saying much. Richard had told Mom what he'd seen and heard at the lightning tree. I was braced for sadness or anger at the suggestion that someone from my biological family was behind it all. But she simply nodded.

I'd always known I was adopted, but only a couple months ago I learned the strange story of how I'd been found by Morfael in a ring of dead trees in Siberia. He'd engineered for my mother to adopt me, after finding no tiger-shifters to take me in.

Before that, Mom and I hadn't talked much about who my biological parents might be. She'd made it clear that she'd chosen me, that she loved me. And that should have been enough for me. She was the best mother anyone could hope for. And when I was ten, Richard had come along to marry her and be a kind of friend/stepfather. I lacked for nothing in my family.

*Then why do I sometimes wake up feeling a huge hole in my heart? Why when I'm in tiger form do I feel part of . . . something else? Maybe all shifters feel that way.*

"Desdemona," Mom finally said, putting down her pad thai. "I have to ask. When you were at his school, did Morfael ever talk about anything like what happened last night?"

I shook my head. "Not like that. That was crazy. I mean, he sent me and Caleb underground once, and made me think you were there when you weren't, but..." I trailed off as they both frowned at me. "But that was all in my head. Probably."

"So, yes. This type of thing has happened before," said Mom.

"But nobody got hurt at Morfael's," I said. "That was an illusion. Last night—I think..." I swallowed, afraid to say what I thought, then said it anyway. "I think that was someone from Othersphere coming through. Like what happened to Caleb at Ximon's compound. He got tired, overwhelmed, and something from the other side of the veil started to manifest itself through him."

"But you stopped it," my mother said. I'd told them most of what had happened during the raid. But I hadn't told them exactly how I'd saved Caleb. That was too personal. Even now, I was blushing, and Mom was squinting at me suspiciously.

"Yeah," I said. "I stopped it."

"That thing mentioned a 'tempest,' " Richard said.

I put down my own plate, not hungry anymore. "That tree is rare. Caleb called it a lightning tree. It's connected to the world next to ours, to Othersphere, but it has a different form there, a shadow form. Over in Othersphere there's no tree, but a huge, permanent storm of lightning and thunder. So what we saw was that shadow form bleeding through the veil between the worlds."

"That thing said it ruled there, wherever it's from. It called you 'daughter.' "

"I know, I heard it." It came out snappish. I took a deep breath. "Sorry. It's just...I don't know what that means. The lightning tree is a connection to Othersphere, so maybe someone used it to talk to me through Mom?"

"I've been having dreams," Mom said flatly, like she was making a sudden confession. "I haven't told you because I thought they were just dreams. It made sense that my sub-conscious would be tussling with everything we've learned in the last few months."

"But now you think they might be more." Richard put his hand on her arm.

She half-smiled at him. "My intuitive husband. In the dream, I feel something deep inside me, like a whirlpool. A churning. It makes me anxious, because it feels so wrong, so alien. . . ."

Goosebumps rose on my chilled skin. That's how I'd felt about my own connection to Othersphere at first. The world on the other side of the veil was utterly unknown and scary. The Tribunal thought our connection to it made us demons or fiends. After what I'd seen that night at the Tribunal com-pound, I could understand that. Even though my own shadow form, and those of my fellow otherkin, was anything but evil.

"I hear a voice in the dream," Mom continued, "low and husky, telling me to just let go, to let it come, this thing that's trying to get out of me. Then the voice says, 'I have a message of importance.' Over and over again, the same words. 'I have a message of importance.' So I reach into myself, here"—Mom pressed her hand against her sternum—"to try and pull it out of me, this thing, this message, but when I look down to see what it is, what I've pulled out—it's my own heart."

She inhaled sharply at the memory. Her distress brought tears to my eyes. Richard, in that gentle way he had, sidled over and took her in his arms. She leaned into him, patting his chest. I could see that she wanted to burrow into him, to escape what she was feeling, but she didn't, so that I wouldn't be too frightened.

"Your dream could be related to what happened," said Richard. "But what was the message of importance? We couldn't hear much over the storm."

"No," I said. "But I'm pretty sure, whatever the message was, it was meant for me."

# CHAPTER 3

The marble-floored, slant-ceilinged lobby of the Luxor hotel was choked with cigarette smoke and bad copies of monumental pharaoh statues. It smelled of dirty metal, alcohol, and menthol. Off in the casino portion, where teenagers were technically not allowed, waitresses in see-through linen skirts set free drinks down next to glassy-eyed gamblers.

*So much noise.* It bounced off all the metal and plastic around me as I paced near the hind end of a sandstone sphinx close to the banks of one-armed bandits. I tried to ignore the clicking of glasses, the clanging of slot machines with fake tumblers falling into place, the *tick-tick* of heels on marble, the *ching-ching* of the simulated sound of quarters falling into metal trays. Occasionally, a buzzer would low like an ox as a lucky winner yelled out in victory.

I was itchy and on high alert. I hated Vegas, with its asphalt and dust and desperation. The metal in the machines set the nerves in my skin on high alert. Plus, Mom, Richard, and I had been followed as we left Burbank in the moving van. It had taken us seven hours to get here instead of five because we had to be sure we lost them.

But it was even more than that. Any second now I'd see Caleb for the first time in weeks. Soon I would touch him, feel his strong hands on me, bury my nose in the crook of his neck to smell his fresh thunderstorm scent and hear the steady, reassuring beat of his heart. I wasn't shaking visibly, but inside me something was thrumming like a violin with a bow running over its strings.

A squeal broke through the rattles and bells. A squeal I recognized. I adjusted my heavy backpack, made sure no security guards were watching, and headed deeper into the forbidden den of slot machines. I kept my head low so the ceiling cameras wouldn't see I was underage, angled past an elderly woman with perfectly coiffed white hair compulsively hitting the button on a one-eyed bandit, and found November bouncing up and down next to Siku as their slot machine shot out a ticket.

She looked miniscule next to Siku's broad-shouldered form, her short brown hair spiking up as if in surprise. Her tight skinny jeans were tucked into short boots with soft soles that I knew from experience made no sound when she walked. She wore a bright red "Anderson's Pawn & Loan" T-shirt under a sleek black leather jacket that hugged her waist, looking eleven times hipper than Siku, who sported his usual wrinkled brown flannel shirt. He was even taller than when I'd seen him last. His shoulders had to be at least a yard wide, narrowing down to hips that barely held up his baggy jeans. His small suitcase sat next to them, November's enormous bag towering over it.

November's squinty eyes lit up as they fell on me. "Stripes! Look, we won!" She threw her thin arms around me, her face burrowing into my chest, where she delivered a raspberry.

"Yeah, but how much have you spent?" I hugged her back as well as I could given the height difference, then lifted my head to accept Siku's dry kiss on my cheek.

"More than this." He held up the tickets of their winnings. "We'll stop now."

"But you can't win if you don't spend!" November let go of me to tug on his free arm.

"Actually, you're not supposed to gamble if you're under twenty-one," I said.

Siku dropped his gaze down to November's, one eyebrow lifting, and she deflated. "Okay, okay. You can't win much at the slots anyway. We should try roulette. Siku looks at least twenty-five!" She bounced up and down like a six-year-old.

Siku lifted his eyes from her jitterbugging to me. "Two full-size Snickers and two Cokes," he said.

November shoved him indignantly. "Don't *explain* me!"

He ignored her, not budging. "Have you seen the others yet?"

"No." I gazed around the lobby, hoping to hear or see either London or Caleb, but mostly Caleb. "Were you followed here?"

"Didn't see anyone," said Siku.

"But we went around the block a few times and all that jazz to be sure before we let the cab drop us off here," November said. "Just like you said, boss lady."

"I'm not the . . ." I shook my head. No point in arguing over nicknames with November. She called us whatever her mood dictated. "My parents and I had to shake a tail on the way here. So the Tribunal might know which town we're in."

"Inevitable," said Siku. "And if they know where our families live, they also know where Arnaldo is. We should be prepared for that when we get close to his house."

"Do we really have to drive there?" November asked, riffling the tickets in Siku's hand. "It's pretty far from here, like, six hours."

"Airports are easier to watch than roads," I said. "It's a numbers game."

"Like gambling." November grinned, showing all her tiny teeth. "It's one of the reasons I like hanging with you, Dez. Life is never dull."

"It's a gamble whether you're hanging with me or not," I said. I wanted to say how much I longed for a dull life, how hard it had been to leave Mom and Richard in their new secret apartment. Their life here was just as much of a gamble as our lives as shifters. But this wasn't the time or place for that. I could talk about such things with Caleb, when we were alone. The ache inside me was growing.

I caught a familiar scent of fur and snow and turned my head. November and Siku must have caught it too, because they also swiveled to look down the row of shiny metal and neon to see London sauntering toward us with that long, loping gait. She was letting the hair dye grow out, so her roots were now three inches of pale blond, darkening suddenly to pitch black down to jagged ends that swung near her shoulders. A new gold nose ring glinted in her left nostril, and she'd added a few pounds to her lanky frame. They filled out her once-starved face and made her silvery T-shirt and jeans cling becomingly. Like me, she wore a large backpack.

"Wolfie!" November practically leaped on London, clinging like a monkey. "Girl, you look righteous." She pulled away, head cocked. "You've been snacking."

"On rats." London smothered November's angry squeak with a proper hug. I embraced the two of them, and then Siku lumbered over to wrap his long arms around all of us.

"Okay, Siks." November's voice came out muffled. "Eventually, we'll need to breathe."

London hugged me a little longer, then pulled away, not meeting my eyes. I went immediately on alert. "I have a message for you."

At the word "message," a chill ran over me.

Could it be something else coming via Othersphere? Or from Lazar? But no, he wouldn't use London for that. "From whom?"

Her thin lips twisted, as if pushing back reluctance. Then she smiled, but it was forced. "Just follow the snow."

She pointed. Puzzled, I saw, falling onto the loud, semi-

Egyptian carpet, a few flakes of snow. I looked up, but there was no hole in the ceiling or snow machine above. The snowflakes were wafting down from nowhere. I caught a whiff of pine sap, and something else—something unearthly, yet strangely familiar.

I walked toward the snow flurry, vaguely aware of London following, Siku and November close behind her. The flakes fell out of nowhere on my face and hands, pinpricks of cold. Others dusted my shoulders.

"Over there," November whispered.

I looked up to see the branch of an evergreen tree wedged between a wall and a plastic sheet which blocked off a quiet area in the dark lobby, marked with an orange cone and a sign that said PARDON OUR DUST.

From the tantalizing scent creeping through the plastic, there were trees and more snow beyond it. I hesitated. *It could be a trap.* London had seemed unwilling to tell me about this . . . whatever it was.

But November was beaming at me like a searchlight. She gave me a shove. "Go on, stupid!"

So I pushed aside the curtain.

And stepped into the winter forest from a dream.

What should have been half-painted walls, pillars, and bare floor awaiting new carpet was instead a moonlit clearing in a woodland hushed with snowfall. Pine trees twenty stories high reached their dark fragrant branches toward a clouded sky that shook snow down upon me.

A fluffy white rabbit, big as a poodle, hopped over a frozen stream that wound between white-outlined bushes and snow-covered grass. And all the clanging and itching that invaded my senses from the machines outside was blown away on a night breeze full of scents I both recognized and did not. It was not a wind from this world. I breathed it in, and something else. A hint of once-stormy sky, of leaves quiet after a rain.

*Caleb.*

He walked toward me, dark eyes burning, his long black coat brushing the snow off encroaching branches. The snow rabbit paused to watch him go by, unafraid. A flood of heat pushed my heart into my throat and filled me with something so light I thought I'd float away, or faint from the pleasure. I tried to say his name, say anything, but I couldn't speak.

"I found all this in the shadow here," he said. His voice was more harmonious in person than on the phone. I felt like I could dive through its depths. "And I knew it was meant for you."

I didn't need to talk. I ran one hand along his strong jaw, up into his dark tousled hair. In his night-black eyes I saw a glint of gold. His lips bent into a knowing smile. Then his arms were around me, warm and strong, our bodies pressed hip to hip, heart to heart.

"I love it," I whispered.

"I love you," he said, in that low murmur that was, yet was not, a whisper. His mouth brushed against my eyelid, soft and warm. I inhaled, taking in all of him; then he stopped my breath with a kiss.

Time held its breath along with me. The boundary between our bodies melted, and the whole world seemed to melt right along with it.

*Tap, tap, tap.*

I brushed at something on my shoulder, wondering vaguely if I could somehow make a living kissing Caleb for the rest of my life.

Caleb looked up and frowned past me. His lips were reddened, his eyes unfocused.

"*I said,* there's an old woman outside wearing an earpiece and whispering into a microphone, pretending not to look at us."

It was London's voice, with a harder edge than usual. Caleb's gaze sharpened, and I turned to look. London stood there, brow creased with embarrassment. "Sorry to interrupt your faery forest and all. I didn't say anything to 'Ember and Siku because the old lady is at the slot machine right next to them."

I blinked. "An old woman with white hair wearing a white sweater with sequins on it?"

London nodded. "Yeah."

"I saw her earlier. She was at least five rows away before. If she's right outside now with an earpiece, she's got to be following us."

"The Tribunal." Caleb swept the forest clearing with a commanding glance, and around us, trees and snow began to vanish. The stream faded away, and a workbench covered with paint cans popped back into existence. Caleb's power had grown since I'd last seen him conjure things from Othersphere.

"We've got to ditch her and anyone else following us before we go to Arnaldo's," I said.

"There's a security door this way," Caleb said, gesturing toward the back wall I could now see behind us. Someone had started to paint it lapis blue. "Amaris is waiting in the car." He took his phone out of his pocket and dialed. "I'll tell her to get ready."

"November and Siku are still out there," said London, starting back toward the plastic sheeting.

"Wait." I grabbed her arm. "If we all bolt, they'll know we're on to them. We've got a better chance of giving them the slip if we don't seem alarmed. Look casual, go out there, and send November in, but don't say why. They're listening. Then you and Siku follow one at a time."

"Why does November get to come back in here first?" London said, frowning.

"Because we need her lock picks," I said. "The hotel's not going to leave security doors unlocked."

London's face cleared into an appreciative smile. "I hate you, smarty pants," she said, then did her best laid-back amble past the plastic sheet.

"No, get the car close to the exit. We'll find you," Caleb

said into his phone, speaking to his sister. He intertwined his warm fingers with mine and pulled me toward the back wall, where I spotted the outline of a door, unlabeled. "You released the parking brake, right? Okay. Just back up slowly out of the space and you'll be fine. *You'll be fine, Amaris.* See you soon."

He hung up and shook his head. "Doesn't officially have her license yet, but it's not a problem."

"She doesn't know how to drive?" I asked.

"We've been practicing for weeks." A flicker of worry narrowed his eyes; then he shook his head. "She'll be fine."

"She'll be fine," I repeated, like a mantra.

November came bouncing up, wheeling her bulging suitcase precariously behind her. "London said to come in, but she looks like she's got a stomachache. Did she catch you guys making out or something?"

"That's not—" I cut myself off and lowered my voice. "That little old lady outside is following us," I said. "That's why London's upset."

November's spiky eyebrows rose. "Oh, Tigger, you are so wonderfully clueless. That's not what's making Wolfie so grumpy. Don't you see how she—?"

"Not now, 'Ember," Caleb said in a warning tone I didn't quite understand. "Focus. See this? It's a locked door, and we need to get through it. Now."

"So we're making a quiet break for it back here?" November showed all her teeth in her hungry smile, and reached into her pocket to pull out three slim metal tools held together with a shiny chewing gum wrapper. "That's my cue."

A large shadow cut across our faces, and I nearly jumped out of my skin.

"London said it would look better if I came in first." It was Siku, his booming voice low. "Who we running from?"

"Little old lady," I said. "White sweater, earpiece, following us."

"Little old lady . . ." Siku looked over his shoulder at the plastic sheet. "At least we can outrun her."

"Probably," I said. "But there has to be more of them than just her. How's it coming, 'Ember?"

November's sharp face was screwed up with concentration as she jiggled the pick in the lock. "Almost there. Maybe I should've raked this baby, but that's risky, and I didn't want to . . . Ha!"

The lock turned, and we all heard the deadbolt slide back. "Wait for London," I said. "In case it's alarmed."

"I'm here, I'm here." London jogged up. "She's talking to some dude in a white blazer now."

November let out an annoyed whoosh of breath. "Even in Vegas these creeps wear white. Don't they know that doesn't make them the good guys?" She yanked open the door, and looked up at Siku. "After you."

He grabbed her bag and palmed the door, pushing it farther open. A cement hallway stretched right and left, lit by bare bulbs. "No. Me last."

"I'm not shy about going first," said London, slipping under Siku's arm and into the hallway.

"Go, go," I said, shoving November. At least no audible alarm had gone off.

November scooted into the hall, turning right after London, just as the plastic sheet behind us trembled and wafted aside to reveal the little old lady. Her rhinestone-speckled sweater glinted, her heavily mascaraed eyes narrowed right at us.

Siku didn't wait, stomping through the door.

Caleb squeezed my hand. I felt a familiar lift in my chest as he pulled me through the door. "Just like old times," I said.

A wry grin lit his face as a heavy-shouldered man in a white blazer with a bulge beneath it loomed behind the old woman. The man reached under his coat as I slammed the door shut and rammed the bolt home.

# CHAPTER 4

Caleb and I ran hand in hand after our friends, our footsteps echoing down the cinderblock hallway. Yellow-green lightbulbs lit the way. My backpack bounced painfully on my shoulders, but my spirits were high. I was on the run with Caleb again, only now we were a team in company with friends. Nothing could stop us.

London skidded to a stop up ahead in front of a door with a push-bar handle and threw us a look. "Here?"

"Sure!" Caleb shouted to her.

London shoved the door open. November reached her, and looked back at Caleb. "You have no idea where it goes, do you?"

"No, but neither does the Tribunal."

"Fair enough." She slipped through the door past London, and we heard her voice echo back. "Stairs. Up or down?"

"Not up," I said between breaths as we came pounding up

behind Siku. "Upstairs will be nothing but long hallways of locked hotel rooms."

"Down we go," said November. And down she went.

As London and Siku followed, I cast a glance down the long hall. The door we'd come through was shuddering, as if from blows. "I think we pissed them off," I said.

We sped down the metal stairs, as silently as they allowed. Ten stairs down and turn, then ten more and turn. We did that four times before we found London stock-still on a landing with her ear pressed against a door marked LL1. Caleb and I looked at each other and mouthed at the same time: "Lower Lobby One."

"Footsteps out there. Lots," she said.

"Go anyway," I said. "This is a busy hotel. Most people won't care what we're doing. Look for a sign to the parking garage."

She yanked the door open, and we stepped out into another hallway, much like the first, only this one had people in it. Two men in white gave me pause until I realized they were kitchen staff, hustling a wheeled cart with a half-eaten lobster, an empty champagne bottle, and crumb-covered plates in one direction. Farther down the hall, three women wearing white tutus and swan-feathered headdresses were walking away from us, spooning yogurt into their mouths and chattering.

"Kitchens must be that way." Caleb pointed in the direction the men were going with the cart.

"Theater dressing rooms that way." I pointed toward the vanishing ladies in the tutus.

"I hear they've got a cool magic show at this hotel," said November. "I vote we go in the theater direction."

We all drew back as a man in enormous green shoes, purple fright wig, and a big red nose clomped past us chewing on a drumstick. His bare arms rippled with smooth muscle, and his red shirt was covered in orange pompoms that helped hide a built-in harness circling his waist.

"Acrobat clowns?" Siku whispered.

"Welcome to Vegas," said Caleb.

"The kitchens will be close to some kind of delivery dock or place where trucks drop off supplies," said London. "We could slip out of the building that way."

"Plus, kitchens usually have cupcakes and pastries in them," said Siku.

"We will need a snack for the road...." November was being persuaded.

"No doubt we can get out of the building via the kitchens," I said. "But that's the obvious way to go."

"The Tribunal will probably send someone to that delivery area to watch for us," Caleb finished my thought. "If they haven't already."

"To the theater!" November scuttled off down the hallway, Siku in tow. "I want a tutu!"

"I want big green shoes," said Siku.

As we hustled after them, I noticed Caleb scanning the ceiling. "Cameras?" I said.

He shrugged. "It's Vegas. They're everywhere."

"You think the Tribunal might've hacked into them?"

"Lazar's almost as good with a computer as he is with a rifle," Caleb said, his voice thickening with anger as he said his half-brother's name. "It's possible."

"You think Lazar's here?" I hadn't had a chance yet to tell Caleb that it had been Lazar who stole my DNA, or about his useless apology.

"I hope so," Caleb said. "Because this time he won't get away alive."

We were passing the women in the tutus. As Caleb spoke, one of them swiveled her head to stare at him with eyes painted like elaborate black-and-silver wings.

"Ssh," I said. "I know you're angry, but this isn't the time to talk about this, let alone confront Lazar or anyone...."

"He killed my mother, Dez," Caleb said. He lowered his voice, but that only made it darker, more deadly. "How would you feel if he killed yours?"

That shut me up. I squeezed his arm and let it go. I'd always been able to tell Caleb everything, and once we were on the road and out of immediate danger, that's what I'd do. Now was not the time for a confrontation.

We rounded a corner and went through a double door, where the population of tutus increased, and several curvy women dressed like showgirls crossed with Mary Poppins adjusted their hats. We passed a black coffin engraved with silver swirls, a human-sized glass cage half filled with water, and another woman with enormous breasts bursting out of the her low-cut Victorian wedding gown, which had been cut away in front to show off her elaborate ivory garters.

But no one told us to stop. Maybe it was the way we hurried, as if we were late to get ready for a performance. Or maybe no one gave a damn.

The space around us opened up into a poorly lit jungle of cables and pulleys. Something hummed, and the four-by-four-foot patch of ceiling a few feet away from me lowered down to reveal an empty electric chair. Above it, another four-by-four-foot slab rapidly closed off the hole, and I realized that we were below the actual stage.

"Do you think there's a show going on above us right now?" London asked.

"Probably rehearsal," said Caleb.

We followed a narrow river of clowns, sexy nannies, and dark-shirted stage crew walking along the wall to avoid the cables. I glanced back at the electric chair and spotted a flash of white behind it. Someone else from the kitchen?

Caleb was staring at the electric chair too. He caught my questioning glance. "It has a powerful shadow," he said. "I think people really died in it. What's that?" He stopped dead, eyes fixed on something near the chair.

A man in a top hat and tails smacked right into him, cursed, and went around. Caleb muttered an apology, scanned the chair again, then turned and moved on.

I searched the shadows near the chair, letting him go ahead. Something flickered, like a dark mirror reflecting gold. Probably some weird stage magic item.

I moved to catch up with the others, who had continued threading their way past men in peacock feathers and a woman wearing a bright red body stocking.

"Desdemona," came a whisper. "Wait." I felt the voice's vibration down to my toes, and I turned, like an automaton.

I scanned the cables and random furniture that filled the dark space beyond. The weird mirrorlike thing behind the electric chair was gone, but closer to me stood a red, wooden horizontal cabinet on a table with strange sliding doors on its sides. It took me a moment to realize it was one of those boxes magicians used to saw ladies in half. The small doors could slide aside to reveal the arms and legs of the person inside.

Lazar stepped out from behind it, wearing his usual white turtleneck and jeans, his thick butterscotch hair tousled. "I need to speak with you for just a second," he said.

"You used your voice on me!" Objurers of the Tribunal and callers like Caleb were trained to use their voices to persuade shifters like me to do things. Lazar's father, Ximon, was so skilled at it that he could get almost anyone, otherkin or human, to do his bidding.

"Only a little," Lazar said. "I wanted to—"

His voice broke off, eyebrows shooting up, as a figure in a long black coat ran past me and cannoned into him. They fell to the floor together, legs thrashing.

"Caleb—!"

Everyone was looking at us.

"Who the hell is *that*?" a woman said.

Caleb reared back and punched Lazar in the face. Lazar's head smacked against the floor. But he didn't try to hit back. He stopped struggling, shook his head slightly, and blinked up at his half-brother. His sun-browned cheekbones were smeared with dirt, the skin around one eye now red and starting to swell.

"Fight back!" Caleb shoved Lazar's shoulders with both hands, then got up, giving Lazar room to stand too. "Get up and fight!"

Lazar pushed himself up to sit and pressed one hand against the back of his head. His mouth twisted in a pained grimace even as he let out a breath of a laugh. "Frustrating, isn't it?"

"Oh, it's that bastard," said Siku. He, November, and London had come back to stand behind me, so that we stood in a semicircle around Lazar, pinning him up against the red cabinet.

"You should let Caleb rough you up every time you go out," November said, her voice biting. "It's an improvement."

Lazar rolled his eyes, but he did not reply.

Caleb kicked at one of Lazar's boots. "We could just kill you right here," he said. "I don't see any backup."

"I didn't bring any," Lazar said. "No one else knows you're in this part of the hotel."

"Lies," said London.

"Hey, you kids!" A large man in jeans and a black T-shirt over by the wall pointed at us. "Get away from those cables! I'm going to call security."

"Come on," I said. "He's not worth the time it would take. Delaying us here is probably exactly what he wants."

"No," said Lazar, looking up at me directly. "I just wanted to be sure you got my message."

Caleb's brow wrinkled as he shot me a look. "What message?"

"I was going to tell you," I said. "Lazar was the one who broke into my house and took my hairbrush. He left me a note, apologizing."

"Like that makes a difference?" London said.

Again Lazar looked like he was suppressing a comment. Caleb leaned over, grabbed his brother by the front of his dirty white shirt, and lifted him bodily to his feet. "You broke into Dez's house?"

Lazar looked him in the eye. His mouth, so like Caleb's own, widened into an infuriating grin. "Yep. And I have to tell you, she was wearing a whole lot less than she's wearing now."

My face got hot. Caleb tensed, then let go of Lazar and struck him with a quick, hard one-two, a cross and an uppercut. The sound of his fists slamming into flesh was sickening. Lazar's head snapped back from the force. He back-heeled into the furniture behind him, and went down.

But he wasn't out. Propping himself up on one elbow, he felt his jaw with the other hand and cocked one eyebrow up at Caleb.

"Coward," Caleb said, and turned, pushing past Siku as if he couldn't stand to be there another moment.

Siku spat on the ground at Lazar's feet; then he lumbered off too.

"But . . ." November frowned at Lazar. "We can't just let him go. . . ."

"Come on." London grabbed a fistful of her sleeve and tugged, and they walked away.

I began to follow, but Lazar spoke. "I meant what I wrote." His voice was rough. I stopped to look back at him. "Please tell Amaris I'm sorry."

I met his deep brown eyes and saw real emotion there, actual sorrow and regret. "Why?" I said. "What changed?"

When he spoke, his voice was almost too quiet to hear. "Back at our desert compound, you asked me to come with you. Back then I couldn't even imagine such a thing. I thought you were crazy. But it planted a seed. I keep wondering what life would be like somewhere . . . else. A life that wasn't all about hate."

Lazar's father, Ximon, was an abusive fanatic, and he'd

shaped Lazar since birth to be the same. I was lucky. I couldn't even imagine such a brutal upbringing, and how it would warp someone.

"Who do you want to be, Lazar?" I said. "You're too old to keeping blaming your father. I hear what you're saying, but words are empty. If you want to be a better person, do what a better person would do."

He regarded me again for a long moment, his jaw muscles clenching. I knew I should go, that Caleb was waiting. But I stood there.

"I haven't told them where you all are," he said. "And I won't. But they'll have someone watching every parking lot exit, every outside door. Be careful."

"I will." I started to go, then turned back, and said, "You be careful too."

His eyes got wide, and it looked like he was about to say something, but I spun away and ran after my friends. Somehow the spark of hope in his eyes was more difficult to bear than the pain.

# CHAPTER 5

London accidentally sniffed out a quiet exit by leading us down a random hallway and opening up a door marked PRIVATE.

We all peered in to see a tall shirtless man in his thirties with shoulder-length, dyed black hair and a web of colorful tattoos running up his arms. He was thin, but a woman with pink hair stood in front of him with an airbrush gun, drawing a six-pack onto the hairless abs above his tight leather pants. A cage filled with pigeons rustled softly on his dressing table.

He looked up at us clustered in his doorway. "What the hell?"

"Hey, you're the magic dude, right?" November asked.

He half-nodded as if he suddenly wasn't sure.

November laughed and pointed at his airbrushed abs. "Makeup's pretty magical, isn't it?"

The makeup lady came toward us, spray gun aimed. "No one's allowed in here!"

We backed up, and she slammed the door.

"Look!" London pointed at a sign at the end of the hall marked EXIT – TALENT ONLY.

Caleb placed his hand on the doorknob. "I'd say we're all pretty talented, wouldn't you?"

"I don't know," Siku said, lifting up his shirt to look at his own ripped torso. "I've never painted on any muscles. Do I qualify?"

"Oh, yeah, you do." November slid her hand up his bare stomach, grinning up at him.

He gave her a look from under his thick brows and pulled away, dropping his shirt. She frowned.

"Can we go now?" London shoved open the exit door.

"I can't help it if Vegas turns me on," said November, flouncing through the door after London.

"Everything turns you on," said Siku, walking stolidly after her.

London tucked her head in close to mine, talking low. "What is going on with them? She's such a flirt, but it's like she means it with him."

"I know!" I whispered back. "And I think Siku likes it, but he's not taking her seriously."

"Wise boy," she said.

We exited into an underground parking garage with sloping ramps and a line of black, white, and cherry-red limousines parked in extra-long spaces. Caleb was already on the phone with Amaris. "It says Reserved, Level One. Where are you?" His attention focused on what she was saying, then he covered the mic on the phone and said to us, "Amaris is one level up, and there's a guy in a white turtleneck driving a white SUV watching her."

"Subtle, aren't they?" November put her hands on her hips.

"What if we steal one of these limos and sneak out in one of them instead? A stretch limousine would look good on me."

"What about Amaris?" asked Caleb. "I could hot-wire one of these for sure, but how's she supposed to get rid of the guy up there?"

"We can't steal a regular person's car," I said, thinking hard. "Then the cops would be after us as well as the Tribunal. And we need to ditch the guy watching Amaris. So we knock him out—"

"And take his car." Caleb finished for me, smiling. Into the phone he said: "Amaris, we're coming up, and the gentleman watching you will soon be donating his car. Is there anyone else with him? No? Good. Sit tight." He hung up the phone. "Okay, she says that if we go up the ramp, we'll see her in our van first, on the right, and about ten spaces up, on the same side, is the guy in the SUV."

"Can we use the parked cars as cover to get close?" I asked, cautiously moving toward the ramp.

"Wait, wait, you big, clunky types." November skittered in front of us, waving us back. "Let me look."

London exhaled, pissed.

"I am not clunky," said Siku.

But we all let her go first.

The ramp sloped upward, then turned sharply left to continue up to the next level. We big, clunky types stuck close to the wall as November crept forward and peered around the blank cement wall to see what was going on up there.

"Lots of cars between us and Amaris," she said. "We can probably sneak up to her without the SUV guy seeing us." She turned and gave us all a glare. "If you enormous people will be careful."

"Now I'm enormous." London pressed herself in close to me, as if to shield herself from November's words. "Big, clunky, and enormous."

"Well"—November gave her a toothy grin—"just in comparison to me. Speaking of which, I'm going to get small and pay the SUV guy a visit. He's got his window rolled down."

I couldn't help grinning back at her. "When she reaches him, the rest of us move in."

Everyone nodded, exchanging glances. November said, "Somebody better bring my clothes and backpack."

"Got it," said Siku.

The air around November seemed to bend, and then her human form was gone. A large, glossy brown rat stared up at us from the pile of her clothes, beady eyes shining. She chittered, waving tiny pink paws with sharp nails at us chidingly; then she scuttled around the corner and up the ramp underneath the parked cars.

"Stay low," I said to the others, stooping down, and followed November. I stuck close to the left-hand wall, knowing that Amaris and the SUV man were against the right-hand wall, with rows of parked cars between me and them. The others scurried behind me, bent double, trying to keep within sight of November's pink, snakelike tail as it vanished under first one car and then another.

We quickly came parallel to Amaris in the white van, the same one we'd stolen from the Tribunal over a month ago. Her back was to us, and I could see the top of her blond head above the van's driver's seat headrest. Four cars up from her sat a white SUV. I got on my hands and knees to scan under the cars. A foot-long whiskered form leaped silently onto the SUV's rear bumper.

"Get ready," I whispered. Still crouched, I made my way between parked cars, getting closer to the SUV. Caleb followed right behind me, while Siku and London split up to approach from the other side.

I stilled, listening, and heard the faint *skritch* of those tiny nails on the car's roof. Risking a glance over the top of a convertible, I was just in time to see November jump down from the white roof of the SUV onto the ledge of the open driver's-side window.

The man sitting there, beefy and balding with biceps that strained against the thick white fabric of his turtleneck sweater, emitted a train-whistle scream and batted at her instinctively with both hands. Too late. November had launched herself to land on top of his headrest, her naked tail slapping against his bare skull.

I ran toward the passenger side of the SUV, Caleb right behind me. Siku and London ran in from the driver's side, as the man in white pushed the door open, trying to get out and grab the walkie-talkie from his belt at the same time.

That's when November jumped onto his neck and slithered down the front of his sweater.

"Gah!" he yelled, scrambling out of the car completely and swatting at the front of his own body as a rat-sized lump wiggled its way toward his belt. "Get off me!" He struggled for composure, his voice deepening. "I call on you, come forth from shadow . . ."

He had great presence of mind, trying to force November out of her rat form even as her little rat hands unbuttoned his fly, her tail poking up out of the neck of his sweater, tickling his ear. It would be interesting to see what happened if she shifted back to human right there and then.

"Reject your dark form, come forth—Ack!" The power of the objurer's call was cut off as Siku charged up and wrapped one arm around his neck in a headlock. The man choked, clawing at Siku's clenched forearm.

November leaped off the man and ran up Siku's leg, squeaking in a way that sounded uncannily like mocking laughter. London got in front and kicked the guy square in the crotch, a move I recognized from our brief martial arts class back in school.

The man gasped, doubling over as best he could with Siku holding onto him.

I opened the passenger-side door as Caleb rounded toward the others.

"Low blow, London," I said.

She grinned. "Yep!"

It kept the man immobile in agony long enough for Siku to release him and for Caleb to land a neat punch to his jaw, followed by an uppercut and a hook. The man crumpled, unconscious.

Caleb shook out the fingers of his right hand. "Haven't thrown this many punches in one day since the last time we all rumbled," he said. "I have missed you guys."

November had run back down Siku's leg and dived into the guy's pockets. But I climbed into the SUV's passenger seat and jiggled the keys that were in the ignition. "We'd better move," I said. "Load everything into this car, and let's get out of here."

In short order, Caleb had backed the SUV up to Amaris's van, and we transferred their stuff from one to the other, tossing in our own backpacks and suitcases.

Amaris got out of the van and threw the keys into a Dumpster before jogging up to give me a hug. She looked ten times better than the last time I'd seen her, disheveled and lost after her father and brother's betrayal and her decision to leave them and join us. Now she was animated, alive, face flushed with excitement. She'd cut her thick blond hair to a layered shoulder-length bob that suited her high cheekbones and huge brown eyes. Now that she didn't have to wear the Tribunal's traditional high-necked white dresses to cover up her amazing figure, she looked like a Victoria's Secret model slumming it in cigarette jeans and a simple green T-shirt.

"Good to see you!" I said, hugging her back.

She pulled back a little and whispered, "We need to talk soon. Alone."

I nodded, puzzled, as she released me and turned to the others, giving them a nervous little wave. "Hi."

They hadn't seen her either since the night we'd destroyed her father's compound, and though they knew she'd changed loyalties to help Morfael and Caleb build the new school for otherkin, there was still a chill of hesitation in the air between her and the shifter kids. They didn't know her through Caleb the way I did, and seeing her as a friend was going to take more time for them.

"Hey," said Siku. He was throwing November's enormous suitcase into the SUV and laying out the clothes she'd left behind when she'd shifted. November leaped into the trunk and, from the rustling in there, I could tell she had shifted back to human and was getting dressed.

"Hi, London." Amaris made a point of catching London's eye. "I like your hair."

London blinked at the compliment. "Thanks."

"Let's get a move on," said Caleb. "I'll drive."

"What, not Dez?" November emerged from the trunk, rumpled and pulling down her shirt. "Don't you want the car to break down in the middle of the desert?"

Everybody knew about my propensity for shorting out machinery. It made life very inconvenient at times. As Caleb took the driver's seat, taking a minute to disable the GPS so the Tribunal couldn't track us, I nabbed shotgun next to him. Siku took up two seats behind us, with November squeezing in beside him thanks to her narrowness.

London and Amaris took the third row of seats in the way back. "You won't make the engine die just from being inside the car, will you?" London asked me as she squeezed her way back.

"Hasn't happened yet," I said. "I think I have to be operating the machine to make it die."

"Remind me never to loan you my phone," said Siku.

We slammed the doors shut, and Caleb hit the accelerator.

As we cruised oh-so-casually out of the parking garage, everyone but Caleb ducked down below the windows, in case there were other objurers keeping watch on the exits. In the Tribunal's car, we shouldn't get as many suspicious glances, but better safe than sorry. And as an extralegal, ultrasecret organization, the Tribunal wouldn't report the theft of the car to the police and risk exposing their own operation.

That's why, when in doubt, we stole from them. Plus, they deserved it.

We kept an eye out for tails for the next few miles, but by the time we hit the freeway we felt sure we'd made it away clean. Caleb got off the northbound 15 and headed south toward the 95. Amaris pulled out some bottles of water and chips, and a contented munching sound filled the car.

"Okay, so that was cool," November said after about fifty miles. "But it would've been way cooler with Arnaldo there."

"Hell, yeah," said London as Siku grunted in agreement.

"What's going on with...all that?" Amaris asked, her voice a little low and timid. "I mean, why do you have to go get him?"

"His dad has cut him off from the world," I said. "His father is...he drinks a lot, and he really hates shifters from other tribes. We don't know exactly what's going on there, but after those Tribunal raids on our houses, we need to be sure he's safe."

"And we're going to steal him from his parents," London said, then glanced around as the rest of us looked uneasy. "Well, that's what's really going on here, right? And only if he wants us to. I mean, most shifters don't like other tribes. Like my parents—they think you all can't be trusted because you're not wolves, but they'll still let me go back to school with you. But Arnaldo's dad is locking him away from the world."

"He hits Arnaldo and his brothers," November said baldly. "It's bad."

"Where's his mom?" Amaris asked.

Silence for a moment. "She's dead," said November. She didn't say that the Tribunal had killed her, but I could tell from the sudden tightening of Amaris's face that she was thinking exactly that.

# CHAPTER 6

Arnaldo's family's house lay next to the still, blue-black water of Alamo Lake. The sun had set not long ago, and in its place the sky thrust up a wall of red-orange topped with fading lavender and indigo.

The building's black silhouette was low and unremarkable except for a narrow tower made of haphazard iron bars and wooden planks that emerged from its center to loom at least five stories up. At the top was nothing but a wooden platform.

To me, it looked like an observation platform, a good spot for an eagle to watch from, to look for prey, and to take off for the hunt. Nothing moved on it now, though for all we knew it held a camera that was even now pointed right at us.

Siku, November, and I had done our best to sneak up to the edge of the backyard, leaving the others in the SUV about three hundred yards back. Now we waited for a signal, keeping an eye on the rusty swing set, the ragged vegetable garden, and the stepping-stone path that led up to the back door.

*Probably the kitchen door*, I decided, peering at it again over some acacia. But I couldn't be sure. There was so much we didn't know. We'd assumed Arnaldo was here, at the only address Caleb could find in Morfael's files. But no one had heard from him in weeks. He could be thousands of miles away for all we knew, maybe a prisoner of the Tribunal.

Or, and I didn't let myself think about this long, he could be dead. We were flying through the dark with no moonlight to show us the landscape.

A sprig of acacia snapped off in my hand with a crack. November glared at me, and I mouthed "Sorry." I was tense. Coming here had been my idea. I'd looked for signs of a setup, just as I'd told my mother I would. I didn't find any, but that didn't mean it was safe. If I was leading my friends into a horrible trap, I had no one else to blame.

Tires crunched on gravel on the other side of the house. It was Caleb in the SUV, with London and Amaris, driving right up to the front door. November cocked her head, catching the sound, then Siku. He cautiously straightened to his towering full height to peer at the house over his concealing shrub.

Heat rose up from the ground around me, released by nightfall. I caught the sound of a stirring creature rustling under the sand nearby, and a faint breeze brought the scent of frying onions. Someone inside the house was making dinner.

Then we heard three raps on wood. Our friends were knocking on the front door. I nodded at Siku and November, and we crept up on our toes, past the vegetable garden. November snuck out her lock picks as I peeked cautiously through the small window in the door.

Relief flooded through me. Arnaldo stood there, all gawky elbows and bony hips, stirring a mix of onions and other vegetables in a saucepan. His head was turned toward the front of the house, so I saw only the back of it. He looked taller, skinnier, and hunched with weariness, as if the last month had stretched him thin. His dark brown hair had grown long, brushing the collar of his plain brown T-shirt.

His skin was the same smooth brown, except for stripes of darker, almost purplish coloring just above his elbow. They looked like bruises, as if someone had grabbed his arm with enough strength and violence to leave a lasting mark. The thought made my blood rise.

Then I caught the muffled voices filtering through the house, the same voices Arnaldo was listening to. He froze, no longer stirring the simmering vegetables.

One voice was unmistakably Caleb's, low and filled with subtle vibrations. I couldn't quite catch the words, but he was answered by another male voice, sharper in pitch, and angry.

November was about to start picking the lock, but I held up my hand, signaling her to wait, then scratched faintly on the door.

Arnaldo whirled toward the sound, as tense and swift as if he'd heard a gunshot. I waved at him reassuringly through the window, but at the sight of me his dark eyes grew wider with alarm, his angular body stiff. I beckoned, but he shook his head and made a shooing motion with his hands.

"What the hell is going on?" whispered November.

Siku grunted, backing up her impatience.

"Arnaldo's alone in the kitchen, and I want him to come with us, but he's trying to tell me to go away." I looked at Arnaldo through the window again and emphatically mouthed: "Open the door."

He glanced back toward the front of the house, every muscle tense, then stepped over, unlocked the kitchen door, and inched it ajar as quietly as he could. He only let it open far enough to poke his beaklike nose out. His bangs had grown out too long, tangling with his eyebrows and catching in his black eyelashes. His voice was low and urgent. "You guys can't be here. My dad will kill you. I mean, literally kill you."

Warm, delicious dinner-scented air wafted past us through the gap between door and jamb. It made November jiggle with hunger. "I didn't know you could cook!" she whispered.

Arnaldo stared at her as if she'd lost her mind. "Did you hear what I just said?"

"We heard you," I said. "Grab a coat and your wallet and come with us."

"Why? What's going on?" Arnaldo looked over his shoulder again. "I can't leave my brothers here."

I frowned at him. "Wasn't your house raided by the Tribunal? All of ours were."

"What? No! No raids here. It's been really quiet. We're fine. Sorry I haven't been in touch, but my dad took away our phones and computers."

Siku shook his head, his long black ponytail swaying. "Why would the Tribunal get DNA from everyone else who raided their compound, but not from you?"

"And you're not fine." I pointed at the bruises on his arm.

Arnaldo slid that arm behind his back, out of view. "It's no big deal. We're really off the grid here, so maybe the Tribunal just couldn't find us. But if my Dad finds *you* here . . ."

"It is a big deal. Get your brothers and come with us," I said. "We won't leave you with him."

"Arnaldo?" A small voice spoke behind him, and I saw a boy of about thirteen standing in the doorway. He had a version of Arnaldo's impressive nose and hooded eyes, currently wide with a mixture of fear and wonder as he stared from me to November's small face at my elbow to Siku towering above, then back to Arnaldo. "Who's that?"

Arnaldo inhaled deeply, as if girding himself, then said, "They're just leaving, Luis. Go back to the dining table."

"Maybe we should go," said Siku. I could hear his feet shuffling uneasily in the dirt behind me.

"Are they shifters from other tribes?" Luis took a curious step toward us. His feet were bare, the cuffs of his brown trousers neatly altered to let down the hem. "You're not a raptor, are you?" he asked me.

I started to shake my head, but Arnaldo moved between us, turning to face Luis. "I said, go back into the dining room now, Luis."

"Papi says the other shifter tribes are thieves and killers," Luis said, his voice getting louder. "Are they trying to hurt you, Arnaldo? I'll protect you!"

"No, Luis!" Arnaldo put out both hands in a calming gesture."These are my friends! I told you, I met other kinds of shifters at the school—"

The front door slammed. Arnaldo cut himself off and threw us a terrified look.

A man's piercing voice called, "Arnaldo?"

Arnaldo's eyes pleaded for us to go. Siku and November backed up behind me, and I started to close the kitchen door, but too late.

A tall man strode into the kitchen behind Luis and stopped, glaring at us. Everything about him was long, lean, and hard. His head was shaved, and his skin, a burnished bronze, lay like a metallic sheet over the bones of his skull, pointed cheekbones, and long, muscular fingers, curled now into fists.

Behind him came another boy, about fifteen, stockier than Arnaldo, with a fuzz of black hair coming in on his upper lip and a large yellow-purple bruise under his left eye.

I stared at it, and then looked over at Arnaldo. He slid his gaze away, lips pressed together into a white line.

Mr. Perez pushed past Luis in one swift but slightly tripping step, eyes darting. I got an impression of great power made sloppy, of intense focus that had been deliberately blurred.

"Papi . . ." Arnaldo said.

But his father ignored him, taking us all in. His thin lips drew up in contempt. "So. You dare to come here."

He slurred a bit. Out of the corner of my eye, I saw November wrinkle her nose, then a strong sweet scent hit me—bourbon. Lots of it. Mr. Perez was drunk.

"We were worried," I said. "The Tribunal raided our houses, so we wanted to be sure Arnaldo was safe...."

"He's safe because I keep him safe!" The alcohol didn't affect Mr. Perez's gaze. It fixed on me like the sights of a gun. "You're that tiger-shifter who pulled him into danger. I'm the one who had to pull him out."

"Danger?" November asked. "Was there recent danger?"

"So the Tribunal did come here," I said. My heart began to race. This was bad.

Mr. Perez jutted his chin out, puffing up his chest. "What was I supposed to do? After you sucked my son into your deadly games, the Tribunal came here. They came to capture or kill me and my family."

Arnaldo's eyebrows drew together in confusion. "They never came here! I didn't see them...."

"While you were visiting your *friends*," he spat out the word, "they came. Dozens of them, dressed in their precious white, bearing their guns, and wearing their sunglasses."

A strange premonition took me. "Yet here you are," I heard myself say. "Alive and well."

"Alive," he said. "My sons are alive because that day I made a deal with the Tribunal." He sneered again, but this time I could see the scorn was for himself.

"No!" Arnaldo lurched forward, hands up, begging for it not to be true. "No, Papi!"

"*Sí,*" said his father. "I pleaded for my sons' lives that day. I promised them anything. So, when they asked, I gave them one of Arnaldo's old hairbrushes, all of our computers and phones, and I swore to them that no one in my family would ever trouble them again."

Siku's voice rumbled. "Maybe we should go."

"Yes," said Arnaldo. He turned to us, swallowing hard. "Go. I have to look after my family."

That was it. We had to go. My thoughts and feelings were tumbling over themselves, trying to find something good to hold onto, but of one thing I was sure. This was my fault. Then my eyes slid over the bruises on Arnaldo and his brother's black eye. Not all of this was my doing.

"Who's going to save your family from you?" I met Mr. Perez's piercing gaze. If I'd had fur, it would have been standing on end. If I'd had fangs, they would have been bared. "We know you beat your sons, sir. We know you drink too much. If you don't allow them to come with us, I'll report you—to the department of Child Welfare."

In the blink of an eye, Mr. Perez swooped across the room, pushed Arnaldo aside, jerked the door wide, and grabbed the front of my T-shirt with his powerful curved fingers. We were nose to nose.

"Then it's better if I kill you now." His hot, alcohol-scented breath poured over my face. I barely had time to remember my training . . . *stomp on his instep, knee him in the groin* . . . before a huge hand reached over me, grabbed Mr. Perez by the shoulder, and shoved him away.

"No killing," said Siku as Mr. Perez stumbled backwards, arms flailing. He would have fallen if Arnaldo's brother hadn't caught him.

"Papi, please . . ." The boy squeezed his father's arm.

"*Cállate*, Cordero," Mr. Perez said. He jerked away from his son as if his touch stung.

In one furious move, November moved around me to get right in Mr. Perez's face. "You're worried about *the Tribunal*?" She had one hand on her hip, the other poking him in the chest. "The man who hits his own children? The man who's all drunk and cross-eyed in front of his kids? What is wrong with you?"

"I . . ." Mr. Perez swallowed with difficulty and then pushed his chin out again. His attempt to cover up his shame was hard to watch. "I love my boys."

I knew then that he did love his sons, and I understood why Arnaldo wanted to stay. Mr. Perez was a desperate alcoholic who just wanted to keep his boys safe from the people who had killed his wife. He was doing the best he could. Too bad it wasn't good enough.

"Come with us," I said. "You and your sons. We can help you."

Mr. Perez frowned as all three of his sons turned to look at me as if my hair had caught fire. November was nodding, though.

"Help me?" said Mr. Perez, as if the words didn't compute. "But . . . you're the problem."

"Alcohol is the problem, Mr. Perez. Getting help for that is smart. Facing up to the real problems is the brave thing to do. . . ."

"Yes, come with us!" November bounced a little on her toes and winked at Cordero. "You know you want to."

"Come with you?" Mr. Perez said, slurring all the more with anger. "Come with cats and rats, to live with wolves and bears? We're nothing but food to you. And you're nothing but trash to us."

"You can trust them, Papi," Arnaldo said. "They're my friends." He looked at me, November, and Siku. "*Son mi familia.*"

I knew just enough Spanish to know what that meant, and how hard it must have been for Arnaldo to tell his father that we were his family.

"This is your family!" Mr. Perez gestured to himself and the boys. "Not those bird-hunters. Only your blood, your tribe, is your family."

"I know what Mama would say," Arnaldo said. At the mention of the boys' mother, Mr. Perez's jaw set. "She would say families don't hurt each other."

"You heard me," Mr. Perez said. "If they're your family, you are no family of mine."

Arnaldo's brown face went gray. Both his brothers gasped.

Luis tried to grab his father's sleeve, but Mr. Perez pulled away. Cordero took Luis by the shoulders and edged him back toward the dining room.

Arnaldo's chin was trembling. "Papi, please. I never meant for this to happen. I'm proud to be your son."

"I am not your father." Mr. Perez's eyes were aimed at him like a spear.

For a minute, I thought Arnaldo would break down crying. But instead he took a deep breath and drew himself up to his full height, taller than his father now, slender and taut. "What would Mama say?'

Mr. Perez winced, as if Arnaldo had struck him. "You are not my son," he said, but it was not as convincing this time.

"Mama would say that you drink too much," said Arnaldo. "I should have told you this long ago, but I was afraid."

His father's eyes were red and bright with unshed tears. The pain behind them made me look away. Somewhere inside, Mr. Perez knew he was failing his children.

"Mama would be ashamed of how you treat us." Arnaldo's voice was shaking. "She would want you to stop drinking, to get help."

Tears streamed down Mr. Perez's face, and his lips trembled, as if saying the words was almost more than he could bear. "Get out," he said, and pointed at the door.

It looked like something out of an old silent movie—the proud father throwing his wayward son out of the family home by flinging out one arm toward the door. For a moment I couldn't quite believe it. But it was all too terribly real.

Luis was crying silently, as if he'd learned not to let anyone hear his sobs, and Cordero stood behind him, arms around his shoulders and chest protectively. "It's okay, Arnaldo," Cordero said. "I'm here."

I caught November's eye and saw she was thinking the same thing. We couldn't leave these boys with this drunken father. "Let Cordero and Luis come with us to the school too, Mr. Perez," I said. "They could learn a lot there, and you could visit—"

"No!" Mr. Perez stepped between us and his two younger sons.

I hesitated. We outnumbered him. We could make him give us the boys.

"Please, go," Cordero said. He was shaking. His voice wavered, but he cleared his throat, determined. "We don't want to go with you."

"Don't you hurt Papi, dirty fur-carriers," Luis shouted. "Get out of our house!"

"You sure?" November asked. "If you come with us, your brother won't get any more black eyes."

Cordero shot a glance at his father, who looked like he might tear November's head off. "I was just playing outside. I fell," Cordero said, his voice dropping, his eyes darting away.

"That's right!" Luis piped up. "Go away!"

"You see?" Mr. Perez brought his chin up. "Nobody wants you here."

"Arnaldo . . ." I said helplessly. It made me queasy to hear the boys defending their father. But what other choice had he given them?

This was too big for us, and I couldn't see any way to make it right. We couldn't force the boys to come with us, not without possibly injuring their father right in front of them and dragging them off, probably in some kind of restraints.

"Let's go," Arnaldo said, and walked to the door. Siku put a hand on his shoulder, and Arnaldo turned to look back at his family. "I'll see you all again soon."

I looked at Arnaldo's father. He put his arms around Cordero's shoulders and hugged both boys to him forcefully; his mouth was twisted in anger and pain.

"You can come with us, Mr. Perez," I said. "And Cordero and Luis."

He glared at me with red eyes. "Get out of my house, cat."

I bit back a smart remark and backed up a step so that I was outside. "We'll take good care of Arnaldo," I said. "Just let us know if we can help you."

Still standing near Mr. Perez, November was seething, her small eyes darting back and forth, her fingers patting her thighs impatiently. I backed up farther, waiting for her to come with me. She took a step, bumped against Mr. Perez, as if giving him one last angry shove, then darted past me and into the open before he could react.

A hundred yards away or so, I heard the engine of the SUV getting closer. Caleb, London, and Amaris were on their way back to get us. And we had Arnaldo. The group would be together once again, safe. But my heart felt like a deflated balloon; my throat was tight. I'd never wanted it to be like this.

"I'm so sorry," I said, walking backwards. "We never wanted to cause problems in your family, but every tribe is in danger from the Tribunal. And if all the shifter tribes can't come together, we don't stand a chance. If you ever change your mind, just let us know. If you ever need help, call us."

"You stupid, foolish girl!" Mr. Perez spat the words out, releasing his sons and pacing up to me, one hand grabbing the door to swing it back and forth in fury. "Do you think you are the first to say all we have to do is 'come together'? Do you really think the Tribunal hasn't utterly destroyed every single one of those like you, who came before and who tried to overthrow thousands of years of tradition? It's your idiotic dreams of uniting the otherkin that will kill us all. Go seek glory and power at someone else's expense. I'll keep my family safe."

He slammed the door in my face. I stood there for a moment, until a quiet hand on my arm turned me around, and Amaris was hugging me, saying, "Come on, now." We walked past the vegetable garden to where Caleb waited in the SUV.

# CHAPTER 7

We stopped in Kingman on the way back north to buy Arnaldo some clothes and a toothbrush. At the store, November pulled out a worn leather wallet I didn't recognize, drew out five twenty-dollar bills, and paid for everything.

Arnaldo stared at her. "You *stole* my father's wallet?"

One corner of November's mouth deepened, as if to say "duh." "I picked his pocket on my way out," she said. "Been practicing on my brothers."

It was London who laughed first, then the rest of us, more in relief than anything else. Arnaldo actually smiled too, though he shook his head at her.

November collected her change from the cashier, then opened Arnaldo's chest pocket with one finger and slid the wallet into it. "I know, I know, it's not ethical and blah-dee-blah. But before you get all weird about it, just remember it's the least he could do, after kicking you out."

I noticed that Amaris wasn't with us. I looked around and

spotted her through the dusty window of the store, barely visible behind our parked SUV. Something about the way she held her head struck me as odd, and I left Arnaldo and the others to buy the clothes and grab some food, and went outside into the cold desert air.

Amaris was pacing behind the car, practically out in the street. I heard her voice speaking, though the words weren't clear, and I realized she was on the phone.

I nearly turned around to give her privacy. But wait— *Amaris doesn't have any friends other than us.* She'd been raised by the Tribunal and was now an outcast. *Who the hell is she talking to?*

I strained to catch even a word of her conversation as I approached. Instead, a deep growl of engines assaulted my ears. Two engines, very large, very loud, coming fast. Headlights swept over us. We turned to see two sets of headlights moving at us much faster than they should have on a quiet street this late at night. One set of lights started to pull ahead of the other, tires smoking.

They were headed right for us. Sixty feet away, forty . . .

I whirled around and leaped at Amaris. She was standing there, eyes wide, still trying to understand the hurtling machines charging at her. I cannoned into her and wrapped my arms around her waist, head down, yanking her with me out of the street, using the bulk of the SUV as cover. We rolled onto the pavement.

Tires squealed, and one car zoomed past, inches away from the rear bumper of our car. The wind from it pushed my hair over my face as I sat up on the asphalt, forearms and elbows bruised from the impact, but otherwise unhurt. Amaris, who had landed on her side, was getting up, brushing pebbles and dirt from her shirt, although it now had a long dark slick of oil across one sleeve.

"Oh, my dear Lord!" she said. That was about as much swearing as ever came out of Amaris. "Have they found us? Was that the Tribunal?"

I stared at the retreating low-slung forms of the muscle cars as they raced away. "I don't think Ximon would approve those modifications on a Mustang," I said. When she looked at me blankly, I explained further. "I think they were street racers, not objurers. Just jerks, not assassins."

"You saved my life," she said. "I've never seen anyone move that fast!"

"Cat-shifter reflexes," I said. "Still pretty good in human form. What are you looking for?"

She had hunkered down, scanning the dark pavement. "My phone. I must've let go of it in surprise. Not that I'm not grateful . . ."

"Maybe it got flung over here." I bent over to look under the truck next to our SUV.

"Don't bother," Amaris said. "It's no big deal."

"It's your phone." My eyes were good in the dark. I spotted a small square object near the back tire of the neighboring car. "There it is."

She knelt down to get it. "Darn, the keyboard's cracked." She pressed a few buttons. "The power's on, but the buttons don't work."

"Bummer," I said, watching her face closely. "Who were you talking to?"

"Hunh?" She glanced up fast, and then looked back down at her phone. She looked distracted, but her eyes flickered strangely. Was that guilt? "Nobody. I was listening to music. I have to hold the phone up to my ear because I don't have earbuds."

"Music?" Until about a month ago, Amaris had led the most isolated life possible in this modern world. The only music she'd ever been exposed to consisted of traditional hymns. Even the religious symphonies of Handel and Beethoven had been forbidden.

Pounding feet announced the arrival of everyone else, coming at a run. "Are you guys okay?" asked November, darting over.

Caleb swept up to me, eyes running over me carefully. His concern smoothed out the frazzled edges in me left over from the adrenaline rush. He gave Amaris a once-over too, face settling as it became clear we were both okay. "We heard the cars, and the tires squeal, and then we couldn't see you."

"Did they hit you?" asked Arnaldo, pointing to the smear on Amaris's shirt.

"Dez pulled me out of the way just in time. 'Speedier than the righteousness of Isaiah drawing near.' " Amaris smiled, as if she'd made a joke.

We looked at her blankly.

Except Caleb. "Isaiah fifty-one five," he said. "Don't let the heathens bother you, Sis. You sure you're okay?"

"Just shaken up," she said. "Thanks."

"Here." London stepped forward and held out a bottle of water. "Scary stuff always makes me thirsty."

Amaris took it with a shy smile. "Thanks."

Caleb opened the passenger door for me, and everyone piled into the SUV.

"Maybe you can show me what kind of music you like sometime," Amaris said to London. "I have a lot of catching up to do."

"Uh, okay," London said, making her way to the seats in the far back again.

As she pulled out her phone and earbuds, I still wanted to know who the hell Amaris had been talking to. But unless I confronted her in front of everyone, the moment had passed. The group's trust in her was tentative enough without me making it worse for no good reason.

*Unless there is a good reason.*

Amaris had been lying. Maybe the reason was unimportant. But maybe it was critical. I'd thought I could handle Arnaldo's family situation, and that had turned out to be out of my league. What if there was more going on with Amaris than I knew? What if I'd been mistaken to let her into our lives? She'd whispered to me earlier that she had something to tell me. Were those things related?

I resolved to get her alone as soon as possible and drag it out of her. Amaris was something rarer than a shifter or a caller of shadow. She was a healer, able to steal power from Othersphere to heal wounds and illnesses. But after she ran away from the Tribunal, her recapture and marriage to a horrible old man had traumatized her so much, she'd been unable to access her skill. She could be hiding things from us out of some irrational fear.

The only good thing about all that guilt and shame was that it made her a terrible liar. It shouldn't be too hard to get the truth out of her once I had her alone. Also, I needed to tell her what Lazar had said, that he was sorry. There hadn't been any time for that either.

On top of that, I hadn't had a second alone with Caleb. So much still to tell him. If I could just be with him, touch him, hear his voice speaking only to me, I might feel like everything could be all right again.

I stewed in uncertainty as we zoomed down the freeway. I felt so useless. There had to be something we could do. I turned in the passenger seat to see Arnaldo staring out the window.

"I was thinking," I said. "Maybe we should call the Department of Children's Services, or whatever it's called."

Everyone in the car stirred uncomfortably, except Arnaldo, who turned his head to look at me with eyes that were still red and heavy with pain. "I know you mean well, Dez," he said. "But no."

" 'Hell, no,' you mean," November interjected. "Shifters can't let humdrums solve their problems."

Siku was nodding. London looked uncertain.

"*Won't* let humdrums help them, you mean," I said. "It's not like he's just going to stop drinking all by himself."

"I said, no!" Arnaldo's voice sharpened and rose, but he

forced himself to remain calm. "Things are bad enough between me and my dad now," he said. "If I did that to him . . ." He shook his head.

Everything was messed up, thanks to me. I turned back around in my seat and stared straight ahead. Maybe I had been wrong to force Mr. Perez's hand. But I couldn't help feeling that Arnaldo's brothers' safety was more important than trying to mend the shreds of his relationship with his dad. Or maybe I was wrong about that, the way I'd been wrong about everything else.

"I'm sorry, Arnaldo," I said.

"I know," he said, leaning his forehead against the window glass. "It's not your fault, Dez."

The drive back to Morfael's school in the Spring Mountains northwest of Vegas took forever, but Caleb wouldn't let anyone else drive. He explained that once we left Kyle Canyon Road, the turns got tricky. He and Morfael had deliberately planned it that way to make the school harder to find, so in the dark after a long day it was better for him to find the way.

Amaris and London took turns listening to music on her headphones till London's phone died. November fell asleep with her head on Siku's elbow, and Arnaldo stared stiffly out the window, not saying a word.

It was past three a.m. when we arrived, pulling the car next to an ancient pickup truck inside an underground garage area. The truck belonged to Raynard, the gruff school handyman and Morfael's apparent boyfriend, though the two of them never talked about their relationship.

Raynard was also compulsively neat. He'd thoroughly organized building tools, saws, and planks of wood against the back wall in stacks or on shelves. The floor was firmly packed earth, the sod over our heads reinforced with what looked like logs from fallen trees. The overhead light was dim, and the automatic door to the outside cleverly planted with grass to look like the rest of the hill.

The others headed out of the garage door, muttering about bed, toward a low hill, which had been partially cut away to reveal a wooden door. That had to be the entrance to the school, embedded in the side of the earth like a human-sized hobbit hole. One by one, they disappeared inside it, like rabbits into a burrow.

I started to follow them out into a cold forest landscape with the stars overhead so clear I felt like I could reach up and stir them around.

Warm hands enclosed my waist from behind, and Caleb's lips pressed against my ear. "You're so beautiful," he said, voice low and soft. "I've waited so long for you."

I turned in the circle of his arms, hands sliding up his chest. "You've been with other people, and I haven't, which means I've waited even longer."

He kissed me, his lips curving upwards in a smile. He smelled like grass after a passing cloudburst, clean and just warming in the sunshine. "Ah, but waiting for you is different. You're not like any other girl. Waiting for you is like saving the best bite of cake for last."

His words and his touch flooded me with a heat so intense, I knew that it was time for the wait to end. We hadn't been alone together in weeks, and we might not have another chance soon. The craving to show my love for him, to satisfy the desire inside me, was overwhelming.

Caleb had been my first kiss, and now he would be my first lover. The images conjured by that thought sapped all the strength from my knees even as it strengthened the need to press my skin against his, to make the union of our bodies match the harmony of our feelings.

"I vote we have a large piece of cake tonight," I said, then lowered my voice to a whisper. "Or maybe the whole thing."

His arms tightened around me, pressing me full length against him, my hip bones grinding into his hips, thigh to thigh, heart to heart.

"If you're sure. I don't think I can wait a minute longer. . . ."

His lips trailed kisses down my neck, hands up under my shirt tracing the bare skin of my back, between my shoulder blades. He was so strong, so certain.

How different things were, how much had changed since I'd hidden from sight and touch because of the back brace I'd worn for so many years. Caleb's unabashed admiration and love, his desire for me even when I'd been wearing the brace, my decision to own my own body, had wiped all of that away.

Caleb's hands stroked the bare skin at my waist. I slid my hand a few inches down the back of his jeans.

"Where can we go?" I said. "Now."

He said nothing, only kissed me again with a craving that pulled the breath from my body. I was light-headed, floating, and at the same time never so certain about anything. His hands were guiding me, pulling me back into the dark enclosure of the garage. "All the rooms inside the school are communal," he said. "There's nowhere else. . . ."

I didn't care. "As long as we're alone," I said.

I leaned back against the side of the SUV and pulled him to me. Something like a groan escaped him as he dipped his head to kiss me again, crushing me against the metal. The boundaries between us were dissolving. I pulled his long black coat from his shoulders, even as his fingers trailed over my neck to grip the collar of my jacket and wrench it off me.

Somehow we were in the backseat of the SUV, me lying half under him. He reached down and pulled my shirt off in one smooth move. Then, with one swift snap, he undid my bra.

*My turn.* I yanked at his shirt, a bit clumsier, till he drew back and tugged it off with one hand, as if impatient to get back to touching me, mouth devouring the skin under my ear, at the base of my neck, at the top of my breast, his hands sliding down the back of my pants to deliciously scrape my skin with his nails ever so slightly. I pressed my body against his, but that wasn't enough. *I need more.*

With trembling fingers, breath coming fast, I undid the top

button of his jeans. God, why had I ever waited? This was so right, so perfect. The world around me rocked. I unzipped Caleb's jeans.

"What is going on . . . ?" a familiar voice began, and then broke off.

I reached for Caleb. What was he worried about?

Then a girl gasped nearby, and it wasn't me. And it wasn't Caleb who had spoken. In fact, he was sitting up, twisting in the backseat of the SUV.

I stared up at Lazar's astonished face.

"What the hell?" Caleb said, throwing my shirt over me to cover me up.

Lazar was half in the driver's side of the SUV, arm braced against the headrest, staring at us over the seats. He wore his objurer uniform of white shirt, white pants, gray jacket. On the passenger side, Amaris was standing by the car's open door, hand over her mouth, brown eyes as round as a startled fawn's.

"Oh, my God!" I said. The change from supercharged love-making to being caught like a deer in the headlights of an on-coming car was dizzying. I froze.

Lazar's face withdrew from view. Amaris slammed her door shut without getting into the car, and Caleb, still shirtless, pants half undone, rocketed up and out even as I struggled into my clothes.

"What are you doing here?" Caleb roared. Something slammed into a wall, and Lazar grunted in pain.

I flung myself out of the car to see Caleb, one hand gripping Lazar's shirtfront, holding him up against the wall of the garage. Lazar, as tall and strong as he, made a twisting move to the side as he slammed his forearm down onto Caleb's wrist.

The move forced Caleb to release him, but he followed up with a step and socked a right cross into Lazar's face.

Lazar's head whipped to the side, but he didn't stumble back. A line of blood trickled from his mouth as he turned and smiled at his brother, brown eyes intent. Then, swifter than I could follow, he punched Caleb, one-two with what looked like a left cross and a right uppercut.

Caleb took the first punch full in the face, but he made a swift move with his left arm in time to deflect the uppercut. His black eyes sparked with furious gold, matching the dangerous flicker in Lazar's, and something savage surged up in me, flooding me with excitement.

*I should be stopping this.* But I was still thrumming from feverish near-lovemaking in the car. Now the skin that had been rubbing against mine was wrestling more violently with someone just as strong, just as determined. Seeing Caleb, bare chested, his jeans unbuttoned, use everything he had to defend me was darkly thrilling.

Caleb's fists loosened, his knees bent, pants riding very low on his hips. He slammed the heel of his hand into Lazar's solar plexus.

Lazar expelled all the air in his lungs with an "Oof!" But he still had enough presence of mind to raise his fists up to guard against the next blow, which I knew from our exercises with Morfael would be aimed right for his throat. If it landed just right, it could kill.

But Amaris shoved herself between them. She screamed, "He's here because of me! It's my fault. Don't hurt him!"

At the last second, Caleb stopped himself from striking and stepped back, breath coming fast, the muscles in his bare back outlined in tension. "*You* invited him here?"

Amaris opened her mouth to speak, but Lazar interrupted. "I followed her here. I was worried about her."

"You were worried?" I walked up next to Caleb. "You weren't worried about her when your father married her off to that disgusting old man against her will. Why would you be worried about her now?"

"He did worry about me then," Amaris said, more heat in her voice than I'd heard before. "You weren't there. You don't know! He begged my father not to make me do it."

"Well, maybe he should've done more than beg," said Caleb. "I'd kill anyone who tried to hurt you."

Amaris turned to me, pleading. "I've been in touch with Lazar for weeks now, talking things out. He was the one I was on the phone with when that car almost hit us in the street. When the call ended suddenly with me screaming, he got worried."

"You've been reconciling with him?" Caleb stared in disbelief at his sister. "After everything he's done?"

"You don't know what it was like being raised the way we were, Caleb," she said. "It can make you do horrible things, crazy things. He's still my brother, and we still care about each other."

"How did he know where to find you?" I said sharply. I was still trying to focus, but I knew one thing. If Lazar knew where the school was, either the Tribunal already knew, or they would know soon. They'd laid waste to our last school, shot Morfael, and kidnapped Siku. We couldn't let that happen again.

"I turned the GPS on my phone off, like Caleb showed me," Amaris said. "But Lazar found me anyway."

"I hacked into her phone, found the nearest tower, and came looking after I heard her scream earlier," said Lazar, wiping the blood from his mouth. "No one else knows I'm here. I turned off the GPS in my own car and on my phone. No one followed me here, and I parked half a mile away and walked the rest."

"Then welcome," said Caleb mockingly, spreading his bruised hands out wide. "Because it looks like you'll be spending the rest of your very short life here."

Lazar lifted his chin, a vein throbbing angrily in his temple, but said nothing.

Amaris, flushed with shame and anxiety, looked back and forth between me and Caleb. "He won't tell them. He promised me. He wants to leave the Tribunal, the same way I did."

Caleb let out a sharp, derisive laugh. "Did he cross his

heart and hope to die? Well, I'm convinced. How about you, Dez?"

"As traps go, it's pretty obvious," I said. "I expected better from you, Lazar."

"They're not going to believe you." Amaris turned to her brother. "You have to tell them what you told me."

"No." Lazar clenched his jaw. I'd seen Caleb do the same thing a hundred times. "I will not justify myself to them. God knows my heart."

"Paraphrasing Luke won't help you," said Caleb. "If you can't prove what you say, you won't leave this place alive."

Lazar drew in a slow, even breath, as if trying to control himself. I could see the bruise where Caleb had hit him darkening his cheekbone. His eyes glittered dangerously. My skin prickled, and I braced myself against the possible power of his voice, ready to shift into tiger form.

Caleb felt it too, Lazar's explosive energy just underneath the surface. And he, reckless with fury, decided to provoke it. "Fine," he said, and took a quick, boxer's step forward.

Lazar saw the attack coming and drove a fist at him.

But Caleb was ready. He faked left in time to draw the punch, then danced right. He grabbed Lazar by the wrist, pushed him around, and shoved his arm up behind his back. Lazar let out a strangled cry of pain; then Caleb pushed him face-first against the wall, wrenching Lazar's arm up to the breaking point.

Lazar turned his head to the side, cheek smashed against the wall, tendrils of dark blond hair wet with sweat curling over his forehead.

I got in close. "That arm of yours Caleb's twisting. Isn't that the same arm Siku broke?"

Lazar exhaled an appreciative laugh. "It just finished healing, actually. Thanks for asking."

Caleb jammed his knee into the small of Lazar's back, eliciting a groan from his half-brother. "Give me one good reason not to break it again," he said.

"Maybe you should tell me what's really going on," I said.

Even smushed against the wall and helpless, Lazar took a moment to assess me, as if weighing what was best to do. I flushed as he slid his gaze over me, remembering how he'd found me with Caleb moments ago. *Why can't the world leave us alone so we can be like everyone else?*

Lazar stopped pushing back against Caleb, as if he'd come to a decision. He said, "We knew you'd rebuild somewhere. So have we."

Caleb and I exchanged a glance. "Where?" I asked.

"Make him let me go first," he said.

I shrugged at Caleb. *Your call.*

Caleb gave me a look that said *I'm going to regret this* and released his brother. He took a step back, breath misting in the cold garage, muscles in his bare arms and shoulders defined and glistening with sweat from the fight. "Where?"

Lazar rubbed his wrist. "About an hour from here, north and slightly east."

Caleb's black eyes flickered with his thoughts. "Near the nuclear test range?" When I threw him an alarmed glance, he said, "They no longer test bombs there. It's just a classified bit of desert now."

Lazar nodded. "Very near there."

*So close to the school.*

"Why there?" I asked. Dread made me shiver. *Could the Tribunal have somehow acquired a nuclear weapon?*

"Tell her, Lazar," Amaris said, and when he didn't speak for a moment, she flared with anger. "When you came here, you not only risked yourself, you put the good things I have here at risk too. If you don't tell them, I will."

Lazar looked down. Apparently, Amaris could shame him still. "No one will tell me why they picked that spot, but the construction's nearly finished," he said. "I didn't know it existed till we moved there last week. It must have cost them millions. But they've built a particle accelerator, a circular collider, underground. Part of it runs right under the nuclear testing range."

"Particle accelerator?" I'd heard the term before, in my AP physics class. Scientists built huge underground tubes where they shot beams of subatomic particles at each other at nearly the speed of light to smash them and see what they were made of.

"Like the one in Switzerland?" asked Caleb.

"Yes, but not that large," said Lazar. "I'm still trying to figure out why."

The Tribunal had a history of using technology against the otherkin, but this was far more advanced than anything we'd seen in their old compound, requiring huge amounts of money and expertise. "How did they build *that*?" I asked. It was difficult to believe.

He shook his head. "I'm not sure. The one thing we excel at is secrecy. Or maybe they bribed or killed anyone who stood in the way. But they must have been working on it for decades."

"And you have no idea what they're planning to do with it?" I forced myself to breathe. This was very bad news. Whatever the Tribunal wanted with a particle accelerator, it had to mean a new level of danger for the otherkin.

"Not yet," Lazar said, then held up a quelling hand as I opened my mouth to protest. "I was going to try and find out and then meet with Amaris tomorrow night. But she wouldn't agree to anything without talking to you."

Amaris nodded. "That's what he and I were arguing about on the phone when the car nearly ran us over."

"So you could still try to get that information," I said to Lazar. "For us."

Caleb shot me a look, dark eyes flashing. "You can't let him go."

"I don't know," I said in what I hoped was a calming tone. "But this is a whole new level of threat. We have to consider it."

"Consider allying ourselves with someone who drugged you and kidnapped you?" His voice grew louder with anger. "You want to make a deal with the piece of scum who killed *my mother*? No!" He swiped his hand in a chopping motion. "He cannot leave here."

"It is risky," I said, looking at Lazar. "What kind of guarantee do we have that you won't just tell your father where we are? That would get you a lot of brownie points with him."

Lazar's lips were pressed together hard, like he wasn't happy with what he was about to say. "I'm done currying favor with my father. He's . . . he's asked too much of me, and I see now it will never stop. I want out. That's your guarantee. I need—" He stopped, reluctant to go on.

"He's got no money," Amaris said. Lazar exhaled in frustration, clearly not happy she was telling us this. "Our father controls every penny and doles it out as needed. Lazar's got nowhere to go, and if he ran, they'd track him down for sure."

Now it began to make sense. "You need our help," I said.

His lips tightened. "And you need mine!" He slammed his open hand on the wall next to him, then gave one sharp shake of his head and paced away in agitation, only to walk back a second later. "I'm sorry," he said, his voice taut.

"It's hard to ask for help," I said. "Especially from people you've hurt."

He looked away. "Yes."

"It takes a lot of nerve," said Caleb. "Unless it's all a long con to infiltrate our ranks."

Reflected in Lazar's golden brown irises, I could see the curve of the white SUV where Caleb and I had almost made love. "I don't expect you to let me come stay here with you," he said. "I'm not a complete fool. But even a hundred dollars would help me disappear. Then you'd never hear from me again."

I had more than that in my own bank account, waiting to use for a college education that, at this rate, would likely never come. "What would we get for our money?" I asked.

Caleb let out a wordless exclamation of protest, stilling only when I sent him an imploring look. Why couldn't he see the opportunity here? It was risky, but with someone on the inside of the Tribunal, we'd be two steps ahead of Ximon, instead of five steps behind.

The tiny, painful spark of hope reappeared in Lazar's face. "They've only let me see a small part of the complex around the accelerator so far. But with a little luck and some hacking, I could get you a map of the entire complex. And maybe find out why it was built. . . ."

"It might start to make up for your past," I said.

He nodded. I studied the line of his throat, the tension in his shoulders, measured the blinking of his eyelids, and the set of his sensual mouth, so like Caleb's. He looked completely sincere. Even the fact that it had taken Amaris to explain his need for money made sense. Lazar was very proud, raised by Ximon to think of himself as special, holy. His father was a bishop in their twisted idea of religion, a man they believed was connected directly to God. To have that illusion stripped away . . . I couldn't imagine how angry and confused it had made Lazar. To come to his worst enemies for money must be beyond humbling.

"Some things can never be forgiven," said Caleb. "Never mended."

I looked over at Amaris. "We freed your sister from the Tribunal. What if we could do that for Lazar, and maybe other objurers too? You know Lazar better than we do, Amaris. What do you think?"

Amaris gazed back at me with wide brown eyes, the twin of Lazar's, but crinkled a bit at the corners with a smile. Her lips lifted up too, hopeful. "I believe him," she said. "And if you don't trust him completely, you can trust me, and trust that he would never do anything more to harm me. He would never tell our father where this school is because he knows it would endanger me and end our relationship."

"I say he's working for his own selfish ends," said Caleb. "To get away scot-free from a life as an assassin for a deranged cult."

"Which is it, brother?" Lazar asked. "Am I trying to trick you for the benefit of the Tribunal or so I can get away 'scot-free' as you say? It can't be both."

"Selfish reasons are trustworthy reasons," I said. "Lazar, if you want to get away from the Tribunal, we'll consider helping you—after you prove yourself and bring us those plans. I'll give you the money to start a new life myself."

"Dez!" Caleb was choking on his rage and disapproval. "How can you do this?"

"He's not lying," I said. "And this particle accelerator is a threat like we've never faced before, technology on an unprecedented scale being used against us, to destroy everyone we know and love. To stop that, I'd make a deal with the devil himself."

He moved up to me, lowering his voice into his own very intimate nonwhisper that always set my heart racing. Close in like this, I could smell his warm skin, and a vivid memory of his hands on my body sent a hot flush over my face. Had that really only been a few minutes ago?

"I know you want to save him. You want to save everyone. But you're putting everyone in danger," he said. "All of our friends in there, Morfael, Raynard . . ."

I took his hands in mine and leaned my forehead against his, as he had with me once when I was in tiger form. "They're already in worse danger than a simple Tribunal attack on the school," I said. "I get why you hate him. But this is bigger than our grievances from the past. It's worth the risk. I need you to trust me."

We breathed each other's breath for a moment, eyes locked across a space of only a few inches, and for a moment we were one again. "Okay," he said. "For now. We let him go and bring the plans back. But if he takes one wrong step . . ." He lifted his head and raised his voice so Lazar could hear. "If he makes one move I don't like, we end this thing."

He didn't say *and Lazar dies,* but the implication was there.

"Did you hear that, Lazar?" I asked. "One foot wrong, and you're done."

Lazar's face had closed down again as he watched us, like curtains drawn over a window. His slightly tip-tilted eyes were cool and calculating. He knew his life was on the line. "I wouldn't have it any other way," he said.

"Okay," I said. "I want those plans in two days." He opened his mouth to protest, but I held up a hand. "If Amaris doesn't get a call from you within forty-eight hours, the deal is off, and you can expect a visit from us. I want the GPS coordinates of the entrance to the accelerator now."

"Very well," said Lazar, and Amaris scrambled to get a notepad. "Thank you."

"I still don't trust you," I said. "You still have a lot to prove. If I get one whiff of anyone else coming with you when we meet, if I hear any objurers breathing within ten miles of here, I'll rip your throat out and be happy to leave the rest of you for the vultures."

He let loose an unexpected laugh, the tension in his shoulders easing. "God help me. Why do I find your threats comforting?"

"Because threats are all we grew up with," said Amaris. "It takes awhile to get used to kindness."

The smile fell from Lazar's face. "I'm glad they're kind to you. You look well."

"I am," she said. "But you'd better not mess this up, Lazar."

"I won't get another chance." He smiled at her ruefully, then took her pad and pen and wrote down a set of numbers. "Here." He sketched a series of lines underneath the numbers, holding the paper out for us to see. "Here's the town of Mercury, just off 95, right on the edge of the federal lands of the Nevada test site. To get to us, turn here"—he made an X on the map—"after you pass the Mercury exit. It's tough to see, but it's a tiny track on the right, after two intertwined saguaro cacti. They actually form an X. Then you dip into a valley, and the entrance is here." He made another X, then looked up at Caleb. "But it's hidden."

Caleb nodded. "In shadow."

"Exactly. The illusion we conjure holds for days unless we disturb it. But there's also a ventilation shaft here." He made another X. "That's how I got out tonight, and how I'll get back in. It's not hidden, but only one, very fit person can get through it at a time. It leads down into a communal bathroom. But I'll get you the complete plans to the place. Soon." He met my eye.

I kept hold of his gaze, trying to see every angle. "Why now?" I said. "What's Ximon done to push you out now?"

He pulled back, handing the paper to Amaris, shaking his head. "It's been a long time coming," he said. "And now I have something to offer in exchange for your . . . help." He said the word as if it stung.

He was hiding something, but it was buried deep. Something had pushed him to get away from his father at last, and although I was curious, its exact nature didn't matter, as long as he was truly desperate to leave and the information he gave us was correct.

"Go," I said. "Take him to his car, Amaris."

Without another word, Lazar walked around and got into the passenger side of the SUV. Amaris gave me a quick smile and got in the driver's side as Caleb and I stepped back.

I took Caleb's hand. "Thanks," I said. "I know this isn't easy."

"If I didn't love you so much, he'd be dead," he said. "I hope you're right."

Amaris was doing something inside the car; then she rolled down her window. "Um. You might need this." She awkwardly showed us the corner of Caleb's shirt.

Caleb gave a short, real laugh, and grabbed it from her. "Thanks."

"I'll be right back," she said, then realized it sounded like she was warning us. "Not that I . . . not that it matters. Whatever you want to do . . ." Shaking her head at her own awkwardness, she rolled up her window, pressed the garage door button, and started backing up the SUV. Caleb put his shirt back on.

Cold air poured into the garage as the SUV turned around and trundled off down the dirt road, disappearing between the trees. Caleb and I grabbed our coats and stood watching them, the silence strange between us, and I realized we'd had our first real disagreement. He was going along with this only for my sake, and the strain of it was palpable.

"I guess we should . . ." I gestured toward the hillside, where the door to the school's underground complex lay shrouded in bushes and grass.

"Yeah, let me show you where you'll be sleeping," he said, and we started walking side by side as we donned our coats. "We'll tell the others in the morning?"

"Yeah," I said. "I'll tell them and face the wrath and the weirdness, since it was my idea."

"Okay," he said. Then he stopped and turned to me, hands jammed in the pockets of his long black coat. "I do trust you, Dez," he said. "You have the ability to see the big picture sometimes when I don't, especially when it comes to—to him." He couldn't quite say Lazar's name. "But I need you to trust my instincts too. We need to approach this very carefully. Okay?"

I took a step into him, our faces close again. "Okay," I said. "I'm sorry it's come to this. But mostly, I'm sorry we got interrupted."

He slid his hands up my arms, sending happy chills down my spine. "Me too. There's the back of Raynard's pickup truck . . ." I could tell he was mostly joking, but also kind of not.

I kissed him, lightly. "Maybe it's better if my first time is somewhere more comfortable and romantic than the back of a car or the bed of a truck."

"You deserve that. Also, it has to be somewhere very, very private." His voice got low, sending a thrilling vibration down to my toes. "Because the next time I get you alone, nobody's going to stop me."

He led me through the rough wooden door into a darkened living room I could barely see, then to a dining area with a kitchen humming to its left.

The sweet, earthy smell of soil faintly permeated the air. The silence all around me was striking. No wind, rain, or traffic. It was as if the outside world didn't exist. The only sound was the faint creak of floorboards as we wound our way down a spiral staircase to a long hallway.

Caleb pointed out the computer room, the boys' and girls' dorm rooms, a general bathroom, and Morfael's and Raynard's rooms at the end of the hall. No lights were shining from under any of the doors, so we said good night very quietly, and I slipped into the girls' room. It was cozy, featuring six beds, a small kitchenette, and a door leading to a bathroom.

November sat up in bed. "So, did you and Caleb finally do it?"

*Oh, God.* No privacy at all in this cursed school. I resorted to London's favorite sentence. "Shut up, 'Ember."

A snort came from London's bed. "Well said."

November was snoring lightly by the time Amaris came in a few minutes later. But I lay for a long time, staring up at the darkness, blood still humming in my veins from Caleb's nearness. *What would it have been like? And what happens now?*

# CHAPTER 8

I awoke alone, blinking up at the intertwining roots in the ceiling above me, trying to remember where I was. *Oh, right, the new school. Underground.* Light filtered down from an ingenious skylight that used the white lime wash to reflect natural light down to us.

I was a morning-hater, always the last one to wake, so the others must have gone upstairs. Hunger bit at my stomach, so I got up, took a lightning-quick shower, and headed out into the empty hallway.

The faint sounds of clinking dishes and voices filtered down the winding wooden stairs. I padded toward them, then stopped, looking at the door to the computer room, seized with an idea. If I was going to do it, now was the time, with no one else around to stop me or overhear.

I pressed my ear to the computer room door. Dead air. *Excellent.* I opened the door to see five monitors and a corded phone.

I hesitated one more moment, and then knew I couldn't live with myself if I didn't. I googled Child Protective Services in Arizona and called the office in Phoenix, the one nearest to Arnaldo's family home. I left an anonymous message saying that I'd witnessed the Perez kids out by Alamo Lake being beaten by their father.

I did it fast, not letting myself think about it, then hung up and sat for a minute feeling a confusing mixture of relief and horror. *No way you can leave those two boys living with an abusive alcoholic.*

If they were taken away from their father, would Arnaldo's brothers be better off in foster care or a home, surrounded by people who didn't even know otherkin existed? I had to believe that was better than getting beaten. And maybe before that happened we could work out a way for them to come stay at the school, or find a home with a different family of shifters.

I made my way upstairs for breakfast, marveling at the building that housed our new school. The walls were made of bales of straw covered in whitewashed plaster, the floors of wooden planks thrown over more straw, with natural tree limbs used to decorate and support, capped by a roof made of turf. The bedrooms were on the bottom floor, dug deeper into the hill. The large living room featured a wood-burning stove and wide, low arched windows with window seats covered with cushions and books. The view gave out onto a bristlecone pine forest.

More noises came from the kitchen. I walked over to find Amaris, Arnaldo, November, London, and Siku blearily preparing breakfast. I paused next to Arnaldo as he waited by the toaster, and put a hand tentatively on his arm. "Good morning."

He looked up at me, his face sagging with weariness, and gave me a half-smile. "Hey," he said.

Still feeling torn about what I'd done, I found Caleb around the corner in a chair at the dining table. A few restless locks of black hair hung down over his face as he gazed into his coffee cup.

I plopped down next to him, leaned in close, and smiled. "Morning."

Smudges of darkness circled under his eyes, a sign that he hadn't slept well. But he smiled back, and took my hand under the table, where no one could see. "Hi." In a low voice, he added, "You smell even better than pancakes in the morning."

I squeezed his hand and forced myself not to plant a giant kiss on him. *Not in front of everyone.* But I wanted to eat him up.

I looked over at Amaris, who was buttering her pancakes. "Should we tell them?"

"Tell us what?" November sucked some syrup off her finger as she set the bottle down. "You two get married last night?"

"What?" Surprise made my voice swoop up. "Don't be ridiculous. We're way too young."

"It's only ridiculous to sane people," said London, pouring herself more coffee. "To shifters it's about average."

I stabbed my fork into a few sausages. "Yeah, but they wouldn't approve of a tiger-shifter marrying a caller of shadow at any age, right?"

Siku nodded, setting his plate, piled high with waffles, down on the table. "True."

"Well, when I said 'married,' what I really meant was 'laid,'" said November. "But now that you mention it, I wonder what kind of crazy babies you guys would produce. We should ask Morfael, you know. Just in case."

"Shut up, 'Ember," Caleb said, his voice sharp as a shot.

November crossed her eyes at him and sat down next to Siku.

An embarrassed flush spread across my cheeks. I cleared my throat. "What happened is Lazar came by the school last night."

Arnaldo's fork clattered to his plate, and London did a spit-take with her coffee.

"It's my fault," said Amaris quickly into the horrified silence. "I started talking to him over the phone a couple of weeks ago because he felt bad about how things ended between us. Yesterday, he got worried about me and tracked me down by hacking into my phone."

"Brilliant," said November. "We've got a healer who can't heal but instead brings in stray homicidal maniacs who think we're demons."

"Back off," Caleb said, and the power in his voice was almost threatening, reminding me of his ability as a caller. The shifters bristled, and the tension level rose. "She's admitted she made a mistake. And you're all still alive."

London's ice-blue eyes were glaring. "So you killed him, right? Where'd you bury the body?"

"We didn't kill him," I said. "Caleb wanted to. But I thought we should turn him into an asset."

Siku set his glass of orange juice down with a click. "That makes no sense."

"This is actually good news," I said. I'd had a lot of sleepless time last night to think about how to approach this moment. "He's sick of life with the Tribunal, but he has no way out. If we help him, he'll give us all of Ximon's plans. He's already told us they've built a particle collider, not far from here."

"Is that like a big gun or something?" November said through a mouthful of eggs. Shocking news didn't touch her appetite.

"Well, it does shoot things," said Arnaldo. He, the geekiest of us, was the most likely to understand the science involved. "If it's a circular collider, it smashes subatomic particles into each other to break them up into smaller particles for study. But that's pretty much all they do. They aren't dangerous. Well, theoretically, if certain aspects of string theory are correct, they could create a black hole or fragments of dark matter."

November mouthed the words "black hole," a worry line forming between her brows.

"No danger there," said Caleb with bite as we all tried to look like we knew what Arnaldo was talking about.

"Those possibilities were all ruled out before they turned on the Large Hadron Collider in Europe," Arnaldo said dismissively. "But what would the Tribunal want with one?"

"And does it have anything to do with their stealing our DNA?" said London.

"Excellent question," said Arnaldo.

"Whatever they have planned, it's big," I said. "It's taken them years and millions of dollars to build this thing. And Lazar's our way in. He's promised to bring us the plans to the place and find out everything he can."

"He won't tell anyone where the school is," Amaris said. "He promised."

"Oh, well, as long as he promised!" London's voice cut like a fang, and Amaris colored a deep red. "I know he's your brother, but he raided our last school and kidnapped Siku. He'd be happy if every single one of us was dead."

"Like my mother," said Caleb, not looking at me.

"No!" Amaris shook her head vehemently. "No, he's not really like that. You don't know all the horrible things our father's done to him, to make him do those things. He's sick of it, like I was. He has to get away or he'll go crazy."

"What a load of crap." London threw her napkin down and stalked out. Amaris looked crushed.

November poked her next bite with her fork. "I hate to agree with Wolfie, but she's right. We probably should have taken Lazar prisoner."

Siku swallowed a bit of waffle. "Or killed him."

Caleb shook his head, his eyes not meeting mine. If he had, they probably would've said "I told you so." The strain that had come from our disagreement last night was creeping back.

"After what the Tribunal did to my family . . ." Arnaldo's long fingers closed into fists. "If I'd been there, I might have done it myself." Arnaldo wasn't usually an angry or violent person; he wanted to be an opera singer. But at that moment, staring down his long nose, eyes glittering, dark hair pushed back from his furrowed brow, he was all raptor, ready to swoop down on his prey and strike.

Siku grunted in agreement.

I looked around at all of them, feeling helpless. "But, Arnaldo, you know this particle collider has to be a big threat, don't you? We wouldn't even know it existed if it weren't for Lazar."

Arnaldo narrowed his eyes, thinking. "If they do have a collider, we need to find out why they built it. But we only have Lazar's word that it exists at all."

"I'm sorry." Amaris was crying. "This is all my fault." She scraped her chair back and ran through a door in the back of the kitchen. I caught a glimpse of gym equipment in the room beyond before the door banged shut.

November waved her fork in the air like a magic wand. "Slamming doors, crying, conflict. It's good to be back."

"We'll see if he was telling the truth when Lazar brings back the information on the collider," I said. "Then you'll know for sure."

"London still hasn't forgiven him for forcing her out of her wolf form," Arnaldo said. "Back at the old Tribunal compound."

"If London smells him anywhere near here, she'll rip his throat out," said Siku. "If I don't do it first."

I'd forgotten how closed off shifters could be to new ideas. My friends had rejected me when I accidentally turned into a cat instead of a tiger because they'd never seen a shifter with more than one animal form before. It had taken facing a Tribunal attack to bring us together again. Maybe once they really understood that, in his own way, Lazar was in as much danger from Ximon as we were, they'd come around.

Or maybe not. I kept pushing the envelope, violating long-held otherkin traditions out of ignorance or because I believed it was best for all. One day I might go too far and find myself without friends or allies again. The balance between doing what I thought was right and maintaining my friendships, even my relationship with Caleb, was getting trickier.

"I need some air," I said, pushing myself away from the table.

"This way," Caleb said, standing up to come with me and pointing at the door Amaris had gone through. As he followed me through the door, I found some comfort in the fact that he was coming with me. Maybe he wasn't happy about what had happened with Lazar last night, but he still cared. He had to. All the emotion in his touch last night couldn't have disappeared overnight because of one disagreement.

The next room was indeed a gym, smaller than at the previous school, with ingenious showers that used gravity to bring water from a nearby river. Beyond that, we made our way through a library or study room lit by skylights, full of all the musty old books and parchments I remembered. The last room was half inside, half out, using the overhang of the hill to shield us from above, and filled with all kinds of growing things—from tomatoes like the ones I'd grown at our house in Burbank to bushes of lavender and a small stand of bristling cacti.

Late morning sun slanted through the surrounding evergreens. There was no sign of Amaris. She must have taken a walk. Downslope from us, several dozen shaggy red-brown elk, some as tall as five feet at the shoulder, had wandered into view, their heads weighed with antlers like coral reefs, pushing aside dead fallen branches with their prominent noses to find something green and edible in the winter forest.

The ground was not yet covered with white, but the cold cloudy air had the tang of imminent snowfall.

Seeing that we were alone, I tentatively took Caleb's hand. "Are we okay?" I asked.

He turned, his face softening, and pulled me in for a long kiss.

"You think the elk would mind if I ravished you out here?" he said against my mouth.

I breathed a laugh. "Who cares?"

He slid his hands down my waist, under my shirt, digging his fingers into my flesh, tracing my ribs. But the freezing air also rushed over me. I shivered.

He pulled back slightly, frowning playfully, and adjusted my shirt to cover me completely. Then he took off his coat and draped it around my shoulders. "Okay, so maybe inside is a better idea for that kind of thing."

I drew the coat around me, and Caleb's warm, airy scent enfolded me reassuringly. "Maybe. And I actually do have some stuff to tell you. Yesterday was . . ."

"Crazy. Yeah. Come over here. It's warmer."

He guided me to sit on one of the benches around a stone table set next to an outdoor fire pit, which glowed with live coals that softly warmed the immediate area. A weight settled on me when I remembered the look on Arnaldo's face as his father ordered him out. "I just left an anonymous message with Child Protective Services about Arnaldo's father."

"Wow." Caleb pursed his lips and nodded. "Okay. But we have to tell Arnaldo."

"Maybe after he calms down, like, tomorrow?" I shook my head. "Don't get me wrong—I'm all conflicted about it. But we can't leave those boys alone with that man. . . ."

"No, I get it." He wrapped his arm around my shoulders. "If it helps his brothers, it's worth it. Maybe we can work it so legally Arnaldo's their guardian or something."

"Thanks," I said, still swimming in a tide of uncertainty. "How did I make everything go wrong so fast?"

"Arnaldo's father's the one who did that, not you," Caleb said. "You're not the kind of person who can stand by while people are getting hurt. That's a good thing."

"Is it?" I turned my head to look at him. "What if I try to do the right thing and end up making things worse?"

"At least you didn't try to strangle your own brother." He stood up, as if the thought of Lazar had pushed him from his seat. He took a few steps to stare out at the forest.

"You wouldn't have gone through with it," I said.

"Maybe I should have." He said it very low, as if to himself.

Instinctively, I drew back. "You don't mean that."

"What if I did?" He turned to look at me, one eyebrow cocked. "What would you think of me then?" When I hesitated, he nodded. "You'd hate me. Then you should hate me now, because part of me wishes I'd put an end to him when I had the chance."

"I could never hate you," I said. "We all do stupid things. . . ."

"Would it be so stupid?" He ran one hand through his unruly dark hair. "He killed my mother and God knows how many others. Maybe it's not so wrong to just kill Lazar and Ximon, and everyone else like them. The world would be a better place without them."

"So you're going to personally kill off everyone you think is bad?" I asked. "If we going around killing people we hate, how are we any better than the Tribunal?"

"Lazar deserves to die!" Caleb moved into me, black eyes sparking with gold in sudden fury. "He and Ximon will do anything to wipe us out, go to any extreme. And if we want to defeat them, we need to be willing to do the same."

My heart was sinking lower and lower as he spoke. "I won't become like them." I made myself meet his eyes without flinching. "I can't and still be me."

"What, so your precious integrity's more important than your life?" He was staring at me in disbelief.

"I don't know," I said. "But if I become what I hate, what's the point of anything?"

He was frowning at me, his gaze flicking back and forth between my eyes, as if he'd find an answer in one or the other. Then he relaxed a little. "I just can't lose you," he said.

I smiled, and my heart stopped sinking, though it still felt heavy. "You won't."

Then I was in his arms. He swooped in and picked me up so that my feet left the floor, wrapping his arms around me to bury his face in my neck. "When you're away it's like a part of me is gone too," he said softly, his lips moving against my skin.

There it was, that feeling I'd been missing. I could breathe again. In his arms I was home.

"I'm always with you," I said. "Even when I'm away."

He inhaled sharply, and then he kissed me with warm, soft lips. I kissed him back, my arms around his neck, fingers tangling in his unruly hair. I could feel the hard line of his body pressed against me, and I pushed myself even closer to him, never close enough. *Closer, please . . .*

Something soft tickled the small of my back. I giggled, wiggling in Caleb's arms, then realized that unless he had three hands, it couldn't be him.

"Whoa!" Caleb pulled his head back, eyes wide and staring behind me.

I turned to see an elk calf, all liquid brown eyes, winged ears, and knobby knees, removing its wet black nose from my skin. I blinked as it snuffled up at me, abbreviated tail wagging. Somehow it had scrambled up the grassy side of the building to join us on the patio.

"Oh, hi," I said, my heart still racing from kissing Caleb. "Where's your mom?"

The calf made a short, high-pitched mewing sound, almost like a bird's chirp.

"We should get inside before Mom finds us," Caleb said. "Elk are—holy shit."

Too late. The mother elk was walking up the side of the hill toward us. She stood five feet tall at the shoulder, with no antlers, just thick brown fur that grew almost into a dark mane around her neck, and legs two miles long that ended in delicate, but substantial hooves.

I began to back away, but Caleb made me stop. "Don't move if you can help it," he said in his quiet voice. "If you startle them, they can knock into you."

So I stood there and breathed evenly as the mother elk walked right up to her fawn and nuzzled it. Then she leaned her long neck over and sniffed my face so that we stood nose to nose. Her eyes were huge, bright, and unafraid.

"Hey, beautiful," I said quietly.

The calf bleated a reply. The mother looked down and made a low rumbling sound; then she turned and walked away with careful, unhurried steps. The calf trotted after her.

I let out a quiet laugh of relief and leaned backwards into Caleb. "What the hell was *that*?" I asked. "Does Mother Nature not want us to make out or something?"

He wrapped his arms around me, chuckling. "I think Mother Nature has a crush on you. Don't you dare leave me for her."

His joking words hit me, and I turned around to look at him. "I have been shorting out gadgets and machines at a record rate for the past few weeks," I said. "And before we moved, the tomatoes outside my room literally broke through the window screen to get inside."

Caleb looked over the top of my head at the elk as they paused to search for grass. "So you think this nature thing of yours is growing stronger? That would help explain what just happened. You're like some Disney princess who has birds come land on her shoulder and make her dresses for the ball."

"Yeah, if Disney princesses set fire to their cell phones," I said.

"You set your phone on fire?" He pulled back to look at me.

"Not on purpose!"

He laughed. "Okay, now there was something else you wanted to talk to me about, right?"

"About my mom," I said. "Something weird happened."

So I told him about Mom channeling whatever-it-was at the lightning tree in the middle of a storm.

"She said I had to learn who I am," I finished. "It wasn't Mom's voice, or Mom's hands—or Mom. At least, I don't think so."

"Her hair looked red, you said?" Caleb was pacing, listening intently.

"It was like the time you channeled that . . . thing from Othersphere," I said. "Something other than Mom was coming through."

"But from where?" He stopped and looked at me. "You have to *grill* Morfael about this. Don't stand for any of his usual evasive bullshit. Your mother's life could depend upon it."

But I didn't find Morfael until everyone came together around noon in the gym for our first class in the new school.

The last time I'd seen him, he'd been lying in a hospital bed, recovering from being shot. His tall alien body was still all pointy angles and cold gray-white skin beneath his cape of black, but he turned as we approached and his opal eyes shone with life. His thin mouth curved into a genuine smile. "Welcome. I look forward to working with you all again."

Morfael wasn't the hugging type, so we smiled back and lined up on the cushy gym mat as he led us through a warm-up, then a vigorous review of martial arts, tapping his carved wooden staff in time with his commands. Amaris kept up with us pretty well, wisps of blond hair sticking to her sweaty forehead as she punched and kicked alongside me. She must've been practicing with Caleb during the past month.

Then a quick shower and shift for everyone except Amaris and Caleb. Shifting had become fairly easy for me, and for all of us, but for some reason I just couldn't wait to shift. I slipped into the skin of my tiger form easier than falling into bed after a long day. It felt so good I nearly bolted out of the girls' bathroom to go hunting, but November bravely got between me and the door and shook her finger at me, calling my name, and telling me not to get a new-moon grade the first day.

Morfael graded us in phases of the moon—and a new moon was the equivalent of an F. No way I could stand the teasing from the others if I ever let that happen, so I forced myself to shift back to human.

We both had to do the same with London, who actually growled at us in her wolf form, then howled before shifting back to human. November was the most easily lured back to her human form; all we had to do was threaten to steal her candy stash.

When we gathered for the after-lunch lesson, all bundled up outside, Arnaldo asked Morfael why shifting felt so different now. The boys must have felt the same thing.

Morfael listened, leaning on his wooden staff, unmoving. The carved animalistic figures on the staff did not seem to move, as they had before. The staff was too tall for me to see the "shadow walker" rune on top. I still didn't know exactly what it meant about Morfael, though the term referred to legendary creatures who could actually travel between worlds. If Morfael was one of them, he certainly wasn't telling. But then he never said a word more than necessary.

"Today's lesson," he said in response to Arnaldo, "is how to recognize places where the veil between the worlds is thin."

He stopped speaking and looked around at all of us, not blinking.

"But . . ." November scrunched up her face in puzzlement. "What about how easy it is to shift?"

"And it was easier to shift to bear form than shift back to human," said Siku. "Why?"

"In this place, we are very close to an area which lies perilously close to Othersphere," said Morfael.

He paused, expressionless.

"Perilously?" said November in a small voice.

"Being a tiger felt more natural than being human," I said slowly. "But what's that got to do with . . . ?"

London's eyes widened in realization. "Shifting is easier because we're in a place that's close to Othersphere!" she said.

Morfael's thin lips twisted with pleasure as we all went "Oh!"

"That is one way to know where the veil is thin," he said. "Your connection to your animal form will become particularly strong. You may feel an overwhelming desire to shift to it and not want to shift back."

"Is it the nuclear testing?" said Caleb. He stood between me and Amaris, hands thrust into the pockets of his long black coat to stay warm.

We all turned to look at Caleb, Morfael included.

"My mother taught me that the veil between worlds becomes thin wherever a huge explosion of power took place," he explained. "Things like volcanoes, earthquakes, meteor strikes, and nuclear bombs—they erode the fabric between this world and Othersphere. And this school isn't far from the Nevada test site. They say they made over nine hundred tests of nuclear weapons in the area, but who knows how many they really set off?"

"They're setting off nuclear bombs nearby?" November asked, her voice rising in alarm. "Great choice for a school location!"

"Don't worry. They stopped testing in the nineties because of the Nuclear Test Ban Treaty," said Caleb. "I looked it up before we settled on this area for the school."

"And it is indeed an excellent location for my school," said Morfael.

"Because it's close to where the veil is thin," I said. "You want us to learn about that."

He nodded, moonlight eyes glinting. "The thickness of the veil between worlds is not consistent. You may discover a spot where it is particularly thin during one of your hikes, or find a place where it thickens. This is something you will learn to detect—without shifting. You will find that the proximity of Othersphere has other, unexpected effects on you and the world around you."

"I—" Amaris started to speak, then cut herself off, blushing.

We all turned to look at her, which made her duck her head, not speaking. Caleb gave her nudge with his elbow. "Go on . . ."

She lifted her chin, still flushed, but determined. "I feel stronger here than I did in Las Vegas, or anywhere else, really. I haven't been able to heal anyone since . . ." She swallowed hard, but went on. "Since my father was injured. But the more time I spend here, the more I feel like maybe I could heal someone again. But, you know, maybe I'm wrong."

"You are correct," Morfael said, and Amaris let out her breath in relief. "As a healer, you draw your power directly from Othersphere, though we are still not sure exactly how. Anything that removes barriers between you and the other world will facilitate the use of your power. In a similar fashion, Caleb and I will find it easier to see the shadow forms of objects and people, and to draw them out."

"Area 51!" I said, and then realized the words had popped out of me without thinking. "Oh, sorry. But that whole thing is probably because the veil here is thin too, right?"

The other kids exchanged puzzled looks, except Caleb, who was grinning at me.

"What's Area 51?" said Arnaldo.

"It's a military base not far from here," I said, "and because of all the crazy sightings in this area of strange lights and weird aircraft, people who believe in UFOs think Area

51 is where the government keeps evidence of alien space-ships and alien bodies and stuff."

"What, so the UFO's aren't alien ships, they're . . . Other-sphere ships?" Siku pursed his lips. "Why would they have spaceships in Othersphere?"

"Not ships, probably," I said. "Lots of the things people see are government aircraft being tested. But since it's also right near where the veil is thin, maybe they're sometimes seeing . . . I don't know, lights from Othersphere, or crea-tures, or something that doesn't make sense in this world."

"You can't *see* through the veil," said November in a scoffing tone. "I mean, callers like Caleb can *sense* shadow through it, but humdrums and shifters don't see animals and mountains and buildings through the veil unless they're called through. Everybody knows that."

"Everybody's wrong." I said, vividly recalling the clash of thunder as lightning had stabbed up between my mother's feet. "There's an old oak tree in my neighborhood whose shadow form is a thunderstorm, and I've seen the lightning without any callers being around. My stepfather Richard saw it too."

Morfael's gaze became very pointed.

"I've been wanting to tell you, but this is the first time I've seen you!" I said. "But I'm not crazy, right? Light and things from Othersphere can appear in our world."

Morfael's eyes narrowed at Caleb, who startled a bit, as if pinched. "Well, your animal forms are manifestations of power from Othersphere," Caleb said. "And for a limited time I can pull a swarm of bees or a forest out of there that feels and acts as real as we do. So seeing lights and shapes through the veil—that could be possible." He turned to Mor-fael. "But wouldn't they need someone drawing on the power to make them visible?"

"It is the thinness of the veil that makes these things possi-ble," said Morfael. "In normal space, a power source such as a caller or shifter is required to manifest the shadow form. But in thin-space, where great power has already been released, shadows may appear randomly, with no one calling them forth. Was there a power source when you saw this lightning?"

"Not that I saw," I said. "The old oak tree is there, of course, and at the time, my mother and I were also there." I saw again my normally tiny mother towering over me, her once brown hair like flames licking her suddenly unfamiliar face. "My mother spoke. But it wasn't her voice."

"Something came through your mother?" London asked. "But she's a humdrum, right?"

"Yeah." I might as well just spill it all. "And whatever it was had red hair like mine, and was taller, and had claws."

Silence fell except for the brisk afternoon breeze rustling through the needles of the evergreens around us. Clouds blocked the sky, threatening snow. I shivered, and Caleb slipped his warm hand into mine. I caught his eye, and when he nodded, felt the courage to look up at Morfael. "Could it have been my biological mother?"

Morfael's eyes looked unfocused for a moment, as if he wasn't quite there; then he blinked and nodded. "It is possible."

I felt as if the breeze were blowing through me. Like my skin and flesh had dissolved to leave my bones rattling in the forest. "But how? From where?"

Morfael did not answer. His hollow face showed no emotion. How could he not care? He'd spent over a year searching for my biological parents after he'd found me in the Siberian forest, and then searching for any other tiger-shifters who might be willing to look after me. He'd found none. Or so he said. After all that effort, wasn't he curious about where I'd come from, where tiger-shifters might still live?

"Could it be a trick?" said Amaris. "Someone pretending to be your real mother, someone trying to manipulate you somehow."

"Oh, my God!" That hadn't occurred to me. What I'd seen that night had felt so real, so sincere.

"That, too, is possible," said Morfael.

"You're thinking it's the Tribunal?" Caleb asked Amaris. "Trying to throw Dez off her game or to use her for some purpose."

"Could they *do* that?" November sounded like she couldn't quite believe it. "I know objurers are basically just like callers with a bad attitude, but still."

"Caleb changed into something else the night we raided Ximon's compound," I said. "Something from Othersphere. Maybe an objurer from the Tribunal somehow did that with my mom, from a distance or something."

"They'd have to be very powerful to do it from far away," said Caleb. "Even up close, it would be draining."

"Yet another reason to find out what the hell the Tribunal wants with DNA from all of us," said Arnaldo.

Snow began to fall. For an hour after that, we walked through the thick, unhurried flurries under Morfael's instruction, focusing on our internal connection to Othersphere. Any change in it could be a signal that the thickness of the veil nearby had changed. This was very hard to do because always at the edge lay the temptation of slipping into animal form. For me, the power of my tiger self felt closer and more irresistible than ever.

A thud and Amaris saying "Oof!" brought us all together again. We found her getting to her feet, brushing snow off the front of her jacket. But her right hand left red streaks on the navy blue fabric. "I'm okay," she said. "I didn't see a log under the snow and boom."

"Your hand!" London darted forward and took her right hand, holding the palm up. It oozed blood from abrasions. "Nothing deep or dangerous. Already it's clotting, so you won't need stitches. Maybe use some snow to numb it up until we go back inside."

"No." Morfael moved through the group of us, up to Amaris. "Heal yourself."

Amaris's eyes popped wide, her jaw dropping slightly open. "I . . . I don't think I can."

"You have done it before," he said.

"Yeah, but not for a long time. I'm kind of . . ." She bit her lip. "I'm broken."

Morfael's face did not change. "Heal yourself."

"Okay." She blinked hard. "I'll try."

London released her hand. "Good luck."

"Thanks." Amaris gave her a weak smile.

"Don't forget, Amar," November said, pronouncing it like "ammer," "the veil is thin here."

Amaris nodded, held up her hands, palms facing her, and closed her eyes.

Caleb leaned into me, his voice low. "I've only seen her do it twice. It's pretty amazing. She doesn't have to hum or anything."

Indeed, the look on Amaris's face had become very placid, almost like she'd fallen asleep standing up. Only a tiny worried line hovered between her brows, and her shoulders were bunched with tension. *Relax,* I thought at her. *You can do this.*

But after about thirty seconds, her eyes flew open and she shook her head. Her hand was still bloody and scratched. "I can't." Her eyes were bright with tears. "I told you."

"It is not *I* whom you told," said Morfael. Then he turned to address us all, back in classroom mode. "Now, you will all continue trying to find spots where the veil is thin. Call out when you have found a perceptible change in space."

We fanned out again, hands out, as if maybe we could feel a change tangibly. London scooped up some snow and put it on the scrape on Amaris's hand. "Just put some antibiotic ointment on it when we get back. No big deal."

"Thanks." Amaris gave her a watery smile.

Morfael took me aside, his normally impassive face show-ing just the slightest twitch. I was immediately on high alert.

"The regional Council of Shifters wishes to speak to you first thing tomorrow morning," Morfael said. "It is time for them to review whether or not they approve your presence here."

I slumped. When I first came to Morfael's school, I'd barely managed to get the Council's approval. The vote had been three to two in favor of me staying, thanks to a last-minute switch by the bear-shifter representative. But I'd stirred up a lot of trouble since then, and the Council was as cautious as a feral cat when it came to the Tribunal. Some of them had wanted to have me killed back then. How much worse must they feel about me now?

"What if they don't approve?" I asked. "Will you kick me out? How much authority do they have?"

"They can't force me to get rid of you," he said, his eyes sparkling with too many prisms of color to count. "But let's not anticipate the worst."

"Easy for you to say," I said.

He regarded me with what might have been amusement. It was hard to tell with him. "You can use the dread you feel right now to tap into your connection to Othersphere," he said. "That will help you find the places where the veil is thin."

It took me a second to realize he was referring to the exer-cise again, trying to determine the thickness of the veil be-tween worlds. *To hell with that.* I opened my mouth to ask him more about the Council, but he had already walked away to speak to Arnaldo.

So I did focus on the dread. Dark thoughts often fueled the black core of power inside me. After about ten minutes of walking around the forest, I realized that it would sometimes pulse and grow, not larger, but *darker*, more chaotic at times. It was like a crazy whirlpool threatening to suck me in. The next time it did that, I stopped and found a very large bristle-cone pine tree in front of me.

I stopped walking. London bumped into me, with a quiet exclamation, and then drew back. I hadn't realized she was following so close.

"There's something here," I said. "The veil is thinner. I think." *If only I could escape through it, so the Council could never find me.*

"Is it the tree?" She looked at the collection of white-dusted cones nestled in the evergreen branches. "How can you tell?"

The others got closer, as I looked at the tree while at the same time focusing on the roiling power near my heart. "I don't think it's the tree. It's coming from something smaller."

"Wait," said November. "I know what you mean. It smells like lemon-lime jelly beans around here somewhere." As London rolled her eyes, she glared. "What?"

A small brown form flicked up the trunk of the tree, and I felt the shift in power inside me. "There!" I pointed at a tiny bird with a fluffy gray body and a striking black-and-white striped head perched on a branch. It cocked its black-capped head and fixed a tiny dark eye on me.

"A mountain chickadee," said Morfael, moving sound-lessly up to gaze at it. "A female. One of the most common creatures in the western United States, and yet, you are right, Desdemona." He reached out one skeletal finger, not that different from the bird's claws, and stroked its feathers once. The bird cheeped musically, but did not fly away. "She lies very close to the veil. All of you, focus on your connection to Othersphere as you look at her, and notice how she behaves. Caleb"—he motioned Caleb to move forward—"tell me what you see."

Caleb came to stand next to me, and under his breath, he hummed something very quietly. We all gasped as the vibration from it, perhaps magnified by the proximity of Other-sphere, thrummed through us.

The bird inclined its head, the black stripe over its eye aimed at Caleb. He pursed his lips, still humming. Then with a sharp exhale, he broke off and stepped back, eyes wide.

"Oh, wow. She's a lot bigger in Othersphere. Like, dragon big. With shiny scales, and eyes like copper pots. Claws as long as my arm." He shook his head and laughed at himself a little. "In Othersphere, this place is inside her cave, and when I looked at her ... she looked right back at me. She knows we're here. I just hope she isn't hungry."

November looked at Caleb uneasily. "Could something come through the veil here and ... eat us?"

"Probably not," Morfael said.

"Probably?" said London. She stood very close to me, as if using me as a shield between her and the chickadee.

"There is a lake in Scotland that lies close to Othersphere," said Morfael. "People claim to have seen a large creature swimming in its waters that could only have come through the veil. But she has not eaten anyone." He paused to think. "That we know of."

We all exchanged looks. Thanks to the Tribunal's prejudices and the shifter community's fear of exposure, Amaris and the shifter kids had all led relatively sheltered lives, often not allowed access to TV or the Internet by their parents. Shifter parents like Arnaldo's dad who didn't want them "tainted" by humdrum culture were common. Of all of them, only November had a phone with Internet access, and even she had a minimal data plan. Still, all of them had heard of the Loch Ness Monster.

"So much for no one traveling between worlds. They say it's impossible, but it sounds like it's happening all the time," said Arnaldo.

"They also say that shifters only have one animal form," said London. "But we've seen Dez shift into two."

"Could we do that?" Siku turned to Morfael.

Morfael did not reply, only faintly raised his nearly invisible eyebrows and smiled his creaky smile.

"The problem isn't just traveling across worlds. With a power source, that's possible. It's got to be much tougher *staying* on the other side of the veil for more than a few minutes, especially without a power source to keep you there," Caleb said, returning to the topic. I moved closer to him, and he smiled down at me.

"There are legendary people or things known as shadow walkers," I said, not looking at Morfael. It was in researching the rune on the top of his staff that I'd come upon this information. "I read about them. They walk between worlds at will."

"My mom used to tell me stories about the shadow walkers," said Siku. "She said they move between all the many worlds, not just ours and Othersphere. They belong nowhere and go everywhere. She said they'd come across the veil and take me away if I was bad. But that's just a story to frighten kids."

"So are werewolves," said Amaris. She threw a smile at London. "Right, London?"

I held my breath. London hated it when people called wolf-shifters werewolves. Those feral blood-crazed stereotypes made her stomp off to sulk.

But the look Amaris sent her was so merry, so knowing, that a smile broke out suddenly from under London's habitual gloom, and she laughed.

"A-wooo!" She threw back her head and howled. The cry was eerie, a genuine wolf call, raising goose bumps on my arms. Then London grabbed my hand and twirled me around, singing the song she supposedly hated most: "Werewolves of London."

I laughed and twirled her around in turn, kicking up snow. November grabbed a clueless-looking Amaris around the waist to dance with us. A second later, Amaris was howling with us, "Ah-woooo!"

General mayhem ensued as Siku swept up both November and Amaris in his arms at the same time, lost his balance, and all three fell into a snowdrift. Arnaldo sang the next verse, perfectly in key, and London pulled me down into the powder with the others. Caleb lobbed a snowball at the back of Arnaldo's head, which put an abrupt stop to the singing and led to a mad scramble for cover and wet handfuls of snow. It quickly became boys versus girls, and with Amaris on our side, we rushed the boys and pounded them mercilessly till they threw their hands in front of their faces, laughing and crying uncle.

Siku rolled over and made the biggest snow angel I'd ever seen, and Amaris lay down next to him to make one that looked like it was holding his angel's hand. We lined up then, creating a linked line of blurry winged shapes in the snow. I rolled onto Caleb as he finished his angel and kissed him with cold lips, clumps of snow falling from the back of my head onto his cheek to melt into tiny streams.

"Morfael just told me I have a meeting with the regional Council tomorrow morning," I whispered, my heart beating fast against his chest. "Will you be there with me?"

"I'll follow you anywhere," he said, his arms tightening around me. "Don't worry. Together we can make it through anything."

I nodded and laid my head on his shoulder, knowing he meant what he said. Maybe everything would be okay between us. Maybe the Council would embrace me and Caleb would forgive Lazar. I opened my mouth to tell Caleb that I loved him, and that we'd work everything out. Then I remembered how he'd said he wanted Lazar dead, and no words would come.

# CHAPTER 9

After dinner I tried to avoid the nauseating mix of guilt and anxiety threatening to boil my brain by going to the library to do some research. Morfael was standing there expectantly, as if he'd been waiting. He held out one pale hand. In it lay a plain leather scabbard attached to a wide silk belt with a tortoiseshell clasp.

"The Shadow Blade," I said, and grasped the carved winged creature on the hilt to unsheathe the dagger. A bone-deep contentment washed over me as I held up the pitch-black knife. As before, its cutting edge was amorphous rather than sharp, as if trailing smoke.

"I have found a way to make it keep its form," said Morfael. "Unless you wish me to reverse the process, it will now always remain a dagger, scabbard, and belt."

"So we don't have to tote my old back brace around everywhere for Caleb to call the blade forth." I nodded. The Shadow Blade had been the shadow form of my back brace, its power sensed and brought forth by Caleb when we raided Ximon's compound. After that, as long as I held it or wore it, it remained a blade. But once I took it off, it reverted to its humdrum form, the brace. Now that shifting had so magically cured my scoliosis and my spine was straight, I didn't need to wear the brace anymore. Having it permanently in knife form would make it much easier to deal with.

As before, when I held the Blade, it felt exactly right, as if it had been made for me. The smoky edge of the dagger cut only through nonliving material. It may have been my imagination, but it seemed to me to hunger for metal or plastic to sink into. I looked around the room for something innocuous and not living to slice into, but the bookshelves were made of wood, the books of paper, the chairs upholstered in leather or wool. Morfael, too, appeared to be alive, though November might have quibbled with me on that. So I slid the blade back into its scabbard reluctantly.

"I want to use it on something," I said. "It's like an itch."

Morfael nodded. "Remember what I said about the effects of thin-space. Many thoughts and feelings will be amplified where the veil is weak. Here."

He drew forth from some pocket in his robes a thin, silver band. A ring. I didn't wear any jewelry because it just popped off when I shifted, and I particularly avoided silver because I had a very rare allergy to it. But Morfael took my left hand and slid the ring onto my index finger.

Immediately, the skin there began to itch horribly. I jerked my hand away and rubbed the finger against my leg. "Why . . . ?"

"Use the Blade," he said.

"Oh. Right." I lifted the Blade in my right hand and lowered the smoky dark edge toward the ring. Even though I knew that the knife would only cut the metal and not my skin, it sure looked dangerous, and I had to force myself to press it down. The murky Blade sharpened to a razor's edge as it sliced right through the silver like a cheese cutter through cheddar, only to stop when it hit my skin. It didn't even scratch me, but felt cool, almost soft. And the itching stopped as if a spell had been cast.

"It doesn't just cut through metal," I said. "It's like it also guards me against it."

He took the ring back, nodding, and slipped it back into his pocket.

"How did you make the Blade stay a knife?" I asked. "I didn't know you could make an object from Othersphere stay permanently in this world."

"The knife is connected to you," he said. "I used that bond to secure it in whatever world you are in."

That made a kind of sense, but as usual with Morfael, it was a pretty vague explanation. "Why is something from Othersphere connected to me?" I asked. "Did my biological parents do it? It can't just be some random thing."

"There is no way to be certain," he said.

Ambiguouser and ambiguouser.

"Do you think the Council knows about the Blade?" I asked. "Or any of the other weird stuff about me?" Even worse . . . I flashed on last night's conversation with Lazar. *Oh, God, if they find out about that, they'll kill me for sure.* Morfael was looking at me. I stuttered nervously. "I-it might make them more nervous if they knew I could also shift into a cat, you know. That kind of thing."

"You've done very well for yourself so far," Morfael said. "Trust that. Now, I require you to describe again exactly what happened to your mother at the lightning tree."

So I swallowed down that set of anxieties and focused on others as I told him everything that had happened with Mom the other night. He listened with his usual watchful lack of expression. A little silence fall after I was done. I resisted the urge to ask questions and just told him the facts while his narrow lips pursed slightly, and his nearly lashless eyelids made slow, deliberate blinks.

"Has anything like this happened to your mother before?" he finally asked.

"No. I mean, wait, yes." Memory sparked an image of my mother rubbing her stomach just before her transformation, and of the discussion she, Richard, and I had had later. "Just before it happened, she said she felt like that sometimes in dreams. And later on, she said she'd had dreams where there was a whirlpool inside her that felt wrong, and a voice telling her it had a 'message of importance.' " I shook my head. "I can't believe I forgot about that."

Morfael nodded once, then began pacing up and down alongside the library's crammed bookshelves, tapping his cane lightly with every other step. I couldn't remember seeing him pace before. He must be quite concerned. "What do you think this message of importance is?" he asked.

"I'm not sure," I said. "But maybe it's about who I really am? That seemed to be what whatever-it-was inside Mom was trying to tell me. But the storm all around her made it difficult."

"Yet it was the storm that allowed it to get through in the first place," he said. "The lightning tree is a very old, very powerful connection to Othersphere. The veil there is thin. I have never heard of a humdrum being used in this way, but the presence of the tree might make it possible. How is your mother now?"

"She seemed okay after some rest, and no other incidents since then." Something in the set of Morfael's mouth, and his half-lidded eyes, made me uneasy. "Why? Do you think she's still in danger?"

His bony shoulders rose in a small shrug. "Now that she has been used as a conduit to Othersphere, some of that connection may remain. She may be vulnerable to other incidents, even away from the lightning tree. Please tell her that if she has another dream like those others, or if anything else strange occurs, she should come here. I may be able to help. Or I may not."

"Okay, I'll let her know, thanks," I said. It was a relief to think there might be some help here for Mom if something happened again. *Hopefully, it just won't.*

Morfael turned to go, heading toward the door, when I realized the other part of what he was saying. "Wait!"

He paused, his cloaked back to me, but did not turn around.

"You're saying then that this message definitely came from Othersphere—not from somewhere else in this world? It wasn't some Tribunal trick?"

He didn't say anything, so I stomped around to look him in the eye. I was nearly as tall as he was, and I kept staring until he met my gaze. "Why is some . . . thing from Othersphere trying to tell me who I really am? I'm a tiger-shifter from Siberia, maybe the last one of my kind, right? Morfael?"

One side of his mouth was turning up, creasing his hollow cheek. I couldn't tell if he was amused or simply smug.

Fear clutched at my throat then. I didn't want to ask it, yet I had to. The words came of their own accord: "*Who am I?*"

The corner of his mouth deepened, and he shouldered past me, no longer pausing to tap his wooden staff, but taking long strides down the hall, toward the front door. I took a few running steps after him, then forced myself to stop as he stepped out into the moonlight. An anxious fury threatened to rise up from my heart and overtake me, and I forced myself to take deep breaths to quell it. The old caller of shadow was still hiding things from me. From past experience, I knew he thought this was for the best. And maybe he was right.

About nine p.m., when most of us were done with homework, we all ended up in the girls' room. All except for Caleb and Amaris, who were having some kind of private lesson with Morfael. I kept glancing at the door, mostly because I couldn't wait to see Caleb again. The meeting with the Council in the morning loomed, and nothing calmed me like being with him. But also wiggling in the corner of my brain was the idea that maybe we could slip away somehow, find a place alone, and see if we could find our way back to those heated moments in the back of the car last night.

Arnaldo hooked his iPod up to a set of portable speakers and blasted songs from a new rock band with classical influences he wanted us all to hear. November bounced on and off Siku's lap in time to the beat until he shoved her away irritably. London sat at my feet and leaned against my legs as I French-braided her hair.

"So what did you do during our little break from school?" I asked her. "Anything fun?"

"Not unless you think chopping wood's a party," she said. "My mom lectured me nearly every day on how I'd endangered everyone in our tribe by helping rescue Siku from the Tribunal, so I went on a lot of very long walks just to get out of the house."

"Meet any cute park rangers while you were rambling around?" I wiggled my knee near her shoulder teasingly. "Or maybe a lumberjack?"

"What?" London's voice swooped up, sounding almost scared. "No! Of course not."

"Why of course not?" I asked. "If your parents ever let anyone outside their little circle meet you, you'd get tons of attention."

London looked down, disturbing my braid-making, tracing the grain of the wood floor with a finger. "You think I'm pretty?"

"More than pretty," I said. "Try striking, gorgeous, beautiful. Please!"

"I don't feel pretty." Her voice was so low, I barely heard it. "Except maybe when you're around."

The door clicked open and Caleb walked in with Amaris. London stood up abruptly, mumbling something about how she'd changed her mind about the French braid, ran into the bathroom, and slammed the door.

"That was weird," I said as Caleb walked up to me.

Nobody said anything for a second, and the quiet got a little odd. Amaris wouldn't look at me while Caleb and November exchanged looks. "What?" I said. "What's going on with London?"

"Ssh," said Amaris. "She'll hear you."

I looked from her to the bathroom door. Did she mean London?

"Yeah, keep it down, Cat-girl," November said in a low voice I could barely hear above the music. She swatted Siku, and then came closer. "You are such an idiot. London's got a huge crush on you."

"She . . ." I blinked. "She does?"

November shook her head at me, like I was the slowest marcher in the parade. "Only since, like, forever. I don't think she's got any real hopes you'll switch teams, and she likes Caleb and everything, but—"

"She resents me," Caleb finished for her.

"Holy mackeroly," I said. I sat down heavily on the bed behind me. "I'm sorry. I didn't mean to . . ."

"It's not you," said Amaris. She looked over at the bathroom door, her wide brown eyes flickering with something she wasn't saying. "People can't help how they feel."

"Boy, that's true," said November. "The truth is so annoying."

"Just don't tell her we talked about this or embarrass her about it or anything," said Arnaldo.

"Siku," I said, turning to him. "Did you know about this?"

He nodded. "She's got good taste."

That made me smile, and I relaxed a little.

Caleb sat down next to me. "I thought you knew."

"No, no, it's okay," I said, leaning against him a little.

"It's really none of our business," said Amaris, her voice harsh. Then, as if regretting how forcefully she'd spoken, she cleared her throat. "I mean. She'll be okay."

The bathroom door opened, and we all shut our mouths and avoided looking at London as she slid out, head down, her hair pulled out of the braids to fall in soft waves. She'd put her nose rings in again, two silver and one gold, glinting against her pale skin.

Amaris stood up, making small clucking noises. "You can't just give up on the braid if it doesn't work out the first time," she said. "Come over here and let me do it."

London shook her head, not meeting anyone's eyes. I'd seen her that way when I first met her, like she wanted to disappear. I'd felt like that a lot when I had to wear the brace. *Ugh. I made her feel that way.*

"No, seriously, my mom taught me how to French-braid and it'll look good on you. Come on." Amaris walked over to London and pushed her shoulders down until she sat on a bed.

Arnaldo cued up another song while I tried not to stare too hard at London. I wanted her to be okay, for her to know that I cared about her, but how the hell could I do that without giving her the wrong idea? I leaned in to Caleb and whispered in his ear, "Why is life so complicated?"

He shook his head. "It'll pass. Just be normal."

Amaris started combing London's hair back, preparing to braid. London was looking anywhere but at me and Caleb. "So your mom used to braid your hair?" she asked Amaris. "Where is she now?"

Amaris looked at Caleb over the top of London's head, then looked down. "She died when I was ten. Breast cancer."

For a moment no one knew what to say. Then: "That sucks," said Siku.

Amaris flashed him a small smile. "Yeah. I could heal small cuts and bruises then, but cancer . . ." She bit her lip, but kept going, as if grinding out the facts. "Later on, I found out that my father refused to let her go to a humdrum hospital for treatment. We've got our own doctors in the Tribunal, but they don't have the latest chemotherapy treatments and stuff. All our scientific research and money goes toward 'the Cause' instead."

"The cause of getting rid of the otherkin," said London.

"Exactly." Amaris began expertly threading locks of London's hair into a smooth braid. "And my mother wasn't important enough. She was just a woman, just a mother. My father wouldn't break the rules against consulting outsiders to help her. It might not have saved her anyway. I don't know."

"But he should've tried!" November hovered near Siku, her skinny eyebrows frowning thunderously.

"Why? She'd popped out a couple of kids just like he wanted, and God was now taking her to heaven." Amaris's eyes were bright as she shook her head. "I think that's when I really started to hate him."

"I hate my parents sometimes," said London.

"Yeah. My dad hates anyone who's not a bird-shifter," said Arnaldo. "That's just as messed up."

"My mom told me that I better marry a nice alpha wolf-shifter soon and start having pups like a good little girl, or she and my dad might throw me out," said London. "She doesn't believe me when I tell her I'd rather kill myself."

"That's what I was going to do, after my father forced me to marry Enoch," Amaris said, her voice soft. "If you guys hadn't come along..."

London didn't turn her head as Amaris kept on weaving the braid through her hair, but her eyes moved back and forth; she was obviously thinking. "Do sworn enemies always have this much in common?" she asked.

Amaris gave a small laugh, and London's lips curved up in a half-smile.

November was giving the two of them a considering look, her lips pursed. She saw me notice and waggled her eyebrows suggestively.

Raynard stuck his grizzled head in around eleven o'clock and ordered the boys out. I hung onto Caleb till the last sec-

ond, unsure of how I was going to sleep through the night before the Council meeting without him. He gave me a sweet
kiss and pulled away reluctantly.

So I let go of my fantasies of picking up where we'd left off
last night and fell onto my bed, punching my pillow into
shape. Things were good between us. But we weren't back to
where we'd been before Lazar had interrupted us last night.
Maybe it was unrealistic to expect to hop right back there in
less than a day, but the memory of Caleb's bare skin rubbing
up against mine kept intruding on every thought. I wanted
nothing more than to feel him that close to me again.

As Siku clomped down the hall without saying anything to
November, she slammed the door, frowning.

"Okay, I admit it. I need some advice," she said. "And not
about silly life-threatening crap. About something more important. Boys."

"Maybe one boy in particular?" London turned from admiring her braid in the mirror with a grin.

"You think?" November stomped over to her bed and
flopped down. "Could I be any more obvious with Siku? I'm
practically stripping his clothes off in public, and he just
smiles and pats me on the head."

"So you're not together?" Amaris got up and grabbed a
bottle of water from the mini-fridge. "I wasn't sure."

"Only if by together you mean I use him like a jungle gym
and he laughs and tells me to get down." November expelled
her breath in a growling sigh.

"I've been wondering what was going on," I said. "Have
you told him you're interested?"

"No!" November flipped over on her back to stare angrily
at the ceiling. "He treats me like it's all a big joke. What do
you guys think? Should I maybe flash him a boob or something?"

Amaris choked on her water, laughing and coughing as she
turned red.

London pounded her twice on the back. "Don't worry. She has that effect on everyone at first."

"I don't think he needs more boob," I said.

November nodded. "I do ooze sex appeal."

"With everyone," I said.

"So?" November shrugged.

"And that's *all* you do," London countered.

November rolled over to stare at London. "What else is there?"

"There's, you know, you," said Amaris.

"Me?" November looked genuinely puzzled.

"The crap underneath the boobs, dummy," said London. "Hopes, dreams. And I don't mean your dream that heaven is made of lollipops."

"Before Caleb, I would push boys away because of the back brace," I said, thinking it through. "But then I ended up in a cage next to Caleb wearing a hospital gown, and I got all angry and mauled Lazar. It was super embarrassing. I mean, I never wanted anyone to see me like that, but Caleb was really cool about it. And later, Caleb nearly collapsed in front of me after he called something out of shadow. Then it was like we'd both taken our masks off, you know? It was a good thing."

"This is not a mask!" said November. "This is me!"

"But you're a big flirt with everyone," said London. "How's he supposed to know that you actually mean it with him unless you show him something you don't show to others?"

"Believe me, others have seen *everything*," November said.

"Did they ever see you scared?" Amaris asked. "Or, you know, vulnerable?"

I saw what Amaris was getting at now. "You have a million brothers, right?"

November snorted. "Damn straight. The whole house smells like a locker room."

"I bet you had to be just as tough and smart-ass as they were, right?"

November considered this, eyebrows drawn, and gave a "maybe" nod.

"Siku's not a smart-ass," said London. "He's more serious."

"You think he doesn't like me because I'm such a tease?" November's voice got suddenly plaintive. "Maybe he only likes stupid gloomy girls."

London and Amaris were shaking their heads, and I agreed with them. I said, "Maybe he thinks you're just playing around. You might actually have to . . . you know, show him what's under the sex appeal."

"Oh, crap!" November buried her face in the quilt on her bed, muffling her voice for a second. "How the hell do I do that?" She lifted her head, lips turned down mournfully. "With my last boyfriend I just wiggled my hips and he came running, you know?"

"Siku's worth a little effort," London said.

"And I think we found what scares you," I said. "Being real with boys."

In answer, she grabbed her pillow, buried her face in it, and kicked the mattress.

I stared at the ceiling, trying not to feel envy. She might be on the verge of something very exciting. As I had been last night, with Caleb. More than anything I wanted to be with him now, discovering more and more about each other, without anyone else around. My whole body got hot just thinking about it. Would we ever get the chance? It was going to be another very long night.

# CHAPTER 10

"What time is it?" I blinked up at Raynard, who was standing in the doorway of our room, rumpled, unshaven, and stern-faced. He'd switched on the lights for some reason. I heard the other girls stirring in their beds, groaning.

"Four a.m.," he said. "Morfael wants you, London, and November assembled outside the front door in five minutes. Amaris can stay in bed."

Then he was gone, thumping the door shut behind him.

"What the hell?" London pulled the covers over her head.

"For once, I agree with you," November said.

Amaris sat up. "I'd go if he wanted me to. You know he always has a reason for the crazy things he makes us do."

"Torture is a reason," said November. "Torture and old-man pain in the ass-itude."

Somehow we stumbled out into the still, snowy night. The deep early morning chill and something else, something darker and crazier, thrummed under my skin.

I looked around for Caleb, who hung back as the other boys emerged, stuffing their hands deep into their pockets and stamping their feet. I padded up to him. "So you and Amaris don't have to participate in this ... whatever?"

"Looks like shifters only," he said, and kissed me on the nose. "But I had to come up anyway to see you and say good luck with whatever."

I gave him a quick kiss back. "Thanks."

Morfael emerged from behind a tree, tapping his staff into the small drifts of snow, clad as always in dusty black, so I trotted to stand with the others. Out beyond the woods something waited. I could feel it like a steady pressure against my body.

"Raynard has set up a course for you to follow using some twine," he said, putting his hand onto a rough bit of string wound around the tree trunk next to him. It stretched from that bristlecone pine about a dozen feet to wind around another tree, then went off into the dark. "One of you will be the leader, while the others will wear these." In his other hand he pulled out strips of black cloth.

A collective moan rose from the group. We'd done blindfolded exercises last term at school with Morfael. They never turned out the way we expected.

"The leader will help the others negotiate the entire length of the course, no matter what obstacles lie in the way," Morfael continued. "I expect you to complete it and be back here in less than an hour."

"Is there some reason this couldn't happen in daylight?" November mumbled under her breath.

"November will be your leader," said Morfael, fixing her with his multifaceted eyes.

November froze. "I didn't mean ..."

"It will be up to you decide whether or not shifting will help you complete your task," Morfael continued, as if she hadn't spoken. "The moon is nearly full and rising. Already the veil between the worlds here is thin, so be warned. I will see you back here within the hour."

Raynard made darned sure our blindfolds were on tight, with no way for the moonlight to creep in. The darkness fell over me like a weight. A faint breeze rustled the trees above us, and I caught a faint scent of pine that was familiar, yet not. I waved in the direction I thought Caleb was standing and heard him laugh.

November tentatively guided us to line up, Siku in front, then London, Arnaldo, and me. "What the hell is he thinking, putting me in charge?" she muttered to us as she placed our hands on each other's shoulders. "I mean, don't blame me if I mess it up horribly. I didn't ask for this." Her voice moved up to the head of our little line. "Here, Siks, put your left hand on my left shoulder like this, right hand on the twine. Everyone else all set to do the same? Okay. Forward, march."

We shuffled forward slowly. I trod on the Arnaldo's heel, tripping slightly. "Sorry," I whispered.

" 'S okay," he said.

"Ow!" Siku grunted in pain. "There's a rock here!"

"Yeah, oh, sorry," November said. "I just stepped over it and didn't tell you about it, didn't I? See? I'm so not right for this. Okay, everyone go slowly past where Siku is. There's a rock sticking up about three inches. Yeah, London, lift your foot a little higher. Now step. Okay, good."

We made our way over the rock, and past the second tree as the sounds and smells of the forest at night enveloped us. Branches grabbed at my hair as we continued winding between trees and stumbling over roots. November scrambled up and down the line of us, trying to make sure we didn't stub our toes too horribly or smack our faces into low-hanging branches.

I could feel when the moon rose. Its rays were the cool equivalent of warm sunshine, only they didn't calm me down.

In fact, my skin crawled, jittering with something. A need. A need to shift.

"We're going so slow," Arnaldo said right in front of me. "I wish we could just shift and follow the twine in animal form."

"An eagle wearing a blindfold, hopping along with string in your beak?" I said. "Not exactly practical."

"I know, I know," he said.

"He just wants to shift," London said. "I want to shift. God, I can smell the deer over to our left, and I just want to shift and hunt. . . ."

"That's because the veil is so thin here," I said.

November piped up from ahead, "And the moon coming out only makes that worse."

"How much you want to bet Morfael planned this at moonrise for exactly that reason?" said Siku.

"It's part of the test." I shook my head, and then realized no one but November could see me.

"That pointy-headed bastard," London said.

"So, we focus." Unexpectedly, it was November saying that. "Feel the twine with your human hand, focus on moving your human feet where I tell you to put them with my lovely human voice."

We hung on to her chattering as we made our way through a narrow gap between two rocks higher than my head. November crowed with victory. A night bird called out an answer, but November's voice choked off a second later.

"Oh, crap!" Her footsteps pattered away from those of us who were blindfolded. "Maybe it goes around or over. . . . No, there's no way over. Damn!"

"What the hell is going on?" London shouted.

Siku grunted. "Just tell us."

November's soft-soled shoes on the soil moved closer. "The twine leads us through this . . . hole in the rocks. A bunch of them collapsed, but they left a kind of tunnel. It opens up after a few feet. But it's too small for me to get through, let alone Siku."

"Could you get through in rat form?" asked Arnaldo. "Morfael said we could decide whether to shift or not."

"Sure," she said. "It would be easy for me, but none of the rest of you could make it. I mean, Dez and Siku are bigger in their animal forms, and even your eagle and London's wolf would be way too big."

"Then how the hell are we supposed to follow the stupid twine the way Morfael told us?" London asked. "This is just dumb."

"Maybe we should just take the blindfolds off and go back," Arnaldo said, his voice hesitant.

"Morfael would know we cheated," Siku said. "You know he would."

A crazy idea was running through my head. "I could get through if I shifted into a cat," I said, trying to keep my voice light, almost as if it was a joke. When I'd accidentally shifted into a cat last term, it had freaked out the other shifter kids so much they didn't want to be my friend for awhile. As far as they knew, shifters only had one animal form. I thought we'd mostly gotten past the weirdness brought on by that episode, but the subject might still be a little sore for them.

A little silence fell. Then London said, her voice emanating resentment, "Well, that would be okay for you. You and November could get through the tunnel. But what about the rest of us?"

"Maybe once they get to the other side, they'll see something over there that will help us," Arnaldo said.

"Morfael does tend to give us problems we can't solve with the usual tools," I said. "What if I'm not the only one who can change into different animal forms?"

"Are you saying what I think you're saying?" November's voice got closer. I could smell the gummi bears she had in her pocket.

"That's ridiculous!" London's voice rose with a rush. Even

though she resented her parents' restrictions more than anyone, she had the hardest time dealing with anything that violated the rules she'd grown up with. "No offense, but Dez is a freak! I'm a wolf-shifter, and I'm always going to be a wolf-shifter!"

"No," came Siku's rumbly voice. "You're always going to be London. Human, wolf, whatever."

My heart jumped at Siku's words. He'd figured out the heart of it. "He's right. When I turned into a cat, I felt and thought the same as I did when I was a tiger, or a human. I was still me—whoever that is. The shape didn't matter."

"Yeah, but I'm an eagle-shifter," Arnaldo said. "That's all I've ever been, and I like it. I don't want to be . . . I don't know—something smaller like a sparrow hawk or even a sparrow. I mean, I could eat those birds for breakfast if I wanted."

"Don't want to be prey, you mean," said November. "Don't want to be like the rats and know how it is to be small and have bigger things threaten to eat you all the time. That might be scary."

"I'm not scared!" Arnaldo said, stung.

"I know it's different; it's uncomfortable; it's weird," I said. "But you only have to do it for a minute, right, November?"

"It's not far," she said. "But sounds to me like Wolfie and Bird-boy don't have the nerve to even try. Go home with your tail and feathers between your legs. Get a new-moon grade and have to come back to school for another term and be a failure. It's no rind off my cheese."

"I didn't say I was giving up on the task!" Arnaldo's sharp voice got even sharper.

"I could try," Siku's voice was quieter, more uncertain than usual. "But the smallest ursines are sun bears and they're still five feet long and about a hundred and fifty pounds. Could I get through it in a form like that, 'Ember?"

"Mmm, probably not, Siks," she said. "If it were big enough

for that, I could just get through in human form, or London could in her wolf form. Sorry."

"Some scientists think bears are actually related to raccoons," I said. "What if you're not limited to actual bears?"

"A raccoon?" Siku sounded skeptical. "They're . . . small."

"Again with the anti-small prejudice!" November stomped closer to Siku. "Here, walk over here, big bear jerk, and feel the entrance to the tunnel. . . ."

I heard Siku's larger tread shuffle after November's. "I don't know, 'Ember," he was saying.

"Here!" November slapped her hands against rock. "Feel that. And see, here's the twine going through it. That's the tunnel you have to get through. Now do you want to get a full moon on this test or not? Hey, Morfael didn't say you could take off the blindfold. . . ."

Cloth slid over hair as Siku said, "It'll come off anyway when I shift into a raccoon."

I pulled off my own blindfold in time to see November smiling up at Siku in delighted surprise. They stood in front of a wall of rock that extended for dozens of yards in either direction. The twine still in my right hand did indeed disappear into a hole in the rock about a foot in diameter. I looked around. We were deep into the forest, in an area I didn't recognize.

"You're going to try it?" November asked Siku, her voice ripe with excitement.

"You showed me small is pretty cool," he said. "And I've always liked those black mask markings on raccoons."

"Like furry bandits!" November clapped her hands. Then she turned on London and Arnaldo, who were slowly slipping off their own blindfolds. "See? Siku's not afraid to be different."

"We'll see if he can do anything at all." Arnaldo's voice was politely skeptical. London snorted. "He's never done it before. No offense, Sik."

"I can do it," Siku said. "We read about raccoons last term

in class. They eat lots of different things, the same as bears. And they fish in streams and ponds, like bears. They just catch smaller fish. If I was catching fish with smaller paws . . ." He closed his eyes, wiggling his big fingers.

For a long moment he stood there, nose out, as if sniffing the air for his catch of fish. Then he was gone. I blinked. *Where . . . ?*

Then I looked down. Standing at November's feet was a dark gray raccoon with roguish black stripes over its glittering eyes, standing only two feet tall on its hind legs.

"Holy crap!" London drew back.

The raccoon dropped to all fours and made a chittering sound of triumph.

"It's still Siku," I said, walking over to put my arm around London's shoulders.

She leaned into me, burying her eyes against my neck. "I'm sorry. I know. I don't know why this freaks me out so much."

"What's freaky is how cute he is," November said, hunkering down to look the raccoon more in the eye. "Good job, Siku. You're a hottie in every form."

The raccoon chirped, then turned, made a very human beckoning motion to us, and hopped up into the hole in the rock.

"You'd be cute too," I said, pulling away from London to catch her eye. "Maybe as a little arctic fox or something?"

"How about a Chihuahua?" November smirked.

London's icy blue eyes glared at her. "A fox could catch and eat a rat," she said, then turned to me. "But what if I can't come back? I don't want to be a fox. I'm a wolf."

"It's like Siku said—you're London," I said. "You're our friend, no matter what. As long as you can find your way back to yourself, you'll be fine."

She swallowed, and took my hands in hers. Her eyes held mine with equal firmness. "Okay. But the smallest fox is the fennec, so maybe I should go for that, just to be sure I can get through."

"Good thinking." I gave her hands a squeeze. "Look at me. I'm thinking about those adorable fennec foxes with those amazing huge ears and that creamy fluffy coat. . . ."

London nodded, then let go of my hands. She shut her eyes, but I could see her irises moving behind the lids, as if searching. "I think I can see the fox, way up ahead," she said. "So small . . ."

"So beautiful," I said. "So perfect."

London let out a small, appreciative laugh. "Flattery . . . works."

Then with a strange warp of the air, she was gone. At my feet sat a creamy tan doglike creature only a foot high, with a sharp, pointed noise, liquid brown eyes, and enormous ears, open wide like wings on either side of its narrow head.

"Oh, my God, you're adorable!" November squealed, scuttling up to London's new form. "You better be careful with this form, London, or every bored housewife in suburbia will want to adopt you!"

The fennec fox lifted its lip in a snarl and gave a tiny growl. I fought back a smile.

November reached out, as if she couldn't help herself, about to pet London on the head. London ducked and ran toward the hole in the rock. Siku shuffled back just in time to give her room to leap up into the hole. She turned to look at us and yipped, as if to say "Hurry up!"

"Guess that's my cue," said Arnaldo. "The smallest bird of prey I know of is the spot-winged falconet that lives in South America. They eat mostly insects, I think." He made a face.

"Still a bird of prey," I said. "Still a falcon."

"Still able to fly," November said, envy creeping into her voice. "That must be really fun."

Arnaldo smiled at her. "It is. I'll take you up one day if you want."

"I want," she said. "Now get your fine, feathery ass through that tunnel." She looked back at the watching raccoon and fox. "Go on through, boneheads. Arnaldo's going to need to fly and you're in the way."

The raccoon made a gesture that looked remarkably like he was flipping her off, but then he turned around and disappeared into the tunnel. The fox stuck out its small pink tongue, then followed after him.

"Here goes nothing," said Arnaldo, and closed his eyes.

"Fly," said November, then started to chant. "Fly, fly, fly, fly . . ."

A smile spread over Arnaldo's narrow face; then in a heartbeat, he was gone, and a flutter of wings shot up into the sky, wheeled, then swooped around November's head.

We both cheered. "Woo-hoo!" The falconet's brown wings were beautiful, spotted with a dramatic pattern of white visible even as he fluttered and danced in the air around us.

"Looks like this form's more maneuverable," I said. "Better for tight indoor spaces maybe?"

"Just hurry up and go!" November said. "I'm tired and it's almost time for breakfast. You coming, Stripes?"

And she shifted into her rat form, clambering up the rock wall to follow the falconet through the hole.

Now it was my turn. It had seemed so easy when I thought of it. But now, alone here with my friends waiting on the other side, it seemed impossible. I was a tiger, right? A tiger and a girl.

Then I remembered how it had felt, sitting on that bookshelf in the form of a domestic cat. I'd had a tortoiseshell coat, and Caleb had stroked my back till I purred. Purring had felt wonderful, and it was something tigers didn't do. It would be pretty great to be able to purr again. I looked down into that roiling realm of darkness inside me that led to Othersphere and found it larger, crazier, more filled with promise than it had ever seemed before.

*The moon and the thinness of the veil.*

Morfael had planned this well. I slipped into the small

form of a tortoiseshell cat and leaped easily up into the tunnel in the rock. My whiskers reached out, assessing the narrow space around me, feeling the currents of air created by the movements of my friends up ahead. My ears pricked, hearing the skitter of November's claws and the beat of Arnaldo's wings.

Then I was out, the light of the nearly full moon shining down on a carpet of white. London shook her huge fox ears, and shifted abruptly into her usual form, a rangy silver wolf with eyes like shiny arctic pools. The rest of us stayed as we were, following the twine only a few dozen yards farther to find it wound us back to exactly where we'd started.

Morfael was waiting. He smiled down at us, eyes crinkling. "I am proud of you," he said.

My heart swelled, and I was very glad to be in cat form. Cats and tigers did not have eyes that welled up with tears when they got a rare piece of praise from Morfael.

"Only the wise and the strong can see themselves as other than they have always been, yet remain true to themselves," he said. "You have proven yourselves strong and wise this night. Now go back to bed. You may sleep an extra hour."

The others got to sleep an extra hour. Raynard roused me at the usual time so that I could clean up and meet Caleb outside the computer room for the Council meeting.

His heavy gaze sent a dark thrill slithering under my skin, for a moment overwhelming the Council-based anxiety in my stomach. "Didn't sleep enough, did you?" he asked.

I tried to ignore the heat threatening to take me over and threw him a pretend glare. "How can you tell?"

His mouth turned down appreciatively, lifting one hand to twist a lock of my hair between his fingers. "Because you look delicious when you're all rumpled."

So he'd been thinking about us being together, just as I had. I leaned into him, and he seemed to be leaning into me, when Morfael's staff tapped a little louder than usual on the nearby steps. We turned to find him surveying us with frosty eyes.

Caleb coughed slightly to cover up a laugh. "Just giving Dez a pep talk before the Council meeting," he said.

That made Morfael's nearly invisible eyebrows lift.

"He's good for my morale," I chimed in. "I want him with me during the call."

Morfael did not respond for a long few seconds, and then said, "Only if he promises not to speak a word." Caleb opened his mouth to promise, and Morfael rounded on him. "Not a word."

Caleb shut his mouth and nodded.

"Very well," said Morfael.

It took him a few seconds to set up the video conference call on the large monitor in the computer room. His long pointy fingers tapped the keys with the speed and sureness of a Silicon Valley nerd.

"Has Amaris been giving him lessons?" I whispered to Caleb.

He smirked, but laid a finger against his lips, reminding me that he'd promised not to speak.

We stood in front of the camera as Morfael adjusted it. I kept transferring my weight from one foot to the other, tapping my fingers against my thighs, feeling like I was about to burst out of my skin. These Council members had way more power over my life than I liked.

If they kicked me out of school and Morfael didn't make me go, the Council could make life very difficult not only for us, but for the kids who stayed here and their families.

If I did leave, it'd be just me, Mom, and Richard on the run from the Tribunal, and any hope of infiltrating Ximon's new compound would vanish. Caleb and I would be physically a lot farther apart most of the time. Would he leave Morfael and Amaris to go on the run with me? How could any of that work?

The monitor blinked, and five faces appeared, sectioned

off each in its own area, with one additional square showing me my own blank, wide-eyed face. I tried not to look at myself much, knowing it would make me self-conscious. I had brushed my hair, but my unruly red mane had a mind of its own.

It had been over a month since I'd last seen the Council, but that experience had been so odd, so full of import, each face was branded in my memory. This time I didn't need Caleb to tell me who everyone was.

The lady lynx, half-smiling at me through her camera, had the same bushy, tufted gray hair and red-brown skin. She was wearing a green flannel shirt this time instead of a blue one, but she looked just as outdoorsy and ageless as before. Shifters could live for hundreds of years, and I suddenly wondered how old she was. Had she been living here when the first explorers from the East wandered into the western part of the United States?

Anyone of them could be that old—the gruff wolf with his crazy red eyebrows, or the hawk with his piercing hooded gaze, or the bear with white skunklike streaks in her long dark hair. They all looked like they'd been that way forever. Only the rat, with her black hair in a messy up-do and traces of cherry-colored gloss on her lips, looked like she might still be maturing, still figuring out the world. The others seemed as immovable as mountains.

Morfael tapped his staff five times on the floor, one time for every shifter tribe still in existence. He bowed his head, and the five council members did the same. I watched them, trying to gauge how they might feel, until the rat-shifter peeked up from under her brows and gave me a playful frown. I hurriedly bowed my head.

"Welcome to this special meeting of the Western Regional North American Council, Morfael," said the lynx-shifter.

"Greetings, Chief of the Council, Lady Lynx," said Morfael in a dry formal tone, exactly as he had at my first Council meeting.

"At the request of my wolf-shifter colleague, we will dispense with further formalities and get down to business," she said. "First, I'm sorry to report that my colleague in the Asian Council has no information that can help us trace Desdemona's family. No one there has been in touch with a tiger-shifter in over two decades, and they have no reports of an abandoned tiger-shifter child. I'm sorry, Desdemona. I had hoped to have news for you."

"Thank you for trying," I said. It wasn't surprising, but still it hurt to hear that even at the highest levels, no one knew who my biological parents were. And yet I almost felt something like relief too. It was like I didn't know what to feel.

The lynx said, "We've all heard there was some excitement at your school earlier this winter, and that you have now reconvened in a new location. I hope the transition is going smoothly."

"Excitement!" The wolf said, in something like a bark. "You call Tribunal attacks on school grounds, helicopters crashing, and the burning of a Tribunal compound 'excitement'? How about disaster?"

"And I hear you're now harboring a member of the Tribunal," said the hawk.

"Amaris has changed her allegiance," said Morfael. "I am satisfied."

"She's the daughter of the Tribunal Bishop Ximon, our most avid enemy," said the bear, her brow furrowed.

"Amaris suffered more at the hands of her father than any of you ever have," I said, unable to keep still. Caleb moved closer to me supportively. "Morfael knows she'd do anything to help us against him."

"Do not assume you know how much others have suffered," said the lynx, startling me a bit with her chastising tone. She'd been my biggest proponent before. "Bishop Ximon is directly responsible for the deaths of many, long before you came on the scene."

"I'm sorry," I muttered. She was right. There was no way for me to know who had suffered and how. But they had no idea of the hell Ximon had put Amaris through.

"If this reckless child isn't prevented from provoking him, Ximon will be responsible for many more deaths," said the hawk.

"Provoking him?" The lynx frowned at her monitor. For a moment, I could see the predatorlike focus in her round dark eyes. "As you may recall, it has always been Ximon who's provoked violence and disruption. He ordered the kidnapping of Miss Grey before she even knew she was a shifter. And he ordered the attack on Morfael's school without provocation—an attack on children from each of our tribes."

"Miss Grey is a tiger, so her kidnapping is no concern of the wolves," said the wolf in his gruff voice. "And if she hadn't been at the school, Ximon's attack never would have happened."

"Yes," the hawk said, steepling his long fingers in front of him. "If others in the Council had voted differently last time, Miss Grey would not have stayed at the school, and that attack would never have happened."

"So now the Council is to blame?" The rat-shifter adjusted a loose lock of her shiny black hair. "Who else besides Ximon would you like to condemn, bird?"

"It is a little like criticizing a rich man for having a nice house when it gets robbed, rather than the thief who broke in," said the bear. "One of my tribe was kidnapped in that raid on the school. He might not have been restored to his family if Miss Grey and the other students hadn't rescued him."

"Not to mention that the Tribunal compound was destroyed, and Ximon forced to flee and regroup," said the lynx. "Miss Grey and her friends achieved more in that rescue than any other shifters in the last two hundred years."

"Only because we all worked together," I said. "Think how much more we could achieve if every member of every shifter tribe cooperated like that."

The rat nodded, looking thoughtful, but the wolf snorted derisively. "The result of this so-called cooperation is that the homes of many of the students in the school were raided the other night by the Tribunal. Laurentia's mother killed one intruder, but another got away."

I had to think for a minute when she used London's true name. None of us called her Laurentia anymore.

"We need to rid ourselves of this girl, the one who started all of this," said the hawk. "Who knows what fresh scheme Ximon is planning?"

"That's exactly what we need to find out!" I said. "Together, children from each of your tribes, along with Caleb and Morfael, stopped an entire Tribunal force intent on capturing or killing all of us. Arnaldo Perez, in his eagle form, brought down their helicopter single-handed. If we can do that, think how much more you adults could do if you just *tried*."

The bear and the lynx were nodding while the rat took her hair down and began to reassemble her bun, a slight smirk on her face. "Imagine a world without the Tribunal trying to wipe us out," she said. "Or maybe my bird and wolf friends prefer to live in fear?"

The wolf growled a little to himself, but said nothing. My heart lifted. It seemed as if the Council members were still three to two in my favor. Maybe it was possible for the vote to go my way.

"Yes, I think the rat representative, the bear, and I see eye to eye on this," the lynx was saying. "Shall we cast our votes on whether Desdemona Grey should be allowed to stay at Morfael's school for the rest of the year?"

"I'd like to inform the Council of just one more point, if I may," said the hawk, lowering his hands and staring balefully into his camera. "Last night an eagle-shifter named Rafael Perez was taken to a jail in Wickenburg, Arizona, on charges of child abuse. His two sons, Luis and Cordero, were put in county foster care and will remain there unless a close relative willing to take them can be found. You see, someone anonymously called humdrum Child Protective Services yesterday morning and told them Mr. Perez was beating his children. When they arrived, they found physical evidence of abuse, and both sons eventually told authorities it was at the hands of their father."

My heart was pounding so hard that I almost couldn't hear his last few words. Morfael turned his head toward me, fingers tightening on his staff. I felt Caleb's fingers cool against the hot skin on my arm. I was burning up from a thousand different emotions. But I stared right into the camera, determined not to look away. I wasn't going to run from what I'd done.

"An anonymous caller reported him—to the *humdrums*?" said the bear, her eyes widening.

"I wonder who *that* could be?" said the wolf, bushy eyebrows thunderous over deep-set eyes now fixed on me.

"The oldest Perez son, Arnaldo, was nowhere to be found," the hawk-shifter continued. "The youngest Perez boy claims Arnaldo was kidnapped by a group of teenagers, while the middle son says Arnaldo went with them willingly."

A small silence fell. I fought the urge to tell them I'd been that anonymous caller, and that someone should have called for help a long time ago.

"So it's possible that Arnaldo called the authorities himself," said the lynx.

"Are Mr. Perez's sons telling the truth?" asked the rat.

"Who cares if it's true?" the wolf shouted. "Did you hear him? Two raptor boys are in a humdrum foster home! I've never heard of such a thing."

"I was in a humdrum Russian orphanage till I got adopted

by a humdrum," I said. "I'm lucky to have found the mother I have."

"Lucky? Look how you turned out!" the wolf said, snarling. "Disobedient, head full of crazy ideas . . ."

"Make no mistake, this is an unacceptable situation," said the hawk. "These boys are no longer connected to their tribe, and the bird-shifters have lost three of their kind in a single stroke."

"They're not dead!" The words burst out of me before I could think. "No one's *lost*. Mr. Perez drinks too much and he beats his sons. It's awful! Everyone here knows that. Now he'll have to stop hitting them. He might even get help to stop drinking."

"I knew it was you who made the call," said the hawk. "As soon as I heard the news, I knew."

"Your people should have made that call long ago!" The words spat out of me with a savageness that surprised me. I was angry, furious that those kids had been left to cope with abuse and alcoholism on their own. "If you gave a damn about those kids, you'd have gone in and taken them out yourself."

I shot a look at Morfael, expecting him to tell me to be quiet. But he said nothing.

"That call was not yours to make," the bear said. She was looking very uncomfortable, like she was sitting on something hot. "You should have contacted us first. The raptor Council member would have taken the matter to his tribe. . . ."

"And done nothing!" I threw my hands up in the air. "The same way you've done nothing about the Tribunal. You're so afraid of anything different that you're paralyzed."

"Afraid?" The wolf leaned forward menacingly. "You dare call us cowards?"

"I don't know," I said, fuming. "All I've ever seen from you is fear—fear of the Tribunal that sends you scurrying into your holes. Fear of the other tribes, which prevents you from working together to get rid of the threats."

"Tiger arrogance," huffed the wolf. "You're not the top of the food chain here, girl!"

All at once the anger whooshed out of me like air from a balloon. I felt very tired, and sad. Caleb's warm hand found the small of my back reassuringly. His eyes were shining, bright with shared anger. His lips were pressed together tightly. He'd promised Morfael he wouldn't say anything, and he hadn't, but it was wearing on him. Our shared gaze gave me some strength.

"I'm speaking as a human being," I said. "To other human beings. If we don't come together, the Tribunal has already won."

Their faces were too much of a mix for me to read: anger, confusion, pity, compassion. It didn't matter. I was doomed. I'd exploded at them, and pushed myself into exile.

"*Are* you human?" the hawk asked pointedly.

My head jerked up. I stared at him.

"I hear you have a second animal form," he said.

"What?" The lynx looked at me, shocked. "That can't be true."

"It is true," said Morfael. "But it is not unprecedented."

"If it's true, then what is she?" The rat peered at me through her camera lens. "Is she tiger or cat? Humdrum or otherkin?"

"Or something else entirely?" the bear said. "Is she some new threat?"

That was it. The hawk had done his job well, turning even my allies against me. I looked over at Morfael, about to tell him to just end this already. I knew my fate. But Morfael didn't look ruffled or worried. In fact, his pale, alien face looked vaguely pleased.

"Desdemona is only a threat to your old way of thinking," Morfael said. "The truth is that any one of you could also take an alternate animal form if you learned how."

The wolf laughed outright. "Are you trying to use this to

recruit more students, caller of shadows? This is the death of your school, and you know it."

"The death of one thing leads to the birth of another," said Morfael coolly. "You could shift into a fox if only your mind allowed it, just as the Lady Lynx could generate a cougar form."

The rat looked skeptical, but at least she didn't look furious, like the rest of them. "Are you saying I could be a mouse if I just believed it?"

Morfael nodded. "Or a squirrel or gopher. I advise you to try for other rodent forms first."

"First?" The bear's voice shot up into the stratosphere. "Are you saying any of us could be . . . anything?"

Morfael didn't reply, but he was smiling.

I looked at Caleb, blinking. He shook his head at me, wonder on his face.

"I've had enough of this nonsense," said the hawk. "I'm a hawk-shifter, nothing else, and never want to be. I ask the Chief of the Council to bring a vote now on whether Desdemona Grey should be allowed to remain at Morfael's school."

"Very well." The lynx's voice was dull, full of misgiving. My heart sank. "I must, with regret, vote against."

"And I," said the bear-shifter, shaking her head. "Most unfortunate, but this girl is clearly a bad influence."

"I vote for her to stay, for whatever that's worth," said the rat. "I'm sorry, Desdemona."

"You all know how I feel," said the wolf. "Throw her out!"

"And my vote makes four against." The hawk's voice was smug. "Pack your bags, tiger-shifter."

"The vote is four to one against Desdemona Grey," the lynx said formally, and bowed her head. "Good luck to you in the humdrum world. For you are no longer a member of ours."

# CHAPTER 11

The next few minutes were a blur for me, but before the lynx hung up, she made it clear to Morfael that I had to be gone within twenty-four hours, or they would ask the members of their tribes to boycott his school. His current students would be withdrawn, and he would personally be shunned by shifter communities everywhere.

"I understand," was all he had said, and ended the call.

*What the hell am I going to do now?*

I leaned against the desk, suddenly exhausted, my shoulder touching the computer monitor as Morfael shut it down. Caleb put his arm around me, and a spark flew upward from the screen followed by a loud pop.

We jumped back as a thin thread of smoke wafted from the monitor.

I sighed. "Sorry."

Morfael's pale eyes traveled from me to the monitor and

back again. "After you have some breakfast, you and I will have a private lesson. You can learn to manipulate this ability with technology."

"Ability? More like a curse," I said. Then what he said sank fully into my brain. "What do you mean, lesson? They just kicked me out!"

He just lifted his eyebrows and nodded toward the door. *Typical.*

I followed Caleb out, feeling sick. I stopped in the doorway and looked back at Morfael. "Should I start packing tonight, or . . ."

"He won't kick you out, will you, Morfael?" asked Caleb. "Those bastards can't tell you what to do."

"We will discuss this later," Morfael said, and the firmness in his voice pushed us out the door.

"This can't be happening," I said as Caleb and I treaded up the stairs. "If I don't leave in twenty-four hours, the Council says they'll tell everyone's parents to pull their kids out—and that's it! I just started feeling like I belong in this crazy world, and now I have to go?"

"I don't know," Caleb said. "If I could get my hands on that damned hawk-shifter . . ."

"What about Mom and Richard? If I go back and live with them, that brings the Tribunal down on them as well. Maybe I should change my name, start a new life. ."

"Only if you take me with you," he said.

I stopped on the stairs, turning to him, and he wrapped his arms around me. I buried my face in his neck. "I can't lose you," I said. "At least here at the school, we're with each other. If I go back home . . ."

"Your mother wouldn't want you anywhere else," he said softly.

*My mother.* He was right. She'd die of worry if I went out on my own. "Okay, so I have to go back to Vegas." I pulled away to look at his face, tugging on his coat. "You'll take me to Vegas when I go back, won't you? It's not a short drive. And maybe you could stay with us somehow, for a little while."

He shook his head. "Don't go there yet. We don't know what's going to happen."

"And just when we're on the verge of maybe finding something out about Ximon!" I pounded my fist on the railing. Anger was creeping in under my despair. "Maybe I should have told the Council about the particle accelerator. Do you think that would help? I could go back and tell them there's this huge new threat, and they'd see I'm just trying to help. . . ."

"Tell them there's a huge Tribunal compound an easy drive from the school?" He frowned at me. "That would just make them want to bulldoze this place."

I sighed. "You're right. What am I thinking?" And I turned to continue up the stairs.

"You're upset," he said. "So am I. But there's got to be a way to figure this out."

At the breakfast table, London wouldn't look at me or Caleb and hadn't touched the lone fried egg on her plate. November was oddly subdued, casting sideways glances at Siku. Amaris dropped silverware with a nerve-shattering clatter at unexpected intervals, and Arnaldo was silent and glum. Only Siku was dribbling honey all over everything and eating with his usual gusto.

I picked at my food as the uncomfortable silence spread out and settled in for the long haul. Finally, it was too much. I had to tell Arnaldo about his family before he heard it from someone else. He might never forgive me otherwise.

"The Council gave us some news on your dad," I said. Next to me, Caleb moved restlessly, realizing what I was about to do.

Arnaldo looked up from his plate, eyebrows shooting up. "Why didn't you say anything? What happened?"

"I . . ." Nothing to do but just say it. "I called Child Protective Services yesterday, and they went to your house, found evidence, and arrested your father for child abuse."

"What?" Arnaldo's brown eyes were like dagger points over his pointed nose. "You got my father arrested?"

"Hitting his sons is what got him arrested," Caleb said swiftly.

Arnaldo didn't seem to hear him. "What about my brothers? What's happened to them?"

I made myself say it. "They're in foster care, until a relative can be found to take them in."

"Foster care?" Arnaldo's sharp voice rose in alarm. "In some home?"

November exchanged a glance with London and mouthed the words "Holy shit."

"I know," I said. "I'm sorry. But maybe that's better than—"

"Living in their own home?" Arnaldo stood up, throwing his napkin down. "They're living with humdrums now. People who don't understand them."

"I live with humdrums," I said. "It's a lot better than being beaten up. And maybe once your father gets some help, he'll be a better—"

"Shut up! What do you know about my father? What do you know about anything?" Arnaldo shoved himself away from the table and strode from the room.

November watched him go. "Nice job, Stripes."

"You did the right thing," Siku said unexpectedly through a mouthful.

"I've been worried about those kids too," London said. "Do you really think they'll be better off?"

"I just couldn't live with myself if I didn't speak up," I said, staring after Arnaldo. "And you guys might not have to put up with me much longer. The Council told Morfael he has to kick me out by tomorrow morning."

"What?" London's forehead creased with distress. "Can they do that?"

November threw down a sausage. "Great. Just when we got the school up and running again. They'll tell our parents, Wolfie. How long do you think your mom and dad will keep paying tuition if the Council tells them to pull you out?"

Amaris leaned over the table toward Caleb. "They don't have any sway over us, do they?"

He shook his head. "I don't think you and I have to worry. Not right away at least."

Siku bit into a strawberry, thinking hard. Still chewing, he said, "Did any of you tell your parents where the school is?"

November pulled her chin in, startled. "No, but what's that got to do with it?"

London gave a quick laugh. "So they can tell us to leave all they want..."

Siku shrugged. "It's up to us to decide if we listen to them."

"Arnaldo won't want to stay now," I said. "He hates me."

"He's just scared," said Amaris. "For his brothers."

At that moment, Morfael glided into the room and crooked a long finger at me.

The others looked at me. "Private lessons in not killing computers," I said, standing up. "For all the good that does me."

As I left the table, the others resumed arguing about just how much control their parents had over them. It all depended on Morfael, really. If he kicked me out, they could stay in school without conflict. Maybe that was best for everyone. Everyone except me and Caleb.

Caleb grabbed my hand as I moved away and walked a few steps with me. "I know it was hard, but I'm glad you told Arnaldo. He had to know."

"I hope he forgives me before I have to leave," I said.

"I hope he forgives you after you stay." He leaned down and kissed my cheek.

I wearily followed Morfael to the library, where he had two watches, an electric hand drill, a battered toaster, and a lamp laid out on the table. He also had a huge fern, which had hung by a window, set on the table next to the mechanical objects.

After getting me to concentrate on my breath for a few minutes, he told me to touch one of the watches and stop it. At first, nothing happened, then like the sting of a bee, my hand itched, and the second hand stopped moving.

"Now place that hand in the soil," he said, pointing at the fern in its ceramic pot.

"Um, okay." Having no idea what he was up to, I slid my hand between the fronds and laid my hand onto the dirt by the base of the fern. It felt cool, soothing. I focused on my breath again.

"Now with your other hand, take hold of the drill and turn it on," said Morfael.

It sounded like the beginnings of a dirty joke, but I said nothing, taking hold of the base of the hand drill. I flipped the "on" switch. It hummed and vibrated slightly, ready to work.

"Now turn it off, using only your energy," he said. "Remember the feel of the soil in your right hand, and direct any excess energy there."

"So you think my green thumb's connected to this whole anti-tech thing?" I asked.

"Did I say to ask questions?" he asked mildly.

Trying to remember how it felt when I'd touched the watch and stopped it, I leaned my mind into the drill slightly. Nothing happened.

"Is it that you think you know better than everyone else?" Morfael said casually, startling me out of my concentration. "Is that why you called Child Protective Services without telling anyone?"

"What? No!" I stared at him, one hand in dirt, the other gripping a rusty tool. "I just couldn't stand thinking about Arnaldo's brothers. . . ."

"That doesn't explain the secrecy," he said. "Are you afraid your friends will reject you if you reveal your arrogance to them?"

"My . . . no!" My grip tightened on the drill, my other hand clutching at the dirt in the fern's pot. "I mean, I'm kind of worried they'll think I'm full of myself. But I have to do the right thing."

"And how do you know what the right thing is?" Morfael took two steps toward me, staff in hand, pale eyes aglow. "Do you plan to turn your leadership role in this group into a dictatorship?"

"Of course not!" I yelled. "Don't be ridiculous!"

The drill in my hand stop-started, like it was shorting out. Morfael leaned in even closer, looming over me. "Quick, direct your emotions into the soil. Now!"

"But, I . . ."

"Now!!

Confused and angry, I shoved my focus to the dirt between my fingers, digging my nails down, feeling them sink deep into the damp gritty earth. The drill wound down its power slowly, then stopped dead. But it didn't turn black or catch on fire. That was progress. The fern's fronds seemed to stretch out another half an inch, glowing a slightly brighter green.

"Good," said Morfael, his eyes crinkling in his version of a smile. "Now let it start up again."

The anger and confusion I'd been feeling floated away as I realized he had deliberately provoked me. I released the soil in my right hand and relaxed. The drill flicked on again. The fern still looked bigger and healthier than it had before.

"You already have more control than you think," Morfael said.

We spent the next two hours going through similar exercises, until I didn't even need to touch the soil or the fern anymore. I could direct excess energy down through my feet to the floor, or imagine it spiraling away from an outstretched hand.

"It's a total contradiction," I said, after about an hour of this. "I have to tap into my feelings but control them at the same time."

"It is the same when a caller manipulates shadow," he said. "Now, go fetch the Shadow Blade."

I did as I was told, and the effect of holding the Blade was like being buried up to my neck in the earth. I felt so calm, so centered, and my emotions were so accessible that I shorted the lamp out with a touch and turned the exterior of the toaster completely black, even as it finished toasting a slice of bread. When it popped up, smelling all warm and toasty, I grabbed it and took a bite. I was ravenous. Ravenous and tired.

"Silver will probably still make your skin itch," Morfael said. "But with continued practice, you should be able to carry a phone for indefinite periods of time, and own a laptop without worrying you'll destroy it in a day or two. Now go do your midday shift with the others, eat, and take a nap. You're excused from other classes until two p.m. We will do this again tomorrow."

"Tomorrow?" My heart jumped in my chest. "Will I still be here tomorrow?"

"You still have much to learn," Morfael said dryly. "And so does the Council."

"But, what if the other kids leave because you let me stay?"

He studied me. "Do you think they'll do that?"

I stared back at him, remembering how quickly they had abandoned me when I'd shifted into my second animal form. But so much had happened since then. We had bonded. We were family. "No?" I said, making it a question.

He didn't reply.

"But what if the Council tries to punish you, or their parents retaliate somehow?"

He nodded. "Actions have consequences. We can't foresee all ends, but we can trust ourselves to deal with what is to come. Now go. You are tired."

For once I slept deeply, dreaming about giant toasters and ferns like green octopi with eyes and fronds that grabbed me like tentacles.

At dinner, Arnaldo sat in his usual place, but didn't look at me. I told Caleb quietly about my lesson with Morfael, and everyone else ate without speaking. Then I said, more loudly, "Morfael's going to give me another lesson. Tomorrow."

London perked up. "Tomorrow?"

Caleb hugged me. "I knew it!"

"Wow, so he's not kicking you out?" November sucked on a chicken bone thoughtfully.

"I knew he wouldn't," Siku said.

I cleared my throat to help my voice sound casual. I thought I knew the answer to the question I was about to ask, but I wasn't a hundred percent sure, especially when it came to Arnaldo. "So if the Council tells everyone's parents to pull their kids out of school tomorrow, what happens?"

"The Council's a bunch of fatheads," said Siku. "I like it here."

"I don't think my parents will care much what the Council says," November said. "We rats are more broad-minded."

"Maybe our parents can't come get us." London let her knife drop with a clank onto her plate. "What about the Council? They could force us out."

"Do they know the school's location?" I asked.

"No," said Caleb with a small smile. "Amaris and I will stay. Right, 'Mar?"

"Of course," she said. "This is our home now."

November grinned, showing all her little pointed teeth. "So they can take their order to leave and shove it."

"Would you disobey your mother to stay?" Siku asked London. He was tearing apart an orange with his large but very dexterous hands.

She thought hard. "I guess maybe I would. You guys and Dez have been way more supportive than my damn family ever was. Mom can scream at me all she wants—from Idaho."

Arnaldo hadn't said anything. He'd looked around as everyone spoke.

November leaned over and stuck her nose in his face. "What about you, Arnaldo?" she asked.

"The hawk-shifter on the Council sent me a message," he said quietly. "He's helping me get a lawyer, so maybe I can get custody of my brothers."

I blinked, a smile beginning to form. Siku leaned over and pounded him on the shoulder.

November stole a grape from his plate and popped it in her mouth. "That would be awesome."

"So I guess I'm the head of my family now," Arnaldo continued. His eyes met mine, and they weren't warm, but they weren't hostile either. "And if I want to stay here until my brothers are ready to come home with me, or have them come here to stay with me, then that's what will happen."

November grabbed a fistful of grapes and threw them up in the air, like confetti. "Hooray!"

Even London was smiling as the grapes bounced down. I sat back in my chair, relief flooding over me.

"So the Council and our parents don't know where we are," Siku said. "But Lazar does."

"Kind of ass-backwards." November stole a slice of his orange.

"He's the key to our fight against the Tribunal this time," I said.

"So let's say he actually gives us the plans to this accelerator thingie instead of betraying us all," said November as she sucked the orange slice. "What then?"

"We should just kill them all," said London. "First we get the plans from Lazar, then we kill him to make sure he stays quiet." She put a hand out toward me as I opened my mouth to protest. "Then we burn down wherever they are, and we hunt down all the other Tribunal compounds and do the same. Sorry, Amaris and Caleb. I know Lazar's your brother, and your father's involved and all that, but it's the only way we can be sure."

"Sure of what?" I said. "That we're a bunch of murderers?"

"Sure of our safety," said Caleb. "Sure of your safety and your mom's and Richard's." He turned to London. "I agree with you."

"If we kill them all, then we've proven they were right about us," I said. "We'd be monsters."

"So you know what's right and wrong better than the rest of us, I guess," said London. "We have our own opinions, you know. We're not all just your servants."

"I never said you were!" I said, standing up. "But I won't be a party to slaughter. These are human beings we're talking about. And if we can become friends with Amaris, maybe . . ."

"We'll just hold hands with the Tribunal and sing 'Kumbaya'?" November asked. "Puh-lease."

"Amaris is different from the others," Siku said.

"Exactly." November nodded. "The Tribunal and the otherkin have been enemies since time began, Stripes. I know tigers are strong swimmers, but you're paddling against the current on this one."

"Never stopped me before," I said. "Good night."

I turned and headed down the steps toward our sleeping quarters, wishing for once I had my own room where I could be alone for a few hours, and not have to justify and explain everything I did and said.

I recognized Caleb's firm footsteps catching up to me. I paused at the bottom of the stairs as he came down. "I'm sorry," he said.

I avoided him, turning to move down the hall to the girls' room. He pushed past me and made me stop, tilting my chin up to force me to look at him.

"Can we talk about it?" he said. "You're acting so strange."

"I'm acting strange?" I jerked my chin from his touch, feeling a rollercoaster mixture of flattery and irritation that he'd noticed. "I'm not the one talking about mass murder."

"We've all had to kill at one point or another, to save ourselves," he said. "It's never easy, and it shouldn't be, but if it helps save otherkin in the future . . ."

"Yes, I've killed," I said. I wish I hadn't but I had. "But there's a big difference between self-defense against an imminent threat and cold-blooded killing against a hypothetical threat."

"Hypothetical?" He pulled back a few inches. "The Tribunal's not a hypothetical threat and you know it."

"All I know," I said, my voice coming out low and heated, "is that I won't make a plan to kill hundreds of people in cold blood. I'll do anything I have to do to find another way. Good night." I pushed past him and shut the door behind me without looking back.

# CHAPTER 12

The girls' room was quiet after dinner. We all pretended to do our homework in silence for awhile. I couldn't concentrate on the book I was reading about how the art and religion of Ancient Egypt, with its many animal-headed gods, had been inspired by its original ruling family of shifters. How could Caleb and I be in such different places when it came to Lazar?

"Hey—" Amaris had just walked in from the hallway. She came over to me, holding an open book, and sat down on my bed. "I've got a question about this history of the horse-shifters."

I sat up, scooching next to her. "Yeah, I read that last term."

She pointed her finger at some text I recognized about how the early horse-shifters had given rise to the legends of centaurs, and said in a very low tone, "I'm talking to Lazar on the computer."

I darted a surprised look at her, then looked around the room. Both London and November were as far away from my bed as they could be, heads down over books, with no sign they'd heard her. "Okay," I said in a normal tone. "Let me show you on the computer."

As we left the room, I looked over my shoulder. Neither November or London had stirred.

We moved quietly down the hall. No noise filtered out of the boys' room, so maybe they were doing the sullen silence thing too. Once in the computer room, I shut and locked the door as Amaris pressed a few keys, and Lazar's face, shadowed with bruises and tinted blue in the light of his monitor, appeared.

I sat down next to Amaris so we could both be seen on the computer's camera. "Hi. We need to be quick. Everything okay?"

"Everything is good," he said, a relieved smile breaking over his face. "I've got the plans. I can't e-mail or send them to you without risking them finding out. What do you want to do?"

"We'll meet you tonight and get them from you in person," I said. "Amaris, can you get on that computer? Find somewhere near Vegas we can all get to, some hotel or something, and we'll meet there at, say, one a.m."

Amaris nodded, sliding her chair over in front of another computer to search.

Lazar cocked his head, his usually sunny hair almost greenish in the strange computer light. "Why can't I just bring them to the school?"

"It can't be here in case you're followed." I didn't want him to know the others were prepared to kill him.

His eyes flicked to the image on his monitor, searching what had to be my face. "You still don't trust me."

"You've got a long way to go to earn that," I said. "You better show up alone."

He nodded. "And you? Will Caleb be there?"

I shot a look at Amaris, whose eyes were wide with apprehension. "Who comes with me is none of your business," I said.

"Found a place, I think," said Amaris, scooting back over to look into the camera on my monitor. "The Naiad Hotel and Casino, on the north side of Vegas." She rattled off the address and Lazar scribbled it down. "There's a bowling alley inside. We'll meet you at the entrance."

"One a.m.," I said. "We'll meet you there."

"Yes, ma'am," he said, his voice tinged slightly with admiration. "See you then."

The monitor went blank. Amaris tapped a few keys to make sure the connection was gone, and then turned to me.

"*We* will meet him?" she asked.

"Just you and I," I said. "For now. We'll need to sneak out around midnight—quietly."

The Naiad Hotel and Casino had a neon sign over the entrance with its name picked out in an Old West font in gold, surrounded by glowing turquoise curlicues that were probably an attempt at evoking ocean waves. A woman with a glittering green fish tail presided, her hair the same blaring gold. Her seashell bra was a frightening blood red.

It was 1:05 A.M. Amaris and I had successfully snuck out of the school, but were running a few minutes late. Outside the Naiad, pedestrians loitered while a man in a toga carrying a trident stood at the door greeting visitors wearing hoodies and board shorts.

"Brace yourself for bad Greek mythology and inconsistent ocean imagery," I said to Amaris as she drove the SUV into the parking garage.

"I'm not sure I'd know the difference," she said as she took a parking ticket from the automatic dispenser. "We weren't allowed to learn the mythology of any other cultures. Morfael put some basic texts on my to-read list, but he said I should read the actual history first."

She was dressed in dark jeans, a long-sleeved black T-shirt, and a waterproof jacket lined with fleece, her thick blond hair pushed back from her face with an elastic headband. I had on a similar ensemble, trying to keep as low a profile as possible while we were out.

"Okay," I said, as she threw the car into park. "We're supposed to meet him near the entrance to the bowling alley, right? You know more members of the Tribunal than I do, so keep scanning the area, in case you see any familiar faces. Also keep your eyes peeled for anyone with an earpiece, or who seems overly interested in you or me or Lazar. Just in case he was followed."

"Got it," she said. She looked a little paler than usual.

"I'll go up and talk to Lazar, with you nearby, in earshot, maybe twenty feet away. If we stay apart, we're less likely to be spotted."

"That's if Lazar double-crosses us," she said. "Which he won't. But okay."

"We hope for the best and plan for the worst," I said, remembering my mother saying something like that to me the day my scoliosis had first been detected. Six months later the worst happened, and they fitted me for the brace. Thanks to my mom, I'd been as ready as anyone could be to deal with it, and I'd worn it faithfully until my first shift to tiger form miraculously cured the curvature. Dealing with that had taught me a lot about being patient, about enduring pain, and how you couldn't always see on the outside what was going on inside a person.

"You've been through way worse than this," I said to Amaris. "Remember how brave you've been so far—facing down your dad, jumping from that plane while it was moving. We're just meeting your brother here. This is nothing compared to that."

She nodded with determination, psyching herself into it. "And if something goes wrong, I run to the car, and drive it to the front entrance to wait for you."

"I'll call or text you if we're separated and the plan changes," I said, holding up November's phone. I'd "borrowed" it on my way out. Fresh from those lessons with Morfael, I hoped I could keep from destroying it. If worse came to worst, I'd get November a new phone. But it was one more thing they'd all need to forgive me for after the night was done.

She nodded. "Okay. Let's go."

As we pushed through the door into the back of the casino, a cloud of smoke enveloped us, followed by the incessant dinging of slot machine bells and the recorded clanking of falling coins.

I forced myself to breathe, even though the air choked me, and led Amaris past a man in a cowboy hat getting a fistful of cash from an ATM and a bent woman who was at least seventy years old screeching at an imperious one-armed bandit that had just swallowed her last quarter.

We passed an entrance to "Billy's Steakhouse" and moved through a glass door to the hotel reception area. Amaris coughed a little at the redoubled thickness of smoke. My tongue tasted like ash. Amaris cast a nervous glance toward the reception desk and hunched her shoulders.

"Just act confident," I said to her, striding across the lobby as if I knew where I was going. "A lot of people come and go in hotels, so they have no reason to think we don't belong."

I angled left, moving past another bar, and found a sign pointing farther left that said MOVIE THEATERS, BOWLING ALLEY, OCTOPUS'S GARDEN ICE CREAM PARLOR—THIS WAY.

The way was paved with craps tables, banks of slot machines, and a rickety roulette wheel surrounded by men in trucker hats wearing rock band T-shirts and women in jackets that easily shed their sequins.

Amaris, who had not come into the Luxor with Caleb, kept swiveling her head around, looking at everything. I leaned in to her, but she put her hand on my arm and said, "I know, keep an eye out for suspicious people. I'm trying. There's just so much noise, so many lights."

She was right. The place reeked of acrid smoke and sickly sweet alcohol. Lights of gold, blue, green, and red flashed and skittered from symbols on the slots. Under the clanging from the machines and the shouts of the dealers, people cursed under their breath or grunted with joy.

Behind it all, under the perspiration and perfume and carpet glue, lay the grimy odor of money. Dollar bills always smelled filthy to me—not the sweet earthy aroma of soil, but like the sweat of a thousand hands and the dust of a thousand cash register drawers had soaked into every crease of the inky paper. That's what Vegas stank like to me, and I hated it.

I almost didn't recognize Lazar. I noted the back of a tall, broad-shouldered blond guy wearing a leather jacket and jeans standing by the door to Caliban's Bowling Lanes and caught myself admiring how his jeans fit. Then with a jolt, I pulled my gaze back up to the shining head of hair. It was cropped to show the clean tan back of his neck as he bent his head down to look at something in his hands.

He turned, scanning the room, and I realized this was the first time I'd seen him wearing anything other than white. Before, he'd always had the look of an arrogant, avenging angel, the kind of masculine beauty the Renaissance painters tried to capture. But in that faded blue T-shirt and brown leather jacket, he could have been the most popular boy in high school—the class president or the captain of the football team.

Only the concerned crease between his eyebrows and almost military stance of readiness gave him away as something quite different. *He'll have a gun under the jacket, even if he's sincere about helping us.*

"There he is," I said to Amaris, nodding toward her brother.

Her eyes landed on him. "Oh." Her eyes got very bright, almost happy. "He kept his word. I guess I should stay here while you talk to him, right? That's what we agreed."

I regarded her for a moment. She attempted to smile and looked past me, her lips pressed together as if keeping something profound in check.

"Go." I patted her shoulder. "Go say hello to him. It'll give me a chance to be sure he's alone."

"You sure?" At my nod: "Okay, thanks!" Her smile became genuine, and she bounded around me toward Lazar.

I inspected the crowd, staying back behind a cluster of craps players. No one seemed to be paying her, him, or me the slightest attention. That was good.

Lazar noticed Amaris approaching, and his whole face opened up for a moment in happy surprise.

Amaris saw it, and she lit up with a sudden grin. She threw her arms around his neck in a hug. He laughed, wrapping his arms around her waist, and I saw that in one hand he held a manila envelope, unlabeled. Had he brought the plans for the Tribunal facility, like he'd promised?

Amaris broke the hug, still beaming, and then turned to examine the room, probably looking for me. She gestured, as if saying, "I need to go keep a lookout now."

He leaned in to kiss her cheek with a sudden, surprising tenderness.

She got very still, biting her lip.

He spoke, and the words looked a lot like "I'm sorry," and then "I love you," and I had to look away, knowing I was observing something incredibly intimate.

When I looked back, Amaris was heading toward me, a little breathless from anxiety mixed with happiness. "I told him I'm keeping a lookout. See anything suspicious?"

"Nothing so far." She nodded, and I walked toward Lazar, who stood looking right at me, his face now unreadable.

"That was clever, having my sister come see me first," he

said as I got close. The familiar, arrogant sneer I remembered from when we raided his father's compound was marring his face. "You got to observe me with my guard down. Maybe it'll help you see through all my lies."

I stopped in front of him, trying to stand in a relaxed way, to make it look like we were friends just hanging out between frames. Through the entrance to the bowling alley came the small thunder of pins being knocked down.

"I *am* an ingenious bitch," I said.

He withdrew a little, blinking incredulously. Like Amaris, he'd been raised not to swear, so I got cheap satisfaction out of shocking him. I continued: "So ingenious that I don't need your sister's help to know when you're lying. Are those the plans to the new Tribunal complex?"

The sneer faded slightly as he narrowed his eyes at me, assessing. "I keep my promises," he said and handed the manila envelope over.

It was oddly close to something Caleb had once said, about how he didn't often make promises, because when he did, he kept them.

"You didn't bring my beloved brother with you?" He looked down at me, brown eyes sparkling with gold, just the way Caleb's black eyes did. "Or should I say 'your beloved'?"

"You really shouldn't say anything about that at all," I said, keeping my voice calm even as my face turned red. "I'd hate to have to kill and eat you in front of all these grandparents."

He studied me a moment. Was that the faint trace of a smile on his face? "I will obey you fully and keep my covenant."

It took me a moment to translate his archaic language. "Were you followed?"

He shook his head. "And I hacked the GPS in my car again."

"Okay." I opened the envelope and allowed its contents to slide into my hand. On top I saw a map of Western Nevada, one part of it marked with a small X. It lay about an hour's drive north of Morfael's school, out of the mountains, and into the desert, perilously close to the air force base closed off to the public.

"That's the location of the accelerator?" I asked, wondering suddenly if Morfael had chosen the school's location for a reason other than the thinness of the veil. Could he have suspected somehow the Tribunal facility was nearby?

"That's the entrance," he said, touching the spot with his finger. "It leads to a series of underground tunnels. The base actually spreads out over an area about this big. . . ." His finger traced a part of the map beyond the lines denoting the air force base.

"You tunneled under a government base?" I looked up at him. We'd moved close to each other to view the map. I noticed a cut on his lower lip that had just started to heal. He smelled like clean skin and fresh-laundered clothes. I took a half-step back.

"That was deliberate," he said. "The accelerator is a circle." He pulled out a second sheet of paper, which showed the floor plan of a complex comprised of a series of rooms and halls clustered on the western edge of a large ring. He ran his finger around the ring. "This is a large circular steel tube to conduct the subatomic particles. We aim them at each other at something close to the speed of light, and when they smash into each other, they break apart into smaller particles and release energy. I'm only just starting to understand what our scientists are talking about."

"This goes under the testing range," I said. "It was once a *nuclear* testing range."

"I know," he said. "When our workers were building certain parts of the conductor, they had to wear special gear in case of radiation, but it's not dangerous in this area. Where we live." He tapped the rooms next to the accelerator ring. "It's just so dark. I miss the sun."

Clearly, Lazar hadn't been taught by Morfael. "The U.S. government exploded nearly a thousand nuclear bombs on this range," I said. "Don't you know the effect that has on the veil?"

He pursed his lips, mulling over what I'd said. "You mean like the Tunguska explosion in Siberia?" he asked. At the word "Siberia" I got a chill. That's where I'd been found as an infant. "That was a meteor, not a nuclear bomb, but it nearly ripped apart the veil between the worlds. Are you saying the veil near our base was torn by the bombs?"

So Lazar was quick, like his siblings. "Yes," I said. "So my next question is: Why build an accelerator close to where the veil is thin?"

His eyes narrowed, glittering with speculation. "I'm not sure, but as particle colliders go, it's small. Nowhere near as large as the one under Switzerland. Being close to Othersphere might make up for its small size and somehow augment the tests they're doing."

"And why are they conducting tests?" I fixed my eyes on him, looking for any sign of a betrayal.

"Somehow it involves your DNA," he said.

So far he was being honest with me. I could see it in his posture, his face, the tone of his voice. He'd made no attempt to manipulate me with his voice, as objurers were trained to do. "That's what we suspected."

"I figured you'd know that's what we were after that night I was in your house. But I don't understand how the accelerator ties into the DNA, or what my father is planning." His eyes narrowed with genuine irritation. "He won't tell me, and the science is too advanced. I've been able to hack briefly into some of the scientists' files, but I don't know what they mean."

"Did you include those files here?" I rifled through the pages in the envelope, but there weren't many more, and they all looked like floor plans and maps.

"I couldn't copy them. They were too well protected, and I didn't have much time." At my skeptical look, he raised his eyebrows, a rueful smile across his lips. "You try sneaking around a closed complex full of paranoid fanatics in the middle of the night, hacking into their top-secret plans. See how much information you get."

I looked away from him for a moment, scanning the room for any signs of trouble to give myself a minute to think. A thumping wash of distant music pounded through the walls, underscoring the distant scrape of the ball falling into place in a roulette wheel and the electronic simulation of slots clanging into place. The fountain show outside must have started. A woman in a Christmas sweater at the blackjack table squealed with delight as she scraped two towers of chips closer.

I looked back at Lazar. He'd delivered on his promise. But he wasn't going to like what I had to say.

"You have to go back," I said. "Tonight."

Incredulity washed over his face, followed swiftly by anger. "Go back? But I brought you everything you asked for. . . ."

"You'll do us a lot more good inside than out," I said.

"So you believe me." Annoyance and maybe a bit of sadness edged his expressive voice. "But still it isn't enough."

"We're going to need to get into this complex of yours," I said. "If you're inside, you can get us inside too."

He shook his head at me, exhaling hard in frustration. "I held up my end of this bargain. Now you need to step up and help me get away from the Tribunal."

"I will personally give you a thousand dollars to start a new life," I said. "But only after you help us put an end to whatever your father is planning."

Lazar got very still, except for his warm brown eyes, which flitted back and forth between mine, as if looking for weakness. "You know it's a huge risk for me to go back there after bringing you this information," he said. "If my father finds out I've betrayed him, he'll kill me."

"The way you killed Caleb's mother," I said, my voice cold. "Without a second thought."

He inhaled sharply, trying to keep his face unreadable without success. "I understand," he said. "Nothing is ever good enough."

"It will be," I said. "Soon."

He was looking at me, faint horror in his eyes. "Now I get it," he said. "I didn't see it before because you're this beautiful girl, and he's my father, but . . ." He shook his head, disbelief now battling with amusement in his face. "You and Ximon are a lot alike."

"What the hell does that mean?" I said, not happy with how my voice rose in anger. "I am nothing like him."

"Every day was like a test with him," Lazar said. "A test of my loyalty, my skill, my commitment to the cause. Nothing I did was ever good enough because of when I—" He broke off, lips going white, and looked away.

"When you what?" I asked. The expression on his face sent my anger leaking away. Whatever he was thinking, it had nothing to do with me.

"Never mind," he said. "I didn't really mean that about you being like my father."

"I think you did mean it," I said. "But you don't have to love me. You just have to help us."

"Love you!" The words tumbled out of him, his face suddenly flooding with color. "I never said that I lo—I never said that!"

"I didn't say you said it," I said, starting to confuse myself. Why had that phrase so flummoxed him? "I just mean—"

"Don't get the wrong idea," he interrupted, putting up both of his hands and taking a step back. A maddening look of condescension took over his face. "Just because I said you were beautiful, and I saw you . . . enjoying yourself with my brother in the back of that car, and I agreed to meet you here alone doesn't mean I give a damn about you personally. You're just a means to an end."

I flushed again at the reminder of how he'd found us

nearly naked in the car. "Fine," I said curtly. "Then we feel the same way about each other."

"Good," he said.

"Good," I said. "But if you're too scared to go back to the Tribunal and do more, I understand."

"Scared?" He spat the word out in surprise.

"I can give you a hundred dollars right now if you'd rather just run away on your own," I said. He'd responded exactly the way I'd hoped. "And good luck to you."

He spun away, took two steps, then paced back to me, clearly furious and not knowing what to do with it. He smiled tightly. "You *are* an ingenious bitch."

I smiled back up at him. "Sweet-talker."

He opened his mouth to retort when, in a blur of motion, Amaris appeared out of nowhere, nearly cannoning into us, her face flushed. "I saw a Tribunal member. I recognized him, coming through the lobby. He'll be here any second."

"An objurer here, now?" I turned on Lazar, fury blazing through me. "What the hell have you done?"

"I didn't know," Lazar said, his face draining of all color. "I swear I looked for anyone following me."

"He hasn't spotted us yet," Amaris said between quick breaths. "He's got a GPS or something. He's looking at it and following it toward us, any second now. . . ."

"They must have planted a device on me without my knowing it," Lazar said. "I promise you, I had no idea."

I had only a split second to decide what to do. Despite everything, I believed him.

"This way!" I grabbed Lazar by the arm, pulling him away from the open area in front of the bowling alley, toward an area crowded with slots and cubicles featuring individual monitors. "Amaris, get to the car! Like we planned. We'll lose this guy, then find you. Don't let him see you."

"Got it!" She angled away from us, back toward the reception area, but taking the long way around the edge of the room.

"You must have a tracking device on you—take this off."
I yanked on the shoulder of his jacket. "Now!"

"Okay, okay!" He started to shed the jacket. "I understand that you're eager to get boys' clothes off, but this is
ridiculous."

I rounded on him furiously, and then stopped, arrested by
a thought. He was about to toss the jacket away, but I
grabbed it, hustling him deeper into the casino. "Wait. Are
you a good actor? Could you convince him you just came
here to gamble?"

He immediately saw where I was going. "Because he probably already reported to the others that I'm AWOL."

"If he hasn't seen you with me yet, then maybe you can
convince him you're just a simple sinner. . . ."

"Not a traitor." He nodded. "Worth a try." He shouldered
back into his jacket. "I'll find a spot here." He indicated our
area, which had several large-screen TVs and a few men
seated at desks in front of smaller screens, pressing buttons.
A sign overhead said SPORTS BOOK. "You hide."

"I'll be watching." I caught him by the sleeve as he began
to move toward a cubicle. "If this works, you'll go back there
and be our inside man?"

"You knew all along I would." He flashed his perfect teeth
in a perfect smile and strode over to a desk with a large monitor. His fake confident walk was as good as mine.

I slunk over to the right, down a different row of cubicles,
and slithered down at one. Its monitor featured a shot of a
jockey in salmon-pink silks on top of a shiny black mare.
Large boards covered in names and numbers loomed overhead, showing me the odds. *Horse races, at this hour?* Then I
saw they were broadcasting from Australia.

I put my hand on the mouse and pretended to watch, hoping nobody would notice the sixteen-year-old girl supposedly
betting on the horses. The wizened old man in a shapeless hat
next to me didn't even look up from his screen as I slumped
in my seat for cover. So far so good.

Two rows behind me sat Lazar. I tuned my hearing in his direction, willing myself not to look behind me. Fortunately, my ears were sensitive enough to catch a heavy tread of foot-steps moving toward him.

A nasal male voice said, "I thought you were too good to be true."

"Oh!" Lazar faked surprise fairly well. But he was an ob-jurer and knew how to manipulate his voice. "Michael. I . . . This isn't what it looks like."

Michael snorted. "I can't wait to tell your father you said that. Come on."

There was a rustle of clothes as Lazar got to his feet. "You don't have to tell him, do you? Does anyone else know that you found me?"

"No, but don't expect me to lie to the Bishop for you. It's not like you ever did anything nice for me." Michael began to walk away.

Lazar took a step. "Maybe I could."

Michael's footsteps halted. "What does that mean?"

"I could give you some of my winnings."

"You won some money?" Michael's voice arced upwards, interested.

"I made a bundle on tonight's big game."

My heart sank. It was midweek in mid-January. There were no big games except the football playoffs on the week-end. Lazar's sheltered upbringing was showing.

"Big game?" Michael paced back toward Lazar. "Which big game?"

"You know—this last horse race game. I bet on the long odds."

I nearly thunked my head down onto the desk of my cubi-cle. Lazar should have shut up while he was ahead. Even I knew the correct term was long shot, and horse races weren't called "games."

"You bet on the long odds?" Michael's voice was soft, and

I knew he hadn't been fooled. I turned, keeping my head low, and peered under the desks behind me. Lazar's brown boots stood about ten feet away, blocked by two desks. A pair of white running shoes walked right up to him. "Did you win the exacta?"

"Exactly." Lazar was vamping now, trying to be clever with puns.

The old man in the cubicle next to me turned his head curiously as I hunkered down on all fours and scuttled under the desk behind me, where no one was sitting. Fortunately, my observer shrugged and turned back to his monitor. I lost sight of him as I neared the back of Lazar's cubicle. Over its wall I could see the top of Lazar's blond head, and the graying hair of another, shorter man facing him. Michael.

"Which horses did you pick?" Michael was asking. His head tilted as he looked up at the big board on the wall above us.

"Horses?" The plural confounded Lazar a little. I should have known better than to expect a guy raised by religious fanatics to lie well about gambling.

"You can just give me the numbers," Michael said. "I'm curious. Exactas can bring in big money. . . ."

He was playing with Lazar now. I ducked under the cubicle between me and them and lunged forward, tackling Michael at the knees. He dropped to the floor with a squawk.

"He knows!" I said to Lazar in a kind of subdued yell. "Knock him out!"

Lazar, startled by my move, took one long second to realize what was going on. Michael, clad in Tribunal gray and white, tried to reach into his jacket for what had to be a gun.

I knocked his hand away and pounded on his solar plexus to wind him, the way Morfael had shown us in class. But my fist slammed into something much harder than skin and bone and bounced back up with no impact.

"He's wearing a vest!" I hissed.

Michael backhanded me in the face, knocking me into the legs of the desk.

Lazar had his gun out, switching grips to hold it by the barrel, and lifted his arm to hit Michael with the butt.

Michael had no such scruples. In one swift move, he pulled his own pistol from under his jacket, pointed it at me, and pulled the trigger.

# CHAPTER 13

A sound like a tree limb snapping, and something smashed into my chest like a sledgehammer. I gasped, but my lungs took in nothing.

I caught a glimpse of Lazar's eyes wide with horror; then he grabbed for Michael's gun.

*Makes sense,* I thought with an odd sort of detachment. *Michael's wearing a bulletproof vest, which makes it tough to shoot him back. And you can't just go around shooting people in the middle of a casino.*

*Or maybe you can.*

I wasn't sitting up anymore; I was lying on my side on the floor. I didn't remember sliding downward. I put my hand to my chest and felt something sticky, but didn't have the strength to pull my hand away to see what it was. I tried inhaling again, and a tiny thread of air squeaked into my lungs.

*Not enough. Not enough.*

Something like the ocean was roaring in my ears, and the

struggling forms of Lazar and Michael were growing fuzzy at the edges.

"Dez!" Through the din came Lazar's voice, sharp as a razor. Somewhere out there I could still see his brown leather jacket, wrestling with a man in a gray jacket, whoever that was. It didn't really matter. My eyelids were made of lead, and my heart had been replaced with a stone.

"Dez, you must shift!" Lazar's voice cut through the woolly fog. "I call upon you to shift now. *Now!*"

That voice could not be denied. It stirred the dark roiling essence at my core that had begun to still. Power, blazing with life, rolled through that portal in my soul, shredding the haze in my mind, pushing the stone from my chest. My hands were not hands, but huge, velvety, striped paws; my skin was now fur, my teeth fangs.

I rolled to my feet, my long tail knocking aside the desk. The monitor on it crashed to the floor. The bullet which had pierced my chest dropped to the floor, and I dug my claws into the patterned carpet, screening out the piercing clang of casino bells, the bright flashing lights, to zero in on the man in the gray jacket. He was thickset and strong. He expertly rolled on top of Lazar, one elbow pushing down on Lazar's windpipe while pinning his legs to the floor with his knees. Lazar heaved up against him, to no avail.

Both guns lay useless nearby, a few feet apart. So Lazar at least had dealt with that part of the problem. I would deal with the rest.

Someone screamed, "Tiger!"

*Yes*, I thought, as a general murmur of panic swirled through the room. *Yes.*

And I roared.

The vibration from it made the floor thrum. Michael's head turned with the suddenness of a marionette's on a string. His eyes widened in fright. His terror pleased me, but it would not save him.

Around us, the sounds of hubbub turned to yells of horror

and cries for help. Michael pushed himself away from Lazar, crabbing backwards on all fours and trying to grab for a gun. Lazar coughed, still alive.

"I objure you," Michael intoned, but his voice was too high and filled with dread. "I forbid you entrance to this world, foul demon! Return! Return to—"

I pounced, leaping over Lazar. One heavy paw to Michael's chest sent his arms and legs flying out from under him.

Flat on the carpet, he tried to grab my jaw, my ears, anything. I just swiped his hands away with my free paw, drawing red lines on his skin. He screamed, "Filth! Demon!"

I sank my teeth into his neck. His blood ran hot and liquid on my tongue. And it was good.

It got very quiet. I let Michael's limp body go and licked my muzzle. Some part of me knew I would regret this, but right now I savored the blood of my enemy. This one, at least, would never trouble me again.

There was movement behind me, and I whirled, snarling, muscles tensed to spring. But it was Lazar, up on his hands and knees.

He froze. I could hear the quickened beat of his heart, the uneven pulse of blood through his veins, his terrified, shallow breathing.

"By God!" He swallowed hard. I could only imagine how I looked, crouched over a dead man, ears back, my striped muzzle awash with crimson. "That's really you. Dez." He said my name as if he couldn't quite believe it. "We've got to get out of here."

"It's over there!" Someone was shouting. "Get it!"

"I'm not going anywhere near it," a man's voice declared in no uncertain terms.

An indignant voice: "You're the security guard."

"All I've got is a pistol. Did you see how huge that thing is? Get everyone out and I'll call animal control. It must've escaped from one of those stupid shows on the Strip."

Lazar started getting out of his jacket. "Here. It won't cover you completely, but..."

There wasn't time to shift. I shook my head at him. As always, it felt bizarre to make such a human gesture in my tiger form, but I had no other way to communicate. Lazar looked puzzled as I picked the manila envelope up gently with my mouth. Then I lashed out one paw and clawed his shoulder.

"Ow! Hey, what..." He jumped back from me in alarm. "What are you...?"

His voice trailed off as I moved away from Michael's body and pointed my nose at a side door marked EXIT.

"It really is you in there, isn't it?" He shook his head. "You just look so... so much like a tiger."

I curled my upper lip in a half snarl and loosed a low growl. *I am a tiger.*

"Don't worry about the security cameras," he said, forcing his voice back to something like normal. "We'll be off the grid soon enough, and whoever watches this footage will be in therapy for years. No one will believe it or ever be able to connect it to us. You go first."

I shook my head again and walked behind where he was sitting on the floor. He didn't move as I got closer, but I could hear his breathing speed up again, his body tense, as I put my forehead against his back and shoved.

He jetted up and forward two steps, and then looked back at me, a light of understanding in his eyes. "Got it," he said. Then he sprinted for the exit, at full speed, as if a tiger was after him.

And I was.

He shoved open the exit door just steps ahead of me. If anyone was watching, it would look like he was fleeing from me, not accompanying me. The door slammed behind us as we pounded into a blank cement hallway that smelled like urine and chlorine.

Thirty feet down the hall, a woman in a rumpled uniform

pushing a wheeled laundry basket pointed at me, screeched like a dying bird, and fled, her clogs clomping.

Lazar laughed and nodded. "I know how she feels."

I bounded past him, toward the laundry basket. He followed, taking long strides. "Oh, look." He pointed through a nearby doorway just as I smelled hot detergent and heard the rumble of clothes in a dryer. The hotel's laundry room was brightly lit and going at full steam at this late hour, getting towels and sheets ready the next day.

"Clothes for you," he said, reading my mind. "But I bet there's a camera in there, to keep employees from stealing. . . ." He startled and pulled away as I used the edge of the envelope in my mouth to scratch at his hand.

He hesitated, then gingerly reached out and took the envelope from me. "This is the strangest day of my life."

But I was already in the room, scanning its upper corners. Sure enough, a cheap camera beamed its little red light on me. I sprang upward, using the wall like a tree trunk, and swiped it with one paw. The camera fell to the floor and shattered. No more little red light.

Lazar walked in. "That's going to look very interesting when they run the footage later. But who knows why tigers do what they do?" He saw me sniffing at a pile of white towels and folded sheets. "No, here, try this."

He held up a cheap terry-cloth robe, the kind hotels provided for their guests. Enough to cover you up when you got out of the shower, but not thick and soft enough to tempt you to steal it.

"And look." He fished a pair of slightly stringy terry-cloth slippers out of a laundry basket. "Is this what they call fashionable out here in the world?"

He threw the slippers down, facing me, on the floor, and then held the robe out, as if waiting for a swimsuit model to step into it.

I made a kind of growling *whoof* sound, something between a snarl and a roar.

He took a step back, going a little pale. I didn't want to just shift to human right in front of him. I wasn't ashamed of my body, but Lazar wasn't exactly a trusted friend I felt comfortable with when I was naked. In fact, quite the opposite.

"Don't you think it's better if you shift?" He swallowed, trying to sound reasonable, but I could see the uneasiness in his eyes as he stared at the tiger in front of him. "And I promise I won't look." He closed his eyes, still holding the robe.

When I didn't move, he peeked under his eyelids and lowered the robe, his face shadowed with remorse. "I know I've given you reason to distrust me," he said. "I didn't mean what I said, about you being like my father. You're quite the opposite. At least in your human form."

I thought about Amaris's story of how her mother had died, and I chuffed at him, the loud, purring noise thrumming in my throat. He frowned, then nodded and stood back up, lifting the robe high so that I couldn't see his face, and he couldn't see me. I turned my back and shifted, reaching back toward the robe.

Lazar guided my arms into the sleeves. I glanced back, expecting to see a knowing sneer, but his eyes were squeezed shut. So he really was being a gentleman about this. His fingers brushed my bare shoulder for a moment, but he pulled away quickly and didn't touch me again.

My face got very hot. Another reason I loved my tiger form. In it, I never wanted to blush and never could. Human form was more complicated. I pulled the edges of the terrycloth together and used the thin belt to close the robe up good and tight as I turned around.

The bruises forming on Lazar's face were standing out more harshly, his cheeks slightly flushed with red. "What I meant to say is that you and my father are both leaders. But that's where the resemblance ends," he said. "He only respects strength and cruelty and devotion to the cause, and if you can't offer him one of those things, you're no use to him."

"Is that what happened with your mother?" I asked.

He drew back, suddenly on high alert, like a cobra hooded and rearing up against a threat. "What do you know about my mother?" he asked.

I tried to make my voice neutral. "Amaris told us why she died, that your father refused to let her get humdrum medical care. That must've been awful."

"Amaris was only ten," he said, not relaxing. "She knows what she was told."

"So your mother didn't have breast cancer?"

"No, she had cancer all right," he said. "She was in agony for months from it. Every now and then he'd allow her some morphine, but only after Amaris or I would beg him for it. He thought it was a waste of money." He let out a sharp bitter laugh. "I tried to sneak her to the hospital one night, all by myself. She could still walk a little ways, so I managed to get her into one of the cars. I even managed to drive it a bit, even though I hadn't learned to drive yet."

"How old were you?"

"Twelve." The harshness left his voice, and his eyes lost focus as he remembered. "He must've heard the engine starting, because he came out of the building, yelling for me to stop. I tried to gun the engine, but in our old compound he'd had spikes implanted in the driveway to prevent people from driving away in the middle of the night, and our front tires blew out. I'll never forget sitting there in the car, listening to his footsteps crunching on the gravel as he walked up to the car. I thought he'd kill me."

"But he didn't," I said.

"No." His voice was cold. "No, he didn't kill me. He opened my car door and dragged me out of the car and beat me. He broke my nose, a couple of ribs, a few other things. My head was spinning, and I couldn't stand up anymore, so he gave up on me and went over to the passenger side of the car and dragged my mother out."

I was frozen in place. I thought I knew how bad Lazar's life had been. I knew nothing.

"She was wearing a nightgown and my father's own robe. I'd stolen it from his closet to keep her warm. She had these clogs on her feet, easy to slip into and out of, and I remember how they slid off her feet because she was too weak to walk. First the left, then the right shoe scraped off as he dragged her by the hair and threw her down in front of me. I thought he was going to start hitting her too, but instead he pulled his pistol out of his belt."

My heart skipped a beat. *Oh, no, oh, no.*

"He made me sit up to do it," Lazar said. He was very calm as he spoke, like he was telling a story. "He handed me the gun, but my right wrist was fractured, so he put the gun in my left hand and got behind me, his hand over mine. He said, 'You're right, son. Your mother's in too much pain. It's better this way. Let God's will be done.'"

Lazar's face was blank, even as he stared right into my eyes. "So we pulled the trigger, my father and I. We had to pull it twice because my hands were shaking. . . ."

I put my hand on his arm. He was trembling.

"It was my fault she didn't die right way," he said. "After that night my hands never shook when I shot a gun. I had killed my mother—what did it matter if I shot Caleb's mother, or anyone else? And if I kept doing what Father wanted, at least for that day he'd still trust me, still love me. I never disobeyed my father, not once." His eyes lost their distant look and met mine. "Not till I met you. You changed everything."

The bruises on his face looked like purple fingerprints against his pale skin. For a moment I couldn't speak. In the space of a few minutes, something had changed, not just between us, but in how I saw the world.

I squeezed his arm, then withdrew my hand, jamming it into the square pocket of my robe. "You're the one who's changed," I said. "Because you're here. It'll be different now."

A door squeaked down the hall and several sets of footsteps started cautiously toward us. I hastily shoved my feet into the terry slippers. Lazar walked up to the doorway just as a security guard peeked around the corner. He visibly relaxed when he caught sight of us.

"You kids better get out of here," he said. "There's a frigging tiger on the loose."

"A what?" Lazar's supple voice was convincingly taken aback.

"I'm not kidding." He motioned us toward him. "You need to go down the hall, into the casino and outside, now." I walked up behind Lazar as the guard gestured the way we'd come. "It's clear that way, through that door, back into the casino. Go!"

"Thanks," I said, and we slipped past him to scurry down the hall and through the door, and back into the smoke and flashing lights.

After our talk in the laundry room, the Sports Book area felt like an alien land. It was completely empty and oddly silent.

"This way!" shouted another guard, motioning us toward the lobby area. "Out, quick!"

We hustled, but slowed down a little as we passed Michael's prone form, lying in a pool of congealing blood. His throat was gone.

I'd done that. I reached blindly toward Lazar as the security guard continued to urge us on. Lazar took my hand and pulled me away.

Then we were out into the cold desert air, being directed by a cop toward the street, where a crowd of gamblers had gathered, cigarettes ablaze, shaking their heads, each coming up with something bigger than the next to compare to the tiger. I dropped Lazar's hand, folding my arms against the cold.

"Here." He handed me the envelope with the maps in it, took off his leather jacket, and draped it around my shoulders, rubbing them with his warm hands. We stood there like that for a moment on the sidewalk, lost.

"Hey, um," Lazar said, his face flushing. "Please don't tell anyone about all of that. I couldn't stand it if Amaris ever found out."

"Okay," I said. "But I think she would understand."

"Maybe someday," he said.

An SUV pulled up to us, and I realized with a start that Amaris was driving, coming to get me exactly where we'd planned. Sitting next to her in the passenger seat, his face set in hard lines, sat Caleb.

# CHAPTER 14

Lazar stepped away from me hastily as Caleb opened the car door and got out of the SUV. He left the door open, one hand on top of it, and looked at us, his face like granite.

His eyes on me made me realize just how disheveled Lazar and I both looked. Lazar was bruised and rumpled, the scratches from my claws on his shoulder now oozing blood. I was severely underdressed in nothing but a robe and another boy's jacket.

"Get in the car," Caleb said to me. I'd never heard his voice so flat, so unreadable.

I took the jacket off and shoved it into Lazar's hands. "Lazar brought me the plans to the Tribunal's new complex," I said. My voice was as shaky as I felt.

"I guess that makes everything okay then," Caleb said, again so flatly that I almost didn't recognize the sarcasm.

Lazar didn't put his jacket on, just gripped it tightly

"Don't blame Desdemona. I made her promise not to tell you about this meeting."

Caleb regarded him, contempt in the slant of his dark brows and the set of his mouth. "So now you're lying for her. How touching."

"I'm not lying," said Lazar, his tone so convincing that I almost believed him.

Caleb shook his head slightly, eyes narrowing. "Dez makes her own decisions."

My heart contracted. How well Caleb knew me.

"It's my fault," I said. "What are you doing here?"

"I heard you sneaking out and followed you," he said. "You've been acting strange. I had no idea you'd be holding hands with *him*."

I bit my lip. I'd promised Lazar I wouldn't tell anyone how his mother had died, and I would keep that promise, even if might be exactly what Caleb needed to hear in order to understand.

"We weren't holding hands." Although we had been, a few minutes ago. *But that was innocent!* "Lazar wants to help us, Caleb."

"So you trust him completely now?" Gold glinted dangerously in Caleb's normally black eyes. "But you didn't trust me enough to tell me about this meeting?"

I opened my mouth, but nothing came out.

"Get in the car," said Caleb, and slid back into the SUV's passenger seat, slamming the door.

Lazar's face wore a rueful look. "I seem to have gotten you into trouble."

"No," I said. "I did that all by myself." I took a deep breath, and couldn't help glancing over at Caleb. He was staring straight ahead. Next to him, Amaris motioned at me nervously to get inside the car. "Call me or Amaris as soon as you're safely back inside the compound. We'll need to strike soon, before your father gets suspicious."

"Good-bye until then," Lazar said, shooting a glance at

Caleb too, then giving me a reassuring smile. "And good luck."

He turned and walked away. I forced myself to stop staring after him and climbed into the backseat of the SUV. Amaris took off too fast, making the tires squeal.

"Sorry," she muttered, looking at me in the rearview mirror. "You okay?"

"I am now," I said. "That objurer shot me, but Lazar used his voice just in time to help me shift and heal."

In the seat in front of me, Caleb's shoulders stiffened, but he didn't turn around. Amaris said, "Michael shot you? Where?"

"In the chest," I said. "I'd be dead if it wasn't for Lazar."

"You wouldn't even have been there if it wasn't for Lazar," Caleb said, still not looking back at me. "Turn here," he said to Amaris, pointing toward an open parking lot. She slowed down with an awkward tap on the brakes and turned right.

"What happened to Michael?" Amaris asked.

"He's dead," I said, a hard lump in my throat. "I'm sorry."

"Don't be," she said. "I mean, I wouldn't wish him dead, but he was a jerk and he shot you."

She stopped the SUV behind a familiar red pickup truck. As Caleb opened his door, I said, "You hot-wired Raynard's truck?"

He didn't answer, just got out of the car.

"I'll follow you back," Amaris said to him, leaning over to try to catch his eye.

He simply slammed the door.

"I'll see you there," I told her, opening my own door. "I should go with Caleb."

"You sure?" She looked over her shoulder at me.

"Yeah," I said. "Thanks."

Caleb didn't say a word to me the first fifteen minutes we were alone in the car together. Anger emanated from him in waves. But finally, I couldn't stand the silence anymore.

"I had to give him a chance, without the rest of you threatening him with death," I said. "All our lives depend on it."

He didn't reply for a long moment, and then said: "Since when has anyone been able to ever stop you from doing anything?"

"You told me you wanted to kill him. All of you!" I stared at his shuttered face as the lights from passing cars skimmed over it. "That would not have been a good way to begin the meeting."

He shook his head. "You should've told me, Dez."

I didn't reply. Maybe he was right. But I remembered all too vividly how he'd shouted at me that Lazar deserved to die.

He was drumming his fingers on the steering wheel as he stared down the nearly empty lanes of the freeway. The land around us was becoming wilder as we drove, the buildings few and far between as the utterly black silhouette of the mountains drew near, blotting out some of the stars in the sky. "You avoided telling me that Lazar stole your hairbrush for as long as you could," he said. "If we hadn't run into him in Vegas, would you ever have told me about that?"

"I hadn't seen you in weeks!" I said. "We barely had a chance to say hello before the Tribunal showed up. There was no time."

"There are phones," he said. "And e-mail."

"Okay," I said. "I could've told you about it right away, that's true. But can you blame me? When you saw him, you almost killed him. And when we talked out by the fire pit, and later with the group—your hatred for him was so immense, I couldn't see any way around it."

"When did you arrange this little meeting?" he asked. "Did you know about it even then?"

"No!" God, this was frustrating. Couldn't he see how his attitude would have ruined everything? "He contacted Amaris via computer tonight, and she told me. It was my decision not to tell the rest of you. I figured that we'd given her a chance.

So tonight I gave him a chance to prove himself. So far, so good."

"You're giving him a chance," he said. "But you wouldn't take a chance on me and tell me what you were doing."

*Damn.* He was guilting me good. But he hadn't seen the murderous look on his own face. And he didn't know what Lazar had been through. Right now, I wasn't even sure he'd care.

"The same way you didn't trust me enough to tell me at first that Ximon is your father?" I shot him a look, and he inhaled sharply. He'd kept his relationship to the Tribunal secret from everyone, including me, until Ximon and his helicopter attacked Morfael's school and took Siku prisoner. "And when I did find out, from Ximon, not you, I still trusted you, because I understood the pressure you were under. You were afraid we'd all turn on you. But we didn't. *I* didn't."

"That was different!" His voice rose, and I knew I'd hit a nerve. "You and I weren't . . . we weren't *us*, then. And my keeping that from you didn't endanger anyone but me."

"I'm not endangering people; I'm helping to save them!" This was agony. Why couldn't he see?

"You're playing with people's lives," he said. "You met with one of the otherkin's worst enemies, and not only did you not tell me, you didn't tell Morfael, or any of our friends."

The whole world sagged around me. "They all hate him too," I said. "There's so much riding on the information he has. And I figured if he gave us the plans to the Tribunal's new compound, it would prove to everyone that he's being honest."

"So we have to trust that you know best," he said, "even though you don't trust us."

Anger stirred inside me. "I was raised by an outsider, so I have a different perspective. You've said so yourself! I didn't inherit the generations of fear and hatred like the rest of you. I knew how you'd all react. You would've done everything in your power to keep me away from him. So I had to do it without you." I leaned toward him, intent. "This isn't about you or me or the kids at school, Caleb. The stakes are too big. That particle accelerator is powerful technology, and it's got to be part of some grand plan to kill off every shifter on the planet. That's more important than who trusts who."

"So it's up to you to save everyone, including Lazar," he said. "That sounds like some martyr bullshit to me."

"Maybe," I said, flushing. "Or maybe I have to do it because you're too caught up in your own bullshit!"

He threw me a hard look. "Maybe you're the one caught up. Lazar had his hands on you when we pulled up."

"What? No, he—!" I broke off, remembering how Lazar had rubbed my shoulders out there in the cold. "He was just trying to help me keep warm."

His lip curled in scorn. "Every boy has used that excuse to touch every girl since the world began."

My jaw dropped. "You're *jealous*? Are you crazy?"

His hands clenched the steering wheel hard. "You hid a call between the two of you and lied about meeting him tonight! How do I know there weren't other calls, other meetings?"

"Because there weren't." It sounded lame, even to my ears. "It's just not like that between us."

"For you, maybe," he said. "But I know Lazar."

"I don't think you do," I said, with heat. "I bet I know him now better than you do."

"Oh, yeah?" His eyebrows shot up challengingly. "Like what? What don't I know?"

I said nothing for a minute, then: "He's just someone who needs help, and who can help us in return. For him I'm nothing more than a way out of hell. That's all."

He shook his head. "I saw the look on his face as we drove up. You're way more than his ticket out."

I almost broke my promise to Lazar then. I opened my mouth to tell Caleb everything I'd learned. The tension between us came from his undying hatred and my keeping secrets. If I told this secret, would it mitigate his hatred for Lazar? Would he be able to see his brother as a human being? I couldn't be sure. So I closed my mouth and sat back in my seat. Lazar's secret was too intimate, too awful for me to betray without permission.

I tried to keep my voice calm, saying, "It was a rough night. But you need to trust me."

"After all the lies?" He pounded the steering wheel once with both open hands. "How?"

I'd never felt this way before—burning with fury and pain at the same time. I looked out the window and we rode the rest of the way in silence. I fought not to cry, not to scream at him, not to beg for his forgiveness, though I still didn't think I needed it. More than anything I wanted to feel his arms around me, hear his voice whisper reassuring words, feel his heart beat against mine. But I didn't see a way for that to happen, maybe ever again.

When we pulled up to the school garage it was nearly four a.m., and my head vibrated with a dozen fuzzy spiders that webbed up my thoughts. Caleb sat up straighter as the headlights swept across a car in the driveway that hadn't been there before. It took me a second to recognize it.

"That's your parents' car," Caleb said.

"Oh, no." The words came out of me without thinking. The car was empty. So they'd gone inside. The horrible buzzing in my head grew hotter and louder. If Mom and Richard were here, that meant everyone at the school was up, that they knew Amaris and I had left. *God, they must be worried.*

"Someone probably woke up and found we were gone," Caleb said. "Then Morfael called your parents."

"Shit." I turned to him. "So you didn't tell them?"

His face was still hard and closed as he shook his head slightly. "I didn't want to worry anyone."

I got slowly out of the truck as Amaris pulled up in the SUV behind us. "Whose car is that?" she asked, slamming her door and walking toward us.

I just trudged toward the front door.

Everyone was in the living room as we walked in. My mother and Richard were seated in a window nook holding hands, pillows all around them, with Morfael standing by. Plump, scruffy-bearded Raynard was creaking back and forth in the rocking chair. Arnaldo, Siku, and November were piled on the couch, while London paced in front of them like a wolf outside a henhouse.

As we entered, heads turned, and the anxiety in the room snapped. They surged forward all at once, talking.

"Where the hell have you been?" London shouted, her eyes like blue bullets in her scared white face.

Arnaldo sagged with relief where he sat on the couch as November pounded Siku on the shoulder and said, "Told you they were up to something." Raynard stopped rocking, and shook his head at us.

Only Morfael's expression didn't change. After assessing us, his pale eyes took in everyone else's reaction, as if it was no more and no less than he'd expected.

My mother pushed in front of everyone, her tiny body burrowing past Siku's bulk and London's betrayed stare. Her brown hair was ruffled, as if she'd spent the last hour running her hands through it, and her hazel eyes were bright with relief even as the corners crinkled downward in anger.

She lifted her hands, grabbed my head on both sides, and pulled it down to kiss my forehead. "I'm thanking the Goddess you're all right," she said, sparing a glance for Caleb and Amaris. "All of you. And now I'm going to be angry with you for worrying us like this!"

"I'm sorry," I said, feeling the way I had as a child when Mom found me up on the roof, about to leap to the nearest tree. "Nobody was supposed to know."

"Unfortunately for you I have to pee three times a night," said November. "When I got up, I saw you and Amaris were gone."

"We thought you'd been kidnapped!" London said, her voice savage with disappointment. "We thought you were dead."

"Then you'd think you'd be happier to see us," said Caleb dryly.

"What are you up to?" Arnaldo stood up from the couch. "There were no signs of violence or forced entry, so I figured you were out—"

"Causing trouble," November interrupted. "Please tell me you were causing trouble."

"Oh, there was trouble," I said. "Amaris and I went to meet Lazar."

An eruption of noise, protests, incredulity followed. I waited for it to die down slightly, and pushed on. "He met us in Vegas and gave us the plans to the Tribunal's new facility."

Amaris held up the envelope, the paper slightly spattered with blood. "Every room, every air duct, every entrance. It's all here."

"*You met Lazar?*" London's voice was filled with loathing. "Without telling us?"

"Yes," I said. "I am sorry I worried you, but not sorry I met him."

"I would have helped you," said London. "But I guess you didn't need me." She spun and paced away from me. Arnaldo got up and took the envelope from Amaris.

Siku stood there, considering, and then said, "You should have told us."

"No shit!" London spat out, then caught a look from my mother and muttered, "Sorry."

"It wasn't your best decision, honey," my mother said, her hands on her hips. "I mean, just you three meeting Lazar secretly? What if he'd brought a whole army with him?"

"It was actually just me and Dez," said Amaris. "Caleb saw us leaving earlier and followed us."

"Well, that's even dumber, then," said November. "It's amazing you're not all dead."

"Lazar would never hurt Amaris," I said. "I've told you he needs our help."

London threw up her hands. "This just gets better and better!"

Mom grabbed my chin and tilted it down so that I had to meet her eyes. "Dez, I know you're a compassionate girl, and that you want to think the best of people, but you've told me about this boy Lazar, and he doesn't sound any more trustworthy than his father."

"Exactly," Caleb said in a low voice that only carried as far as me and Mom.

I jerked my face out of her hand, but Mom was not to be deterred. "What if he'd captured you? Not only would you be dead or worse, but he might have been able to make you tell them where this school is, where your friends are, where Richard and I live."

"That would never happen," I said, my voice rising. "We were ready."

"So ready that you got shot in the chest," said Caleb.

"What?!" Mom's hands dropped. Her face, already creased with weariness, crumpled further. "Lazar shot you?"

"Not Lazar," I said. "An objurer who followed him. But I'm fine! I shifted and healed. That objurer isn't going to tell anyone anything."

"You killed him?" Her eyes dimmed with sadness. "Oh, God, Dez, what are you becoming?"

Stung, I pulled away from her. "What do you know about it?"

"I know you, honey." She was shaking her head, tears in

her eyes, and put her hand on my arm. "I know you want to do what's right. You're also incredibly stubborn and determined once you get an idea in your head. But you can't just go off and risk your life and everyone else's because you believe a boy can change."

Her disappointment was worse than anything, worse even than Caleb's anger. I shook her hand off. "He has changed," I said. "You've never even met him!"

"I know you better than anyone—" she started to say.

"No, you don't," I said, choking back threatening tears. No way I would give her or anyone else here the satisfaction of seeing me cry. "You don't know anything. You didn't even know I wasn't human! You just pretended everything was fine while all my life I had no idea who I was or where I came from. Even when I got the brace, you told me everything would be fine. Except I wasn't fine! Every single moment I wore that thing was torture."

Mom shook her head, as if she didn't want to believe me. "You never said anything. You never asked me about your origins. I just wanted to help you be strong. I didn't know you felt this way."

"You should have," I said. "Maybe it's because you're not really my mother."

Mom's mouth opened, but no sound came out. Bright spots of red burned in her cheeks, as if I'd struck her.

Someone laid a warm hand on my arm. Caleb. "Dez . . ." he said.

"No, no!" I pulled away from him. "You don't trust me either. None of you do! And you're wrong, you're wrong!"

Mom was clutching her stomach, backing away from me and shaking her head. Something inside me was glad to see how I'd hurt her. That would teach her to doubt me when I was right.

An odd choking sound came from her, and she doubled over. My own stomach lurched as I realized that was exactly what she'd done that night by the lightning tree.

Richard was on his feet, every fiber alert as he recognized the signs too. "Caroline?" He moved toward her.

"Goddess help me," she said through clenched teeth. "The dream. It's like the dream." She jerked upwards, throwing her head back in pain. The air around her bent, like heat waves over a desert mirage. Then she was tall, taller than I was. Her skin glowed from the inside, like a lantern when the wick is lit.

"What the hell . . . ?" London backed away from her. The other kids were poised to move, whether to flee or help I couldn't tell.

"It's happening!" Richard said, stopping in his tracks as Mom writhed, gleaming brighter now. "Dez, it's happening again!"

"Get away from her," Morfael's voice cut through the confusion in my head, and we all took three steps back from my mother, leaving her alone, towering over us all and blazing with internal light, in the middle of the straw-strewn floor. "Arnaldo, Laurentia, November, Siku, and Amaris—go downstairs. *Now*."

London whipped to the stairs instantly, with Siku, Amaris, and Arnaldo moving more slowly, but following. November hesitated, till Siku lumbered back over, grabbed her arm, and hauled her with him.

Caleb took a step away, and then found me with his eyes. "I can go," he said. "If that's what you want."

"No!" I choked out. "Please stay."

"Caleb, I will need you," Morfael said in a voice that brooked no argument. "Come."

Caleb gave me a quick, encouraging nod. Then, allowing Mom a wide berth, he made his way to Morfael's side.

The transformation going on in my mother was strangely silent this time. Without the lightning and thunder, it was all the more eerie to see her change, standing as if in a spotlight, her short brown hair growing long and red, her limbs lengthening as the hem of her dress rose, and the seams at her shoulders ripped to reveal luminous skin. It was like a shift in slow motion, only Mom wasn't a shifter, and the alternate form wasn't animal, but something very close to human.

The radiance inside her subsided a bit, like a light on a dimmer switch, and she lifted her head. Her eyes were wide, gold-green, and unfamiliar, but fixed right on me. She smiled, but it wasn't my mother's smile. The teeth were too white, too sharp, the skin too smooth and ageless.

When she spoke, the smoky voice was not her own. "I found you again," she said. "My lost little cub."

# CHAPTER 15

"Mom?" I couldn't help saying it, even though I knew she wasn't there.

"Sarangarel," she said, holding her hand out to me. The nails were long and pointed.

"What does that mean?" I looked over at Morfael. His moonstone eyes glittered, his spindly fingers gripping his staff so hard the knuckles were pink.

"You look well," said the thing that used to be my mother. She took two steps toward me, moving with an inhuman grace, taller than me by at least six inches, hair drifting around her shoulders like a live thing. Any remnant of my own small mother was gone; the woman before me looked a lot like . . . me. I didn't want to think how close the resemblance was. "You are beautiful, my child. I'm sorry it has taken me so long to find you."

"So long?" I felt very stupid all of a sudden. "I don't know you."

"The shadow is pouring off her," Caleb said. His eyes were narrowed, as if facing into a very bright light. "This is not a Tribunal trick."

"Your boy is clever," said the mom creature, bending a smile on Caleb that reminded me of how November smiled at her lunch. Her luminous eyes turned to Morfael, radiating something far more dangerous. "I trusted you, shadow walker."

Caleb stared at Morfael as if seeing him for the first time.

Morfael appeared unmoved. "You may not stay here," he said. "Go."

"You are the worst of all," she said, her voice rising to shake the furniture. "Your betrayal will be punished!"

"You leave my mother alone!" I said, my own voice escalating to match hers. "This isn't right!"

"Not right to see and speak to my own, my only?" In a flash she was calm; her eyes were bright and full of such alien fondness that I recoiled. "You must know that I have longed to see you. As much as I know you wished to see me. You must not fear me. Everyone else shall." Her gaze swept the room, taking in Caleb, Morfael, Richard, and Raynard before returning to smile at me. "But not you."

Richard took a step toward her, facing the woman who had been his wife. "Whoever you are," he said, "go back to where you came from."

She didn't even look at him. "I will find a way to bring you back to where you belong," she said to me. "That day is coming."

"I'm not going anywhere," I said. "And I won't allow you to use my mother like this."

Caleb hummed a low note, then slid it up the scale to settle on one harsh tone.

"Yes," said Morfael.

"Your mother?" The redheaded woman looked down at her own hands, and then nodded. "Of course. Your relationship makes this possible, for that is something she and I share. And I am grateful to her."

The hair on the back of my neck was standing straight up, goose bumps prickling my skin. It was what I'd suspected all along. I'd known it somewhere inside myself, but still I resisted. "Are you saying . . . *What are you saying?*"

She beamed at me, and my heart contorted, for her eyes, although the wrong shape and color, held the same expression my mother's did when she said she loved me. "I think you know."

Morfael sounded a note near to Caleb's, but oddly dissonant. The intonation rounded through their throats, spreading out to every corner, and took over the room. The sound's weight descended on me, and I had to clench my fists against it or be crushed.

The woman in my mother's body pivoted smoothly to face them, muscles gathered as if to spring. "No," she said. "I won't go! Not yet!"

"You have to," I said, teeth gritted against the unholy resonance. Any minute it might blow me away. "I don't want you, whoever you are."

"But you do!" Her tone was pleading, even as her eyes narrowed against the vibration from the callers of shadow. "For no one in this world understands you as I do. Inside you there has always been something missing, something stolen away. I can give it back to you, make you whole."

*Is this my fault? Did it happen because I said those awful things to Mom?*

"I didn't do this!" I said. "I don't want this!"

Morfael's voice shaded a semitone lower in a vibration so profoundly irritating, so very wrong, it took everything I had not to run, not to scream. The redheaded woman's face convulsed in pain. One long-nailed hand clutched her stomach, and for a moment, she looked much shorter, her hair brown, her eyes hazel. Hope rose in me. Mom was somewhere in there.... I hadn't banished her.

"You're hurting my mother," I said. "*You let her go.*"

She lifted her head, her skin white and stretched with agony, the tendons in her neck straining against the force of the din around her. Her eyes were pools of yellow-green, sparking for a moment like the bolts from the lightning tree. "I love you, my own little cub," she said. "I never stopped. But I will do as you ask. We will meet again. Look for me, where the veil is thin. I will find you...."

Like a trick of the light, the air around her buckled. She collapsed as if all her bones had vanished. The horrible sound coming from Morfael and Caleb cut off, as if a "stop" button had been pressed.

A foggy weakness clouded my vision, and I staggered and fell back against the wall. Richard lunged toward my mother, who lay where she'd fallen, now a sickly version of her true self. Morfael and Raynard helped him get her off the floor and onto the couch while Caleb came over, picked me up as if I weighed nothing, and carried me to the cushioned window seat. I didn't want to lie down, but when I tried to remain sitting, blackness closed in. I woke up to find Caleb adjusting the pillow under my head, his anxious face frowning down at me.

"Wow," I said, my voice coming out thinner than normal. "That was some crazy noise you made."

"How do you feel?" he asked.

"Did I faint?" When he nodded, I managed a grin. "Fainting sucks."

"Your mom's okay. Right, Raynard?"

I turned my head to see Raynard checking Mom's pulse while Richard kissed her forehead. "Whatever had her is gone," Raynard said. "But it would be better if this didn't happen to her again."

"Raynard," I said. "Master of understatement."

"She will heal with rest," said Morfael, walking over to look down at me. "As will you."

"What was that sound?" I asked. "It was like eight hundred fingernails on a chalkboard."

"Banishment tone," said Caleb. "You need more than one caller to do it. It's supposed to be so horrific to denizens of Othersphere that they leave this world and never return."

"It's pretty sickening for the rest of us too," I said. "But it got rid of her, so thank you."

Caleb and Morfael exchanged a look, but said nothing.

"It wasn't sickening for me," Richard said, straightening up to look at me. "It was loud, but to me it sounded kind of reassuring."

A wind blew through me. "But . . ." I shivered and looked up at all of them as Caleb drew a blanket over me.

"The sound is unbearable only to those who come from Othersphere," said Morfael. "We refined it to have its greatest effect on her, but you were also affected."

"I . . ." The world got blurry, and I realized my eyes were filling with tears. "I'm from Othersphere?" All the recent events circled in on me like a hovering vulture finally coming to land on a kill. That mom-creature had said she loved me, that I was her lost little cub. She looked just like me, and she was from Othersphere, which meant . . .

"In 1908, a meteor or comet exploded over Tunguska, Siberia, killing trees for hundreds of miles around and ripping a hole in the veil between worlds," said Morfael. "Fifteen years ago, that is where I found you."

I lay there, not speaking. Caleb sat down and took my hand. "So whoever that was just now is probably somehow related to you."

"My mother," I said, though my lips felt numb. It felt horribly true as I said the words. "That was my biological mother."

Caleb took a deep breath. "Maybe."

"You saw her!" I half sat up, but the room began spinning, so I fell back down. "You heard what she said." I stared up at Morfael. "She knew you!"

"She thinks I should have sent you back to her," Morfael said. "She is wrong."

"But . . . but why would she think that?" The questions were crowding my mind, too many to choose from. "Who are you?"

"They know of me in many worlds," he said. "I am not of them, but I may walk between them. I am a shadow walker."

Caleb nodded. "You are not from here."

Morfael slowly shook his head.

"And you're not from Othersphere either?" I asked.

He smiled a little and shook his head again. A small, stunned silence hung in the air. Then Morfael said, "You need to rest now. We will talk later. Raynard"—he turned to his boyfriend, as thickset and down to earth as Morfael was thin and otherworldly—"is your room ready for Desdemona's parents?"

Raynard nodded, moving toward me. "I'll help Desdemona down to bed."

Incredibly, they were acting as if it was time to go to sleep. But my head was about to explode from what I'd just seen and learned. "But why now?" I said. "Morfael, you can't just drop a bomb like that and send me to bed! What does she, that creature, want? Will she be able to come back?"

Morfael paused at the top of the stairs, looking older than he ever had before and leaning a little more heavily on his stick. He turned, his face gray, though his eyes still held their wild opalescent sparkle. "She was able to manifest through a humdrum because your mother is closely connected to you and because she is here, where the veil is thin," he said. "Clearly this person is very powerful, so she may return, although not through your mother. I believe we have warned her away from trying that avenue again, but your mother should go back to her home tomorrow and stay away from areas where the veil is thin."

"She said..." My mouth was very dry. "She said she would find a way to bring me back. To Othersphere. Can she do that?"

"She thrust you through the veil once before," said Morfael, and walked down the stairs.

# CHAPTER 16

"Dez?"

I was rocking in a tiny rowboat on a dark sea. Above, a full moon hovered too close, craters black and unfamiliar, its reflection in the ocean somehow larger than the moon itself. I tried to steady the craft, but the waves kept washing me from side to side. All around the air was glowing, pressing in on me. Any second I'd lose my balance, fall in, and drown.

"Dez, wake up!"

I opened my eyes to see Arnaldo standing over me, thick eyebrows drawn together in concern. I sat up too fast, and my head spun.

"What is it?" I said. "What's wrong?"

"Your mom," he said. "They're taking her to the hospital."

"What? What happened?" I threw back the blankets, shoved my feet into the stupid terry-cloth slippers left over from the Naiad Hotel, and grabbed for a shirt and jeans.

Arnaldo stepped back to let me get dressed, not even blinking at me in my underwear. Shifter kids took that kind of thing in stride.

"Is she worse?" I was walking toward the door even as I zipped up my jeans.

"I don't think so. But she's not better either." He followed me as I broke into a run. "They're getting her into the SUV now. She won't wake up."

I took the stairs two at a time, and ran without a glance past the other kids clustered in the kitchen and out the front door toward the garage. There I saw Caleb helping Richard gingerly lay my mother down in the backseat of the SUV. Raynard was already climbing into the driver's side as Morfael watched, leaning on his staff.

"What's going on?" I ran up as Caleb stepped back. "Why didn't you get me?"

Richard was leaning half in the car, adjusting a pillow under Mom's head. Her eyes were closed, dark rings like bruises shadowed under them. Her skin was so pale and thin I could see the tiny veins and capillaries threading over her forehead and nose. She was wrapped in a large gray blanket, like a mummy, but she looked more like a child, so tiny and vulnerable.

"We sent Arnaldo to get you," he said. "About five minutes ago I tried to wake her, and when I couldn't, we decided to take her to a hospital in Vegas."

"I'll sit with her," I said. "I can put her head in my lap."

"If you're sure you can get away," Richard said. His voice was mild, but he wasn't looking me in the eye.

I looked down at the muddied snow at my feet. An arctic breeze lifted my hair off my neck. "Don't you want me to come with you?"

"She's going to be okay," he said. "At least I think so, from what Morfael says. And I know you have things you need to do around here."

"Nothing's more important than Mom." I tucked my

hands into my armpits and turned to Morfael. "What's wrong? Why won't she wake up?"

"Your mother's body is in excellent health," Morfael said. "And the entity which possessed her is gone. But some part of her consciousness has not yet returned from Othersphere. I believe that if she is taken to an area where the veil is thicker, she will return to herself."

"Then why take her to the hospital?" I looked back and forth between Morfael and Richard. "If she's going to get better as soon as she's out of this area, just take her home."

"We don't know how long her return will take," Morfael said. "Probably not more than an hour or two, but she hasn't eaten or had anything to drink in awhile, so it's best she get fluids and other sustenance with an IV until she can eat and drink on her own."

"And the sooner the better," Richard said. "I didn't want to wait for you to get ready and eat breakfast. I'm sorry."

"No, no, I'm sorry. I don't need to eat. I don't need anything else. I'm coming with you."

"Okay," Richard said, his face softening. "Good."

"Dez?" I looked over to see Amaris walking up warily, as if unsure of her welcome. "If you're going, do you want my coat?"

"Yeah, thanks." I walked over to her as she shed the heavy coat she had thrown over her clothes. I was jittery, but not just from the cold. I couldn't quite grasp that we were on our way to the hospital again with my mother.

Amaris handed me the coat, getting her mouth close to my ear, and said quietly, "Lazar is on vid conference downstairs on the computer right now. What do you want me to tell him?"

Oh, God. *Of course he's calling now.* I closed my eyes. *Focus.* "Does he have any news?"

Amaris helped my left arm find the coat sleeve. "He says he does. Big news. I don't know what it is yet, but he says we need to go in tonight."

I glanced over my shoulder at Caleb. He wore the same closed expression and stood too far away to hear us. "Tonight? Why?"

Amaris shook her head, moving around to help me with the coat's zipper. "I haven't had a chance to ask him yet. I ran up here to grab you before you left. He says he might not be able to find a time he can talk to us again. Do you think you'll be able to get back here tonight?"

"I don't know."

Richard had finished settling Mom in the back cab, and had one leg up on the step into the passenger's side of the truck. "Are you coming or not?" he said.

"He has an idea of what the particle accelerator is for," Amaris said. "And it might be online as early as tomorrow." She looked up at me. "You should go with your mom. We can handle this. Caleb could talk to Lazar."

I took a deep breath to stay calm. Any second now Lazar could be forced to hang up the call in order not to be found out. If I missed this chance, we might never be able to stop Ximon. "No. You know that would never work."

Amaris stamped her feet in the cold, eyes darting from me to Richard and back again. "Well, no. But if you need to go . . ."

I turned to Richard. "I'll be right there."

"What do I tell Lazar?" Amaris asked in a very low tone. "Maybe he can try to call us back later?"

I glanced over at Caleb, still far enough away not to hear me, dark eyes staring out at the snow-dusted forest. I made sure to keep my voice very low. "Tell Lazar where I'm going, and why. Tell him to meet me there, if he can."

"Oh!" Amaris's eyes popped wide and shot over toward Caleb before she tamped down her expression. "Just Lazar?"

"Yes," I said. "No one else. If he can't get there, we'll have to find a way to text him or e-mail him when I'm available to talk."

"Dez!" Richard stamped his feet to stay warm. "Get in the car!" Then he opened the passenger door and climbed in.

"I have to go." I squeezed Amaris's arm. "Tell him I'm sorry."

"He'll understand," she said.

I tried to smile and moved to the car. Caleb stepped over unexpectedly and opened the back door for me. "Thanks," I said.

He leaned in, helping to arrange my sleeping mother so that I could get in the car and settle her head on my lap. "Let me come with you," he said, his velvet voice like a steady, supportive wall.

I jerked my gaze up to his face in surprise. His brow was furrowed, his black eyes warm and worried. "No," I said. "It's okay. But thanks."

"I can huddle in the very back," he said. "I promise not to get in the way. You know how fond I am of your mother, and if I can be of any help . . ."

"That would mean so much to her," I said, putting my hand on the black wool covering his arm. *I wish you could come with me. I need you now.*

But if Lazar managed to find me at the hospital, having Caleb there would probably lead to a fistfight, or worse. I wanted him there more than anyone, but getting the information from Lazar about the collider was more important. "And it means the world to me that you offered. Really. But we'll be okay."

He looked thoughtful, but obediently stepped back and shut my car door. I rolled down the window. "I'll use Richard's phone to call and let you know once we're settled down there," I said. "You make sure everyone here stays safe."

He nodded. Behind him, Amaris was already running back toward the school to tell Lazar what was happening. Would my going to the hospital with my mother jeopardize all my plans to stop Ximon's mysterious plot? Maybe. But I couldn't bear to do anything else.

As Raynard backed the SUV up and turned around, I took

one last look back to see Morfael standing there looking as alien and expressive as a Giacometti statue. *But then he really is an alien.* Caleb had his arms crossed, and his black eyes were skeptical.

It took nearly as long to check Mom into a room at the hospital as it had to get there, even though Richard had called ahead. By early morning, the neurologist was once again recommending antiseizure medication, and couldn't understand our reluctance to agree. Otherwise, he said her brain function looked normal, and that once she was better hydrated, there was no reason to think she wouldn't wake up. But time would tell.

*Too bad there's no such thing as anti-shadow medication.*

Sitting in a hard chair in our half of the puke-tan hospital room, I glanced over at Richard, not saying those words, but seeing the same thought in his tired eyes. Mom was breathing steadily and quietly, the IV in her left arm dripping in the silence. I kept having to fight the urge to crawl into the bed and hold her close, as if somehow the life in my body could pass into hers. Richard, sitting opposite me holding Mom's small right hand, probably felt the same.

"Why don't you go get us both some coffee, and maybe get yourself a sandwich," he said, reaching into his pocket and pulling twenty dollars out of his wallet. "Don't worry, I won't leave her."

I really wanted to be there when Mom woke up, but I was starving. And Richard looked like he could use the caffeine. "Okay." I took the money and headed for the door. "I won't be long."

My footsteps bounced off the long walls of the hallway outside. The nurses and aides all wore scrubs in happy colors like pink or cheerful prints of tiny roses or baby toys. But under the fluorescent lights and set against drab beige walls and even drabber beige floors, all the bright colors were incongruous and jarring.

In the clatter of the cafeteria, I ignored the damp tuna sandwiches and wilting salads, and found a decent-looking bowl of hummus and side of pita bread, shoved them in a bag, grabbed two bottles of water and two large coffees, and headed back toward Mom's room. As I passed our nurse's station, the reed-thin aide named Mauricio, who'd helped us settle Mom in, looked up from his computer screen as I passed by and said, "Did he find you?"

I halted and turned, and he must have seen puzzlement on my face, because he explained, "A tall young man was looking for you." His gaze drifted past me, focusing on something down the hall. "Oh, there he is."

Heart leaping, I whirled to see a long lean form with tousled blond hair and a brown leather jacket thrown over his white pants walking toward me. Our eyes met, and relief washed over me.

"Thanks," I said to Mauricio.

He winked at me and shot a look back at Lazar. "Cute. And considerate."

Lazar had reached me, and I saw he was holding a small bouquet of pink and white cosmos down by his side.

"You made it," I said.

A smile broke over his face like dawn over a winter lake. "Thank God," he said, and his voice made it sound like an actual prayer. "It wasn't easy, but I made sure to check my clothes for tracking devices this time." His wide brown eyes and butter-gold hair were shining, but the bruises on his jaw and cheekbone had darkened into black and purple, standing out like splotches of dark paint on a pale canvas.

"Thanks for coming," I said over the too-loud patter of my heart. My eyes drifted down to the flowers.

"For your mom," he said, his voice tentative, his long fingers around the flower stems curling and uncurling. "A guy was selling them outside the hospital parking lot."

"Smart location for a florist," I said. "That's very nice of you."

His brown eyes studied me. "How is she?"

"The doctors think she'll be fine. Let me just check on her and give this to Richard." I held up the coffee, and he followed me as I moved down the hall to our room. When I walked in, he hung back. I gestured to him. "It's okay. Come in for a second."

Richard looked up, eyes going gratefully first to the cup of coffee in my hand, and then darting over warily to Lazar in the doorway.

"This is Lazar," I said, handing Richard the Styrofoam cup. "Lazar, this is my stepfather, Richard."

Lazar's eyes moved from my mother's tiny form huddled under the blankets on the bed to Richard's solid bulk in the chair beside her. Recognition sparked in his face before he smoothed it away, and I remembered with sudden dismay that Lazar had led the group of objurers who'd tried to kidnap my mother and Richard not that long ago. But Lazar had been wearing a face mask, and Richard had been quickly sedated. So Richard showed only signs of curiosity as he stood up.

Lazar shook Richard's hand. "Nice to meet you, sir. These are for your wife." He held out the flowers. "Oh, and here's something to put them in." His other hand drew out a small vase from his jacket pocket.

"Thank you," said Richard. "That's very thoughtful."

Lazar walked over to the sink in the room, running water into the vase and adding the flowers, while I handed creamer and a sugar packet to Richard and kissed Mom on the forehead. I could hear how steady and strong her heartbeat was, and smell the warmth of her skin. She was getting better. But the room still held the uneasy quiet that comes with waiting.

"Her color looks good," I said. My words felt awkward and weighty, when I had meant them to be light.

"Mmm," Richard said through his coffee cup. "I think the fluids are working."

"Here." Lazar's brown boots clicked over the tile as he walked over and handed me the flowers.

"Thanks." I set them down on the table next to Mom's bed.

"They're cheerful," Richard said. "Thank you."

Lazar nodded, keeping very still and looking down uncomfortably.

"Okay, so I just need to have a quick word with Lazar," I said. It sounded clumsy even to my ears. "I'll be right outside in the hallway if she wakes up or anything."

Richard nodded, sipping his coffee, and Lazar and I slipped out into the hallway and then to a small alcove a few feet down, where two semi-padded chairs sat under a not-terrible painting of the desert beneath a full moon.

"God, hospitals make everything weird." I plopped down in my chair. "Here, hold this."

He obediently took my cup of coffee as I used both hands to dig open the container of hummus and tear apart the bread.

"Did Amaris try to heal your mother?" he said, sitting down in the other chair.

"No," I said through a mouthful of pita, then chewed and swallowed. "She hasn't been able to heal anyone, not even herself. Would you like some?" I offered a piece of bread.

He held up a hand as if to say "no, thanks." "I think I was the last one she healed," he said.

"Oh, right," I said. "From when I knocked you out that time in my house."

"Yes." He looked down at the cup of coffee, hands clenched around it. "When I tried to kidnap your mother and that nice man in there and shot you. I'm glad he didn't recognize me from that night. I always wondered why you let me and the others live."

I dipped a triangle of pita into the hummus. "Well, I did kill that one guy, and I'm sorry about that, but he was a threat at the time. After I knocked you unconscious, I wasn't going to rip your throat out unnecessarily. That's murder, not self-defense."

He nodded and finally met my eye. "I'm grateful. I woke up surprised to be alive. Mercy from a shifter was not what I was brought up to expect," he said. "But then you're never what I expect."

"That was only the second time I ever shifted," I said. "I had no idea what I was doing."

"I'll never forget the sight of you, this huge tiger, pure vengeance and fury. It was the most frightening thing I've ever seen."

I smiled over my pita bread. "Scared you, hunh?"

"Maybe a little." He held out the cup. "Coffee?"

"Thanks." I took it from him. My spirits were picking up. Maybe it was the food, or knowing that a plan to foil Ximon still might come together. "So. Amaris said you found out what the accelerator was built for."

"Yes, and it's even worse than I thought," he said. "I was able to read part of a hard copy file in my father's office. I didn't have time for all of it, but you were right. They have big plans for it. They think, somehow, they can use it to cut off all connection to Othersphere."

I frowned, trying to get my mind around that. "That makes no sense. Do you mean, they're going to cut themselves off from Othersphere?"

"Not just themselves—everyone." He reached into his pocket and pulled out a small notebook. "I wrote down what I read as soon as I could after, so I wouldn't forget. The file said something like, 'If experiments go as we predict, we will sever all connection between Othersphere and our world forever. Without access to this hellish place, the fiends who call themselves otherkin will never again be able to change into their demonic forms, and the so-called callers of shadow will no longer conjure forth other devils and unnatural objects. Everyone will be forced, in God's mercy, to walk the earth as our Maker intended.' Sorry." He looked up. "That's how our scientists tend to phrase things."

I still wasn't quite grasping this. It was too big, too impossible. "So they don't intend to just reverse the effects on the veil in their area," I said. "They think they can cut us all off—everywhere?"

"Exactly." Lazar flipped a page in the notebook. "I saw the phrase 'chain reaction' in there, and a lot of stuff I didn't understand about dark matter and interaction of particles between universes."

Dread clawed over my skin.

"It gets worse," he said. "The accelerator will be online tomorrow. I have access to the scientists' schedule, and they're set to gather in the main computer room at seven-thirty a.m." He looked up from his notebook, his lean face drawn. He'd probably had even less sleep than me. "If you can't make it tonight, I could try to take the accelerator off-line myself. I'm not exactly sure how to do that, but I'm pretty good with a gun." His look was grim.

I thought about it. "That's a generous offer. Not to sound coldhearted, but if you failed, and they caught you, we'd never get another chance to take them by surprise. Assuming nothing else happens with my mom, I'm going to gather our group to come in tonight."

"Generals need to be a bit coldhearted." He tore a page from the notebook. "Here's the code to get you in the front door. There's a guard in the watchtower able to see anything within three hundred yards of approach, and two guards outside the front entrance."

"When's their first shift change of the night?" I asked.

He cocked his head, as if surprised at the question. "Six p.m. The shift after that starts at two a.m."

I looked up at the ceiling, calculating. "Then we should try to get there around one in the morning or so, just before shift change when they are most tired and most eager to get to bed, and when everyone else is dead asleep. Once we get inside the front door, where do we go?"

He was looking at me, impressed. But it was just the way I thought about things. "I'm starting to see why my father's so worried about you. I'll meet you in the foyer, because you'll have to pass a hand scan to get anywhere interesting after that, so you'll need me. Where will you want to go?"

"We need to download as much information as we can, then destroy their files and all relevant equipment, including the accelerator itself," I said.

"So nothing too ambitious." Lazar grinned at me.

I couldn't help smiling back, shoving away the dismay his news had brought to concentrate on what I could do about it. Taking action always made me feel better, even if the action brought its own risks. Anything was better than sitting passively by and anticipating the worst. I'd done that for years, hoping the brace would prevent spinal surgery, unable to do anything but wait. *To hell with waiting.*

There was nothing I could do to help Mom, or to make Caleb trust me again. But I could do my damnedest to stop Ximon's plan. If he succeeded, I'd never again be a tiger, never again feel the power of shadow pulsing through me. *Never see your biological mother again* . . . Was that a good thing or a bad thing? I wished I knew.

"Can you get us into the main computer room that controls the accelerator?" I asked. "And into the accelerator itself?"

"No," he said. "I don't have access. But I can access the scientists' bedrooms, and the scientists."

He was thinking ahead too. Good. "This just might work," I said.

"There are over thirty armed objurers in the compound other than myself and my father," Lazar said. "As well as four scientists. It won't be easy."

"What happened?" I asked. At his puzzled look, I went on. "Something made you realize you had to leave. I know you were talking on the phone with Amaris, that seeing her having a life outside made you think that was possible for you too. But there was something else, wasn't there?"

"My father." He looked down at the scuffed floor between

his feet, elbows on his knees, then leaned back, eyelids clamped shut, as if trying to block something out.

"Did he hurt you somehow?"

He shook his head. "No, worse than that." He opened his eyes. They were like dark saucers, staring off into space. Whatever he was seeing in his mind's eye wasn't pretty. "He told me that after the experiments are done, assuming they're successful, the Tribunal will let go of the workers and scientists who built the accelerator, since they won't be needed anymore. But he was afraid that once they got out in the world, they might reveal where they'd been, and what they'd done, and who had led them. So he told me they would be my responsibility. It would be up to me to release them . . . to God."

"All of them?" I put my food down, no longer hungry. "He wants you to kill all of them?"

He nodded. "That's over a dozen people, Dez. Father would give me the signal, and then I was supposed to shoot them as they slept."

"My God," I said.

"He said that would be the most humane way to do it—so they didn't feel any fear or pain. That's my father's version of mercy." Lazar's tone was lacerating in its bitterness. "A bullet in the head while you sleep."

"Did you consider maybe telling them about your father's plan?" I asked gently. "It might stop the accelerator from going online at all. They might even sabotage it for you."

"They'd never believe me," he said. "I thought about it a lot. But they only respect me because I'm Ximon's son. He's their pathway to God, and if I spoke against him, they'd tear me to pieces."

"Then, in a way, we'll be doing some of them a favor by going in," I said. "Though, they'll probably never know it."

"That's another reason I had to get you to believe me," he said.

I hesitated, then said: "But still, people you know and care about . . . your father, they could get hurt."

"I know." He folded his hands together, thinking. "Sometimes I hope Father does get hurt. Then I think about what you said to me, that night you rescued your bear-shifter friend and took Amaris away. Do you remember what you said?"

I shrugged. "Just—that you could come with us, I think. I meant it."

"You also said: 'You don't have to follow your father. You can be your own man, a better man.' " With a sudden, restless move, he got to his feet and paced to the far wall and back. "It didn't sink in right away. I was too confused, I guess. But after a few days without Amaris, I realized that she'd gotten what she always wanted—a way out. I knew my mother would be happy she'd gotten away from marriage to that awful man, and then I thought . . ." He stopped, swallowing hard as his eyes got very bright.

I put down the food and my coffee. "Your mother loved you too, Lazar. She would have wanted you to be happy too."

He inhaled deeply, steadying himself. "Until then, I didn't think I deserved it. And now, seeing your mom here . . . sorry, but seeing her being so well tended, I can't help wondering what life would have been like if we'd gotten my mother the help she needed." His voice caught as he stuffed down another surge of emotion. "She might have lived."

Before I knew it, I was standing in front of him, taking his hands in both of mine, gripping them tightly. "You were a child in the hands of a madman," I said. "Forgive yourself. And remember that you don't have to be like him. Now that you're older, you can fight him, stop him."

"Or die trying," he said, his voice very low. His fingers, a bit cold in the over-air-conditioned hospital, curled around mine.

"What a touching scene."

It was Caleb's voice, silky and insidious.

I dropped Lazar's hands, a cold sweat forming suddenly between my shoulder blades. Caleb stood not ten feet away, leaning one shoulder comfortably against the beige wall, as if he'd been there, watching us, forever. His black eyes were narrowed at me in a venomous look I'd only ever seen when he was dealing with Lazar. He must have overheard everything these last few minutes. He had seen me take Lazar's hands.

"Caleb . . ." I started to say.

He sauntered forward, ignoring me, coming to stand before his brother. "So glad to see you're mending fences, bro. When's my turn to get the 'forgive me' speech?"

Lazar didn't back away as Caleb approached, the bare emotion in his eyes now replaced with a watchful glint. For a moment, the two half-brothers stood face-to-face, the same height and build, the same carved cheekbones and expressive lips, light and dark, but so alike.

"A month ago you were trying to kill us," Caleb went on. His voice, normally so low and soothing, now cut like a knife. "And now you want to help us. Tell me, Lazar. Why are we so lucky?"

Lazar took a moment to respond, as if trying to keep his reaction under control. "I'm the lucky one," he said. "I have a chance to start to make up for some of the things I've done."

"Don't con a conman." Caleb leaned into him, their faces close. "This is a trap and you know it."

Lazar didn't flinch. "Dez knows the risks," he said. "All I know is that I don't want to live this way anymore."

"No," said Caleb. "That's not the only reason you're doing this. I know you too well. And men have done stranger things to try to impress a girl."

"Oh, come on," I said.

But both of them were ignoring me now. Lazar raised his eyebrows. "Which one is it, *bro*? Am I laying a trap for the otherkin or trying to steal your girl?"

Caleb's dark eyes were derisive. "Why not both? One will make you Daddy's favorite, and the other will give you the illusion you're a man."

Lazar's fists clenched, and his chin went down, a sign he was ready to fight. Caleb, too, was coiled like a panther about to spring. I was starting to get angry—at both of them. The last thing we needed was for them to start another brawl, right outside my mother's hospital room.

"Nobody's *stealing me*." I said, shoving my way between them as much as I could. "I'm not a candy bar."

I forced them both back a few inches. Lazar's eyes remained fixed on Caleb's. "Dez changed my life," Lazar said. "The same way she changed yours, and Amaris's. By thinking outside the box and showing me life was possible outside. Get over it, Caleb. You're not the center of the universe— hers or anyone else's."

"I don't need to be," said Caleb, pressing forward toward Lazar. I could feel the violence inside him stirring. "You're the one who's taking over her life."

"That's enough!" I placed a hand on each of their chests, and shoved them both back. "You're both being ridiculous."

Even in my human form, I was a lot stronger than I looked. They both reeled back two steps, giving us all some breathing room. But the look on Caleb's face made my stomach clench. *Does he hate me that much now?*

"Now I see why you didn't want me to come with you." His tone was mocking. "Lazar volunteered first."

"It's the only chance I had to talk to him," I said. "And I knew you'd mess it up if you came, like you're doing now."

"Don't worry, Dez," Lazar said. "Not even Caleb can stop me from helping you."

"So noble," said Caleb. "Tell me, Lazar, whose mother will you kill tonight?"

Lazar went white to the lips. I almost put my hand on his arm, but stopped myself in time. Caleb hated Lazar for killing Caleb's own mother, Elisa. He had no idea that years earlier Ximon had forced Lazar to pull the trigger on his own mother. Caleb's words cut far deeper than he knew. My promise not to tell anyone that truth was making life tougher for me every day.

Caleb paused, assessing us. "No smart-ass comeback for that one, I see. Maybe you have formed the remnants of a conscience, or maybe you just don't want Dez to see how you really feel."

"Caleb," I said, forcing my voice to a reasonable tone, "Lazar is risking his life for us."

"And you are risking us all," he said.

"I'd better go." Lazar's voice sounded slightly strangled, as if speaking at all was grueling. "I'll be waiting for you at one a.m., Dez."

I blinked, forcing myself not to take his arm or say something too reassuring or too kind. Anything might set Caleb off now. "Good. Contact Amaris if anything goes wrong. But even if nobody else will help us, she and I will be there at one a.m. tonight."

He gave a short nod, taking in my face with one last lingering glance. "I'll be waiting."

He left, boots clicking farther and farther down the corridor. Caleb stood stock-still, waiting till the sound died away and Lazar disappeared around a corner.

"I needed to talk to him," I said. Anger simmered inside me. "And I knew if I told you about it, or let you come with me, that *this* would happen."

"What would happen?" he asked, eyes sparking. "Someone might confront you with the truth? Yes, how *dare* I do that?"

"Good God, Caleb! There are more important things here than your ego. You could have ruined everything! If Lazar wasn't so resolute, so certain this is what he wants, you could have turned him back to Ximon and ruined any chance we had to stop him."

"My ego?" He took an exaggerated step back, tucking in his chin and looking at me through narrowed eyes. "So the fact that you've lied and lied and lied to me is a problem because of my *ego*? Bullshit."

I swallowed. "No. I know. That's a bad pattern," I said. "We've been at odds about Lazar, but I was hoping we could get past that."

He squinted, his face hard. "So, from now on, you'll keep me in the loop?"

"Yes, I promise!" I held out both hands, spreading them open. "I never meant any of this to hurt you. And if I've mistreated you or lied to you about stuff . . ."

"If?" Both of his black eyebrows lifted with devastating mockery.

"It won't happen again," I said. "I swear to you. . . ."

"You won't lie to me from now on, right?" The sarcasm in his voice cut through all my defenses, into my heart.

"Caleb . . ." I didn't know what to say. He was right, and yet he was so wrong.

"Right." He took two steps down the hall, and then turned back to me, stuffing both hands in the pockets of his black coat. "I'll be back at the school, along with everyone else you haven't been talking to. And from now on, that's how you should think of me. As just another anonymous soldier for you to use in your war. Because I can't trust you anymore. And I won't be with someone I can't trust."

Then he was walking down the hallway, his back stiff and straight. He didn't look back.

# CHAPTER 17

I didn't allow myself to cry for long. After the sobs ebbed, I found my way into the empty, echoing bathroom, put my hair in a ponytail, and splashed cold water on my face. I looked pale and haggard, and felt even worse. The emptiness inside me felt bottomless. I was like a summerhouse abandoned in the fall, after all the furniture is put in storage and the windows locked for winter.

I stared at myself in the mirror and forced myself to think about the future. Even a future without Caleb at my side. Because tonight, if everything went as planned, we would stop the Tribunal's most destructive plan yet, or die trying. That's what mattered now. The issues between me and Caleb would have to wait.

I made my way quietly back into Mom's hospital room and handed Richard one of the bottles of water.

He took it from me, searching my face. "Brothers fight," he said. "Especially if they both like the same girl."

My face got hot. "I'm sorry if you overheard that."

"Well, I don't claim to understand it all," he said. "But don't let them take over your life. Do what you need to do for yourself."

"Thanks, Richard," I said, my voice small. "You almost sounded like Mom there for a second."

As if on cue, Mom groaned and turned her head from side to side. My heart jumped as Richard grabbed her hand. "Caroline?"

I circled around the bed to take her other hand. "Mom?"

Mom licked her lips; then her eyelids fluttered open, hazel irises moving back and forth between us. "Hi," she said. It was almost a question.

My throat got tight as Richard brought her hand to his lips. "Hi, sweetheart."

Within the hour the neurologist pronounced her on the road to recovery, and told us she could go home in the morning. I used Richard's phone to text that information back to November, who could tell everyone, and to call Raynard, who had been out running errands in the SUV, to see if he could take me back to the school. Until he showed up, I sat with Mom, who lay there, quiet and quizzical, as we told her what had happened.

She remembered nothing, including the horrible thing I'd said to her just before her transformation. I was so grateful for that, I laid my head down on the edge of her bed and breathed a prayer to the Moon, or the universe, or to the Othersphere. It didn't matter whom. I was thankful.

"You're doing something dangerous tonight, aren't you?" Mom said when I was getting ready to go.

"Probably," I said, leaning over to kiss her forehead. "I love you, Mom."

She let go of Richard's hand to put her own on my cheek, pulling me in close to her. "I love you too," she said. "And I'm not going to say good-bye. I'm also not going to tell you not to do whatever it is. I know how stubborn you are. But I am going to tell you what I always tell you."

I nodded. "Trust yourself."

"Exactly." She pushed my cheek to make me look her right in the eye. "You're going to make mistakes, Desdemona. Everyone does. But you have to trust yourself to know you'll make it through them and come out wiser than before."

"I will," I said. Her words made a kind of sense, but I was in too much turmoil to ponder them. "I'll call Richard in the morning and come see you."

"We'll be home. Aren't you worried about the Tribunal following you to our new house?" she asked.

"After tonight, we won't have to worry about the Tribunal in this area again," I said. "One way or another."

I found everyone outside at the fire pit, wearing thick coats and huddled around a roaring blaze. They were sipping hot cocoa and passing around a Tupperware container full of cold slices of Raynard's homemade pizza. The air smelled like both fire and snow, even though no flakes were falling and the last rays of afternoon sunlight still filtered through the trees. Everyone sat on the benches around the fire, except for London, who walked around anxiously, breathing on her gloveless fingers.

As I was about to join them, I heard her say, "She thinks she's better than us. I am so done with her."

"About time." That was November. "There are plenty of other rabbits in the forest to chase, Wolfie. Available rabbits."

"Shut up, 'Ember."

I fought the urge to turn and run away. I couldn't really blame them for talking about me. But if London was moving on, maybe one tiny good thing could come out of this.

"She knew you guys wouldn't support her," Arnaldo said. "I mean, if these plans for the particle collider are real . . ."

"We should give those plans to the Council," Siku said.

"Yeah, let them do the fighting," said London. "They're the grown-ups."

I pushed the door open and walked out into the sharp air toward them. London glared, her intense aquamarine eyes radiating cold resentment. She'd arrayed her nose rings all in one nostril and painted her fingernails black, her version of war paint. She turned on her heel and walked to the edge of the patio, where the flagstones met brown grass, staring out at the snowy wood with her back to us all.

Amaris moved a bit closer to Arnaldo to give me enough room on the bench to sit down. I kept my head down and didn't look at Caleb, who sat on the opposite side of the fire pit, long black coat buttoned up to his throat. The flames licked upwards between us, and the air shimmered.

"Good news," Arnaldo said, leaning over to me. "My dad's been sentenced to probation because he agreed to go into outpatient rehab and anger management classes."

"That's great!" Hope pushed past my sadness and trepidation for a moment, heat from the fire edging back the cold. Arnaldo was looking much happier, and speaking to me as if nothing bad had happened between us. "Did you get that lawyer you talked about?"

He nodded. "I talked to him on the phone. Apparently, the hawk-shifter on the Council went down and talked to Dad himself. Persuaded him to get help."

"The hawk-shifter on the Council went down?" I pictured the man's guarded face from that recent video conference call, the clever hooded eyes and how he'd stood against me from the start. "Wow. He hates my guts, but I guess he's smart enough not to let that get in the way of helping someone he represents. Any word on your brothers?"

"The lawyer thinks I can get custody of them, and we can all live in our old house. There's some kind of program that will help us out financially for awhile." His long face brightened. "I am an adult to the humdrums, and they try to keep families together if they can."

"That's wonderful!" I got up and hugged him. I couldn't help myself.

He squeezed me back. "Well, we'll see."

"We're all keeping our paws crossed," said November.

"It'll work out," said Siku.

Amaris nodded, and quiet took over as we all stared into the flames. I remained standing, girding myself for what I had to do next.

"So I need to talk to you guys about the Tribunal," I said.

"Amaris already told us about Lazar," November said, her breath frosting as she spoke.

"I figured the sooner they knew what was going on, the better," Amaris said.

"And maybe better we hear it from Amaris," said Siku. "Since most of us are pretty angry with you."

Leave it to Siku to say out loud exactly what everyone was thinking.

"Why'd you go rogue, Stripes?" November hunched close to Siku's warm bulk. "What are we, stale gumdrops?"

"I'm sorry," I said. "I don't blame you for being mad. But you all hate Lazar so much, I didn't think you'd go along with what I wanted to do unless I got the plans from him and proved we could trust him."

"Still no guarantee of that," Caleb said shortly, his face a blank behind the fire.

"Well, he's going to meet us and help us get into the accelerator tonight," I said. "He's willing to trust a bunch of people who hate him. If he makes one wrong move, you can jump on him. And then you can all tell me how wrong I was."

"How wrong we both are. Except we're not," said Amaris.

I flashed her a grateful look. "Also, I found out tonight that after his plan is successful, Ximon plans to have all of the extra laborers and scientists working there killed, to keep them quiet. He told Lazar he would have to murder them all in their sleep."

"Whoa," said Arnaldo.

"That's messed up," said Siku.

"So that's why he needs our help so desperately!" Amaris stood up. "I had no idea." She sat back down, shaking her head. Caleb put his hand on her arm, and she looked at him. "How can such a man be our father?"

"So Lazar's telling Dez secrets he doesn't even tell Amaris, hunh?" November made a *tsk*ing noise. "You'd better watch your back, Caleb."

Caleb didn't answer, but his eyes shot over to me, then settled back to stare at the fire.

"What, exactly, is Ximon planning to do with this accelerator?" Arnaldo asked. "And how does this tie into their taking DNA from all of us?"

"If you don't know, how the heck are we morons going to figure that out?" said November.

Now was the time to tell them. I just hoped I could convey how much danger the otherkin were facing. "Lazar found out a few things and just met me at the hospital to let me know," I said. "The Tribunal scientists think they can cut off access to Othersphere, all over the world."

Everyone stirred as I said this, exchanging disturbed glances. I went on. "He's not exactly sure how it works, or how our DNA ties into it. But the collider will be online tomorrow. The scientists meet at seven-thirty a.m., so we have to stop it before then. Then we download everything we can and destroy the files."

"Holy shit!" said November.

Siku took a bite of pizza, chewing thoughtfully. "How can they do that? Stop us all from shifting?"

"And Caleb from calling forth from shadow, and me from healing." Amaris's voice was laced with anger. "Not that I can heal anymore, but that's still none of their business!"

"That can't be right," said November. "Because they'd stop their own ability to push our animal forms back to Othersphere too!"

"We wouldn't have any animal forms," I said. "Don't you see? All of us would be humdrums, so the Tribunal's objurers won't need to have special powers. They will finally have achieved their ultimate objective and rid the world of otherkin. The report talked about forcing us all to walk the earth 'as our Maker intended.' They won't have to fight us anymore, because to them we'll stop being demons."

Amaris was nodding. "Exactly. To my father, this is merciful."

November snorted. "Merciful, my ass."

"Yeah," said London. "It'll make it easier for him to kill us all, you mean."

Arnaldo frowned in concentration, as if doing calculus in his head. "Einstein called it 'spooky action at a distance' when quantum particles interact across vast distances with seemingly no connection. So the Tribunal's theory must be that we're connected to Othersphere via quantum teleportation. That makes sense. But I don't see how the particle collider could cut off that connection. Unless they've discovered the exact nature of dark matter. . . ."

"Spooky action at a distance?" November's thin eyebrows climbed upward. "Sounds like a horror movie shot with the camera too far away."

"The point is that they think they've figured it out," I said. "And they're going to try to do it tomorrow. They might be wrong—I don't know. But we can't let them try. If they're right, everything we've fought for, everything we are, changes completely."

Caleb stood up, his face set in challenge. "So you want the seven of us to just walk into the Tribunal's armed, top-secret facility and destroy miles of high-tech equipment stored hundreds of feet underground." He snapped his fingers. "Just like that."

"We have the plans to the facility and a man on the inside," I said. "Lazar."

Caleb uttered a short, derisive laugh and then said no more.

"But why does it have to be us?" Siku licked his fingers clean, and then held his large hands out toward the fire. "We should tell the Council and let them do it."

November was nodding. "Imagine how cool a whole army of bear-shifters would be. They'd take care of the stupid Tribunal in a hurry."

Before I could argue, a voice drifted in from farther away.

"The Council will never believe us."

We all turned to London, still standing at the edge of the flagstones of the patio, almost in the forest. Between the curtains of her two-tone hair, her cheeks were spotted pink from the cold. She looked pissed off, and her voice was thick with reluctance, as if she spoke against her own better judgment. "The Council already told Morfael to kick Dez out of school. If we go to them now with a plan of hers based on information from Lazar, a member of the Tribunal, they'll banish all of us and tell our parents to lock us up and swallow the keys."

She walked toward us, blue eyes glowing. "Well, tough shit. I won't become a humdrum. If we tell the Council now, we'll never get a chance to stop Ximon." Her voice got louder, more resolved. "I'm a wolf-shifter, and no one's going to take that away from me."

Siku grunted thoughtfully. Next to him, November stirred. "But you were the angriest of all of us."

"Yeah, I'm pissed that Dez didn't tell us what she was doing," London said. "I'm going to be pissed off for awhile. But this isn't about her." She took a deep breath and exhaled it in a cloud into the frosty air. "They don't get to decide who I am. Nobody does that but me."

"Amen," said Amaris, and her voice reminded me of Lazar's in prayer.

Everyone turned and looked at me. With London's pro-
nouncement, something had clicked into place. I closed my
eyes for a moment in a tiny wordless prayer of thanks of my
own. A silent, crushing weight I hadn't wanted to acknowl-
edge lifted and I could breathe again. My friends had come
through for me again. Now a jittery anticipation was taking
me over. We were going to do this, and soon.

I opened my eyes. "Okay," I said. "We need to leave here
by ten o'clock tonight, so we can drive there, do some reconnaissance of the area, and take out the guard they have in a
watchtower and two others directly outside the entrance by
one a.m. Lazar gave us the code and will meet us inside at
that time. From there, we find a scientist and use him or her
to get past the hand scanners and into the main computer
room."

"Dibs on the guard in the watchtower," said Arnaldo,
grinning.

"Everyone should study the plans we got from Lazar," I
said. "I'll make some copies."

"What if they catch him before we get there?" Amaris said,
her voice tight. "He risked a lot meeting you at the hospital.
What if they see him sneaking back in?"

"They could be expecting us." Caleb stood up, unnerv-
ingly tall and forbidding in his long black coat with the wind
ruffling his unruly dark hair. The flames sparked in the
depths of his eyes.

"We still have to go," said London.

"If he's not waiting for us behind the first locked door,
we'll know something has gone terribly wrong," I said. "Be
ready to adjust the plan."

"But how will we get past all the high-tech locks if he can't
walk us through?" Amaris shook her head. "November's
good at picking locks with keys, but these are different. We
need Lazar."

I shot a knowing look at Caleb to find him looking right
back at me. Recognition flashed between us. The Shadow

Blade could cut through any metal. Unless the locks were made of wood, we could get through them. Then, as if we both remembered the state of things between us at exactly the same moment, we looked away.

"We do need Lazar," I said. "But if worse comes to worst, I can get us through the locks. Oh, and one other thing."

They were all getting to their feet or moving toward the door back into the school. But I had to tell them now. One more secret would break us, and that would not only ruin my plan, it would break my heart.

"You probably already suspect this after seeing what was happening to my mom last night," I said. "Or maybe Raynard or Caleb already told you."

I took a deep breath to steady myself and saw, from the corner of my eye, Caleb bow his head. He knew what I was about to say.

"Tell us what?" asked Arnaldo. "Your mom was channeling something weird, that's for sure."

"The thing that came through her was definitely from Othersphere," I said. My lips were trembling. *I could really use Caleb's steady arm around me now.* "And I'm pretty sure that thing was, or, I guess, she *is*, my biological mother."

Arnaldo gulped audibly, and Siku let out a sharp but understated "Hunh!" Amaris's hand flew up to cover her mouth, and November blinked hard a few times. Caleb looked at the snow-scuffed flagstones at his feet, his face thoughtful.

Strangely, it was London who was nodding to herself as her eyes scanned me up and down, as if everything suddenly made sense. "That explains a lot."

"Yeah," I said. "But it doesn't change anything, not really."

"That means that you're from Othersphere," Arnaldo said, voice full of wonder. "Wow."

"I think so," I said. "Yeah. Turns out I'm even weirder than I felt back in high school."

Siku looked at me, eyes filled with a reckoning. "If you're

from Othersphere, what happens to you if the Tribunal's plan works?"

Caleb looked up from the ground at him, suddenly alert. "You mean, if they actually do shut us off from shadow?" He turned to me. "Would that trap you here? Or would it . . . ?"

"Send me back there forever." I finished his sentence, as I had a million times before. Only this one sent a bone-deep chill through me. "What do you think, Arnaldo?"

"Nobody's ever come across the veil and stayed so long before. Nobody we know of anyway," he said. "There's no way to know what will happen."

"So we don't let it happen," said London. "It's simple."

I smiled at her. I couldn't help it.

Her frown dissipated, but she fought to keep a remnant of it in place. "I'm not saying that for your sake," she said.

"I know," I said. "But thanks anyway."

"There are those legends of shadow walkers," November said. "Hey, Dez, you're a shadow walker!"

"Not exactly . . ." I said, again looking over at Caleb automatically. This time he didn't return the look.

"She's like the Loch Ness Monster," Siku was saying, a slow grin breaking across his face.

"And Bigfoot," said November. "And UFOs!"

"No. Arnaldo's the Unidentified Flying Object," said Siku. "Because he flies."

November put her hands on her hips, staring up at him. "Oh, clever. That means you're the closest thing we've got to Bigfoot."

Siku crossed his eyes and held his arms out in front of himself, stiff like a zombie. "I am the Yeti!" He stiff-walked toward her, a low abominable snowman growl coming from his chest.

She giggled and ran around the fire pit. He chased her, still doing his best Frankenstein's monster imitation, and then followed her inside.

"That went better than the last time we found out some-thing new about you," said Arnaldo. He patted me on the arm and headed inside too.

Amaris fell in next to London. "What's that mean?"

London opened the door for her. "Oh, one day last term Dez turned into a cat instead of a tiger, and we all flipped out. Especially me. . . ."

The door clunked shut behind them. Caleb and I stood there without speaking, not looking at each other. The last rays of sunlight played across his wind-tossed hair, etching shadows under his cheekbones, and my whole being ached because I was with him but could not touch him.

"You got what you wanted," he said, his tone neutral. "But you usually do."

His night-black eyes were stormy with sparks of gold. A feather touch of cold hit my cheek, and white flakes filled the air.

"I didn't want *this*," I said, my hand tracing the distance between us.

He looked away, and then up at the cloudy sky, blinking into the snowfall. "You're lucky. The moon will be full."

"I know," I said. "It rises at midnight, just before we meet Lazar."

"Of course. You already thought of that." A reluctant smile bent his lips. "I should have known."

I caught his eye. "Are we going to be able to do this thing tonight, together?"

His gaze brushed over me, unreadable. "We have to go in and stop them, even if Lazar is lying, even if it's a trap." His square jaw hardened. "You were right. About that at least."

Then he turned and left me as the flurries descended.

# CHAPTER 18

I stood there alone for several minutes, staring out at the snowfall in the dying light of sunset. Perhaps it was the thinness of the veil, the knowledge of my deep connection to Othersphere, the pending full moon, or the coil of sadness twisting deep inside me, but I felt like I was going to jump out of my skin.

Hoping the cold of the falling flakes would calm me, I wandered down the hill from the patio, palms and face lifted toward the sky to catch whatever touch of snow I could.

A large white hare hopped in front of me about twenty feet away, and I froze. It wasn't as unnaturally enormous as the rabbit in the snowy forest Caleb had drawn from shadow for me back in Vegas, but it was quite large and a startling pure white except for the sharply black tips of its long ears.

Impulsively, I squatted down and held out my hand. The hare lifted its head, black eyes shining at me as its nose twitched inquisitively. I held my breath as it hopped toward me on back feet shaped like furry white kayaks. Then the ever-sniffing nose was touching my fingers.

"Hello," I said, keeping my voice very quiet.

The hare hopped closer, coming to huddle between my knees, as if using me as shelter from the wind. Hesitantly, I reached down and stroked its back. The fur was soft, like liquid against my skin. The hare nosed my fingers, then began grooming itself, tiny pink tongue wetting its front paws before running them over its long, translucent ears.

It had to be a dream. Had I fallen asleep and ventured back subconsciously to the time Caleb had cared enough for me to conjure an enchanted forest from shadow? I lifted my head and nearly fell over backwards as a huge red-brown elk sporting a chandelier of antlers trotted over the snow toward me, stopping just a few feet away. Its large brown eyes glinted as snowflakes decorated the rack above its head.

I stood up slowly, which didn't seem to disturb the hare, and extended my hand. The elk eyed me, decided to ignore my gesture, and then lowered its head to rip out a few pieces of drying grass still poking up through the snow.

Something crunched in the snow behind me. Almost afraid of what I might see, I twisted at the waist to find a spotted cat with a stumpy tail peeking around the trunk of a pine tree at me. It was a bobcat, with powerful haunches and white spots on the back of its ears. It took a few steps toward me, then sat down, yellow eyes aglow in the twilight, till a flutter above drew its gaze.

A chunky winged form whooshed overhead and came to rest in the branches of the tree nearest me. A great horned owl folded its wide gray wings, pointed ear tufts shaking in the breeze, and regarded me with perfectly round golden eyes.

My whole body was aglow with wonder. A music just beyond the edge of hearing connected me to each of these creatures, just as they were bound to each other, and to the grass, the trees, and the falling snow.

The rim of the sun dipped below the horizon, and the light in the sky swung from golden tangerine to fiery orange tipped with indigo and deepest purple. In a few hours, the moon would rise, and I felt deep in the roiling black center of my being that if I took one step in the right direction, I would part a curtain in the air and step into a forest greater and darker than this.

I trembled on that brink, wanting to reach out, to widen the space inside me. I knew that if I did it, all the rest of my life would fall away. And I was sorely tempted to move beyond all the pain and conflict and judgment. Was this Othersphere—this enveloping union with everything?

As night fell, a light in the window of the school flicked on, sending a white beam into the woods. The elk turned his head with weighty majesty in that direction, and the owl took flight with one silent beat of its wings. The bobcat disappeared behind a clutch of sagebrush with a flick of its abbreviated tail. Only the snowshoe hare calmly finished washing its ears before casting a beady glance up at me.

"Not yet," I said, though the thought wasn't mine. Was I speaking for the hare, for myself, or for someone . . . something else?

As if its job was done, the hare bounded off, leaving faint tracks in the snow before it vanished.

I reentered the school in a daze, my cheeks and fingers wet with melted snow. I'd glimpsed that feeling before in tiger form, but never so strongly as a human.

*But you're not human. Not even in "human" form.*

At first I barely heard, let alone paid attention to, the voices coming from the kitchen. Then I heard Siku mutter, in a more annoyed tone than I'd heard from him in ages, "I told you I'm not hungry. We don't have a lot of time before we have to go do this crazy thing."

A plastic bag rattled, as if someone were digging into it. "I know, I just wanted to talk to you real quick," said November. Her voice got low and intimate, and without my cat-shifter hearing, I never would have caught her next words. "It's important."

I paused in my progress toward the stairs down to my room, not wanting to interrupt by walking past them as they talked. But if I stayed here, I'd be eavesdropping. I looked behind me. *Should I go back outside for a few minutes?*

"Are you okay?" Siku asked, his annoyed tone vanishing to become something warmer and more intimate than I'd ever heard from him. "You've been weird lately. Distant."

I could hear fingers unwrapping something in plastic. "I know," November said. "It's because I don't know how to act around you, exactly."

"What did I do?"

I padded forward as silently as my training allowed. This was clearly a very personal conversation, and maybe I could sneak past them down the stairs.

"It's not what you did," said November. There was a tiny clatter, like a marble rolling on a floor, and I envisioned her dropping a round hard candy on the kitchen counter to play with. "It's what you haven't done. What you won't do."

"What do you mean?" Siku's bass voice dropped even lower. "I'd do anything for you."

"You would?" November's quiet delight gave me goose bumps. "I didn't know that."

"You're hard for me to read," he said. "I can't tell what you're thinking."

"Mostly I'm thinking that you're . . . you know, wonderful. The most wonderful guy in the world, really," she said.

"Yeah?" He took a heavy step. I imagined it was toward her.

"Yeah." Her voice was so small, so vulnerable. "I think I love you, Siku."

My heart swelled, and my eyes pricked with tears. She'd done it. Brave girl. And as happy as I was for her, I couldn't help remembering when Caleb had said those words to me. It was the most amazing feeling in the world. I would never feel it again.

There was a little silence, during which I forced myself not to inch forward to see what was happening, though I couldn't help straining my ears for any clue.

"Get over here," Siku said, a sly smile in his voice.

November let out a tiny, thrilled squeal, and then another kind of quiet descended. I heard clothes rustling and Siku whispering, "I love you too."

I stifled a delighted laugh and bounced gleefully on my toes. Okay, now that they were safely making out, maybe I could sneak past them. I padded as quietly as I could toward the stairs, and caught a glimpse of them in the darkened kitchen. Siku's beefy arms rendered November's tiny form nearly invisible, though I could just see her hand in his hair and one of her legs wrapped around his waist.

A floorboard squeaked beneath me, but neither of them seemed to notice. I slipped down the stairs without breaking the mood.

I found Morfael in the computer room, his long fingers poking at the keyboard with surprising speed. "Yes, Desdemona?" he said, not looking away from the monitor.

"We're going into the Tribunal compound tonight," I said. "But you probably already knew that."

He stopped typing and fixed his pale eyes on me. "Yes. You'll be taking the Shadow Blade with you, I presume."

"Yes," I said. "Of course."

"Good." He eased back toward the monitor and started typing again as he spoke. "The collider is positioned very close to where the nuclear testing took place, so the veil will be even thinner there than it is here. The urge to shift and for Caleb to use his powers as a caller—these things will be magnified. You all may find yourselves more irritable, more violent, closer in personality to your animal forms than usual. You may also see things which disconcert you."

*As if things won't be difficult enough.* "Great. Just great. I'm guessing that means my anti-technology aura will be worse than ever too."

He paused for a moment to turn his head, a faint smile creasing his thin lips. "Exactly."

*Why does he always look so pleased when he says bad things?* I wasn't quite sure how to put my next question, so I just asked. "Will you come with us? We could use a shadow walker like you."

His spare eyebrows lifted gently, but he said nothing.

"Did you know me over there, or my parents?" I asked. "Do you have any idea why I'm *here*?"

His eyes glimmered under nearly translucent lids. "You are at my school to learn what I can teach you."

"Oh, come on!" I fought to keep myself from shouting. His evasiveness was unnerving. "We're heading into an underground facility filled with objurers armed with silver. I might not come back. Don't you think it's time for me know who I am?"

"You know who you are." He resumed typing, fingers like bird beaks pecking at the keys. "I insist you come back. I'm not done with you."

"So that means 'I won't talk to you about this now, ' and 'I'm not coming with you.' " I heard myself sigh. "This isn't going to be easy, Morfael."

"No," he said. "It will test you to the utmost, but there is something else I must do."

"Now?" I didn't want to whine, but I was getting close to it.

"Yes. I must go." He finished typing with a flourish, and then stood up, all bony angles and dusty black robes. Looking at him now, it was easy to believe he wasn't from this world. "Raynard and I will take his truck and leave the SUV to all of you."

He pushed past me to the hallway. I turned, incredulous. "You're blowing me off so you two can have a date night?"

His opal irises slid over to me, and he tapped the floor with his carved staff irritably. "Your irreverence has its place," he said. "This is not one of them."

"Sorry," I muttered. "But something weird happened just now. I was outside, feeling pretty crappy, and all these animals came over to me. A hare, and an elk, a bobcat, and an owl," I said. "I felt—different. Like I was connected to them, and to everything."

"The natural world here helps link you to that feeling," he said.

"But if I were in Othersphere, would I feel that way all the time?"

He considered this. "Othersphere does not contain the blocks to the natural world that this world does, so that feeling would be more accessible to you there. But you can overcome the blocks on this side of the veil. That's part of what you must learn here."

"If you walk between worlds but don't come from any of them, where *do* you come from?" I asked, praying for once he wouldn't evade me.

He looked mildly amused. "Any other questions?"

"A million!" I said, throwing up my hands. "But go do whatever you have to do. I'm sure it's super important."

"I'm not abandoning you, Desdemona," he said. "All your life I have worked to help you, and it gratifies me to see how worthy of that you are."

My throat tightened with emotion. "Thanks," I said. "Keep being this nice and you'll start to worry me."

"What you attempt tonight will be more difficult than you imagine, in ways you cannot foresee," he said. "But there is little point in worrying."

I couldn't help a small, sad laugh. "I should've let you go while I was ahead. Wish us luck."

He shook his head very slightly. "There is no luck. I wish you learning and love."

We were a little late getting on the road because at first we couldn't find Siku and November. They finally emerged from the garage, rumpled, sweaty, and holding hands. Envy jabbed me. They'd found a couple of hours to be together alone there, the way Caleb and I had not, and now never would.

The dopey, happy looks on their faces made even London, very tense before heading off into battle, grin widely. "So, finally, you two?" she said.

"What do you mean, finally?" Siku asked.

"Never mind," I said. "Find whatever you need, fast. We have to get on the road."

Crammed into the SUV with Caleb driving, we drove for awhile listening to nothing but November crunching on caramel corn and sucking soda through a straw. The anxiety of knowing where we were headed didn't seem to affect her, and it was oddly comforting to see her chowing down as usual. She was practically on Siku's lap, seat belts be damned.

Amaris and London sat together in the very back, heads together over London's playlist, sharing earbuds and distracting each other with music talk in low tones. Arnaldo continued to pore over the plans to the complex, using a tiny flashlight. Our backpacks, with changes of clothes, binoculars, rope, lock picks, and more snacks, were jammed in the trunk.

I'd automatically taken the shotgun seat. Then I realized that I was no longer Caleb's girlfriend, with no automatic right to that seat, and no reason to sit next to him everywhere we went. I felt hyperaware of his every movement, keyed into the rhythm of his breath, trying to guess how he felt sitting next to me now. He seemed restless, tapping his fingers against the steering wheel and constantly looking in the rearview mirror to make sure no one was following us.

I stared straight ahead as the road wound down out of the mountains, gripping the hilt of the Shadow Blade to calm myself. It worked. The same centering effect it had on me when dealing with technology spread outward from my core now, tamping down the tumult of sadness, anger, and pain competing for space inside me, and allowed me to focus on what lay ahead.

The Blade. It came from Othersphere, just as I did. Had it belonged to my biological family over there? Maybe that was why it felt more like an extension of myself than a weapon. It couldn't cut through skin or fur or flesh. It only harmed whatever did not come from the natural world. If it came to defending myself against an objurer, I'd have to rely on tiger strength and tiger claws. With my hand on the hilt of the Blade, I trusted that would be enough.

The road met the desert, which lay spread out under the starry night sky like a bumpy brown blanket. No snow lay here, though the wind blew cold, and just over the horizon I could feel the moon lifting inexorably toward the horizon. Already the appetite for shifting gnawed at me. I'd shared what Morfael had told me about how the thinness of the veil here might affect us, and we were all on edge.

"Okay, so do you guys think the space there could be so thin that we'll, like, spontaneously shift or something like that?" November asked, digging near the bottom of her box of caramel corn for the last kernels.

"I'm more worried your stomach might explode," said London, her voice edgier than usual.

"This is going to be a lot tougher to pull off than burning down the last Tribunal compound," said Arnaldo. "The thinness of the veil might make us more powerful than usual in our animal forms, but it will also make it more difficult for us to return to human."

"According to Morfael, it could also make us grumpy," said November. "Not that you could tell the difference with London."

"Also," Arnaldo continued as if she hadn't spoken, "we can really only enter the complex in force through the front door because the rest of it lies underground."

November leaned over to look at the plans lying in Arnaldo's lap. "What about that air shaft Lazar went in and out of?"

"We can't risk going in single file, one at a time," I said. "The odds of someone spotting us are high, and if one of us is caught without the others able to help right away, that person could be captured."

"And used as a hostage to control the rest of us," Siku said.

"I bet you they wouldn't notice a rat sneaking through the shaft," November said. "I could go in that way and do reconnaissance and meet up with you inside."

"Lazar says they thought of that," I said. "If you'd read all his notes, you'd see they were worried about rat-shifters infiltrating, so they built a series of heavy mesh screens into the air shaft. It takes Lazar half an hour to climb the shaft, removing and replacing each screen as he goes in or out. It's something only a human or a monkey could do, and it would be very time consuming."

"November's like a monkey in her human form," said London.

"No one's going in alone!" Caleb's voice, uncharacteristically snappish and loud, almost gave off sparks. "We can't risk splitting up. So shut up with the alternate plans and get ready. We don't have room for stupid errors."

Uneasy silence fell. Caleb had never barked at everyone like that before, and the power in his voice did actually shut everyone up for an awkward minute. It reminded me sharply that as a caller he had the potential to control us all with his words if he wanted, as did the objurers we would soon be facing.

"Someone needs a tranquilizing dart," November finally said under her breath.

Caleb's hands clenched the steering wheel. Was it the thinness of the veil, our breakup, the danger that lay ahead—or all three—making him so short-tempered? Could we all keep it under wraps long enough to do what we needed to do tonight?

We passed the spare lights of Indian Springs and Creech Air Force Base. A few miles later, we saw the turnoff for the town of Mercury and signs pointing to Desert Rock Airstrip. Underneath the airstrip's name, I could make out the words PRIVATE. FOR USE OF UNITED STATES DEPARTMENT OF ENERGY ONLY.

It was like we were heading right into the jaws of the government, which had used this land for some of the most violent scientific experiments ever devised. Yet this was where the supersecret Tribunal organization had chosen to build its facility. Ximon's audacity was breathtaking. The Tribunal had to have been digging here for years, maybe decades, without the government knowing. There must be some very powerful objurers involved to shield their efforts so completely. That and maybe a lot of money for bribes.

Caleb slowed down, pulling off the road to come to a stop, then switched off the headlights. "We're getting close," he said, unsnapping his seatbelt. "Dez should drive, so we can do it in the dark."

So now he wasn't even addressing me directly. "Fine," I said, getting out of the car to walk around and switch seats. "Arnaldo, time for you to grow some wings."

Caleb and I passed in front of the car without looking at each other, the chill dry wind blowing his long black coat back like a cape. As I climbed into the driver's seat and adjusted the mirrors, my hands shook a little.

How different this raid on the Tribunal was from our last one. Then Caleb and I had been an unshakeable team, excited to be heading into action together. Now there was a wall between us thicker than the veil between the worlds. We shared a goal tonight, at least. But without the unspoken accord I'd leaned on in the past, would we be able to coordinate through the dangers ahead?

Arnaldo had gotten out, climbed onto the SUV's roof, and

swiftly shifted into his eagle form. He thrust his clothes down through the moonroof using his long yellow beak, the snowy feathers on his head waving in the wind. His talons, as long as my hand, curved around the edge of the moonroof for balance.

"Keep an eye out for the two cacti that form an X," I said to him. "We should be pretty close now."

He emitted a sharp chirp, and then pushed against the car to leap into the air with two swift beats of his wings. The SUV rocked from the power of it. I turned back onto the road to follow the faint form of the raptor, visible to my night vision as the starlight glimmered faintly on his pale head.

Arnaldo's eyes were the sharpest of any of ours, and when he flew low in front of me, then zoomed up to circle, I knew to slow down and keep an eye on the right side of the road. Sure enough, a spearlike silhouette sharpened against the sky, tall as a tree, and as we passed it, the second cactus became clear right behind it, its long green arms reaching out toward the other to cross in an X.

*X for Ximon*, I thought, and saw the faint wheel track a few yards later just as Arnaldo swooped down right over it, so close to the ground that the tips of his wings brushed the dirt. He followed the track, away from the road, coasting over the uneven sands as if he were trolling a lake for fish.

I slowed down to turn, and everyone held onto something as the SUV bumped and rattled over the desert floor. We headed up a long slow incline, past the rattlesnake weed and ghost flower, thumping past rabbit burrows, lizard dens, and tarantula nests.

My skin buzzed, and I fought the urge to roll down the window to smell the air, to call out to the creatures and plants right outside, to stop the car and join them under the stars. I blinked, focusing back on the mission. Othersphere was close and getting nearer.

"God, are we there yet?" November asked, her voice

pitched in a chirping whine. "I just want to . . . I don't know what. But I have to do *something*."

"That's the thinness of the veil," said Caleb. His voice was normal now, dropping only as the car bumped hard over a rock. "It's put us all on edge. Don't let it distract you. Especially now, because I need to roll down the window."

Maybe that was the closest he'd come to an apology for shouting at us earlier.

Caleb's window lowered with a faint whirr, and the cold, powdery air of the desert flowed in. London, Siku, November, and I all took deep, happy breaths, as Amaris huddled deeper into her coat. As shifters, we could detect the scent of the monkey flower and brittlebush, still winter dormant, but silently working toward their spring bloom. Out there lay dusty gopher snakes, breezy red-tailed hawks, and musky desert kit foxes. Even at night, the desert was no wasteland, but a living place, full of its own silent drama. The black core of me that connected to Othersphere churned hotter and darker than before, wanting to spread out and take me over, to shrug off my human form and stalk through the night as a tiger.

*Soon. Soon I will hunt.*

Caleb hummed low under his breath and scanned the blackness outside his window. Just over the horizon the sky glimmered brighter, and I felt the moon there, like a bride just outside the chapel door about to sweep down the aisle.

"There," Caleb said, pointing straight up the low hill we were climbing. "Over the hill. Something big."

"Oh, thank the Moon," said London, biting at one of her cuticles. "If I don't shift soon, I'm going to split wide open."

Arnaldo dropped down, coming to rest on another saguaro that stood like a disembodied giant's hand at the top of the incline. I let the SUV slow down without pressing on the brakes, downshifting until we came to a gentle stop a few yards downhill from the cactus.

Like a dam breaking, doors clicked open as everyone piled

out. "Careful!" I said, voice low. "They've got someone watching down below."

We crept up the last few yards of the incline, cheeks cold in the breeze, to peer over the crest of the hill. It was less a valley below than a shallow basin. Above, the stars glittered like diamond dust, and I could see that there was nothing down there but more desert, except at the far end of the basin, metal glinted in a wavering line across the horizon. It was a fence, cutting off public lands from the government lands of the former nuclear test range.

"There." Caleb's sleeve brushed over the tips of dry grass as he pointed to a seemingly normal patch of desert. The Tribunal's objurers had drawn a curtain of shadow over the area so exactly that I could see no difference. Only Caleb, with his ability to feel vibrations through the veil, could have found it. Only Caleb, who was here because we needed him, but not because he cared for me.

I turned to see the faces of my friends. They looked exactly as I felt: on edge, fearful, but ready to go.

"Welcome to the most nuked patch of land in the world," I said. "Let's go."

# CHAPTER 19

The full moon rose, fat and yellow, as we approached the door to the Tribunal's compound from an angle.

With Arnaldo high above, we spread out ten or twenty yards apart, following Caleb's lean dark-coated form, using boulders and clumps of sage as cover as we got closer. I swallowed down an instinctive need to be at his side and forced myself to think about our plan. Lazar hadn't said there were Tribunal patrols in the area, but I preferred to be extra cautious.

London and November had slipped into their wolf and rat forms as effortlessly as expert divers slicing into the surface of a pool. After a moment of severe concentration, Siku shifted into a raccoon, since he would have been larger and easier to see as a bear. November sat on his back, long pink tail wrapped affectionately around his neck. London, a ghostly silver in the moonlight, trotted with her ears perked straight up, her eyes like eerie blue lamps.

The Shadow Blade's touch kept me from following them into my tiger form. I held it with one hand as I advanced over burrow weeds and dormant fuchsia, trying to disturb the chipmunks and desert tortoises sleeping underground as little as possible.

Amaris kept closest to me. Before we'd crested the hill and headed down into the basin, she'd asked me if I was sure she should come. She felt useless.

In response, I'd dug into a backpack in the trunk of the car and handed her the gun Raynard had purchased last term. Everyone in the Tribunal, Amaris included, had extensive training with sidearms. She'd looked a little relieved, knowing that with a gun in her hand she could do us some good. We only had two extra clips of bullets, but she didn't need to go on a shooting spree. The intent was to kill as few people as possible.

*But we'll do whatever we have to.*

Ten yards ahead of me, Caleb stopped and waved us forward, even though the ground in front of him looked no different from where I was standing. I moved up till I was about ten feet away from him, Amaris not far to my right. The other three crept closer too.

A vibration from Caleb hummed through my chest and down to my feet. Seeing him out here in the desert, calling out to shadow, I couldn't help remembering the first night we met, when he had drawn forth a ridge of white marble to keep the Tribunal from capturing us. The effort had made him collapse. With the moonlight on his face, he'd looked so beautiful that I think that's when I started to fall in love with him. Now the vibration from his voice was a painful reminder of the gulf that lay between us.

High above, I could just see Arnaldo's silhouette blotting out bits of the star field. Everything seemed more distinct here. Sounds echoed strangely. The touch of the breeze felt like a cold hand on my skin, and the light of the moon fell with a substance and weight such as I'd never felt before.

Caleb stopped humming, and turned one hundred and eighty degrees to sweep us all with a glance. His eyes glowed a molten gold without a trace of black. Tiny sparks of black smoke issued from his fingertips. The nearness of Othersphere had empowered him as well. His look told us to be ready.

I nodded, making sure my hand lay on the hilt of the Shadow Blade to brace myself. Directly ahead of Caleb had to be the shroud of shadow the Tribunal had called forth to disguise the entrance to their facility. Here, where the veil was thin, a disguise like that could last for a day or more if it was undisturbed.

Caleb was about to disturb it. He swept around to face north once more, lifted a hand, and called out a thunderous note. It throbbed in the very center of my being, and if not for the Shadow Blade, I would have shifted there and then.

Siku shifted again—into a bear. The call to become his most familiar form must have been too irresistible. One moment November sat on a dog-sized gray raccoon with a black robber mask, the next moment a bear as big as a truck stood there. November squeaked in surprise, and then ran along his back to perch on top of his head.

London threw back her head and howled, and the piercing call, instead of interrupting Caleb's vibration, joined it like two instruments in a duet. Then, as if wiped clean, the desert scrub in front of us was gone.

In its place sat a wide metal door set at an angle into the ground, big enough for a large truck to fall through if it was opened. The door had been painted desert brown, but rust marred its scratched, weather-beaten surface. It looked as if it had lain there since nuclear tests started nearby in the 1950s. But that was part of its disguise, in case the shadow camouflage failed.

Next to it sat a large shallow cement pond filled with inky water. Lazar had told us it was used for runoff in cooling the accelerator. The enormous yellow moon on the horizon floated in reflection there, its rays gilding the smallest ripples.

Between them sat a tower, set on an open structure of metal struts, about thirty feet tall, with a simple open box on top. Caleb had told us that the objurer guard there would not be able to see us until we dropped the shadow façade.

I looked up. A white face above a white jacket was righting itself from where it had been resting against the side of the box. The man had been sleeping. I had time to see him gape down at us, the whites of his eyes shining in alarm. Then he lifted his hand to press on the button on his earpiece.

But Arnaldo was ready. Like an arrow, he shot down from above, directly at the man in the tower. The furious flapping of his wings obscured my view, but he struck as the man lifted his hand. A strangled cry rose up, and then was cut off.

The man slid from view into his box, and Arnaldo hopped to perch on the edge of it, holding something in his beak. I ran to stand directly below him and held out my hands. He let the small thing drop, and I caught the man's earpiece in the palm of my hand.

I gave him a thumbs-up, walked over, and gave it to Amaris. "See if you can hear anything on this," I said, as she wiped away a trace of blood on the black plastic. "Just don't let them hear you."

She fitted it into her ear, pretending to zip her lips together. Siku lumbered over on all fours toward the door in the ground, November on top of his flat head like a figure on the prow of a ship. When they reached it, she jumped down and ran over to a small pad of numbers on the right-hand side, tiny pink-clawed paws poised over it, waiting.

Amaris shook her head. "We're good. No chatter on the radios at all. And the mic on this piece isn't active, so he never got a chance to sound the alarm."

I glanced over at Caleb, instinctively wanting to share this good news with him. But he was staring down at the door, hands jammed into his coat pockets. His eyelids half hid the glow in his eyes, but energy still eddied around him, as if gathering to explode.

I glanced at my watch: 1:02 A.M. "Do it, November."

November was normally our lock-picker, but her tools and skill only worked on regular tumbler locks. Still, she had wanted to maintain her role as door opener, so she had memorized the twelve-figure code Lazar had given us for the front door. She now tapped out the code on buttons as big as her paws. Lazar had explained that they used a less sophisticated-looking keypad on the exterior, one that did not require a handprint scan, to make the door look less like one to a top-secret, high-tech bunker and more like an old government shelter, in case their shadow smokescreen ever dropped.

As we all gathered around the edge of the door, November pressed the last key, chittered at us, and pressed "enter."

The metal slid up soundlessly, disappearing into the dirt at its top to reveal an asphalt-paved tunnel wider than a truck slanting down into the earth. LED lights in the ceiling flicked on, illuminating nearly thirty yards of empty passageway before turning to the right, in the direction of the nuclear test site.

We waited. Thanks to Lazar, we knew that two men patrolled this area, with their guard post just around the bend in the tunnel. The lights must have alerted them to someone entering. They would investigate in moments.

We all kept well back of the doorway, not wanting them to see us peering down at them. All except November, whose head was tiny enough to avoid notice. Arnaldo still circled overhead. Amaris took the pistol out of the waistband of her jeans and checked to make sure the safety was off.

Another protracted moment passed. I longed to shift and bound down that tunnel, to find the guards and deal with them and put an end to the deep agitation in my heart. London paced, and Siku placed both front paws, with their black, daggerlike claws, on the edge of the door, clicking them against the metal, as November scampered around the edge of the door and ran up his foreleg to perch once more on his head.

"Yo!" The man's voice from the depths came as a relief. "Stop there! You're not authorized!"

Footsteps echoed up from the tunnel. "Unless they are authorized and someone forgot to tell us," another man's voice added. "Remember the other day when Ximon's kid reamed us for not expecting him?"

"That was previous shift's fault for not marking down that he left," the first man replied, then lifted his voice, coming nearer. "Hey! Who goes there?"

"How much you want to bet Lazar left to visit the Bunny Ranch?" said the second voice. They were less than ten feet from the entrance now.

*Bunny Ranch?* I crouched down. Siku had stopped tapping his claws, and London's back leg muscles were tensed to spring. "He's a young man, trapped in a bunker in the middle of the desert, and I hear the lovely ladies there are very welcoming."

*Oh.* Prostitution was legal in Nevada. Not that Lazar would ever visit a whorehouse . . . although, for some reason, the thought made my face grow hot. Damn it. Everything was heightened where the veil was thin.

"Sounds like you're the one who wants to visit the Bunny Ranch," the first man said. "Ximon's kid's as upright as the Bishop."

"Careful near the entrance now," said the second man. "How can there be nobody here? And why didn't we get a call from Rivers?"

"I can see the stars," the first man said. "What about the shroud? Should I be able to see the stars?" He poked his head and the point of a pistol over the edge of the door, like a prairie dog sticking its head out of its burrow. "The shroud has dropped! Call reinforcements—whoa!"

Looming big as a shed, Siku swiped at the man's face with one giant paw. He didn't use his full strength. Instead of taking the man's head clean off, he knocked him across the width of the tunnel mouth, slamming him against the far side. His head made a horrible thump against the metal doorsill. Then he crumpled and lay still.

His friend had time to raise a gun at Siku. He fired just as London smashed into him. The bullet went wide. He fell to the ground with a horrified cry, disappearing beneath her rangy gray form. A muffled snarl came, then a wet ripping sound. Blood sprayed against the tunnel wall, and he too lay still. London stood over him, licking her red muzzle with a long pink tongue, eyes hot with a thirst that one kill hadn't even touched.

I felt it too, the thrill of the kill, even though I was still in human form and had not lifted a hand. "Well done," I said. "Now, inside! Caleb, help me with this guy."

London, Siku, and November padded farther down the hallway as Arnaldo swept in to alight on Siku's shoulder. The grizzly was big and strong enough not to be slowed down by the weight of a larger-than-life bald eagle and a rat the size of a small dog. Amaris searched the dead objurer, head turned away from the gore where his throat had been, and came away with his pistol and two mags of bullets. She followed the others, gun pointed expertly at the ceiling.

Like a black hole in the night sky above him, Caleb stood for a moment in the doorway. We were alone. The breeze whipped his black hair around his cheekbones, brows fierce over molten eyes. He looked like some ancient god of power. He caught my eye. We both paused, and my stomach clenched as a current ran hot between us.

I caught the taste of him once again in my mouth, felt again how one of his hands had cradled my lower back as his other hand ran a burning line from my sternum to my belly, dipping below the edge of my underwear. *God, if we could . . . if I could only . . .*

He ripped his eyes away from me and leaned down to grab the shoulders of the unconscious objurer. I snapped back to the present, wind biting my face, and forced myself to take the man's feet. Together, we hustled him deeper into the tunnel. The wind cut off abruptly as we dipped down into the earth.

I looked over my shoulder to catch one last glimpse of the stars, and instead saw the moon, glowing as gold as Caleb's eyes, perfectly framed in the doorway. We had decided to leave the door open. We might need to make a quick exit. All of the biggest threats still lay inside.

We passed under a camera on the tunnel's ceiling. I had to trust that Lazar had taken care of electronic surveillance, as he'd said he would. Caleb reached the corner and we set the objurer's body down. November, still perched on Siku's brow, leaned forward to peer around the corner. Studiously ignoring me, Caleb moved up to join her, stealing a quick glance as well.

"Empty guard station and another door," he said.

"You're up, November," I said.

But she was already hopping off Siku and scampering around the corner. I brushed past the massive bear so that I could peer around to watch her, which brought me right up against Caleb. The warm airy scent of him added to the ache in the center of my chest. He was so close, and yet so far away. I'd heard the phrase "broken heart" before, but never understood it till now; an endless source of pain there welled up at the slightest provocation.

He recoiled from me as if I were radioactive, pressing back against Siku. I bit my lip to keep from bursting into tears, and kept moving forward. I squinted around the corner to see another ten yards of tunnel dead-ending at a large door big enough for trucks and, set next to it, a human-sized door. Both were constructed of heavy, reinforced metal. Lazar should be waiting just beyond the regular door for us, if all had gone as planned. The truck entrance led to storage and construction areas that were sealed off from the more secret control rooms.

Two empty folding chairs sat next to a small table covered with playing cards in the middle of a game and two steaming cups of coffee. November scurried past that to the regular door and, gripping the doorframe with her tiny claws, climbed up to another keypad. This one featured a pad of numbers with a screen just below it.

November chittered and beckoned us forward with her paw.

"We're up," I said to Caleb, keeping my voice neutral. We grabbed the unconscious man again to haul him over to the locked door. With the Shadow Blade I could have cut right through the lock, but that was likely to set off alarms. The longer we could hold that off, the better. As we approached, November punched in the code, and Caleb took the man's wrist, positioned his hand over the lock's sensor, and pressed it down.

The door clicked open. November leaped to the floor and threw her small frame against the bottom of it, but it wouldn't budge. Caleb and I set the man's body down as the others jogged up. Caleb took the second gun from Amaris, checking to make sure it was loaded and ready. She slipped the extra mags into his coat pocket.

I scanned the faces around me. London's blue eyes were wide and feral. Siku's small black eyes were focused, with Arnaldo tensely gripping his shoulder above. At my feet, November danced on her back legs with nervous anticipation. Amaris stood with the gun in both hands, blond hair pulled back, face serious. And Caleb, silver gun now tucked in his belt, reached his hand into the internal pocket of his coat, as if making sure whatever he had was still there. Their attention narrowed to my face, and for a moment, we were united.

"This is it," I said. "If we stop them here, we just might stop them forever. Let's go."

I pushed the door open, using the doorframe as cover, and we all looked inside. Nothing but a small hallway lay in front of us, furnished with a mini-fridge and a hotplate with a half-filled coffeepot set on top. The door at the far end snapped open, and I nearly jumped out of my skin as a figure in Tribunal white appeared.

It was Lazar, a finger to his lips, brown eyes sweeping over us apprehensively. The sight of him sent a new kind of tension through the group. For me, the relief at seeing him made my knees weak. So far, our plan was going better than I'd hoped.

Lazar motioned us forward, stepping back to give us room.

I shot a look at Caleb, who still had one hand stuffed into his internal breast pocket, eyebrows lowered, eyes black but specked with gold. His other hand clenched into a fist, and I thought he might cast something at Lazar and call forth shadow to injure or kill.

Then he turned his head and our gazes met. The moment seemed to last an eternity, and I saw a dozen thoughts flash behind his eyes: anger at Lazar, anger and something more complex at me, a murderous itch, and finally a conscious effort to rein in those feelings. His eyelids fell to veil his eyes as he took his hand out of his pocket, empty. Then he motioned to me, inviting me to go first.

Had he given up the thought of killing Lazar, or was he biding his time? Uncertain of almost everything I'd once taken for granted, I stepped forward into the Tribunal's top-secret underground bunker at last.

# CHAPTER 20

Lazar held the door open for me as I entered a small, brightly lit room. I brushed past him, aware of the stamp of fatigue under his eyes, the trace of golden stubble on his jaw. One half-open door led to a bathroom next to another small space that looked like a closet full of brooms, buckets, and other janitorial supplies. The room was otherwise bare, painted a stark white, except for a black metal door in the far wall.

I turned to Lazar and held out my hand, feeling grim, but wanting to cement my gratitude. He took my hand, eyes focused and determined. The handshake became an agreement: *We will do this*. Siku walked in with his cargo of eagle and rat, followed by London and Amaris.

Lazar did a double-take at the sight of Siku, who even on all fours was as tall at the shoulder as he. The bear's fuzzy bulk took up half the room. Caleb walked over to stand by Siku, as if making it clear where his sympathies lay.

Lazar was somehow still holding my hand. I dropped his

grip, flushing and, marshaling whatever composure I had, raised an eyebrow at him inquiringly.

He pointed at the black door and spoke in a low tone. "Long hallway through there, leads down past various bedrooms."

"We'll be quiet," Amaris said.

"But odds are good we'll wake someone up," I said. "So be ready."

Lazar went on. "I'll get us through the security doors until we reach the scientists' rooms. We'll need one of them, preferably alive and awake, to get through the last door to the mainframe computer and then the accelerator itself."

"And if none of them happen to be available both awake and alive?" Caleb asked, his voice flat. His arms were folded across his chest. His whole stance was an objection.

"We can still get into those rooms using their handprint, just like you did with Noah there." Lazar gestured in the direction of the unconscious objurer we'd left outside. "But it'll take longer to download the information, since I don't have access to the pass codes."

"Awake and alive if we can then," I said, and then nodded at Lazar. "Let's go."

We clustered to the left of the door as Lazar stepped up to the keypad on the right, punching in the code, then pressing his palm to the sensor. Something buzzed faintly, and the door lock clicked open. Lazar laid his hand on the knob, but I shook my head and pushed his arm away.

"Behind me," I whispered.

His jaw set. He was about to object, but I squinted a warning at him and shook my head once.

He glanced over at my assembled friends, then back at me, and his face relaxed. He bowed slightly at the waist, conceding that I was in charge. I believed he was truly here to help us, but even so I couldn't take the chance he would charge ahead and lead us into a trap. Also, my dubious friends would feel more comfortable with him in their midst, where they could keep an eye on him.

I held up my hand to show I was ready, taut with anticipation. The door pushed inward, and I used it as cover for my body as I swung it slowly open to find a long hallway that sloped down. It was empty of life and decoration, ten feet wide and a hundred feet long, set with one door to the right side and series of doors on the left. It also descended at a sharp angle, as if eager to plunge into the depths of the earth. Greenish fluorescent bulbs were set in the ceiling, though only half were lit, probably because it was the middle of the night.

Behind me, my friends were craning their necks to see. I opened the door fully and moved down, keeping my steps on the cement floor as silent as possible.

With a bit of scuffle from Siku's nails, we progressed down the hall. Heading down at such a steep angle, it felt like we were entering an ancient Egyptian tomb that some obsessive-compulsive archaeologist had dusted and paved.

I ticked off where the doors led to in my head, recalling the plans Lazar had given us. The utility closet lay to the right, containing a generator and tools. On the left lay a lounge, the kitchen, dining area, and the gym, with its showers and restrooms. Past the gym lay one door, decorated with a huge golden cross: the chapel. There the hallway ended in another metal door identical to the one we'd just come through.

I reached it, still not quite believing we'd gotten this far without being detected. Over the door I spotted a camera. I turned to Lazar, who was following right behind me, and pointed at it, a questioning look on my face.

He made a cutting motion across his throat. So he'd hacked that camera.

I mouthed the word "Good" at him, then ushered him to the keypad next to this door. My friends were lined up in single file, waiting, the Siku express coming first, then London, and Amaris, with Caleb dourly bringing up the rear like some black-coated messenger of doom.

Lazar unlocked it exactly as he had before, and this time he stepped back to let me open it. As I laid my hand on it, he reached into his jacket and pulled out a shiny silver pistol.

Siku growled a low warning. I dodged to the right, expecting a bullet. Caleb flew into Lazar, tackling him to the floor with a muffled thump.

"Wha—?" Lazar started to say, but Caleb had one hand over his mouth, the other locked around his throat from behind, legs pinning Lazar's to the floor.

November jumped down off Siku's head and onto Lazar's. She thrust her whiskered face right up to his and chittered furiously. He struggled in vain against Caleb's grip, words stifled.

My thoughts came together. Caleb had been incredibly quick, but not quick enough. Lazar had had plenty of time to shoot me, or any of us, if he wanted. I squatted down in front of him and whispered, "Were you going to shoot?"

He shook his head as vehemently as Caleb's grip allowed.

"Were you pulling out your gun to help us in case we needed it?"

He nodded, relief in his eyes as they flew from me to Caleb, then going a bit cross-eyed to focus on November hanging upside-down over his forehead.

"Drop the gun," I said,

Metal clinked somewhere underneath his body as I hissed back at everyone else, "Be ready in case they heard us!"

Amaris turned to face the length of hallway behind us. I reached under Lazar, hand brushing against his waist, and pulled the gun out. The silver stung my skin and, remembering Morfael's training, I imagined the itch of the metal flowing down through me, out through my feet, and into the floor. It made the pain of contact bearable for a little while at least. I stood up.

"Let him go," I said to Caleb, waving at November to get off.

November skittered back to Siku. Caleb's grip tightened around Lazar's throat for a second in warning; then he let go and got to his feet.

I leaned in so only Caleb could hear, and said, "Thank you."

He gave me a curt nod, but didn't relax his guarded stance over Lazar.

Lazar massaged his throat as he stood, the front of his white shirt and pants imprinted with gray dust from the floor. I expected him to be angry, but instead he looked disappointed in himself.

"Guess I asked for that," he said, speaking softly. "My father's quarters are the first on the left through that door, and I wanted to keep you covered."

I nodded and handed the gun back.

Caleb hissed in objection. I kept my eyes on Lazar, ignoring Caleb. "Don't do anything without indicating to me first," I said. "For your own safety as well as everyone else's."

"Got it." He hefted the gun, pointing it at the ceiling in a style similar to his sister's. "After you, General Grey."

The door was still unlocked. They all looked ready to jump out of their skins, so I pushed it open.

The hallway extended for another forty feet, then turned left. Only one door stood to the left, and that, I knew, led into Ximon's quarters.

Nearly on tiptoe, I passed that door and peered around the corner. The others followed suit. Despite that little misunderstanding, things were going far better than I'd expected. Somehow the scuffle in the hall hadn't drawn attention.

To the left, the hall stretched fifty feet, dead-ending in another security door. The regular door halfway down on the left led into the scientists' quarters. According to Lazar, four people slept there. The other two doors, on the right, led to dorms for Tribunal guards and technicians. By my count, twenty-five of them were housed in there. One wrong move and we'd alert them all and bring them down on us en masse.

I pointed at the door to the scientists' room, and Caleb, Amaris, and London moved around me, positioning themselves on either side of it. London prepared to spring, and Caleb took out a salt shaker.

Lazar frowned in puzzlement. I held up a finger to him, telling him to wait, and then motioned to Siku. He trotted forward with his heavy rolling gait, to stand in front of the security door at the end, November and Arnaldo still riding him like the world's craziest circus act.

I leaned in to Lazar, mouth to his ear. It was weirdly intimate. My nerves were pulsing with the buzz of impending action. "Cover the first door on the right," I told him.

He blinked, still puzzled, but whispered, "Aye, aye." He moved to point his gun at the door leading to the room full of sleeping objurers.

I crept past Lazar to the second door on the right. Behind it lay more sleeping objurers and technicians. The lock next to it looked exactly the same as the others had—a keypad with a hand scanner. I pulled the Shadow Blade out of its sheath. Cool certainty washed over me as if I'd dived into a forest pond. I hefted the knife with its smoking black edge and sank it into the keypad to the hilt.

Sparks flew from the lock as the wires fizzed. I thought I heard a startled shout from behind the door, but I didn't wait. I sprinted the few strides to the door Lazar was covering and knifed that lock too. Smoke rose.

I turned to Lazar. His gun didn't waver, though he was staring in astonishment at the Shadow Blade. "Cover your father's door now, please."

He swiveled with professional grace to train the gun on Ximon's door as I sprinted back and gave its lock the same treatment with the Blade. "Should take them a little while to get out." I jogged back around the corner to where the others waited outside the door on the left. "Scientists?"

As if I'd commanded it, the door to the scientists' room swung open. A fiftyish woman in white flannel pajamas stuck her head out, squinting in the greenish light of the hallway. "What the . . . ?" She froze as Amaris pointed the gun at her head and London showed her teeth.

"Hello." Caleb brandished the salt shaker, sprinkling her. "Good-bye." And, humming a quiet note, he lifted a finger and a spark of black flew at her.

She opened her mouth to scream, but when Caleb's power touched the salt, a web of sticky yellow goo exploded outward, encasing her. She tried to give a dampened scream, but her mouth was encased. Caleb pried a bit of it away from her nose so she could breathe. "Sorry about that."

Voices called out from the room behind her. Caleb picked her up bodily and set her wiggling form out of the way as London shot through the door in a silver streak. Amaris followed her and several male voices bellowed in alarm. Caleb followed her.

"Hands on the back of your heads, gentlemen!" Amaris shouted.

I reached the doorway to see three rumpled middle-aged men in white pajamas in a room about twenty feet by twenty furnished with four slept-in twin beds and several stand-alone wardrobes. The walls, as usual, gleamed starkly white, the only decoration a cross over each bed. One of the three lay on his back on the floor, with London standing over him, paws on his chest. She pushed her teeth closer to his throat, snarling. The other two huddled in the back corner, faces pale.

"Please!" said the one on the floor, trembling and digging the back of his head into the floor in a vain attempt to get away. "Call off your dog!"

London growled.

"Wolves do as they please," I said. "Stop calling her a dog, and you might live."

"Sorry," he said up at her. "I'm so sorry!"

"Otherkin!" the fattest man said, hands out in front of him, as if warding us off. "How did you get in here?"

"Easily," said Caleb. "Now, which of you is in charge of this little project?"

The three men exchanged nervous looks. "What project do you mean?" asked the balding one standing next to the fat man.

Caleb took a slingshot out of his pocket and then, as they all watched in horrified fascination, took out a handful of buttons. "Which do you want?" he asked, holding his hand out flat so they could see the buttons, red and blue, arrayed there. "Ice or fire?"

"What do you mean?" the fat one asked, after a brief hesitation that made it clear he knew exactly what Caleb meant.

Behind us I could hear pounding on the doors of the rooms I'd locked up. "No one's coming to help you," I said. "Quit stalling and help yourselves."

"We—we don't know anything!" the fat man said. "We're just hired workers."

"Lazar," I said. Behind me, Lazar walked to stand in the doorway, the light from above haloing his gold hair. "Which one's in charge?"

"Dooley," said Lazar.

"No, not me!" the fat one said, backing into the wall behind him. "I can't tell you anything."

"Reverend Lazar?" the bald scientist said. "Have you betrayed us?"

"It was the only way to save you." Lazar paced into the room. "Tell them what you know or they'll use your hands to open the doors without you attached."

"Do it!" shouted the man on the floor with London looming over him.

As his friends hesitated, Caleb rolled his thumb over one

of the blue buttons in his hand. "I'm told the cold takes longer, but doesn't hurt as much. The fire is faster, but, oh"— he smiled, selecting a red button—"the pain is terrible." He fitted the button into the band of his slingshot.

"All right, all right!" Dooley moved away from the wall. "Don't hurt us, and I'll take you to the mainframe."

I relaxed slightly. Convincing him had been easier than I'd anticipated. Maybe too easy. Dooley's eyes were shifting left and right, but I couldn't tell if that was from anxiety or because he knew more than he was telling us.

"Excellent choice," Caleb said, aiming the slingshot at his head. "My trigger finger's itchy. You came *this* close." He stretched the band back, released it, but as the button flew, his hand shot out to catch it in midair.

Sweat was dripping down Dooley's temples. "I'll cooperate."

"Part of me wishes you wouldn't." Caleb cocked an eyebrow at the huge wolf still menacing the man on the floor. "Isn't that right, London?"

She barked in the man's face, then whirled and lunged at Dooley, coming within inches of his arm as he flinched backwards.

I wanted her to jump up and rip his throat out. I wanted to shift and sink my own fangs into his neck. The thirst for it rose up from the dark heart of me, and that was nearly the end of them all. My hand brushed the hilt of the Shadow Blade, and a still tranquility cloaked my wild thoughts.

"If you lead us into a trap, there will be consequences," I said. "As a scientist no doubt you know the thinness of the veil here brings out the more . . . untamed side of the otherkin. Step very carefully."

"I will," he said, jowls shaking.

"Good. Lazar, bring the woman back in here. Dooley, out into the hallway."

Dooley grabbed a robe from the foot of his bed as he scuttled out of the room, London at his heels. Lazar picked up the goo-bound scientist and set her gently back inside the room. We all backed out, then shut the door.

I took the Shadow Blade and sliced into the lock. Its wires hissed. Dooley saw Siku looming at the end of the hall, decorated with a rat and an eagle, and he shied away. Lazar had to catch him by the shoulders to steady him.

I kept my voice light. "I believe we need your handprint to get us through that door at the end of the hall, Mr. Dooley. If you please."

"Okay." He shuffled slowly toward Siku, pressing against the wall to keep a few precious inches between himself and the bear. As he squeezed past, Siku grunted and pawed the ground, claws rattling.

Dooley leaped about five feet in the air and shot forward, slamming bodily against the door and pressing back against it, as if trying to push through it. Trembling, he turned to punch in the code with shaking fingers, pressing his sweating palm up against the sensor.

The door clicked open. Dooley laid his hand upon it, but Lazar said, "You don't move unless we tell you to."

"The door to the mainframe's the second on the left," Dooley said through trembling lips.

"Anyone in there?" Caleb tossed his slingshot end over end to catch it by the handle.

"No! Not that I know of."

I looked up at Caleb. "Come with me." It sounded awkward and weird, too much like a command. "Please."

His black eyes ran over me. "Just a soldier in your army, General," he said. "Let's go."

My heart contracted at his cold tone. The gulf between us was larger than ever. The loss of him washed over its edge and threatened to take me over.

*The veil. The veil is thin.*

I remembered Morfael's warning about the effects of Othersphere and put my hand on the Shadow Blade's hilt. Its centering touch allowed me to straighten up and walk past the others to the door. I paused, listening at the crack for a moment, and then pushed it open.

Another thirty feet of hallway lay half-lit before me, with two doors on the right and the left. I knew Lazar had never been to this part of the complex before.

I was taller than Dooley by several inches. I put my hand on his shoulder, feeling his damp sweat soaking through his robe. "Tell us what's behind each door," I said.

"On the right there's a closet and the lab." He pointed to the first and second doors on the right. "On this side, the bathroom and the computer room." He pointed to the left. "The mainframe's in the computer room."

"How do we access the tunnels of the particle accelerator itself?" Caleb asked.

"There's a door inside the computer room, on the right-hand wall," he said.

"The computer room, please."

With my hand still on his shoulder, Dooley walked tentatively toward the second door on the left. Caleb walked right behind me, then Siku and his entourage, Amaris, London, and Lazar.

Dooley input the code into the lock in front of the computer room, and then pressed his hand against it. As always, the door clicked open.

"This is going better than I thought," Lazar said.

Caleb tensed as his half-brother spoke. "A little too well."

I agreed with Caleb, but said nothing. So far our plan had gone with unaccustomed smoothness. I was braced for the punch line.

The computer room was empty except for a series of huge computer monitors and linked hard drives on shiny metal desks, dotted here and there with a file cabinet or a chair. A palpable hum vibrated through the room like a tide, the whirr of many electronic motors keeping themselves cool and running. In the far right-hand corner lay another security door. If Dooley was telling the truth, that led to the tubes of the particle collider itself. This was the control room.

"Log on," I said, prodding Dooley in the small of his back.

"All right, all right!" He padded in his bare feet to the largest monitor and pressed a button on the keyboard next to it. Lazar kept right by his side, gun at the ready, but his eyes on the monitor. It sprang to life, showing a space for a password. Dooley typed in a long series of keystrokes, and the view cut to a bright display of many intersecting lines of yellow, red, and blue that looked almost like a galaxy as seen through a high-resolution telescope.

Dooley went to hit another key, but Lazar caught his hand. "No. Don't touch it again unless we tell you to."

I walked up, and pushed Dooley back toward Siku, then stared at the monitor. "Arnaldo, I think we need you back."

Dooley eyed the eagle nervously as he flapped off Siku to the floor and Amaris began to pull spare clothes out of her backpack. "What. What is that bird going to . . ."

He flinched and stumbled back a step as Arnaldo shifted back into his human form, using a desk for partial cover, got dressed, and walked over to examine the monitor.

"This display shows the results of a particle collision," Arnaldo said, tapping the keys. Dooley blinked nervously at his words. "They've already used the collider."

I turned to Dooley, who was sweating profusely with Siku staring down at him. "So you've used the accelerator already," I said. "I think it's time you stopped lying to us, and so does Siku here."

Dooley swallowed noisily, then nodded. "Yes, we've tested the collider at lower speeds, and successfully smashed particles into each other."

"Exactly what are you planning to do tomorrow to cut us all off from Othersphere?" I asked. "And what does it have to do with our DNA?"

"DNA?" Dooley blinked, using the back of his hand to wipe off the sweat beads under his nose.

I got in Dooley's face, pulling his watery eyes back to me. "How, exactly, does this machine cut us off from Othersphere?"

A fine tremor ran through his entire body. I could see his skin trembling. "Th—the thinness of the veil here," he stuttered. "It changes what happens in the collider."

Arnaldo was squinting at the display. "Pre-strangelets?" He turned to Dooley. "You think if you speed up the collisions you'll produce actual strangelets?"

Dooley's anxious face took on a startled look. Arnaldo had impressed him. The rest of us kept our faces still, clueless. "I—I couldn't say, really."

Caleb strode over to Dooley, grabbed his lapel, and shoved him up against Siku's furry side. Dooley shrieked, trying to shrink away as Siku turned his head and gave him a big wet sniff. November let out a piping cheep very much like a laugh.

"You will say," Caleb said, his flexible voice low and deadly. "You'll say it now."

"Okay, yes! Don't hurt me. We're almost certain we'll produce detectable strangelets, but not the same kind other colliders might produce."

Arnaldo was tapping the computer keys, moving into other files. Amaris handed Lazar a flash drive, and he plugged it into the hard drive to start copying the information.

Arnaldo let his hands drop from the keyboard, and when he turned around, his face was drawn and serious. "So the nearness of Othersphere will affect the properties of the strangelets," he said. "They'll find all matter connected to Othersphere and convert it. Into regular matter."

"Y-yes." Dooley dipped his head cautiously.

November let out a stream of chirps, waving her pink paws angrily. Arnaldo swiveled in the chair and gave her a condescending look. "What that means is that the particle collisions they do in this accelerator create subatomic particles called strangelets. The strangelets will be strongly attracted to particles connected to Othersphere, called O-particles. The strangelets will be drawn to the O-particles like magnets, and when they touch, the O-particles will be converted to ordinary matter. That is, matter unable to connect to Othersphere. They'll also create more strangelets."

"So if the Tribunal releases these strangelets into the world . . ." Caleb began.

"They'd start converting the nearest O-particles, creating more strangelets, which will find other O-particles."

"A chain reaction," said Lazar.

"Obliterating all O-particles from this universe." Dooley lifted his quivering chin, his voice tinged with pride.

"Cutting all the otherkin and objurers off from Othersphere," I said, though it was more like a question for Arnaldo.

"Yes," he said. "Forever."

The room got very quiet except for the hum from the computers. Arnaldo turned back and began searching the files. "Somehow this is connected to our DNA. This says something about a biological virus?"

*BAM!* The door burst open. Two objurers lowered tranquilizer guns at us and fired.

One dart slammed into the back of Arnaldo's chair. The other buried itself in Siku's side, right next to Dooley's head.

Behind them were many more, all dressed in white.

# CHAPTER 21

Arnaldo and I threw ourselves behind the nearest desk, scrambling for cover.

Lazar leveled his gun and fired. A splotch of red appeared on the forehead of one of the objurers. He dropped.

Fangs bared, London leaped for the other man in the room. He yelped as he sprawled on the ground, his gun flying.

Siku roared out and smacked Dooley in the head, sending him to the floor unconscious, face bleeding. November, shrieking, ran along Siku's back and yanked the tranquilizer dart out of his side.

Amaris crouched to make herself less of a target and fired at a third man starting to come through the doorway. She hit him in the center of his chest.

As he fell back, blocking the men behind him, Caleb pulled out his slingshot, armed it with a red button, and fired it.

"Come forth!" he commanded, and the flying red disc morphed into a fiery sphere the size of a basketball. It struck the man Amaris had shot. The man's clothes burst into flame. Then, with a whoosh, his entire body was engulfed in fire. The blaze swallowed up the doorway as someone yelled for everyone to step back.

"Lava spheres," Caleb said, with a grim smile. "Better than barrels of oil and matches any day, eh, London?"

London's muzzle was red with blood again. The man at her feet lay still. She gave Caleb a fierce, joyous bark. With a thrill, I too remembered the enormous bonfire of the first Tribunal compound we'd burned to the ground.

*Stay calm, focus.* This was a different compound. It was under the ground, and we weren't done with it yet. The fiery doorway would only give us a brief reprieve.

"How's Siku?" I asked, running up to him.

November threw the dart at Dooley's body as I looked into the bear's shining black eyes. They were clear.

"You okay?" I asked. The Tribunal had needed three darts to subdue him when they'd kidnapped him, but they might have improved their formula.

Siku huffed, nodding his huge head. I patted his bulky shoulder.

Beyond the burning doorway, I could hear someone yelling about a fire extinguisher. Then, without warning, water burst from the ceiling. Cold drops soaked quickly through my hair, running down my scalp, trickling underneath my clothes. I looked up to see sprinklers raining down on us. Ximon had planned his facility well.

The flames in the doorway winced and retreated. Through the smoke, I could now see figures in white.

"Get through the other door to the accelerator!" I shouted. "No time to download information. We need to destroy this thing and get out of here!" The water, at least, would take care of destroying their hard drives. But they had to have a backup server. We needed to somehow dismantle the accelerator itself.

Bangs dripping into his eyes, Arnaldo looked furious. "Dammit! That virus information was important!"

Amaris was already running to the door. "It's locked!" she shouted.

*Of course.* I moved toward Dooley's body, about to ask for help with it, but both Caleb and Lazar were already coming over. I gripped the man's beefy shoulders as both of them came to stand uneasily near one of his legs, hesitating. I stared at them angrily. *How the hell had it come to this?*

Caleb's hair lay in dark whorls across his forehead, drops circling his thick brows and clinging to his black lashes as he avoided looking at Lazar. "We should just cut off his hand."

"He's still alive," I said. "No."

Caleb glared at me. I stared right back until he looked away.

Water turned Lazar's white shirt transparent, outlining his broad shoulders and narrow waist. He had pushed his hair, a darker gold when wet, back from his face. He put the gun in his waistband and grabbed one of Dooley's feet, waiting for Caleb to take the other.

Caleb's eyes flicked from Lazar to me and back again, his face set. I wanted to yell at him that now was not the time for animosity to get in the way, but I knew that would only make it worse. He turned his gaze to the doorway. The flames there were almost small enough to let the men through.

"I'll cover the door," Caleb said, moving swiftly to get between us and the milling men in white. He pulled a blue button from his pocket.

Lazar shot him a heated look and grabbed Dooley's other foot. What Caleb was doing made tactical sense, but his real motivation came from distaste for me and Lazar.

*Fine.* Bearing the fat man's considerable weight, Lazar and I shuffled toward the other door. Siku followed, carrying a bedraggled November and keeping his bulk between us and the door.

The water continued to pour down, and I glanced back. The flames were dead, and the men in white zigzagged through the door, guns pointed at Caleb. Before they could fire, he snapped the button at them, calling out a single chilly note. A black cloud of power shot from his outstretched hand and struck the button.

It shimmered like a diamond, and then shook itself, stabbing outward. A wall of icicles appeared like a freezing monolith in the doorway. Shining daggers of ice speared the two men in the way, knocking them bloody to the floor.

We neared the door. Amaris hastily punched in the code as I hoisted Dooley up. Amaris grabbed the man's wrist and lifted his hand to the scanner. The door snapped open.

Lazar and I put Dooley down, and I pushed the door open, peeking inside. No sprinklers watered the metal staircase here. It descended into darkness. My eyes adjusted to the dark as I stepped through the door, water pooling at my feet. The stairs jogged down left and right twice, ending in an unlit room with two doors on opposite sides. They didn't have locks that required hand scanners, so I motioned Lazar forward. Siku followed, the stairs barely wide enough to accommodate his huge frame, with Arnaldo, London, and Amaris following closely behind.

I paused in pounding down the stairs to glance up, waiting for Caleb.

Lazar paused on the step above me, followed my glance, and said, "He can take care of himself."

I didn't say, "Except when he's trapped in a silver cage," or "Except when a demon thing from Othersphere takes over his body." I'd helped Caleb through both of those situations. Just because he wasn't mine to help anymore didn't mean I stopped wanting to. Then I caught the swirl of his black coat as he slammed the door shut behind him. It got very dark until Amaris snapped on a flashlight, gun still in her right hand. Heartened, I continued down.

There wasn't time to worry about which door to go

through. The one on the right was locked. I drew the Shadow Blade, inserted it into the space between door and jamb and cut through as if it were pie. The knife's edge grew more distinct as I pulled it out. It liked eating through metal. I shoved the door open to see a few more metal steps going down.

Beyond, a dozen objurers armed with tranquilizer guns were waiting. I had a second to take in a large underground parking garage before all ten fired at me.

My cat-shifter reflexes had always been fast. I jerked the door shut as the tranq darts thudded into it.

"They were waiting for us!" I said.

"It's like they want us to go through that door." Lazar was right behind me, pointing to the door on the left. My heart sank. He was right. We were being funneled somewhere. Ximon must have started grouping his people as soon as I cut the lock on his door. He was out there somewhere nearby, directing all of this. But as long as wherever he led us was close to the accelerator, we still might be able to shut it down. Then we'd have to fight our way out.

"I'm worried about this virus," Arnaldo said, a few steps up from me. "What if we're heading toward it and it somehow infects us?"

Above, an arm clad in white opened the door to the computer room. Caleb whirled in a swirl of black, humming, and sent another ball of fire hissing at the door. It shut abruptly as flames exploded all around it.

"Looks like it's our only choice!" I said, slashing through the lock. "Go!"

Gun ready, Lazar kicked the door open and went in, reaching along the wall to click on a light. It flickered, showing more stairs down.

"Clear!" he said.

Arnaldo and London visibly hesitated in the doorway. London's hackles were up. She turned her icy blue eyes on me, lip curling to show a bit of fang.

"If you smell someone else down there, bark now," I said. "Otherwise, we don't have a lot of choices."

Arnaldo said, "Come on, London," and followed Lazar. She took a few sniffs, then went after him. I breathed in relief. At least she hadn't sensed more objurers in the immediate area. I waited and let Siku, November, and Amaris go in before me. Caleb came last, his normally dark eyes flaring a gold so bright they were almost neon.

"I don't like this," he said. But he went through the door. I followed and shut it behind us.

The steps went down, back and forth, and farther down. The walls that rose around us were earth, plastered over and whitewashed, not unlike the walls of our school.

As we descended, my skin prickled with something darker than static electricity. It was tugging at me, inside, wanting me to not just go farther down, but somehow to go farther in. I'd had a similar feeling out in the forest when the animals came to me—a sense of infinite possibility, of magic, if I just stepped through.

A cement floor appeared below, but the stairs didn't stop, heading down through a mesh trapdoor. Amaris shot the hinges off with two clean shots, as footsteps clattered above. More objurers giving chase.

Arnaldo shoved the door aside, and down he went.

As soon as he passed through the trapdoor, an earsplitting buzzer went off. Arnaldo hesitated, halfway through.

"I was wondering when we'd hit an alarm!" I shouted over the claxon. Way up the stairs, flashlights swiped through the dark. Flashes of legs in white pants were running down after us.

"We could fight them on the stairs here," Amaris screamed.

"No. We have to keep going!" Caleb could make his voice loud without shouting. "We have to find a way to disable the accelerator."

"There has to be a backup server," Arnaldo yelled over the

din. "If we can access that, we can hack in and set up some kind of self-destruct."

I caught everyone's eye, and we were all agreed. Down we went.

The space closed around us. The beam of Amaris's flashlight showed we were in a tunnel of concrete. The steps ended on an asphalt walkway with the curved wall of the tunnel on one side and a thick metal tube about four feet in diameter on the other. As far as the light shone, the tunnel curved onward in both directions, the metal tube glinting.

"Looks like we found the particle accelerator," Arnaldo bellowed, catching his breath as we all paused at the bottom of the stairs. The alarm kept on with its dreadful clamor. "It probably goes on like that for miles."

"Just a mile and a half," said Lazar, his voice also effortlessly loud. "According to the blueprints. It circles around and comes back here."

"Are there other exits?" Caleb's voice was terse. I knew what he was thinking. Were we trapped hundreds of feet underground in a circular trap?

"Not that I know of," said Lazar. "But they never let me down here, and the blueprints I saw could have been purposely inaccurate."

"How the hell do we destroy it?" asked Arnaldo at top volume, walking over to run a hand over the metal surface of the tube. "I don't see any computers. Wait. Look, there!" He pointed.

"What?" Squinting in reaction to the blasts of sound, I followed his finger to see small holes in the ceiling that had tiny pipes jutting out of them. "What are those? They look like spray nozzles or something."

Caleb was looking too, eyebrows drawn together. "You said something about a virus?"

The alarm beat down on us. I bowed my head, the racket banging against the inside of my skull. It was maddening. As a cat-shifter, my hearing was extremely sensitive, although the blare was enough to drive anyone insane. *It has to stop. I can't think. Make it stop . . .*

Arnaldo shook his head. "It doesn't make sense. Goddamn it! I can't think with this noise!"

Fury reached its black tentacles out along my every limb, extending out beyond my skin. . . .

"Enough!" I screamed.

The alarm died in mid-honk.

Blessed silence fell. I took a deep breath. *Much better.*

I looked up to see Caleb eyeing me in surprise. Lazar looked wary. In fact, everyone was staring at me. *Did I do that?* Could my anti-tech-fu work without even touching the machine involved? It had never occurred to me to even try. Or maybe it was just a coincidence. . . .

Arnaldo's face cleared in the blessed quiet. Then a realization hit him. His eyes widened with dismay. "That's got to be it. They said something about a virus. DNA plus strangelets from the accelerator. I could be wrong—but they could have altered our DNA and used it to genetically engineer a virus. A virus aimed at us."

"Welcome," said a familiar voice, channeled through a speaker. Fluorescent lights winked on along both sides of the tunnel, illuminating our haggard, sweating faces, the metal tube, and a window ten feet wide and three feet high set into the side of the tunnel opposite us.

Behind that window stood a handsome older man with a thick head of pure white hair and perfect blue-white teeth that flashed as he smiled at us through the thick glass. Ximon.

Near him two men in lab coats were busy with some shiny equipment. One said, "The injectors are ready, Your Grace. We will go on your mark."

Ximon's smile faded. He looked almost sad. "Welcome to my little experiment, shifters. Welcome, my children. Welcome to the end of the otherkin."

# CHAPTER 22

Caleb didn't hesitate. Using his slingshot, he fired a red button at his father's smug face, intoning a perilous note. The button flared into a sphere of burning lava and smacked into the glass. It hung there for a second, flames licking its surface. Then it slid like a fiery slug down the window, leaving the glass unharmed.

Lazar was only a second behind. He pointed his pistol at Ximon's face and fired. The gunshots echoed loudly through the narrow chamber, but the bullets bounced off the window. Bulletproof glass.

Ximon let out a sorrowful laugh. Caleb's lava fell heavily onto the asphalt on the other side of the tube from us and began to burn a hole down into it. "My only sons. And my beautiful daughter, Amaris. You look so much like your mother, my dear. I've been expecting you. But still. Seeing you here breaks my heart."

All the blood drained from my heart. I was hollow. *I've*

*been so wrong.* "That's why they only shot at us with tranquilizer darts. They wanted us alive. Ximon wanted us here."

Amaris made a small, sad noise in the back of her throat and reached out to put a hand on London's furry back, as if to steady herself.

Above, a metal hatch slid into place, cutting off our escape. Siku roared up at it, and then turned the roar on Lazar.

"I didn't know," Lazar said, backing away from the bear. "I didn't know!"

"It's true," Ximon said, turning his melancholy gaze to me. "I saw how he looked at you that night you burned my compound down, Amba. I heard you offer to take him with you. I saw the hesitation in his eyes, and I knew then that one day he would betray me. Lazar"—Ximon's voice caught slightly as he said his son's name—"after your brother left us, I prayed you would carry our quest and the family name with honor. I loved you. I still do."

"Love is more than words," said Lazar. "And your actions have not been those of a loving father."

Ximon shook his head, his eyes bright. *Were those unshed tears?* After everything he'd done, he still loved his children. Somehow that made everything even more appalling.

Nausea twisted my stomach. Ximon had been expecting us. So everything, from the first contact with Lazar onward, had been a trap. He'd used Lazar to get us here. I'd helped him get exactly what he wanted.

A man in a lab coat leaned in toward Ximon. We could hear his voice faintly over the loudspeaker. "We're ready on your mark, Your Grace."

"Then await my mark!" Ximon snapped. "Can a father not speak to his children one last time?"

Siku and London exchanged desperate glances. November's transparent ears trembled. Arnaldo's throat convulsed as he swallowed down his fear. Caleb stood on the bottom step, his eyes still aglow, staring up at his father.

"What are you dosing us with, Ximon?" he asked.

Arnaldo shot Caleb a look, as if he'd been wanting to ask that same question.

"My cleverest child." Ximon shook his head. "There was a time you called me 'father.' "

"Does the virus cut us off from Othersphere, *Father*?" Caleb's tone was biting. "Is that the real reason you built this monstrosity?"

Ximon's dark eyes surveyed Caleb regretfully. "Your mother was equally brilliant. It was my grievous fault when I failed to convert her. I might have reached this important point in my research earlier with her help. Then you never would have left my care or met the Amba. But your mother was stubborn, as you are. As Desdemona Grey has proven to be."

Arnaldo leaned in, lips close to my ear. "It's got to be what Caleb said—Ximon's going to infect us with a quantum virus he created by combining our DNA with the strangelets and O-particles. Once we're infected, it will alter the DNA that connects us to Othersphere. We'll be cut off. Then, when we go back to our homes and communities, the infection will spread . . . to everyone."

*To everyone.*

All the shifters, everywhere, and any callers who came into contact with Caleb or Lazar. All of them would have their abilities, their identities wiped away

I looked up at Ximon almost in admiration as my horror grew. He'd played it so smart, using Lazar's compassion by telling him he'd have to kill extraneous Tribunal members when the experiment was over. Ximon had known that would send Lazar to me for help.

And Ximon knew me too. It made me shiver to think how well. The last time he'd seen me, Ximon had said my compassion would be my undoing. I never expected it would be compassion he wanted me to feel—for Lazar. That, and that alone, had brought me here and doomed my friends. And everyone they knew and loved.

"And my only daughter, my once-in-a-lifetime healer, Amaris." Ximon had eyes only for his children, ignoring the rest of us to lean forward and look down on Amaris. "The praise and thanks we gave when your powers were discovered!"

"That's all I ever was to you, a healer. Not a daughter," said Amaris.

Ximon shook his head. "You don't understand. You were a gift from God, until these servants of Satan spoiled you."

"God made shifters as they are, Father," she said. "Who are you to unmake them?"

"I'm God's best servant," he said. "I understand what he requires. And in his mercy, he has found a way for me to preserve your lives and to wash your ultimate sin away. You will return to the fold, Amaris, and rejoin your husband."

I looked over at Amaris in despair. We couldn't let her fall back into the hands of that disgusting man.

Amaris choked, fingers white on the grip of her gun. "I'll kill him. I'll kill myself before I let him touch me."

London threw her head back and howled.

The sound brought me out of my hopelessness. Somewhere in the back of my mind, I knew I was missing something. There was a solution somewhere nearby, if I could only see it. I'd allowed Ximon to take the lead for precious minutes now. *Think, think, Dez!*

"Once you are taken care of, we will use this accelerator to continue our work," said Ximon, "Which is to cut this world off entirely from the devilish influence of Othersphere. We will thicken the veil around this world and keep it safe."

No more lightning tree.

No more snowshoe hares grooming their ears at my feet.

No more nights prowling as a tiger, hearing a snowflake touch the earth, tasting the breeze from the north, smelling the sap rise within the trees.

No more contact with my biological mother. I would never

know her now. Never understand the part of me that came from her.

No more worrying about setting my cell phone on fire.

The air around me seemed to contract and fracture.

*That's it.*

I'd been so blind. The very thing I'd thought of as a curse, my tendency to destroy technology, was the answer to our problem. I'd turned off that head-splitting alarm with a thought. What else might I be able to do, down here where the underground nuclear tests had torn the veil to shreds? The thing that had felt so dark, threatening, and strange, was now the remedy.

I'd been a fool.

*Othersphere is close.*

It lurked in the corner of my eye. I heard the deep hum of it in the earth. Its music stirred the churning black center of power that always lurked inside me.

The metal of the accelerator tube, its wires and gears, the pipes ready to blow sickness over us, the filaments in the lights, the triggers on the guns, the hinges on the trapdoor above—I felt them all, saw them clearly in my mind, scratched their itch against my skin.

*They are nothing. Destroy them.*

Ximon was saying, head bowed, "I'm sorry I could not keep you safe, my children. I do believe that to be my own greatest sin."

"The lights are about to go out," I said to my friends. "Head up the stairs."

Ximon stood up a little straighter, dropping his hands at his sides. "What did you say? No, they're not." Alarmed, he flapped a hand at the technician. "Ready the injectors!"

London turned her laser-blue eyes on me, and I swear her wolf mouth smiled.

"Mark!" Ximon shouted, pressing his hands against the bulletproof glass, staring down at me. "Spray them with the virus, now! *Now!*"

His technicians scrambled to obey, their hands moving over the console in front of them.

I laid my hand upon the metal tube of the accelerator. Reaching deep inside myself, I let the darkness out.

Blackness flooded me, and I felt the *wrongness* of the metal in the tube, how it had been wrenched from the earth, melted, refined, and shaped by hands that did not love it and could never understand it. I heard its voice, sighing, a prisoner. But I sought out a different voice—bypassing the computers in Ximon's room above, the tubes in the lights, the pipes, and coming to rest on the injectors forced into the concrete walls.

*I free you.*

The blackness inside me flowed into the tube, flew up into the lights, and followed the wires and pipes in the walls.

The lights went out. The hum of machinery died.

From behind the glass I heard a muffled, "No! Damn it!"

"Nice." Caleb's voice came through clear in the darkness. It shouldn't have warmed my heart, but it did.

"Hold still, everyone," I said. "We're getting out of here." I brushed past Amaris and London, moving around Lazar and Arnaldo by remembering where I'd seen them last and feeling for their shoulders. Even in human form, my senses were sharper than normal. I couldn't see in total darkness, but I could hear breathing, feel how the air changed when people moved, smell the cotton in their clothes, or in Caleb's case as I approached him on the stairs, the wool of his long black coat, damp now from the sprinklers.

"Let me get up to the door and cut it open," I said. I put a hand on Caleb's back to move past him up the stairs. His heart was beating fast but evenly. I said, "I think the power's out throughout most of the complex. Amaris, don't turn on your flashlight unless you absolutely have to, and keep hold of London. Her nose and ears will get you out of here. Caleb and Lazar, do the same or hang onto Siku."

I unsheathed the Shadow Blade, feeling above my head for

the metal door. "As soon as I cut it open, move out fast. Don't wait for me."

I slid the knife into the cold metal above me. It sliced through it, growing colder and happier in my hand. Below me, my friends arranged themselves. The voices up behind Ximon's window were still yelling at each other, muffled through the glass.

Amaris said, "I've got London here. We'll go first. If they've got a light source and see us, I'll shoot them. Lazar, where are you?"

"Back here with Siku," Lazar said. "Dez, why shouldn't we wait for you? You need to come too."

"No," I said, cutting another right angle through the metal, making my own door. "I have to destroy the entire particle accelerator."

"*What*?" Lazar said. "No, you can't stay down here alone. It's too dangerous. I'll stay with you."

"No." I was almost done. I traced the cuts with my free hand, ready for the metal square to fall into it. "You know the complex better than anyone. You have to make sure everyone gets out safely."

"On the way, we'll destroy that laboratory across from the computer room," Arnaldo said.

Siku grunted a deep agreement and November chirped. The only one I hadn't heard anything from was Caleb. Did he hate me even more now that I had failed them all so terribly?

The large metal square I had cut fell heavily into my hand. I threw it over the railing in the direction of the accelerator's tubing. It clanged into the metal there.

"Go," I said, moving aside, feeling for the nearest person to find London's soft, wet fur under my fingers. "Stay safe."

London yipped and trotted up the stairs through the open space I'd created.

A taller presence moved by her side, smelling of gunpowder. "See you soon," said Amaris.

Long fingers found my shoulder, and I heard Arnaldo's

unique breathing as he fumbled and found my hand, holding it tightly for a second before he moved up through the door. I squeezed back and let him go.

Siku came next, walking on all fours, smelling like a fur rug left out in the rain. He grunted, touched his nose to my hand, then lumbered upward. November's claws tickled me as she ran up the length of my arm, mussed my hair, and raced down the other arm to hop back onto Siku's back.

Somewhere, far above, footsteps clattered clumsily on the stairs. Objurers were trying to gather up there. One of them shouted something to another, and then cursed the darkness. "Try one of the flashlights from deep storage. What kind of black magic is this?"

Then Lazar was there, smelling like clean laundry airing on the line. He found my shoulders with both hands, leaned in, and pressed his lips to my chin. He'd probably been aiming for my cheek. "This is all my fault," he said, pulling back.

I reached for his face and found his tousled wet hair, then slid my fingers down to wrap them around the back of his neck. "No," I said. "He fooled everyone. Mostly me. Keep my friends safe."

"I will," he said, like an oath. Then he moved along with Siku.

I waited, my heart beating loudly in my ears. Then I felt a familiar presence and caught the scent of the forest before a thunderstorm. *Caleb.*

"I messed up everything," I said. "I'm sorry."

His hand brushed mine, and I couldn't tell if it was deliberate or not. His footsteps paused. "Better go tiger. What you're planning won't be easy."

A tiny thrill passed through me. Even after all this, Caleb knew me better than anyone, and he must care just a little if he was offering advice.

"Good idea," I said, my voice thick, forcing myself not to say *good-bye.* "Thanks."

I turned and ran down the steps, not missing one, even in the dark.

Caleb was right. As Othersphere pressed in on me from all sides, I reached toward it. All the sadness I felt about Caleb, the confusion over what Ximon had said, they only increased the propulsive surge inside me.

I shifted, clothing shredding across my new shoulders. As I inhaled with larger lungs, I could feel that my tiger form was bigger than it had been before, stronger, faster, senses even keener. I dug my claws into the concrete, piercing it as easily as cloth. I whipped my tail, bumping it into the cool metal of the accelerator tube. My fur rippled, irritated from the steel so close.

I held completely still, ears cocked. Above, my friends climbed the stairs, their footsteps light but audible to me. Soon they would clash with the three other sets of footsteps coming down toward them.

Up behind the observation window, Ximon's voice called out, "I don't care why, just get that backup generator going!"

A fist smacked into flesh, followed by a painful grunt. He must be taking his frustration out on his subordinates. My whiskers caught a stir of air. Far ahead, around the curve of the tunnel, someone was coming toward me.

I dipped my head, calling upon the link to Othersphere at my heart, and then sent it flaring outward. I roared, and the vast set of heavy pipes around me rattled like teacups in their saucers. Metal hissed and sluggishly began to sag, like warm rubber.

I sprang forward, running down the asphalt trail next to the accelerator and sending out waves of rippling destructive force toward everything man-made in my wake. It felt so good. I'd once tried to rip my back brace apart with my bare hands and failed utterly. Now, here where Othersphere was close, I could do so much more.

I didn't go at my full speed, keeping my ears cocked for

sounds up ahead, whiskers fanned out like peacock feathers to catch the slightest change in air pressure. The path curved as I traced the circumference of the accelerator. As I rounded one section, feeling the metal next to me melting like butter in the sun, three lights winked ahead.

A beam illuminated my stripes, and a shout went up: objurers, armed with flashlights. My first flash of destructive power must not have touched them.

A shot rang out. A bullet pinged into the tubing.

I growled, and hurled the force of Othersphere forward like a dark blanket. The face of one man, only ten yards ahead, was briefly illuminated, his eyes widening with fear as they traveled up my huge frame to find my narrowed yellow eyes. Then his light went out.

He screamed and tried to fire at the place where I had been. But his gun was blackened dross. Then I was on him. My paws were bigger than his head. I dug claws into his shoulder and side, and sank my teeth into his flesh, cutting through the sinews of his throat, splitting his spine. Blood gushed out, coating my tongue with coppery saltiness. I gulped it down and felt the power within me renewed. Dropping him like a doll, I looked up to see another man holding a rifle with a flashlight strapped to its barrel, aiming at me.

I snuffed out his light and leaped upon him.

Light hit my eyes and something whistled past my ears. I ducked, releasing the limp objurer, as a third man aimed yet another silver rifle at me. If he hit me with silver bullets, this could be the end. I hoped I'd destroyed enough of the accelerator to render it useless forever. I could die knowing I'd accomplished that, at least.

Then a fourth man, dressed in a long black coat, stepped out of the shadows and punched him in the face.

*Caleb.*

The objurer reeled back. Caleb jerked the rifle out of his hands, pointed it at him, and fired. Blood splattered against the wall, and the man slumped, eyes rolling back.

Caleb wrenched the flashlight off the rifle barrel and ran the light over me. His wet dark hair clung to his temples, his chest rising and falling rapidly from what must have been a dead run. His eyes in the reflected light were bright gold, assessing me clinically. "Damn, you're *bigger*. Amazing. Othersphere effects, I bet. You're uninjured? Good."

Joy rebounded through my heart. I butted my head against him, and his look of focus and ferocity morphed into a reluctant smile. "It didn't make sense for you to do this alone," he said. "The otherkin need you alive."

My happiness contracted, but only slightly. So he was here for the greater good, not because he loved me. *Or so he says.* Hope fluttered inside me, like a baby bird that still didn't quite know how to fly. I didn't know if I should encourage the feeling or not.

Caleb turned the beam of light to the accelerator tubing, and I finally saw my handiwork. What had once been shiny and perfectly cylindrical was now a molten, blackened mass, oozing like a dying slug as far back as the curve of the tunnel allowed us to see. Could all that be because of me? For a moment, even I was awed.

He shined the light up ahead, where the unblemished tube continued on. "Maybe another three quarters of a mile to go. Shall we?"

I roared in delight. *Caleb and I are working together again!*

He winced at the volume of my excitement, cast me a joking look of reproof, then clicked off the light, dropped the rifle, and put his hand lightly on my shoulder. "Let's go."

So we ran, side by side, through the tunnel. With Caleb there, my energy was boundless. It boiled up and sent the metal before us melting and popping like molten lava. It felt like no time at all before we were back where we started, still in darkness. The entire accelerator lay in ruins around us.

No sounds came from the window where Ximon had been. He must have left to try to muster his people. Caleb and I found our way to the stairs and began the long climb up. Caleb still seemed as invigorated by the thinness of the veil as I. We panted as we ascended, but our pace didn't flag.

Near the top of the stairs, we came across three bodies lying draped over the railing or head down on the stairs.

A quick sniff confirmed for me they were none of our friends. As Caleb ran his hands over one of them, I mewed in a way I hoped was reassuring.

"Not them, eh?" he said, getting my meaning immediately. "Good."

We traced our steps back to the place where we'd seen the door down into the garage. I was about to continue up the steps to the complex, but Caleb paused.

"Wait," he said. I heard his hand land on the door to the garage. "Let's grab one of the trucks and drive it up. Assuming I can hot-wire it. We'd get to the surface a lot faster, maybe be able to join everyone. Do you think any of them will start?"

Remembering how I'd gotten machines to turn back on during my lesson with Morfael, I trilled back at him encouragingly. If we made it to the surface in a truck and our friends weren't there, we could go back down into the complex faster than if we climbed up on foot.

"Here we go." He pushed the door open, feeling his way to the stairs down into the garage. I could tell from the absence of other sounds that no objurers lurked there.

I reached out, feeling with my mind for a light, and released it. Illumination flooded the wide-open area of the garage.

"Woo-hoo!" Caleb jumped down the stairs three at a time, coat sailing out behind him.

I bounded from the top of the stair right to the bottom, beating him down. I lashed my tail at him and crouched as if ready to pounce.

"No fair!" he said, his tone playful. "Oh, wait!" He began to take off his coat. "Did you want to . . . ?"

I shook my head. I didn't want to shift back to human yet. Being a tiger felt too wonderful, especially this close to Othersphere. And something about being in tiger form made it easier for Caleb to be with me. I couldn't let that go. Not yet.

"Okay. Then we'll need a slightly larger vehicle." His liquid eyes lit upon a large pickup truck. "We can bring it back for Raynard! Let's go."

Pulling his coat over his fist, he smashed it into the driver's side window of the truck. The glass flew. He opened the door, got inside, and reached under the dash for the wires to get it started.

I leaped into the bed of the truck. It rocked like a boat in a storm, and I mentally released the truck's engine from the dark binding of Othersphere.

The engine roared to life. Caleb turned and pounded triumphantly on the back window of the cab at me. I put my paw up to the glass, and roared. He gunned the motor, and we took off.

# CHAPTER 23

We wound our way upward by the twin beams of the head-lights, which meant some of the power around us was work-ing again. It worked well enough to lift a metal door for us when we hit the sensor. As we drove past where we'd first en-tered the complex, I saw four slumped bodies dressed in white near the table with the playing cards. We'd left one there, and one at the top in the desert. So three of them were new.

Which meant that some or all of our friends had made it that far on their way out of the complex. Impatience beat on me as the truck curved up the drive to reveal a square of starry sky above. The rush of cool fresh air was a blessing. *They must be okay, all of them.* Or I would never forgive my-self.

Caleb slowed as we approached the exit. The objurer Lon-don had killed still lay to one side, but there was no way to know what else had happened up here. Some kind of animal noises and shouts came from not far away. Caleb stopped the truck just below ground level.

I jumped out and padded up beside the truck to peer over the edge.

The light of the full moon blazed down onto the desert, casting a hard black shadow from the observation tower. The shallow pool of water nearby reflected the silver beams like a mirror. Everything was shockingly sharp to my eyes, as if I'd suddenly put on glasses after years of quasi-blindness. The nearness of Othersphere heightened everything.

Something scuffled far behind me. I turned and crept out farther to look. Then in the distance: a ferocious bark and whine. *London.* A furry brown mountain moved into view, chasing something two-legged in white. *Siku.*

Caleb raised his eyebrows inquiringly at me, and I nodded. Then I sprang back into the bed of the truck. The tires spun, and Caleb peeled out, swerving in the direction I'd been gazing in.

I put my front paws up on the roof of the cab, wind ruffling my ears, to get a better look as we thumped over hillocks and small cacti. From here, I could see Siku turning from the prone body of an objurer next to a truck, which acted as a shield between him and seven other armed objurers.

Amaris was peeking around the back of the truck, taking shots at the men in white, pinning them down. I didn't see Arnaldo or November, but London was limping near three prone figures in white. She weaved slightly, like she was drunk, and then fell over. My stomach clenched. Was she drugged or something much worse?

"Shit!" I heard Caleb say inside the truck. He floored it as one of the objurers fired three shots at Amaris. Another person in white, a woman, ran toward London.

Nearby, two objurers were moving in, using the truck and a large cactus as cover, to surround Amaris. They had holstered their regular pistols and pulled out tranquilizer guns. Ximon's orders must be to capture her alive. The other three people in white were moving around the end of the truck, two of them firing darts at Siku. The small lump on his back had to be November. The other one was firing real bullets at Lazar.

But they hit nothing, distracted by a winged streak of feathers falling out of the sky. With an earsplitting screech, Arnaldo grabbed the silver gun in his talons and flew away. In the moonlight I tracked him as he zoomed back up, leaving an objurer with a bloody, empty hand.

"You get the one on London!" Caleb shouted, swerving to avoid a clump of saguaro. "I got the ones on Amaris."

As our truck approached the prone wolf, the female objurer near London turned, hearing our engines. She raised her tranquilizer gun as I launched myself into the air, using the truck's momentum and my own power to leap over thirty yards. She gaped at me, firing almost as a reflex, and her dart whizzed past my ear. I cannoned into her so hard the impact sent us both rolling like tumbleweeds.

I got to my feet to see Caleb speeding the truck right at the two men stalking Amaris. They veered in different directions to avoid getting run over, but one of them was not fast enough. The truck rammed him, hurtling him thirty feet to lie broken on the ground. Caleb swerved to track down the other one.

My objurer had rolled to her side, blood pouring down her face, and fumbled with trembling hands at her gun. I gathered up the darkness inside me and growled at her.

Up here, the veil was slightly thicker. I could feel it. And the well of power inside me that could destroy technology without a touch was drying up. But the gun in the objurer's hand blackened and warped. She dropped it as if it burned her. The silver cross around her neck sizzled. She screamed, tore it off, and threw it away from her.

"The devil!" She pushed herself away from me, face pale. "You're the devil himself."

*Herself,* I thought. But I settled for a derisive tiger snort.

From the angle of her left arm, it looked like her collarbone was broken. She was no longer a threat. I looked for Caleb and saw him drive down the other fleeing objurer. He braked and downshifted just enough to bump the man hard. He fell with an audible snap. Caleb had to haul on the wheel to avoid running over him.

Closer to the Tribunal's empty truck, Lazar had gotten one of the objurers in a headlock, using the man's body as a shield between him and the other two.

Meanwhile, Siku, with November on top of him, moved with his surprising speed around the truck to come up behind the other men. One turned and fired. The dart buried itself into Siku's front leg. The other objurer ran.

That saved his life, for Siku let loose a bellow of rage and lashed out at the man who had shot him. His long claws hit the man near the neck and tore his head off with a heavy spurt of dark blood.

I ran over to where London lay. One sniff told me she was unconscious but not dead. *Thank the Moon.* A dart had speared her shoulder. Her jaws were covered in blood, but from the odor, I knew it was not her own. But her front paws were bloody from dozens of cactus quills. Reverting to her human form would cure those wounds and push the needles from her body, but she was out cold and unable to shift.

*Caleb.* He could send her wolf form back to Othersphere. He was turning the truck in a wide circle, bringing it back toward the objurer who had fled Siku. Lazar had knocked out the man he'd had in the headlock and dropped him to the ground.

In the distance, I heard other engines, at least four large ones, coming from the entrance to the accelerator. The Tribunal was coming, in force. *We have to get out of here.*

There were other noises too, coming from a different direction, that didn't make sense to me. *No time to worry about that now.*

Amaris came running up, holstering her gun, to kneel beside London. "Is she . . . ?"

I shook my head as she felt for a pulse. Tension drained from her as she found it, and she buried her face in the wolf's fur. She'd been even more worried than I had been.

I mewed. *No time for that!* She sat up and wiped angrily at the tears running through the desert dust on her face. "She needs to shift. Her paws are shredded. Or maybe we can get her into the truck. . . ."

I uttered a short, negative growl.

"What? Oh!" She saw what I was looking at—four sets of very bright headlights coming our way. I had no idea how we were going to get out of this.

Lazar yelled from where he was taking ammunition off the objurer bodies, "Four trucks full of men coming any second now!"

Off in the distance Caleb's truck knocked the running objurer to the ground.

I butted Amaris with my head, then nosed London's bloody paws.

"She stumbled into the cactus because she was saving me from those three." Amaris pointed back at the three bodies I'd first seen as we drove up. "It's my fault."

I sniffed London's paws again, and then pushed my nose up against Amaris's hands.

Amaris's eyes lit with understanding, then despair. "Heal her? No, I can't, I . . ."

She looked up at the headlights approaching. Caleb and Lazar were still far away. Siku was galloping toward us, but it would be nearly impossible for him or for me to carry London away with our claws and teeth without hurting her even more.

Amaris looked at me, her jaw set. Her dark eyes turned steely. I'd seen a similar look on Caleb's face many times. "I have to do this," she said. "I love her, you know."

I nodded, and took a step back. Amaris closed her eyes and

held her hands out, palms up. She grew very still. Her face took on a look of utter peace, as if all the love in her heart had poured outward.

The headlights of Ximon's trucks were fanning out into a semicircle, hoping to pin us against their empty truck. I placed my long, striped form between Amaris and London and the nearest truck, now fifty yards away.

Amaris gasped, and her eyes flew open. Instead of warm brown, they glittered silver, bright as the full moon rising over us. Her skin took on a sheen, then a glow. Light trickled from the ends of her hair and streamed from the tips of her fingers. She looked like a creature made of moonlight. The wave of power echoing inside me told me that she had accessed something very powerful in Othersphere.

"Amaris!" Lazar shouted in alarm from over by the truck. He began running toward her. "What . . . !"

I growled a warning at him. He slowed, bewildered.

Caleb's truck rumbled between us and the oncoming vehicles. A pop, then something pinged into the truck. *Bullets.* I remembered the sound from the first night I'd met Caleb. The Tribunal had fired at us then too, as we'd stolen Lazar's BMW to get us to safety.

Amaris was smiling. The white radiance made her look like an angel or some benevolent alien. She ran a hand lovingly over London's furry head, then down her shoulder to touch her front paws. Wherever the silver light touched, the wounds disappeared. The cactus spines were pushed out by the healing flesh. She leaned over and whispered into the wolf's ear. "Wake up."

London lifted her head, ears erect, then scrambled to her feet, wagging her tail furiously. In the light coming from Amaris, her fur sparkled silver.

Amaris's smile widened. "Hey, beautiful."

London's wild blue eyes took her in, shining like a star; then she barked joyously and licked her face. Amaris laughed.

"We're surrounded!"

It was Caleb's voice. Siku, November, and Lazar had run up closer as one of the four trucks circled around behind us. Caleb's truck sort of shielded us from two of the vehicles, but there were headlights aimed at us from the four corners of the compass.

The light from Amaris dimmed. She blinked, wavered, and then shook her head as if about to pass out. London dipped her head under Amaris's arm to act as a support.

I knew how Amaris felt. I, too, was growing weary. I'd drawn on my own reserves time and again to destroy the technology ranged against us. And given the slightly thicker texture of the veil aboveground, I didn't have near enough power to stop the trucks, douse their lights, or melt all the guns pointing at us. But I couldn't despair yet. *We'll find another way.*

"Get in the truck!" Lazar pointed toward Caleb's truck.

It was our only chance. He was right. But there were too many of the enemy. I could see the same thought on everyone's face. Not all of us would get away.

"Surrender and you might live," came an amplified voice we all recognized. Ximon. I could see his snowy white head and broad shoulders climbing out of the cab of the truck to the east; he stood on the running board. He wasn't using a megaphone or mic. His voice only sounded as if he were.

Lazar was helping Amaris to her feet. She could walk, but kept one hand on London's back and the other arm around Lazar's neck for support.

Siku turned his back to us, facing out toward the truck to the south, and bared his teeth. November huddled on top of him, using his shoulder blades for cover. A growl rolled out of my throat, echoed by a snarl from London. Beyond Siku, four figures in white poured out of the truck, lining up to aim rifles at us. If there were four in each truck, that was sixteen objurers, plus Ximon, to deal with.

Caleb moved from his truck toward us as Amaris stumbled forward. A bullet hit the ground at Caleb's feet, and he stopped dead.

"Don't move," said Ximon. His tone was the most reasonable in the world, and I felt a lethargy weighing down my limbs. Lazar, London, and Amaris came to a stumbling halt.

*Why would I move? Moving would be silly.*

"In fact," Ximon said, "why don't you lie down? You're so very tired."

I curled my tail around my body, bending my knees to lie down. I could see the others doing the same.

"You've fought so well, so bravely. Lay your burden down now. Rest."

*Resting will feel so good.*

I sat, stretching my forelimbs out luxuriously. *Just a little nap.* Near his stolen truck, Caleb wavered, eyes fluttering as if about to fall asleep on his feet.

"Rest, and know that you are safe. . . ." The voice was so soothing. It was my father's voice, a voice I had never known. He had found me at last, and he would protect me. "You are safe with—*Aah!*"

The soothing tones broke off. An explosive cry pierced the calm. I snapped alert as an eagle dived from the sky to rake its talons across Ximon's throat. He fell, and others rushed to help him.

*Arnaldo?* I got to my feet. Caleb straightened, and London urged Amaris again toward the truck.

There was a flurry of movement within the trucks. Guns were raised.

Another penetrating screech descended like a thunderbolt as the eagle somehow was also behind me, falling upon one of the men facing Siku.

But wait—Arnaldo was still to the north, hurtling back up into the sky. There was a second eagle helping us, one even bigger than he.

A battery of shots came from the objurers. Dirt kicked up around us. Hot pain sliced into my shoulder. A bullet. No time to think. I moved anyway, putting myself between London, Amaris, and Lazar and the truck to the east. I looked over at Siku. He glanced over his shoulder at me. I nodded.

We were the muscle. We would cover as they escaped in the truck.

Siku's huge head dipped in a small nod to me, black button eyes shining. Turning back to the men arrayed in front of him, he snorted, pawed the ground, and charged. November clung to his back like a rodent rodeo rider. I silently wished them good luck.

There was a flutter of silent black wings over by the truck to the west as what looked like a giant owl swooped down, grabbed a man by the shoulder, and carried him, screaming, into the air. His legs kicked. The men around him ducked, staring up at the sky with dread. Two of them tried to aim at the huge, feathered creature, but couldn't fire for fear of hitting the man it carried. He tried to shoot it too, but it dropped him. He plummeted fifty feet to the ground. A cloud of dust lifted as he hit.

To the north, a man shrieked as a huge furry black form— not Siku's—lunged out of the darkness and bit his neck from behind. *What the hell?* He dropped instantly, and the black bear reared, clawing the next man across the chest.

The objurer next to him aimed his rifle at the bear, but something low to the ground and covered in spikes smashed into the back of his knees. He fell over backwards, bullet shooting harmlessly into the sky. His astonished whoop turned into a yell of pain as he fell onto the spikes of the animal. He rolled off, and the giant porcupine, for that's what it looked like, waddled over and raked its long claws across his throat, chittering with what sounded like glee.

*Otherkin?* It had to be. But I couldn't imagine how. Then, near the porcupine, I saw a bony figure in black tap a long wooden staff on the ground. The truck engine burst into flames. *Morfael!* This all had to be his doing.

Ahead of me, a woman in white was helping Ximon to his feet, a cloth pressed to his throat and shoulder, stemming the blood from the wounds Arnaldo's talons had inflicted. He could still walk, so he wasn't as badly injured as I'd thought. The truck's driver had climbed out to help him into the cab. Two other men stepped out, lowering rifles at me.

I leaped.

Aiming for the larger man, I swerved in midair to avoid a bullet and landed on top of him. His cry muffled by my fur, he thumped to the ground. My claws, longer than fingers, found his carotid artery. Blood gushed from his neck, and I left him, gurgling toward death, to find the other armed man wrestling with a mountain lion. *A mountain lion?* Astonishment made me hesitate.

Ximon was in the truck, leaning heavily on the driver, who had shoved it into gear. The woman who had helped him was climbing into the passenger side when a lithe, spotted, four-footed form leaped onto her back and sank its teeth into her shoulder.

She yelled in pain and surprise, batting at the creature. It was a lynx, its tufted ears strangely familiar. It crawled up her back to rest its front paws on her head, back paws on either shoulder, curving its head down to bite her nose.

The woman squealed, trying to hoist the huge, velvety cat off her, and fell over. The lynx swiveled its head to catch my eye, and I swore it winked. On the other side, the mountain lion was finishing off its prey.

I mentally shook myself as the truck engine revved. The wheels pushed it forward. It was coming right at me, about to run over the body of the man I'd just killed. I could see Ximon's eyes, so like Caleb's, glowering down at me.

"Go!" he shouted to the driver.

I stood my ground, glaring into the headlights, and wrenched deep into the whorl of darkness inside me. There wasn't much left to draw on. *But maybe just enough . . .*

I roared it out, and with a force almost physical, it slammed into the front of the truck. The lights flared and went out. The engine sputtered and died.

My power against technology was gone, I could tell. If I did such a thing again, I might be forced to shift back to human. But it was worth it. In the sudden dark, my eyes adjusted to see Ximon's flabbergasted expression.

"God will damn you, Amba!" he shouted at me through the windshield. "You are damned to hell!"

I lifted my upper lip in a snarl and leaped in a single bound onto the hood of the truck.

Ximon and the driver startled back against their seats reflexively. The driver scrabbled at his door, and then shied away as the mountain lion stood on its hind legs and placed its forepaws on his window.

I drew back my right paw. Smashing into the glass would cut me, but it would be worth it to feel Ximon's face under my claws. I couldn't wait to see the look in his eyes as I killed him.

A high-pitched squeal, far away, hit my ear, making its way past the frightened beating of the human hearts in front of me, past the thundering lust for blood pulsing through my own heart.

*November.*

Another shriek, this one more desperate than the last.

I pivoted, leaped off the truck, and bounded over the desert toward the sound.

Two men lay dead on the ground as Siku sluggishly swiped a paw at a third. He missed, but came back with the other paw, hitting the man in the shoulder, knocking him down, to lie bleeding and cursing on the ground. A fourth man was getting up at that same moment, reaching for a rifle that lay a few feet away.

Siku was bleeding from his left shoulder and his right haunch. I spotted two darts lodged in his fur. A foot-long pod-shaped bundle of fur and whiskers leaped right onto the face of the fourth man, clawing at his eyes.

Yelling in panic, he tried to grab November bodily, but she wiggled away and slid down inside the front of his shirt.

"Gah!" he yelled, plucking at the cloth.

He pulled a pistol from a holster on his hip and pointed it at Siku, who was turning his way with heavy effort. But the man winced as something bulged down near his belt; he writhed, and fell, grabbing desperately for November.

No mysterious otherkin had showed up in this group to help. Siku and November were fighting for us all. And I was almost there.

A fifth man, the driver of the truck, left the cab and ran out, pistol drawn. He wavered, first pointing the gun at Siku, then at the rodent in his ally's pants. Siku stumbled and fell on his side, chest rising and falling in huge, uneven gasps.

*Oh, no. Please, no.*

Satisfied that the bear was no longer a threat, the driver turned the pistol on the squirming protuberance traveling over the body of his friend, trying to angle the shot to hit only November.

The man on the ground put his hands up toward the gun, kicking himself backwards. November squirmed back up into his shirt. "No!" he shouted. "Don—"

The driver fired.

His friend screamed, clutching his chest. The bulge that was November wiggled down the leg of his pants. He fell back, blood spreading in a red pool around him.

"Damn it!" the driver said; his face blanched. He drew a deep breath, girding himself. "You won't die in vain." He pointed the gun once more, right at November.

I was still too far away.

"Hold still, little demon. . . ." The driver closed one eye, finger tightening on the trigger.

Behind him, Siku thrust himself off the ground, eyes glinting red, looming like a ziggurat.

Too late, the driver sensed something and turned. He screamed in terror, and fired point-blank.

Then the bear fell upon him.

The man disappeared beneath a hillock of fur, blood, and muscle. Bone cracked, and everything was still.

I ran up. November peeked out from the pants leg and saw Siku lying next to her. He wasn't moving.

She chirped once, a question, and scuttled over to place a pink paw on his ear. She chirped again, more urgently, crawling up his neck.

The air around Siku warped and bent. The bear was gone. A tall boy with wide muscular shoulders lay there now. His broad chest was marred by a gaping hole near the heart. His long black hair fanned in wild disarray around him. His dark eyes stared out at nothing. He was dead.

# CHAPTER 24

*Siku's dead.*

I was standing, on two human legs, wrapped in a heavy black cloak, staring down at the body of my friend through a kind of tunnel. He looked very far away, even though I knew he lay right at my feet. Someone had covered most of him with the white coat taken from a dead objurer.

November, also human and wearing a long black coat, lay next to him, face buried in his neck, sobbing. London, clad in rumpled sweats, tears coursing down her cheeks, crouched behind her, patting her back helplessly. Amaris hovered nearby, her blood-spattered hand pressed to her mouth, as if trying to stuff down her feelings.

I tasted salt. Someone pressed something into my hand. A handkerchief. Mechanically, I raised it to wipe my eyes and my nose. An angular face, hollow with weariness and covered in brown dust, appeared in the circle of my vision.

*Morfael.* It was his cloak I was wearing. I must have shifted involuntarily when Siku died. November had done the same.

*Oh, November.*

Dizziness overwhelmed me. I dropped down to squat on my heels. "I think I'm in shock," I said. My voice was strangely clear. How was speech even possible now that Siku was dead? How could anything go on?

Morfael hunkered down next to me. His opalescent eyes glittered with what might have been tears, his nearly transparent hair waving in the cold wind. "Yes," he said. "That's why you feel so distant from everything. Why you can speak about it."

I looked over at November. Her narrow fingers clutched at Siku's black hair as deep, inconsolable sobs wracked her body. Her moans sounded like they came through a filter, as if my ears didn't want to hear them.

She was wearing Caleb's coat. He'd put it on her, unless . . .

"Caleb!" I said. "Where is he? Is he . . . ?"

"He's fine," Morfael said. "He's getting the truck. No one else was badly hurt. You had a bullet in your shoulder, but it healed when you shifted. Ximon has fled."

A round-bodied woman with gray tufted hair dressed in jeans and flannel shirt walked up to stand behind Morfael. I'd seen her recently, glaring at me through a computer screen. Now she gazed with pity down at Siku, shaking her head. Then she looked at me, and I recognized the tufts of her hair, just like the tufts on the ears. . . .

*Lady Lynx.*

It must have been she, jumping on that objurer's back, along with the mountain lion. But what was she doing here?

I got to my feet, Morfael's hand at my elbow to keep me steady, as Arnaldo walked up, wearing a set of clothes that didn't fit him too well. Next to him was another familiar face, dark eyes sharper than I'd seen them before, bronze bald head gleaming under the moon.

"Mr. Perez?" I asked.

It was Arnaldo's father. An unusually large red-tailed hawk swooped down, hovered above them for a moment, then landed on Mr. Perez's shoulder. It turned its head to gaze at me with one bright eye that also looked familiar. With the lynx here from the Council, I could only think this was the hawk from the Council as well. But how could that be?

"Yes," said Mr. Perez. "I'm sorry we came too late to help your friend."

I looked at Morfael, amazement bumping up against my sorrow and shock-induced detachment. So that's where he had been going as we headed off to the accelerator. Somehow Morfael had gathered some adult otherkin to help us.

Arnaldo, his eyes red, had moved over to put one arm around London, the other hand reaching out toward November. Caleb's stolen truck pulled up behind them. An enormous black bear shuffled up. Was that the bear-shifter from the Council? Although she wasn't a family member, she halted at the sight of Siku, then uttered a mournful huff and ruffled the boy's hair with her nose.

"I'm so sorry."

Behind me a petite young woman walked up, twisting her long black hair into a slippery bun. *The rat from the Council.* The only one who had voted in my favor in the last meeting. She gazed down sadly as November tried to huddle closer to Siku, stroking his hair.

"Poor girl. I e-mailed her parents that she's uninjured, but that's not really true, is it?"

"What . . ." I struggled against the tightness in my throat. "What are you doing here?"

"Morfael told me you needed some help tonight. I told Jonata there. . . ." She pointed at the lynx. "And she gave the rest of the Council a stiff lecture. The wolves were no help, but Alejandro found out Arnaldo's father wanted to help." She indicated the hawk on Mr. Perez's shoulder. "Add in the bear from the Council, a mountain lion, and an owl I haven't yet been introduced to and you've got yourself a nice little army of shifters swooping in to save the day."

"Well." She squinted hard down at Siku, as if that might keep her from crying. "Maybe saving isn't quite the right word. But Morfael did help me learn to take on a second form. Did you know porcupines are rodents?"

So she had been the huge porcupine I'd seen earlier. Even the adult otherkin were learning how to shift into more than one form. It was another piece of information to process through my numbness.

"You did it, Dez," Caleb said, walking over from the truck in his shirtsleeves. He didn't look as if he felt the cold. Behind him came Lazar.

Arnaldo looked up at me. "At least you brought some members of the shifter tribes together, Dez. I know it may not look like much, but my father . . ." He choked up as emotion overcame him. "My father came."

"This is unprecedented," the lynx, Jonata, said. "It's a tremendous beginning."

Mr. Perez cleared his throat. "It's kind of a miracle," he said. "And I just wanted to add my thanks, and to apologize."

I shook my head at him. Him apologize to me? I was the interfering one, the one who caused all the trouble, the one who got Siku killed. But Arnaldo gave his father an encouraging glance, and he took a step toward me.

"I was wrong to say those awful things to you when you came to my house the other day," he said. "I've been deeply mistaken about many things lately, and I have a lot of work to do. But I wanted you to know I'm sorry." He bowed his head, shutting his long-lidded eyes almost in prayer.

I dipped my head. "Thank you for coming." I had no idea what else to say.

"If there's ever anything you need from me, just ask." He

turned to his son. "I should get back, Arnaldo. Lots to do still. But walk with me, and we'll talk about your brothers?"

"Sure, Papi," Arnaldo said. "Let's go."

He put his hand on his father's shoulder. They walked away with similar strides. One day soon Arnaldo's gawkiness would smooth out into something like his father's angular grace.

"Here." Wiping her eyes, Amaris pulled my spare set of clothes out of her backpack. "Come back to the car and you can put these on."

I looked around at them all, standing in a circle around Siku. The intense light of the moon, now directly above us, hollowed out their eyes and cast their shadows in starkly outlined puddles at their feet.

London pulled at November's shoulder. "Come on, 'Ember. It's time to take Siku home."

November, her face puffy and red, turned and clung to London, who pulled her gently away from Siku's body and toward the stolen truck. The rest of us looked down at Siku, lying there alone.

"Help us," said Morfael to the bear.

I turned away as the others moved in to lift Siku up. Amaris and I walked back to the truck. London was helping a blank November into her clothes. I threw on jeans, shoes, and a hoodie, then wrapped my arms around November. Somehow London and Amaris were there too, and we all huddled for a long time silently together.

Lazar walked up, his eyes gentle on November. "They're taking Siku back to his family...." He pointed to a different truck. I could just see Caleb shutting the door. A woman, the black bear-shifter, was driving.

"Take me!" November broke away and ran toward them.

Caleb saw her coming and leaned in to speak to the driver.

" 'Ember, wait!" London grabbed November's backpack full of candy and raced after her.

Amaris's eyes followed London, and I said, "Go with her." And she was gone too.

Lazar's tip-tilted brown eyes furrowed with concern. I shook my head. Something too horrible to speak of welled up within me. Then he took a step forward and put his arms around me.

Three or four great sobs wracked me. *I failed them. He's gone.*

Something brushed the top of my head, and through the tumult, I wondered if it was Lazar's lips.

I pushed him away, wiping my nose on my sleeve. "I need a minute," I said. And he let me go.

Then I started walking. I didn't look where I was going. But I had to move. A terrible confusion jittered around inside me, and if I stayed still, it might shake me to death. I stumbled forward, unable to see anything but Siku, falling like a redwood to crush the man who had killed him.

I bumped my toes and stumbled over the shallow pool near the entrance to the Tribunal's compound. My hand brushed the surface of the black water, sending moonlight-tipped ripples down its length.

A shadow moved behind me. Caleb was there, catching me by the elbow before I could fall in. He was so close. I had a vision of his arms wrapping around me, holding me to his heart, his lips close to my ear telling me it would be all right.

Instead, he made sure I regained my balance, then took his hand away. He was wearing his long black coat again, and he stuffed his hands into his pockets. The space between us felt suddenly like a huge canyon, and he'd just cut down the bridge.

"The rat-shifter's going to take November back with Siku to his family," he said. "The others are almost ready to go."

"What about Arnaldo?" I asked.

His eyes were mostly black, except for a single golden spiral in each. "His dad has to go to rehab every day for the next three months, and if that goes okay and he stays in the program, he might get custody back. In the meantime, that hawk Council member thinks their lawyer will get Arnaldo declared guardian of his brothers. So he'll go back with you to the school tonight, but probably head down to Arizona tomorrow."

"He'll come back with us, you mean?" I cleared my throat. I didn't want it to sound like an appeal. "You're coming with us too, right?"

He shook his head very slightly, eyes narrowed and veiled. "Lazar will take care of you," he said. "And I have things I need to do."

My heart dropped. Caleb must have seen me in Lazar's arms a few moments ago. "He was just being nice! Siku's..." I choked. I couldn't say it.

He nodded, eyes cold. "He died saving November," he said. "At least she'll always remember his complete loyalty to her."

His words cut into my heart. "I was never disloyal to you!"

He lifted one eyebrow skeptically, then tossed something at me that jangled. I caught it: the keys to the SUV we'd driven here. "I'm taking the pickup truck," he said. "It's the least Ximon owes me. Amaris knows I'll be in touch with her."

With her. But not with me.

I wanted to plead with him to stay. I wanted to smack him across his stony face. Pride kept me from doing either one.

"Good-bye, Caleb," I said.

"Good-bye, Dez."

I turned away as he walked off. I willed myself not to cry, not to turn around, not to run after him, staring down at the reflection of the moon in the still water of the pool.

I blinked. Something was different. The great white disk of the moon looked even bigger in the pool, and it looked... *wrong*.

We'd studied the moon in Morfael's classes, its influence on our ability to shift, how its phases augmented the power of Othersphere. It had distinctive craters, and the same side always faced the earth so that we never saw the dark side. The near side had distinctive areas that were darker than others, called "seas" by early astronomers, but now known to be basaltic plains darker than the highlands thanks to their iron-rich content.

The moon reflected in the pool had no gray seas. Instead, it had seams of darkness, branching out like veins full of black blood across the whiter, fleshlike surface. As I stared down, the water rippled, and the moon pulsed, like a shining heart.

A current, like electricity, filled the air. The hair on the back of my neck stood up.

I lifted my eyes to stare up at the real moon, not a reflection. It looked the same as always, silver with darker silver splotches, like giant freckles, not veins.

*Wait. It's not supposed to be there.*

The reflection in the pool was in the wrong place. The normal moon was directly above us. But the reflected moon's angle meant it mirrored something over . . . there.

A chill took me. When I turned, a second moon hovered on the horizon, a different moon, bigger but darker, threaded with a thousand pulsing black capillaries.

It was not our moon. The light shining on me came partly from the reflected light of our moon. The other part came from a different moon altogether.

*Have I crossed over?*

My skin prickled. The power here was triple what I had felt before. The ground I stood on was still familiar, but for how long?

"Sarangarel."

The voice, low and husky, came from behind me.

I turned back toward the pool. A slender woman even taller than I stood there in the center of the other moon's reflection, water up to her knees.

Her fiery orange hair, striped with black and white, wrapped around her in the breeze, revealing a pale face nearly the twin of mine. She wore a long dress, green and gold like her eyes, that looked like it was made out of interwoven leaves. The light from the pool flickered up around her with an unearthly glow.

"It is time for you to come home," she said.

"Mother." My voice was a whisper. "You're *not* my mother."

The smile spread slowly across her face. "There's nothing for you here anymore." Her voice was throaty, a growl. "Come back. We need you. We love you still."

*There's nothing for you here.* That was true. I'd failed everyone. Siku was dead, November devastated, Caleb gone.

My biological mother held out her hand. "You have always wanted to know me. Throw away the artifact we gave you, which now resembles a blade. Forsake it, and you may cross over to be with your family again."

"The Shadow Blade?" I put my hand on its hilt, feeling the cool calm it emanated stealing over me. "You gave it to me?"

She nodded. "To keep you safe, we decided to send you across the veil. Morfael agreed to take you. But we needed an item of power that would anchor you there until it was safe for you to return. It takes on whatever form you need, but you need it no longer. Morfael refuses to bring you back. Now is the time, daughter. Destroy or drop the blade and come with me. We are in danger. Our world may not survive. Only you can help us."

"Don't believe her!" Lazar's voice rolled out over the desert. He pounded up to halt at my side, breath coming fast. "You don't know who that really is, Dez. You can't trust her."

The woman in the pool laughed. "She knows me well. She called me here, where the veil is thin. And I have answered. She is more powerful than she knows."

I couldn't help staring at her—so like me and yet so different. Could I ever look like that, sound like that—*be* like that? If I did, maybe I wouldn't feel so small, so sad, such a terrible failure.

Lazar grabbed my face with one hand and turned it, forcing me to look at him. "Dez, listen to me. You belong here. You've defeated Ximon. You've begun to unite the different shifter tribes! We need you."

"Fool," said my biological mother. "You may need her, but my daughter doesn't need you. She needs me. She needs her true family. Come, Sarangarel. You'll find everything you need here with me."

*Sarangarel.* "Is that my name?" I asked. She was right. I needed to know who I was. "What's your name?"

"*Dez!*" Lazar took me by the shoulders and shook me. "You can't leave. Think about your mother! Remember what this . . . thing did to her!"

*My mother.*

Something in me snapped awake, as if the light from the other moon had sent me into a dream.

My mother had nearly died because of this woman. And now she stood there smiling, expecting me to leave everything behind, for her.

Lazar's brown eyes widened as he saw realization come to me. "That's it. Remember?"

"I remember." I turned to my so-called mother. "You used my mother like some kind of puppet. You could have killed her."

"*She* is not your mother." Her arched brows frowned dangerously. The faint veins beneath her pale skin darkened. "You are one of us. We are Amba, and we are at war. Will you doom your true family to extinction?"

"I have family here," I said. "This is my war. And I won't let you endanger them again. Go back!" I waved my hand at her, pushing my mind against the dark current of Othersphere pressing in around me. "You don't belong here."

Lazar hummed a deep, disturbing note. My biological mother winced, a ripple of fear crossing her face.

The note alarmed me too. But I placed my hand on the Shadow Blade and leaned into the vibration. I found something resonant inside me. "Get out of here!" I shouted. "Begone! Go! I don't want you here!"

A cloud seemed to pass over the moon as the ambient light around us dimmed. The figure in the pool writhed. "Look for me!" she cried. "I will send for you."

Then she was gone.

I collapsed. I would have fallen completely, but Lazar fell to his knees to catch me. "You're here," he said, his voice soft with happiness. "You stayed."

He cradled me in his arms and pressed soft lips against my forehead like a benediction. This time I didn't pull away.

# BEYOND
# THE
# STORY

# THE TIGER

*It is better to have lived one day as a tiger*
*than a thousand years as a sheep.*
—Chinese Proverb

Imagine you're a beautiful striped creature weighing 700 pounds and that you can move in silence, sprint up to 50 mph, kill a bear with your paws, and crush bones with your jaws. You live completely without fear and know how to hunt humans better than they can hunt you. After all, tigers have attacked helicopters; they've charged cars. They learn fast and will change tactics if the situation requires it. They know no master, and when challenged, will annihilate the threat if they can.

Who wouldn't want to know how it felt to be *that*?

But for me the tiger's allure is more about being a badass. You see, tigers are never insecure. Wearing a back brace during my teenage years was a recipe for squashing down my feelings, for worrying that people would think I was a freak. We all know how that feels in one way or another.

But a tiger doesn't care what you think of it. A tiger doesn't have to follow rules or repress its feelings. It follows its instincts without apology. If it hides, it does so because hiding fits the tiger's agenda, not because it is ashamed. Because of all this, the tiger was the perfect animal for the self-doubting character Dez to shift into. She and I have learned a lot from tigers.

I came to care about these great cats even more when I learned they are critically endangered in the wild. The tiger may be evolution's ultimate predator, but it is also terribly vulnerable to poachers and environmental changes. In an attempt to impart my awe and love for these animals, I've compiled a few facts to share with you.

- The tiger is the largest species of cat. The Amur, aka Siberian, tiger (designated *Panthera tigris altaica*) is the largest of the five remaining tiger subspecies.
- In the 1940s the Amur tiger was on the brink of extinction, with no more than 40 tigers remaining in the wild. Thanks to vigorous anti-poaching and other conservation efforts by the Russians, with support from many partners, the Amur tiger population recovered to its current numbers, close to 400.
- With poachers still able to make up to $30,000 for a tiger carcass, the Amur tiger and all other subspecies remain in grave danger of disappearing from the wild forever.
- Tigers can weigh up to 720 pounds (363 kilograms), stretch up to 6 feet (2 meters) long, and have a 3-foot- (1-meter-)long tail.
- The mystacial whiskers on the tiger's muzzle are so sensitive that they can detect the slightest change of air pressure or help the tiger find the prey's jugular vein.
- Tigers see about as well as humans during the day, but at night their eyesight is six times better than a human's.
- Tigers hunt primarily at night.
- Each tiger has its own distinct pattern of stripes, like fingerprints on a human.
- The word tiger came from the Greek word tigris, which is derived from a Persian word that means "arrow." This is probably a reference to the tiger's speed and deadliness when attacking.
- Fast as they are, tigers rely mostly on stealth to hunt. Their ability to vanish and travel unseen, despite their size, is notorious among the people who live near them.

*A tiger will see you a hundred times before you see him once.*
—A SAYING IN THE RUSSIAN TAIGA

- Humans may be easy prey, but tigers do not consider them a normal source of food. Most man-eating tigers have been wounded by humans, or are old, infirm, or missing teeth, which renders them incapable of eating their normal prey.
- In 1997, a male Amur tiger was wounded by a poacher named Vladimir Markov. The tiger then tracked Markov, found his cabin, destroyed everything containing his scent, laid in wait for days, and assassinated him.

> *Do not blame God for having created the tiger,*
> *but thank him for not having given it wings.*
> —INDIAN PROVERB

- The illegal trade in wildlife is the third largest in the world, after drugs and arms.

> *When you murder a tiger, you not only kill a strong*
> *and beautiful beast, you extinguish a passionate soul.*
> —SY MONTGOMERY, in "Spell of the Tiger:
> The Man-Eaters of Sundarbans,"
> in the *Washington Post*

- To save tigers, we must save the places they live—Asia's last great forests. These incredibly diverse wild lands provide thousands of other species, including people, with food, freshwater, and flood protection.
- The tiger is the national animal of both India and Bangladesh.

> *When you see a tiger, it is always like a dream.*
> —K. ULLAS KARANTH, director,
> the Wildlife Conservation Society, Indian Program

- The Tungusic people of Siberia considered the tiger a near deity and refer to it as "Grandfather" or "Old Man."

- In a poll conducted by Animal Planet, the tiger was voted the world's favorite animal.

For more information, and to learn how to help preserve these animals in the wild, visit:

www.21stcenturytiger.org
www.wcs.org/where-we-work/asia/russia.aspx
*or* www.panthera.org

# GREAT BOOKS, GREAT SAVINGS!

When You Visit Our Website:
## www.kensingtonbooks.com
You Can Save Money Off The Retail Price
Of Any Book You Purchase!

- **All Your Favorite Kensington Authors**
- **New Releases & Timeless Classics**
- **Overnight Shipping Available**
- **eBooks Available For Many Titles**
- **All Major Credit Cards Accepted**

Visit Us Today To Start Saving!
## www.kensingtonbooks.com

All Orders Are Subject To Availability.
Shipping and Handling Charges Apply.
Offers and Prices Subject To Change Without Notice.